# WILDE TYPE

A NOVEL

HK JACOBS

# DEDICATION

To Mamaw,

who would be extremely proud and slightly appalled

# CONTENTS

# ACKNOWLEDGMENTS

This book was a labor of love and would not have been possible
without the following wonderful people:

My friends Tammy and Erin for making this book infinitely better
with your creative influence,
My editor Stacy Kinney for polishing the text into something
beautiful,
My friends and colleagues around the globe who have blessed me
with their hospitality and kinship,
And mostly my patients, who change my life on a daily basis.

# ONE

The polished, aged wood cooled her temple, and she exhaled in the form of a long, cleansing sigh. After a long exhausting week, all the energy she could muster was just enough to sit as still as possible and admire the woodgrain in the bar supporting her head. She stared through her empty glass of beer at the distorted images of people laughing raucously in preemptive celebration of the weekend and felt as distant from that scene as the view through the glass made it seem.

She was entering her seventh month working in Botswana as a critical care physician specializing in children. With the longest track record of civil stability of any country in Africa, Botswana had the added benefit of a rapidly expanding economy. Right in the middle of its most accelerated economic growth, the HIV/AIDS epidemic had hit Botswana hard, and the country was responding with a vengeance. As part of a collaborative partnership between Princess Marina Hospital in Gaborone and the Children's Hospital of Philadelphia, she trained local pediatricians to care for seriously ill children with pneumonia, diarrhea, or whatever else happened to show up on their doorstep. Although the work was grueling, especially when resources became limited, Alex had honestly never been more in her element. At the end of every day, she was grateful to be part of the team learning to care for these children and promote their long-term survival.

After a long week of holding teaching sessions, rounding on the wards, and staying well past midnight to stabilize a few of the sicker children, Alex found herself as she often did on a Friday evening— lightening the burden on her heart with the magic elixir of a good beer.

"Alex …. alexandraaaa!"

1

Her name resounded, high school musical style, from across the bar. She had always preferred Alex to Alexandra, a name she reserved only for life's necessary pomp and circumstance. She enjoyed simplicity, brevity, and names that one could utter in a single breath. Her mom, a lover of television dramas, had christened her "Alexandra" after her favorite character on her favorite television show, which she just happened to be watching when she went into labor. Thoughts of her mom brought a twinge of homesickness. Months had passed since she had seen her mom, and she could still clearly see her encouraging yet distraught face through the open passenger side window as she had waved Alex into the airport.

"Alex ... Alex, that better be you."

As if emerging from an underwater dream, she surfaced back to the present. Reluctantly picking up her head, she swung around in her barstool to see one of her favorite people shimmying through the crowd to take the empty seat next to her.

"Hi Rox," Alex said warmly and was folded into a spectacular hug with her friend and kindred spirit. She had only been in Gaborone for a week when she serendipitously met Rox at the hospital café one morning, both in search of a much-needed caffeine jolt. Rox had ordered a flat white in a wonderful Canadian accent and a voice that made Alex think of warm maple syrup. Alex had sidled over to the counter where Rox was distrustfully eyeing a display of lumpy mounds of fried dough on little plates. Before Alex could get a word out, she whipped her head around, revealing a huge crooked smile, and assessed Alex with a pair of sparkling eyes, made up to perfection.

"I'm Roxanne...Roxanne Clarke. These things look awful. So much worse than last week. Ten times worse than anything I have ever eaten. Come on then—let's walk down the street. I know a great little place where they sell flat cakes."

Words tumbled around Alex's mouth, but nothing actually came out. After an awkward pause, she finally started, "I'm Al—"

"Alexandra Wilde! I know! I heard all about you from Dr. K's secretary—you know the hospital director guy. Anyway, I am so glad I ran into you. It was meant to be."

Rox could not have been more correct. They spent the next few weeks grabbing coffee, meeting for drinks after work, cooking awful dinners, and overall becoming inseparably bonded for life. Rox was Canadian to the core but had trained all over the world as an obstetrician. She had finished up her residency in Australia and then hopped over to London for a prestigious fellowship in high-risk pregnancy. Her passion for improving care for mothers and babies in less resource-rich parts of the world had landed her in Gaborone. This was her "single gal gig", as she put it—working in a setting with a high incidence of complicated deliveries until she met the man of her dreams.

Alex had never met a more thoroughly beautiful individual than Roxanne. Her heart and personality were magnanimous. Outwardly, she was tall and curvy with muscle definition from growing up on a working farm in the middle of nowhere, Ontario. She laughed loudly and loved fiercely and had quickly become Alex's best friend. She told stories like she was unveiling a movie plot and had everyone hanging on the edge of their seats until she revealed the climactic finish. Much to Alex's chagrin, she was thoroughly obsessed with the opposite sex and had no qualms showing it. In a room full of people, Rox was the sun.

Ending their hug, they each plunked down on a barstool, ready to settle in for a night of venting, gossiping, and reveling in the fact that neither one of them had work tomorrow.

"I'll take two more beers, Jeff." Alex flashed two fingers at the robust, bald man tending the bar. Jeff was the head bartender at the popular local bar where all of the ex-patriates in Gaborone seemed to gather on a nightly basis. The appropriately named "Ex-Pats" had become a proverbial stomping ground for Alex and Rox, who frequently met there on Friday nights to enjoy the music and libations in the alfresco patio under the southern hemisphere sky.

"Here's to the start of a glorious weekend," said Rox, tipping back her beer and taking a generous gulp.

"Cheers!" said Alex and let the cold frothy liquid fill up her mouth with foam.

"How was last week?" asked Rox in a slightly more somber tone.

"It was—," Alex started and had a flashback reel of late nights with crying children weak with fever, sometimes straining to breathe. "It's over. Let's just have fun tonight. I desperately need a break from sick babies."

"If distraction is what you want, distraction is exactly what you will get," taunted Rox playfully. "I happen to be an expert in the art of making things fade into the rearview." She pantomimed adjusting the rearview mirror of a car and tossed her blonde bob provocatively.

"Yes … you absolutely are," Alex muttered, thinking of all the times she had woken up with a throbbing headache after a night of putting things in the "rearview" with Rox.

Rox generated fun and drew people in like shrimp in a net. Where Alex was quiet and prone to pensiveness, Roxanne Clarke was exuberant and lively. She tended to draw in a crowd where Alex was, quite literally, forced to manage the overflow. Not that she minded. Rox was confident and trendy and knew how to create the best smoky eye that Alex had ever seen. Alex was content to be along for the ride.

Running her hands through her long deep brown locks with outgrown layers, she eyed Rox suspiciously. "What do you have in mind?"

"Tequila…salt…limes." When the middle-aged bartender didn't respond fast enough, she leaned her voluptuous top-half over the bar and yelped, "Jeff, this is a bloody emergency!"

Four empty shot glasses and a carnage of limes later, Alex's head was a floating balloon attached to her body with a mere string. The bar had exploded with a hefty crowd jockeying for drinks, and a guitarist started plucking loud rhythmic notes into the air. Her brain welcomed all the stimuli that served to drown out the memories of last week.

"So, Roxy," Alex said a little too loudly, "how are things with Fen?" Fen was a general surgeon at Princess Marina, or "PM" as the local physicians called it. Rox had been shamelessly flirting with him for weeks, much to his discomfort.

"Fabulous. I have, in fact, been invited on a date this weekend." Rox gave a sly grin and ran a hand through her textured layers. "We are going to a concert and then out for drinks and then hopefully to breakfast." Her brilliant hazel eyes sparkled with delight. Rox loved a challenge, and Dr. Fen Mosweu was quiet and intense but ridiculously attractive. She had played subtle predator to his prey for weeks now.

"I'm thrilled for you. Don't do anything I wouldn't do," teased Alex.

"Oh, I plan on doing lots of things you wouldn't do," she teased back.

Being the more introverted of the pair, Alex felt herself often living vicariously through Rox's romantic interludes. Focused and ambitious to a fault, she had never minded being alone. Growing up in a small town with a small life and very little financial comfort had pushed her to rise to an incomprehensible level of self-expectation. She had been born with an enviable work ethic—one that catapulted her to the top of her high school class, then her college class, then her medical school class.

Alex was now completing her specialty training in critical care medicine at the Children's Hospital of Philadelphia and, in a little over a year, would fulfill her dream of being a pediatric intensivist. She would be able to take her place among the heroes that she so admired, the doctors who walked into the chaotic maelstrom of a dying child and saved a precious life while calming everyone in the process. This opportunity to come to Botswana had been her godsend. Alex had traveled many places to care for sick kids, but here she had discovered a second home. The minute she disembarked from the plane after landing in Gaborone, she inhaled the warm dusty air, and it settled in her soul forever.

"It's been a while. I am definitely in a dry spell," whined Rox, bringing Alex's focus back to the present and the humming bar that had become even more crowded in the last hour.

Alex threw up her hands. "When have you ever been in a dry spell? You might as well be the freaking rain forest, Roxanne!" They both shared a dizzying laugh. "I, on the other hand, have taken up permanent residence in the Sahara…during a drought."

"You don't have to, you know," she said through pursed lips. "You could live a little … thaw the ice for a bit, sister."

Alex sighed and stared down at the salt, now crusted into a little pattern atop the woodgrain. She felt like a lost cause somehow, but the desire to be intimate had never outweighed her desire to remain invulnerable. Being invulnerable had saved her. Real intimacy came with a price that she could not afford. She picked at the salt.

"But it's so much fun having a ringside seat to your impeccable shenanigans," she retorted, not able to keep a smile from gracing her features. A devilish expression crossed Rox's face, and Alex's tequila-ridden brain took a minute to process her next words.

"I think it's time to play the game."

"The game" was somewhat of a social experiment that Rox had picked up while living in Australia and was her favorite way to torture Alex after a few drinks had muted her frontal lobe inhibitions. Fiercely competitive, she had never deferred a challenge, but this game made her stomach roil. The rules were as follows—one friend chose a guy in the bar for the other friend to kiss. The guy should be unattached with no wedding ring or girlfriends in sight to avoid unnecessary drama, and the kiss must happen spontaneously— without asking for it with words. Whoever received their kiss in the least amount of time was declared the winner. The loser had to buy the drinks for the rest of the evening. Alex always ended up buying the drinks.

"It's time to end that losing streak, dear. Don't be the Red Sox or the Cowboys or whatever that team is that loses all the time." Rox gesticulated into the air with each sports reference.

"Rox, do not pretend you know anything about American sports," Alex muttered.

"Truthfully, I don't care about sports...except for the sport of foreplay." In response to Alex covering her face with her hands, Rox continued, "It is a sport, Alex, with a special set of skills that can be taught...even to an ice queen." Rox widened her hazel eyes and batted her lashes a few times for effect.

Alex could not help but be filled with an overwhelming wave of admiration for her friend. Her boldness was infectious, and she knew how to accentuate her curves with her outfits, most notably with a large piece of jewelry that led the eye to the top of her cleavage. Tonight, it was a string of enormous turquoise beads.

"Now—choose a man and let me show you how to be the MPV."

"MVP, Rox. Most...valuable...player," Alex corrected.

"No, sweetie. Most...powerful...vixen," said Rox as she slid off her stool and applied a coat of gloss over her petal pink lipstick, all in the same fluid movement.

With her head still spinning from the tequila shots, Alex leaned over in a fit of laughter, tears threatening to leak from her closed eyelids. Abruptly straightening, she feigned intense concentration as she scanned the bar for an ex-patriate that might be up for the challenge. She skimmed over the jacketed businessmen smoking in the corner—too stodgy—and past the unshaven backpackers sharing a table in the back—too dodgy—until her eyes rested on a tall fellow in jeans tipping back a beer bottle while he glanced periodically at the television.

"Him." Alex pointed toward the sandy-haired loner. "He looks in desperate need of some entertainment."

As Rox sauntered off to pounce on her prey, Alex ordered another beer and settled in for the show. Upon sensing her arrival, the man turned his full attention to her, as if her face were some sort of homing beacon. She noted a few sideways glances from Rox, one head toss, and a single well-manicured fingertip trailing the man's muscular forearm. Exactly one minute and thirty-two seconds later, Roxanne's parted lips were greeted by a second pair of lips, the unsuspecting sandy-haired man shocked by his own kiss. Not surprised in the least, Alex shook her head in admiration. He had not stood a chance. Satisfied, Rox turned, and without a backward glance, strode over and slid into her seat.

"You are a force to be reckoned with," said Alex, a touch of awe in her voice.

"It's the lip gloss," said Rox, winking and intensely dissecting the various groups of men for the next worthy candidate.

"You know I hate this," Alex whined. "Why do you like seeing me squirm?"

Rox continued to scan the crowd. "Because it's the only time you do squirm. You are so *in control* all of the time." She made actual air quotes with her hands.

"It's my job to be in control," Alex grumbled through gritted teeth. "And it's not easy to turn it off."

"Consider this a therapy session," said Rox patiently, "like getting over your fear of heights or spiders or clowns. I will make you do uncomfortable non-Alex behaviors until they feel normal."

"Since when did you trade in your speculum for a psych degree?" teased Alex.

"Him," said Rox assuredly. "He is the one."

"Where?" asked Alex, twisting her head from side to side.

Rox pointed to an elevated patio through the screen door leading to the back part of Ex-Pats.

Dressed in dark jeans and a black t-shirt, he leaned casually on the small outdoor bar with his left forearm. Alex could barely make out his profile but could see that his face was relaxed underneath his dark aviators as he talked on his cell phone.

"Go on, then, love." Rox nudged her encouragingly and winked. "Don't take less than a hundred."

Alex stiffly removed herself from her barstool and began making her way out to the back patio, hearing Rox's soprano in the background. "Pretty woman, walking down the street…"

She cast a few furtive glances back toward her friend, who shooed her forward like a mother hen. She wished she had opted for anything more glamorous than bootcut jeans and a blue t-shirt that read Baby Blue's BBQ. As Alex drew nearer to the stranger, she saw that his hair was dark, so brown that it was essentially black, and styled in a messy fashion that made it look like he had just rolled out of bed. His muscles were lean under the black V neck t-shirt, and his jeans hugged his hips seductively. When she ventured close enough, she could feel the heat emanating from his back and could smell the hint of freshly washed skin mixed with a touch of sweat. Alex froze like a gazelle that had just detected the whiff of lion—this man was dripping sex. In the instant that it took her brain to signal her feet to start backing away, he turned and smoothly removed his sunglasses to reveal the most heart-stopping eyes that Alex had ever seen.

# TWO

His gaze locked onto Alex's face with relaxed intensity, and his eyes, as blue as an ocean sky, seemed to be studying her features as his mind formulated questions. Alex took a selfish moment to evaluate his face. It was clean-shaven with a straight nose and a chiseled jawline that ended at a set of full lips. His face was perfect except for a subtle scar over the bridge of his nose, and some part of Alex's doctor brain wondered what had happened—bike accident, maybe? His lips parted slightly, and his dark eyebrows furrowed like he was thinking of something creative to say.

"I Ii, I'm Ian," he said as he cocked his head to the side and gave her an unconcerned smirk.

"I'm Alexandra." She cringed at the sound of her own name. "But most people call me Alex," she blurted awkwardly.

"Alexandra," he repeated. Her name on his lips sounded richly sexy, like a silk dress tumbling into a pile on the floor. He sounded American but without an accent that would geographically place him in a particular region. His voice was smooth, sultry, beckoning even.

A few more moments passed with neither of them saying anything. Alex narrowed the distance between them with an uncharacteristically bold step. She drew close enough to acknowledge more of his physical presence. He was tall—probably just under six feet—with lean, well-defined muscles. Most striking were his eyes, round blue pools that were the color of a limitless, perfect sky. Alex felt her tension rush out through her feet, and her mind was unnaturally quiet as she felt her lips widen into an unprovoked smile. Without diverting his eyes from hers, he made a slight movement with his head, indicating that she should take a seat on the stool next to him. They both sat, not quite facing one

9

another, a tense column of air between their torsos. Ian motioned to the bartender with two fingers, and the older gentleman smiled warmly as he placed two napkins and matching highball glasses with sparkling amber liquid in front of them.

"Cheers," said Ian lifting his glass and turning to face Alex.

"Cheers," replied Alex and sniffed the vapors wafting from the glass. She took a tiny sip—bourbon—good bourbon. The liquid burned a satisfying fiery trail deep into her belly.

Under Alex's observation, Ian tipped back his head, simultaneously taking a hefty swallow of bourbon as he cast a sidelong glance at her.

"So, Alexandra, what are you looking for?" said Ian. The words seemed casual but, coming from his lips, they were soaked with innuendo.

*What kind of question was that?* "I have no idea," she whispered, mostly to herself, but he heard her anyway. Her brain felt muddled, and it wasn't just the alcohol.

"Let me take a guess, and if I'm right, you can buy me a drink," he replied with a mischievous yet purposeful look in his eyes. He quickly scanned her over, and she noticed that he lingered over her face before moving down her body, seeming to commit it to memory.

Alex felt like a horse brought for auction. Though not terribly self-conscious, she was well aware of her faults, and for some reason, they seemed to be clamoring for attention right now. She knew that she possessed an enviable figure, thin but strong from the hours of running she did every week plus the hours spent on her feet in the hospital. Her long dark chocolate locks framed a heart-shaped face that was always slightly pale. Her eyes, a bit too large for her face, were blue like the color of a fathomless ocean and permanently shadowed from lack of sleep. Her makeup was minimal rather than the professional level care that Rox frequently displayed. Although the epitome of poise and control at the hospital, she felt awkward in most other environments, even to the point of being downright clumsy.

Alex didn't answer him right away and instead took another sip of bourbon to sustain her liquid courage. She was supposed to be practicing magical female wile to convince this divine man to kiss her. Instead, she was on sidetrack highway having a near-existential crisis.

"Well, you aren't looking for sex," he said with a raise of one eyebrow as he nearly emptied his bourbon glass.

Alex sputtered into her drink, which thankfully broke the half-trance she had been entertaining, and she turned in her chair to face him. Although her heart thundered and her insides felt like they had been scrambled, she donned her calmest, most in-control façade. "How do you know I'm not?"

"Because, Alexandra, a lot of women want me, and I can always tell when they do," he answered matter-of-factly with a wry smirk briefly contrasting his beautiful face.

She answered with a raise of her eyebrows and a mild glare that gave off her unspoken disdain. He wasn't exactly wrong. She was not here looking for Friday night post-debauchery sex. However, despite her preference living within a formidable ice fortress, her body felt anxious to betray her. Her mouth felt paper-dry, and a slight sheen of sweat was rapidly accumulating on her palms. She wiped her hands over her jean-clad thighs, a movement that caught Ian's eye.

Looking up at him, she startled a bit at his expression which was curious and sincere with interest, quite different from a moment ago.

"You're right," started Alex. "I am definitely not looking for sex." She flicked her eyes down to the bourbon for comfort rather than continuing to let herself be enraptured by his face.

"Let me tell you what you are looking for," he said in a husky, bourbon-soaked voice. He leaned over now so close that Alex could feel his breath on her cheek. She didn't dare meet the eyes that looked down at her through half-closed lids. *Was he going to kiss her?* She held her breath and felt everything stop for a moment, including her heart. In fact, it seemed to take forever for it to squeeze another aliquot of blood into her arteries.

"You want an epic love story…a love that is timeless…immortal. You want a love that frightens you and inspires you," he whispered into her ear. His face retreated from hers then, and his nose barely skimmed her cheek as he did so. "And I hope you find it," he finished, genuinely smiling at her, without a trace of his previous bravado.

Thoughtfully, her blood hammering a symphony in her ears, Alex put down her drink and stood up from her perch at the bar. Gathering a tremendous amount of practiced self-discipline, she calmly said, "Thank you for the drink, Ian," and turned away from him, willing her feet to gain momentum.

The clamor of the frenetic bar atmosphere rushed into her consciousness as she stepped away from the intangible bubble that they occupied just moments ago. After a few steps forward, she turned once to look back at him and caught him staring at her with those flame-blue eyes, a bemused expression on his face.

She drifted back toward Rox, who was, by then, regaling bartender Jeff with her latest escapades. He was trying to hold a laugh in his cheeks as he wiped down the bar. Rox raised one eyebrow mid-sentence as she sat down as carefully as she would slide into a church pew. Quiet and composed, at least on the outside, Alex gestured toward the door.

"Rox, I need to get out of here."

Rox, appearing worried, sprang into action, dropping down a bill for their drinks and grabbing their purses from under the bar.

Once they were outside, warm, cleansing air entered Alex's lungs, and she was finally able to inhale large, purging breaths that filled her bloodstream with oxygen and cleared the supernatural feel in her brain. He was just a guy—a guy who was charming and sexy and really good with words. Alex had never experienced such an intimate moment with a stranger, and it left her shaken. In truth, she had never had such an intimate moment with a boyfriend, either. No matter how close she seemingly grew to the boys and then men she had dated, the relationship always remained superficial. The impenetrable ice wall always stood. It was how she managed to survive her childhood. It was how she functioned so well in her job with its hefty burden of death and suffering and tragedy. Disturbed, she realized that in a matter of minutes, this random stranger with the burning blue eyes had peeked over the wall and caught a glimpse of what lay on the other side.

"I'll grab a cab, and then you are going to tell me why you have an expression on your face like you just encountered Jesus in the flesh," said Rox as she looked at her friend suspiciously.

Inside the cab, Alex tried, albeit unsuccessfully, to fully describe her interaction that evening with Ian.

"That was it?" exclaimed Rox. "So, in summary—incredibly drop-dead gorgeous, sexy as sin, ingeniously insightful man buys you a drink, takes a gander into your idealistic little heart, and then you just leave…without knowing his last name…or his number…or how to get in touch with him ever again!" Her voice had become almost shrill at this point.

"It wasn't like that, Rox." Alex chewed on her lip thoughtfully. "We had a singular moment. A brief metaphysical connection that passed by like an eclipse." She spoke more confidently now. Her words actually sounded believable. "It was meant to be this way. One perfect moment in the floating panacea of all the other moments in life that never quite live up to our expectations. I'll just accept it for what it was."

Rox eyed her speculatively. "Don't be too cerebral about this, love. It's okay to feel something for an almost complete stranger."

Alex exited the cab and leaned down to hug her bestie. "The only thing I feel is ridiculous. I'll call you tomorrow. Have fun with Fen!"

"Goodnight and sweet dreams, dear," Rox called as the cab pulled away from Alex's small rental home.

She used her remote to open the gate and walked into a small courtyard that contained a simple three-room enclosure that she had called home for the better part of the past year. Almost every home in her area was privately gated. Crime had been on the downswing the last few years, but physicians were certainly prime targets and couldn't be too careful. Alex had stumbled upon the very best burglar deterrent around in the form of her gangly, protective Rhodesian Ridgeback puppy. She had found him stranded on the side of the road one day along her favorite running route, abandoned by his former owner and in desperate need of nutrition. Alex had taken him home and gently nursed him into the seventy-five-pound floppy puppy sniffing her jeans with vigor. She and McCartney, named for her favorite famous Beatle, shared a person-canine bond that was therapeutic for them both.

"Hi, boy! I sure missed you." She reached down to give him a loving scratch behind his ears, which sent a fresh wave of wiggling all the way to his tail.

After letting McCartney have his private moment in the grass, Alex entered her home away from home and tossed her purse on the kitchen island. The house was simple but charming with walnut hardwood floors and whitewashed walls. The living room contained a lumpy purple couch and a first-generation flat-screen television, which she had never turned on. The kitchen was basic, consisting of a tiny electric range, microwave, and refrigerator connected by white cabinetry. A small wooden table with two mismatched chairs looked out over the best spot in the house, a large window where the sun rose each morning and bathed the entire house in a rosy glow. Alex retreated into her bedroom, a sanctuary of sorts with its iron bedframe containing a squeaky mattress covered in yellow floral sheets and a wooden desk piled high with a myriad of textbooks, medical journals, and framed photos.

She picked up one of her and Rox at a winery in Stellenbosch during one of their weekend trips earlier this year. They held glasses of a pale gold beverage with emphatic smiles on their faces. She remembered being delightfully tipsy while, from their enviable spot on the wine shop balcony, they had watched the sun set over the valley below. Her adventures with Rox had truly been some of the happiest times of her life. Rox had a way of inspiring a passion for life and made it her life's mission to squeeze every drop of fun out of the world when she was not working. *Work hard, play hard*—a well-known mantra that most doctors she knew lived by. It was a way of life that made work bearable. The cumulative pain and suffering that she and her fellow physicians swallowed every single day had to be balanced out on the altar of sacrifice by living life to its fullest.

Alex picked up another photograph of her friends from medical school, innocent and wide-eyed, on the steps of the university as they received their match letters for residency. The photographs served as evidence that Alex had definitely done her share of living. She picked up the remaining pictures in turn—atop a camel in Mongolia during a heart surgery mission, in a tuberculosis ward in Port au Prince, in the mountains of Guatemala delivering food and medicine. Alex felt a wave of gratitude for the divine intervention and hard work that had presented her with all of these incredible opportunities. Immersing herself in other places and cultures had allowed her to experience a depth of humanity and strength and hope that she could never have imagined.

Her last few months in Gaborone had been productive. The pediatric ward staff was bright and enthusiastic, and, most importantly, deeply invested in improving childhood survival. Kids could survive almost anything given a fighting chance, and Alex wanted more than anything to make sure they got that chance. She knew the general direction her life was going—to finish her training and dedicate her life to saving kids from the evil maladies and tragedies that lay in wait. This singular purpose had meshed with her identity until they were one and the same. She had always been content with that choice.

So, why, in the literal midnight hour, was she so unsettled? The restlessness in her heart had become tangible, and she refused to believe it had anything to do with meeting Ian. Maybe it was just the alcohol and its irritating effects on the sympathetic nervous system. In a vain attempt to shake off this twisty nervousness, Alex shed her bar clothes and took an obnoxiously long shower. She let the water heat her skin to the point of being painful and observed, satisfactorily, that her lavender soap ferried her feelings right down the drain.

Once dressed in her favorite soft flannel pants and a white t-shirt, she initiated her nightly tradition of snuggling in her bed, her feet wedged under McCartney, who had already become a snoring red lump of fur. Alex grabbed a book off her nightstand and planned to read until she passed out with her bedside lamp still ablaze. Tonight, she surveyed her choices—*Twilight* or *The Coming Plague* by Laurie Garrett. Giving *Twilight* a derisive snort, she picked up the latter and began to delve into the story of the Lassa fever epidemic and how it was eventually quelled. After about five minutes, she realized that she had been reading and re-reading the same passage.

Irritation clouded her vision, and she snapped the book closed. Against her better judgment, Alex let her mind wander back to the night at the bar and replay the events. She delved into the tiny sensory-driven moments at first—his spiced breath on her face, his expression as he enjoyed her bewilderment, the lithe, muscled body under his t-shirt that begged to be touched, and those eyes—eyes that burned like a blue flame. Eyes that burned everything they touched, and now she was left longing for something to ease the burning sensation she felt every time she thought of him. He had kindled a spark, and Alex was enthralled yet terrified of being engulfed by a fire she couldn't control. A fire that promised to melt her precious, protective ice.

Luckily, it would be a non-issue as she was likely never to see him again. He certainly did leave an impression, though. How could a total stranger evoke such deep and complex emotion? She had spent less than ten minutes with the man, and he was causing her to question how she lived her life. She had always practiced meticulous censorship with her feelings, even to the point of being potentially pathologic. In reality, she felt deeply—intensely—and had learned, over time, to dilute her emotions so that none of them ranged to the heights and depths that they should. Her pain and suffering had required containment but unfortunately so had her joy. However much this benefited her professional life, it was a death sentence to her personal life.

Alex had dated and truly enjoyed the perks—good conversation, great food, and the exciting possibility of potential chemistry. She had even had a few boyfriends over the last decade, but none lasted. Eventually, all relationships reached a critical altitude, and rather than reveal her deepest and darkest, Alex had always decided to pull the ripcord. Her most recent relationship had ended over a year ago. *Wow, had it been that long?*

She had met him at a local music venue showcasing a Beatles cover band right after moving to Philadelphia, and they had bonded over their mutual love for everything McCartney and Lennon. He was easy on the eyes and actually quite interesting. He had landed his dream job as a financial analyst and was on his way to becoming quite prominent in his company. Pursuing her with vigor, he had invited her to the art museum, soccer games, and even sailing. At that point, she was working almost a hundred hours some weeks, not counting the extra reading she did outside the hospital plus her research responsibilities. The demands of her career eventually took their toll on his patience, and she let it happen. It was easier that way. Just another relationship that became a job-related mortality.

Was Ian right? Did she ever want more than a surface level relationship that was doomed before it really began? Rather than delve into that question tonight, she let it float around in her brain as she succumbed to sleep and dreamed of eyes as blue as flames…as limitless as the sky.

# THREE

Alex stepped onto the pediatric ward at Princess Marina hospital on Monday morning with a renewed sense of purpose. After all, throwing herself into work had always had a certain therapeutic benefit. She entered the small, makeshift conference room where she and the pediatric interns met every morning to go over the admissions from the night before as well as the current patients admitted to the ward.

"I hope everyone had a great weekend, including those that had to work," she said enthusiastically. "Now, let's get started."

Mercy, a quiet, intellectual powerhouse and one of the rising stars of this year's intern class, took the lead. "Good morning, Dr. Alex. We had two admissions overnight—a six-year-old boy with respiratory distress and a two-year-old girl with diarrhea and marasmus."

Marasmus and kwashiorkor were the terms used to describe children with severe malnutrition. Marasmus indicated that the child had total calorie malnutrition whereas, in kwashiorkor, the child had enough calories but not enough protein and presented with a distended abdomen and swelling. Kwashiorkor literally translated to "disease of the deposed child" and meant that once another baby was born, the older child was weaned from the breast and might not get enough protein-rich calories. Malnutrition was way too common in the rural villages outside Gaborone and complicated the clinical care of over a third of the children admitted to the ward.

"Let's discuss each case and come up with a differential diagnosis," encouraged Alex.

Diagnostic tests, including laboratory and radiology services, were limited, so Alex usually made her interns rely first on the history and physical exam findings to direct care. They spent the better part

17

of an hour discussing the possible causes of illness in the two children and formulated a treatment care plan that Alex found acceptable.

"Remember to first address the most life-threatening conditions, stabilize the patient, and then you have some time to think about the diagnosis and what testing you might need." Eyeing the silhouette that had just darkened the doorway, she called after them as they headed over to the ward to prepare for rounds. "I'll catch up with you guys in a few minutes."

"*Dumela,* Dr. Alex," called her supervisor and friend from the doorway. Dr. Kefentse Kenosi, affectionately known as "Dr. K", had recently accepted the position of hospital Chief Medical Officer and, in doing so, had become Alex's boss. He was a true leader with a progressive vision for the hospital and was incredibly supportive of Alex's work with the pediatrics program. His smooth, unblemished face belied years of wisdom and experience working with Botswana's national health services department. He was tall and lean with just a hint of gray at his temples and possessed the kindest eyes that Alex had ever known. In addition to supervising the entire medical staff at the hospital, he made time for his five grandchildren, who frequently accompanied him on weekend trips into the office.

"*Dumela,* Dr. Kenosi," Alex responded with the traditional Setswana greeting along with a huge beaming smile. "It's great to see you, sir."

"And you, Alex," he said in turn. "I was wondering if you had a moment to speak with me."

"Of course. I have a few minutes before rounds."

"Excellent—can I buy you a coffee, perhaps?"

"I am not one to turn down a coffee," Alex said warmly as they began walking through the covered open-air corridor toward the hospital coffee shop.

Despite the comfortably warm weather, Alex was perpetually cold, and the steaming chai latte felt warm and comforting between her palms. Next to her on the bench, Dr. K gently sipped his black tea, careful not to spill a drop on his pristine white coat. She patiently waited for him to speak, allowing him one last opportunity to percolate on his thoughts.

"Alex, I have been very impressed and very pleased with the work you are doing with our pediatrics program," he began.

"Thank you, sir. That means a lot."

"Yes, but I am aware that you, at times, are, shall we say, disheartened by the level of advanced care that can be provided here at Princess Marina," he continued.

*Where was he going with this?* "I..." Alex struggled with what to say, and her heart rate picked up its tempo. "I am...but only because I want better outcomes for these kids, and I see such potential for making that a reality. I deeply apologize if I ever offended anyone." Alex felt threatened by the prick of tears in her eyes.

"No need to apologize, Alex. We want the same things, you and I, which is why I have asked to speak with you today. There is an opportunity to achieve the ability to provide for our kids like we so desire. If you had your wish, what would you create here?"

"A dedicated intensive care unit for kids," she said assuredly. Resources to care for the sickest of the sick, she thought. Monitors, ventilators, IV pumps to start, not to mention an organized training program for nurses and physicians. "I would create a system of sustainable resources and staff support so that these kids would always have the very best care available," she continued, her voice rising in excitement.

"I thought so," interrupted Dr. K. "Our hospital, specifically its pediatric division, has been chosen as a finalist to receive a substantial grant from the Devall Foundation. An analysis team is planning to evaluate our site and determine if it merits their generosity."

Alex's mouth involuntarily opened in shock. While she remained vocally quiet, her mind had started spinning, creating and recreating the possibilities that could become a reality over the next five years. When she still failed to speak, Dr. K eyed her speculatively and continued with his monologue. "I would like you to meet with this team. I can think of no one better to enlighten them as to how special our children are. They will be here on Thursday." With that, he abruptly stood, buttoned his coat, and strode toward the office, leaving a still incredulous Alex sitting outside nursing her lukewarm tea.

During rounds that morning, Alex was admittedly distracted. "I am so sorry, Mercy. Could you please start over?"

"Of course. This is a six-year-old boy with no past medical history admitted for respiratory distress and chest pain for the past few days, and here is the chest radiograph." Mercy popped a plain film of the boy's chest into the lightbox. "What do you see?" asked Alex, mentally regarding the radiograph and quickly coming to her own conclusions.

Mercy chewed on her pencil a moment then answered carefully, choosing her words. "The airways look normal, but the bases of both lungs have opacifications. Pneumonia?"

"Very good thought. Now take a look at the heart," Alex said as she traced the enlarged cardiac silhouette.

"The heart is big and dilated, and the liver is enlarged," remarked Mercy. "Could it be heart failure?"

"It looks that way," concluded Alex. "Can we get an echocardiogram and confirm? In the meantime, let's go see our patient."

Alex led the group of interns over to the bedside of a small, quiet six-year-old boy. His eyes were tightly shut, and he clutched the hand of his mother, who sat in a rattan chair near his bed. His breathing was noticeably labored, coming in quick, shallow bursts. Alex exchanged places with his mother and took his wrist in her hand. His pulse was rapid and weak, like a pair of butterfly wings tapping against her fingers instead of the typical thrum generated by a healthy child. She quickly listened with her stethoscope and heard the telltale sound of crackling paper with his every breath—pulmonary edema.

Alex made eye contact with the team and said in a clear voice, "Let's send some bloodwork and get the echo. In the meantime, we need to place him on oxygen and give medication to get rid of the extra water on his lungs. Khobi?" She turned to the nearest intern who was scribbling notes on a sheaf of paper. "What medication would you like to give?"

"Furosemide, Dr. Alex. Ten milligrams," he said with fervor.

"My thoughts exactly." She nodded and smiled at him in affirmation. "I'll stop by after lunch and check on him again."

She touched the boy's hand again, sending healing vibes through her fingertips, and wished for the thousandth time that her Setswana was good enough to explain the treatment plan to his mother. "Lesedi," Alex called to the nurse in charge of the ward, "would you mind telling his mom that we think his heart may not be working quite right, and we are doing some tests to find out?" Lesedi was one of Alex's favorite nurses. She remained calm and focused even in the worst of circumstances.

"Of course, Dr. Alex," Lesedi said smoothly.

Alex smiled and reached into the pocket of her white coat to check her buzzing phone. It was Rox.

*Meet me in the courtyard for lunch xoxo*

*Be right there*

Rox, who was already seated on a concrete bench enjoying her unwrapped lunch, scooted over when Alex plopped down next to her to give her a side hug.

"I have some news," Alex started, "but first, I want to hear how Saturday night went."

Rox smiled conspiratorially and took her time swallowing a bite of peanut butter sandwich before answering. "The concert was great—totally my jam—and Fen was fun. He's different though. A bit intense, but I think he's secretly longing for someone to help him let loose. There is a panther/lion combo in there just waiting to be unleashed." She took another enormous bite.

Alex clutched her sides and shook with laughter. "If anyone can do the unleashing, it's you, Rox."

"I know. Timing is everything," Rox said with a coquettish smile. "Now, spill the news, sister."

Alex filled her in on the impromptu meeting with Dr. Kenosi, gushing about the grant opportunity as if she was a lovesick teenager. "This could change everything, Rox," she said, her eyes shining. A once elusive dream now within their grasp was an intoxicating feeling. Alex let her imagination unfold with the vision of a row of occupied hospital beds with advanced monitoring systems, centralized oxygen delivery, and teams of well-trained medical professionals performing heroic saves.

Rox plucked her from daydreaming by swinging a frosty can of Diet Coke in her line of sight. "Where in the world did you get that?" asked Alex, immediately reaching for the can. Ice-cold drinks were impossible to come by, and Alex had adjusted to drinking everything mildly tepid while at work.

"I might have nicked it from Kenosi's office while his administrative assistant wasn't looking," she said proudly. There were definite perks to Dr. K's new position, and apparently, an endless supply of cold drinks was one of them.

"You are a lifesaver." Alex practically swooned as she felt the exquisite burn of the cold soda in her throat. "Do you think it's pathologic that I basically plan my day by which caffeinated beverage is due next?" she asked, critically eyeing the top of her can for dirt.

"Yes, as a matter of fact, I do. Now before I have to run off and check if my laboring ladies are ready to push out some babies, what was the name of the foundation about to make all your wildest dreams come true?"

"We haven't gotten it yet, and I don't want to jinx it, but Dr. K said it was De—something. Devall foundation, I think," Alex answered.

Rox looked pensive as she checked her phone. "Do something for me—google it when you get home. It can't hurt to know some background, maybe what they might be looking for," she said with a wink.

The idea was brilliant, and Alex paused to place it on her mental to-do list. Her attempt to fully process the secretive smile on Rox's face was interrupted by her name being shouted from across the courtyard.

With surprising agility, Alex tore across the grass to the sidewalk, turned the corner alongside a breathless Mercy, and raced down the hallway to the pediatric ward. They arrived at the bed of the young boy who was suspected of having heart failure, and Alex pushed her way through the crowd gathered there. She immediately reached for his wrist. It was floppy and pulseless.

She stepped back from the boy, raising her voice above the din, "Mercy and Khobi, I need you to start CPR. Lesedi, I need a dose of adrenaline now." Alex kept her hand on his femoral artery as Mercy and Khobi took turns compressing his chest. She could feel them forcing the blood out of his heart with every solid compression, but every time they paused, the regularity of his pulse faltered and staggered into nonexistence. Fifteen minutes went by. One more dose of adrenaline given. Twenty minutes passed then thirty.

"Can anyone think of anything else we should try? If not, we are going to stop the resuscitation," Alex said calmly. A heavy silence ensued, punctuated only by the muffled sobs of the boy's mother, who was standing at the periphery of their tight ring around the little boy. Alex's heart broke, a tiny shard floating down into grim oblivion.

"Time of death is 1:32 p.m.," Alex said as she stepped to the boy's head and wiped his face clean. Placing a palm on his forehead, she whispered a quick prayer—for him, for his mom, for herself. Lesedi brought his mother over, and the nurses made short work of arranging his body in a bundle of sheets so that it seemed he was just napping and might wake at any moment. Placing a hand on the mother's shoulder, Alex gave her a silent, sorrowful squeeze and left her to grieve in peace.

The packed dirt felt good under Alex's sneakers as she turned off the street onto an unpaved path that wound its way from the back of the hospital all the way to the first village outside Gaborone. She found the solitude she often sought on this largely unused road with her only companion a statuesque donkey that stood within a muzzle's distance of getting razed by a truck were one to come along. He had been standing in the same spot during every single run she had ever taken since moving to Botswana. She ran past the donkey who never acknowledged her presence, not even with a simple blink of his overly large eyes. For some reason, she felt a strange kinship with this masochistic mammal, like at times she herself was a chin hair away from being bowled over by some unseen force. She continued on, pounding out a therapeutic rhythm, a melody of grief and distress, that trailed behind her all the way back to her house.

Once in her favorite sweats snuggled up next to her favorite canine on the lumpy purple couch, she allowed herself a long exhale and a monumental swallow of chilled white wine. Stellenbosch was known for its Chenin blanc, and she had taken the opportunity to stock up during her most recent trip with Rox. As she sipped the wine, swirling the divine liquid around her palate, she rewound through the day's events, specifically focusing on the young boy who had suddenly died this afternoon.

Alex was no stranger to death. Sometimes it was peaceful. Sometimes it was quite ugly. No matter how it occurred, it was always shocking and painful for those watching it happen. Death served as both a friend and an enemy, delivering comfort to the dying and excruciating heartache to the living. Children were not supposed to die—but they did and, sometimes, despite her best efforts. Alex had also witnessed kids survive the most horrendous illnesses and injuries when their medical team had said otherwise. The more she learned about death and survival, the more she

23

realized how out of her control it truly was. What she could control, however, was preventing kids from ever having to stare death in the face at all.

Hearing Roxanne's voice in her ear, Alex flipped open her laptop and typed "Devall foundation" onto the Google homepage. She began scrolling through photos of a white-haired, dapper gentleman in a black Armani suit shaking hands with the Botswana minister of health. The caption read "Devall Mining CEO, F. George Devall, was honored recently by the Botswana Ministry of Health".

Devall Mining Company—the name did sound familiar now. They were the largest mining conglomerate in Africa and were known for the partnerships they formed with local companies to make a positive economic impact in the countries they mined. The Devall partnership with the Tswana diamond company had brought millions of dollars, not to mention jobs, into Gaborone. Alex continued scrolling through various news articles from the last five years. "Devall company merges with competitor to become largest mining company in Africa." "Devall mining pledges $1M to fight malaria." "Devall named world's most eligible bachelor."

She smiled as she clicked on the link to that page, expecting to see the attractive, older man in the black suit pop up on her screen when, much to her absolute shock, a familiar face housing a pair of sky-blue eyes smiled seductively back at her.

# FOUR

*What the actual hell?* Alex siphoned up the image in front of her. There he was—blue eyes peeking out from dark tousled hair and a day's worth of stubble highlighting his jawline. He was wearing a white button-down shirt that exposed his neck, and a dark gray sportscoat over low-slung jeans.

"Ian Devall," she read haltingly, "heir to the Devall mining fortune, was named the world's most eligible bachelor last year by the *UK Daily Mail.*" After a second of hesitation, she plunged into the proverbial rabbit hole of internet gossip and scrolled through a hefty collection of paparazzi photographs—at the Met Gala last year posing on the iconic staircase, walking out of Starbucks, one hand balancing coffee while he held the door for a leggy blonde who Alex was pretty sure was a Victoria's Secret model, next to Mr. Devall senior and a crowd of young Kenyan girls in school uniforms as he cut the ribbon in front of an orange-brick schoolhouse.

Alex continued to scroll furiously as picture after glossy picture of Ian flashed across her screen—Ian as a teenage model, Ian surrounded by a crowd of guys holding up a large stein of beer in a college bar, Ian brisk and businesslike as he talked on the phone while crossing Trafalgar square. His entire life had been carefully curated for Alex to peruse. Before her obsession intensified any further, she poured another glass of wine, drank half of it in one gulp, and dialed Roxanne.

Rox picked up on the second ring and immediately started recounting the trials of her day when Alex cut her off abruptly. "Did you know who he was this entire time?"

"Know who who was, my dear?"

"The guy in the bar," said Alex through stressfully clenched teeth.

25

"The Devall Foundation...that he...that they..." She floundered miserably.

"I'm right around the corner. Be there in a jiff."

After five excruciatingly long minutes, Rox was seated on the purple couch next to Alex and McCartney, sipping her own wine and luxuriously reveling in her friend's discomfort.

"The short answer is no. I had no idea who he was from the delicious view of his backside that I had at Ex-Pats, but I keep up with social media, and I knew of him and then when you said Devall foundation yesterday, I thought—hmmm."

"And your 'hmmm' was not important to share! To warn me before I googled myself into a state of insanity!" Alex was pacing the room at this point, taking a gulp of wine every few steps and just waiting for some type of aneurysm to explode in her electrostatic brain.

"This is so good for you, Alex," she said wickedly. "I've never seen the bent out of shape version of you before."

"I was fine. Completely fine! We had a moment and I had a mini-identity crisis...and then I realized that I would never...see... him...again! And it was fine!" Alex was practically yelling.

Roxanne settled further into her suede purple couch haven and accepted into her lap the anxious brown puppy who was unsure what to make of his owner. The increasing level of alcohol in her bloodstream transitioned Alex from a state of panic to intense purpose.

"Thursday is a huge day. This grant could potentially change everything, and I will not let anything, or anyone, be a distraction. He probably will not even remember me. He probably hasn't spent one second thinking about me since he ..." she paused, flustered with what words to choose.

"Enraptured you? Mentally sexed you? Twisted you up like a pretzel?" Rox offered with a smirk.

A giddy Rox laughed silently and held up her wineglass as a pillow sailed in her direction.

Alex spent the next two days in relentless pursuit of any information she could find on Ian Devall, his family, their company, and their charitable foundations. The results were admittedly impressive from his grandfather's rise from middle-class businessman to mining mogul to the substantial amount of money they had contributed to further the projects of various nongovernmental organizations. They had donated millions of dollars to the International Pediatric AIDS initiative, built schoolhouses in every single country that they had a mining operation, and, from the looks of it, maintained an exclusive elephant reserve in Tanzania. Then, there was the true juicy pulp of their story packaged up in the ridiculously attractive, sexually charged heir to the Devall empire. Racy photographs and gossip columns written about Ian seemed to emerge around the time he graduated from Cambridge University. Every picture shared the same theme and was just a slightly different version than the one before—Ian impeccably dressed at some ritzy event, holding a glass of sparkling liquid, surrounded by women with perfect tresses and flawless faces. She noticed that no woman appeared twice in any of the snapshots of his life and, for some reason, felt a sense of satisfaction. There were a few more casual images, Ian always in jeans and a t-shirt with tousled bedroom hair and one, in particular, she liked of him out running with a cute Jack Russell terrier at his heels. She pored through interviews he had given various magazines, noting that his answers were mostly glib and vague, never revealing anything too personal.

> *From GQ magazine:*
> *Rob (Editor GQ): Tell me Ian—as the world's most*
> *eligible bachelor any special lady who might change*
> *that?*
> *Ian: All the ladies are special to me, Rob. I could*
> *introduce you to a few if you like.*
> *Rob: (laughing) I'm sure you could -but let's talk about*
> *the next five years. Where do you see yourself?*
> *Ian: Everywhere (said with a smirk and a shrug)*

Alex clicked on the link to the Devall Foundation website, which contained a list of past and current projects, various grant applications, and photos of star-studded charity events, many of which included a tux-clad Ian. The words of his recent interview with GQ rang true—he was everywhere, including permanently embalmed in Alex's brain. Did he have to look so heart-stoppingly gorgeous? Shaking her head, as if she could thrust him right out of her disobedient thoughts, she opened up the most current foundation newsletter and read aloud.

"The Devall Foundation recently named Ian Devall as the new

chair of the board of trustees, replacing his father, F. George Devall, who stepped down after twenty years of leadership."

That confirmed it. Ian would most likely be at the hospital on Thursday to evaluate the pediatrics program, and she would be more than ready.

Alex popped one eye open and turned her phone on its side to see the time—5:40 a.m. The sun was just beginning to tint the horizon with a pink hue, and the neighborhood rooster was belting out his welcome call to the morning. Sitting up groggily, Alex realized she had fallen asleep with her laptop still open on her chest. McCartney had already jumped to the floor and was thumping his tail excitedly, ready for a trip outside. Feeling the catecholamine surge that happens with too little sleep and over-caffeination, Alex began frantically preparing for her day at the hospital, which included rummaging through her chest of drawers for clothes, tossing journal articles into her bag, and patting her pup's head between chores for emotional support.

Unlike other mornings, Alex actually sat down in front of her bathroom mirror and carefully applied some mascara and a hint of lip gloss. She plaited her thick brown locks into a simple braid that hung over her shoulder and slipped on a navy sheath dress and a pair of nude calf-skin heels, the only nice outfit she had brought to Africa. Shrugging on her long white lab coat, the pockets filled with her medical treasures like her beloved stethoscope, she headed out into the chilly dust-laden morning. Rox, who had offered to meet her for coffee before her big meeting with the foundation, let out a relieved sigh when she saw Alex tromp through the door.

"I'm cutting to the chase, love. How are you? Nervous? You look phenomenal by the way," Rox said with a proud smile.

"Thanks. I am nervous," Alex stuttered, right as her emotions welled up to the surface. "I can think of all kinds of things I would rather do today—like, oh, I don't know—jump into a pit of snakes. I have never felt so unsettled. My insides are all butterflies." She shakily perched on the edge of a wobbling plastic chair.

"You will be brilliant," gushed Rox as she sipped her latte and glanced at her phone. "I have to run, but I promise that I will meet you at Ex-Pats afterward to hear everything." With a flourish of her silk skirt, she scooped up her day planner, phone, and steaming latte and strode out of the café.

Alex clutched her mug of chai and let the warmth soak into her palms and grow her courage. She took a few mouth-searing gulps interspersed with deep calming breaths and mentally rehearsed her speech to the foundation committee.

A few hours later, Alex was standing nervously in the courtyard at Princess Marina, a crisp fall breeze ruffling her hair. With Dr. Kefentse in the lead, a small group of men and women dressed in business attire made their way toward her from the administrative offices. Once they were near enough to warrant introduction, Dr. K announced, "Everyone, please, I would like to introduce Alex Wilde. She is the brilliant doctor that I have been telling you about. She will be touring you through the pediatric ward and answering all your questions today."

Each of the foundation members reached forward, in turn, with an open hand for introductions. Alex committed each face and name to memory as they took turns offering her a greeting.

A short, attractive young woman with copper hair smoothed into a bun stepped forward. "Hello, Dr. Wilde. My name is Lydia Fisher. I am the director of the grants evaluation program for the Devall foundation". She spoke with a lilting Scottish brogue, and her green eyes were warm and kind. Alex liked her immediately.

Next was a tall, aging gentleman in his sixties with a lovely British accent and a thick shock of white hair. "George Harris. Lovely to meet you. I am the legal counsel with a specialty in Tribal Law."

The next two came in quick succession—Rachel, director of children's initiatives, and Rahul, executive assistant to the board of trustees.

Alex had been so consumed with memorizing names and engaging with their coordinating faces that she felt mentally unprepared for the sight of Ian Devall. Suddenly he stood right in front of her in a charcoal gray suit, dusty rose shirt and maroon tie, like a page from *GQ* magazine had expanded to life-size. His eyes found hers and held them for a moment, and she searched for a flicker of recognition. Then, almost to her disappointment, he held out a smooth hand and said, "Ian Devall" in a voice that was so low and sexy that it made Alex's ears tingle. He smiled assuredly as if he expected her to know who he was and exhibit some fantastic reaction.

Instead, Alex willed her body into quietude and simply took the proffered hand.

"Nice to meet you. Thank you for coming, Mr. Devall." Alex was the quintessential professional, if nothing else. Ian seemed bemused by her response. Laughter, along with something else, flared in his eyes as he let go of her hand.

"I am so grateful that we are being considered for this generous grant. If everyone will follow me," Alex announced to the small group, "I can take you to our pediatric ward."

Alex led the group, albeit painfully slowly in her heels, down the sidewalk to the hospital wing that housed the eighteen-bed pediatric unit. Externally, she remained upright and poised as the foundation members followed along, asking questions along the way about the organizational structure of the hospital and the number of children they cared for each year. Meanwhile, a tiny group of neurons in her cerebral cortex fired with questions regarding Ian—did he remember her from the bar? Why did she care so much if he did? Was he as self-assured and arrogant as he seemed? Exceedingly grateful for her skills at multi-tasking, she attempted to impress the group with her answers while pondering the insanely attractive man walking in her shadow.

As they entered the pediatric ward, Alex beamed with pride. The interns were scattered about the unit examining their patients, while the nurses, clad in navy and white uniforms, performed their daily tasks of patient assessment, charting vital signs, and administering medications. There were twelve patients in the unit today, a representative cohort of the epidemiology of the region, with diagnoses including diarrhea, pneumonia, and one new onset seizures.

"Welcome to our pediatric unit. We are the regional center for seriously ill children," Alex explained. She walked toward the center of the open space, surrounded on the periphery by a cacophony of crying children. In her peripheral vision, she noticed Ian reaching in his pocket for his phone and frowning as he started furiously texting some unknown entity. Alex internally bristled at his lack of interest and began a passionate monologue about the potential capabilities of the pediatric program given the right resources.

"These kids are fighters," she heard herself proclaim loudly across the noisy din. "But in order to give them the best possible chance of survival, we have to address the limits of our physical resources as well as the barriers in creating sustainable educational interventions."

Ian continued to monitor his phone while glancing up at her periodically, a curiously tense expression on his face. Alex's eyes swept from Ian to the many mothers seated at their children's bedsides, helping to change them or feed them spoonfuls of yellow porridge. Her heart, filled with compassion, kept driving the words exiting her lips while she silently willed the foundation committee to understand the potential of this place. The Devall group stood close by in a tiny cluster, listening with rapt attention or taking notes on their clipboards—all except Ian, who absently stared out the nearest window.

"Well, Dr. Wilde, it has been a pleasure to see the great work you are doing in action." The gentle lilting voice came from Lydia. "At this point, we usually sit down together and ask a few questions. Would that be acceptable?"

"Of course," responded Alex, "I can take you to our meeting room." The room, already small, seemed to get smaller once everyone was seated on the upcycled elementary school chairs that served as the only seating options. Alex opened the window to allow a breeze to circulate and then took a chair opposite the half-moon seating configuration.

"Dr. Wilde, if awarded this grant, please tell us how it would be used," began Rachel, who beamed a genuine smile across her lightly freckled face.

Alex spent several minutes mapping out her vision for optimizing the care of any critically ill child that presented to PM. Right in mid-sentence, as she was describing a training program that simulated scenarios to improve nursing competence, Ian interrupted.

"I have a question." He paused, leaning back in his chair, before continuing. "Everyone thinks they can make a difference, but in reality, not many people actually pull it off. I want to know what makes you different?"

Alex stared at him for a moment and then uttered the most ridiculously honest statement she had ever made. "I don't know." The room received her answer in complete silence. As the words abandoned her lips, she felt a somatic disconnect with her body, as if her mind were denying it had any relationship with the idiot who had just spoken.

She cleared a throat that was threatening to close. "I don't know what makes me different…but I do know how to help the children here survive past age five and have a chance at life." She caught her breath, willing herself into calm. "Thank you again for your time today. We are grateful that you were willing to come."

The foundation members rose as one, many of them eyeing her empathetically, and she walked mechanically to the door to bid them goodbye. The inevitability of her failure nestled itself in the pit of her stomach, waiting to surface until a more appropriate time when she could let the tears fall freely and without judgment.

"Thank you very much for the visit, Dr. Wilde."

"Thank you, Dr. Wilde."

"A pleasure, Dr. Wilde."

One by one, they shook her hand, murmuring their appreciation, and exited the doorway.

Ian was last to leave. She both dreaded and was relieved by this final interaction with him. He would become a nagging reminder of her failure at the bar, her failure here today, and her complete ineptitude at life outside, and apparently inside, the hospital walls. She forced herself to meet his gaze one final time and was surprised that he was intently staring back at her, eyes searching and finding what they sought. His face cracked into a sideways grin.

"You still owe me a drink, Alexandra."

# FIVE

Alex stared down at the golden liquid brimming over the top of the shot glass, and the frosty bottle of beer gathered like a pair of commiserating old friends. She couldn't decide which one to drink first. Señorita tequila won out, and she threw back her head to let the burn spread like wildfire to her toes. He had definitely recognized her—the arrogant jerk. She felt justified in feeling betrayed. As she reviewed the day's events in her mind, she saw him standing apart from the group, distracted by his phone, unengaged during her speech, thoroughly disconnected from the sick kids right in front of his face. Then he had the audacity to ask her an impossible question that made it seem like she lacked self-awareness and lacked passion for what she did. Both of which were entirely untrue. She could only be angry with herself for the latter. In the spirit of self-flagellation, she tipped the cold bottle up to her lips.

Halfway through her beer, she caught sight of Rox weaving her way through the growing Thursday night crowd at Ex-Pats. Rox looked stunning in a flowing red silk skirt and black sleeveless top, a chunky red-lacquered necklace resting atop her décolletage. She tossed her leather handbag on top of the bar and eyed Alex up and down.

"Empty shot glass...hunched posture...missing shoes." Rox *tsk'ed* as she tilted her head toward Alex's heels that had been shed haphazardly under the barstool. "Jeff!" she belted authoritatively, and seconds later, Jeff, with a secret smile on his face, wiped down Rox's section of the bar and plunked down a bottle of tequila, a bowl of limes, and a shaker of coarse sea salt.

Rox took her time pouring the tequila into a Lilliputian-sized glass and then pushed the bottle toward Alex. After draining the glass and squeezing a fresh lime provocatively into her mouth, she licked her lips and honed her senses onto her best friend.

"So...how did it go today, love?" she asked gently.

Alex gave an audible groan and then launched into a detailed recap of her day, from the polite, diverse members of the foundation committee to her ridiculous flub during the interview portion thanks to Ian.

"He acted completely aloof during the tour today. Who does that in a children's ward?" When Rox failed to comment, Alex continued her rant, aggressively squeezing a slice of lime into her beer. "He is an arrogant ass that tries to hide behind his flirty comments and seductive...hair."

Rox bore a thoughtful expression, as if her thoughts were weighing themselves on the wisdom scale, competing for which ones would be revealed. "He is toying with you, Alex. And he is toying with you because he wants you...and he wants you because he can't have you...or perceives he can't."

Alex rolled her eyes in part annoyance and part disbelief. "Number one—there is no way that he wants anything to do with me—a socially challenged, neurotic doctor with no fashion sense." She held up her hand as Rox started to interrupt. "No, Rox. I have googled until my eyes were blurry. I know his lifestyle and the kinds of ladies he is photographed with and how attractive," she paused and swallowed another gulp of beer, "he is."

"Number two," she continued, her tongue much looser than it was an hour ago, "I just completely screwed up this grant for our pediatrics program, partly because I was distracted by Ian Devall and his sky-blue eyes and twisty sex appeal." She paused long enough to drain her beer and let the alcohol unhinge the doorway to her emotions. Alex wanted to feel loose and carefree right now but regret and crushing disappointment were edging them out.

"The staff...the kids...Dr. K...they were all depending on me," she said as tears threatened her vision and her nose burned with the sense of devastation.

"Alex," Rox said smoothly, accepting an ice-laden beverage from Jeff that contained a little purple umbrella. "You are about the furthest thing from a disappointing human that I have ever met. Now—" she said, changing her tone from empathetic to businesslike, "go in the bathroom, wash your face, and convince him what everyone else already knows." Rox tilted her head toward the door. "That you are a dedicated, brilliant physician who can't possibly fail."

Alex whipped her head around to see Ian talking and laughing as he made his way through the crowd. She wasn't sure how long she remained in a state of suspended animation, staring in complete disbelief.

"Go!" Rox hissed, thrusting a crystal tube in her direction. "And put on some lip gloss."

Fifteen minutes later, a refreshed appearing Alex emerged from the ladies' room, a fresh sheen of pink gloss on her lips and just enough circulating alcohol to raise her confidence a notch.

"Okay," she said, a bit breathless, "how do I do this? I need the cliff notes version of Rox 101."

"I thought you'd never ask." Rox's eyes gleamed, and she launched into her favorite subject: manipulation—emphasis on the man part.

"Make brief eye contact—just enough to acknowledge his presence but not enough to seem like you're keeping tabs. Whatever you are doing, even if it's the most boring thing in the world, smile and laugh. Flirt but don't intimidate. And for goodness sake, keep your heels on. Never take them off! You have great calves."

"Got it. Eye contact...ha ha...flirt...shoes on...game on," Alex summarized, smiling to herself.

"And Alex, you have to act as if he is the last thing on the planet you would want," Rox added.

"That will be the easiest part," claimed Alex boldly, "because he definitely is."

Rox rolled her eyes dramatically and excused herself to the ladies' room. Alex watched her leave and then, in her current state of debauchery, briefly mused why this all seemed like a good idea.

"Good evening, Ex-Pats," rang a loud South African accent over a crackly speaker system. "It's time for our Thursday night dart tournament. Sign up at the bar and make your way over to the dartboard."

In a wild moment of delusional overconfidence and the desire to do something out of character, Alex hopped off her barstool and boldly scribbled her name on the sign-up sheet. As she sidestepped through the seated patrons toward the back of the bar containing the billiards, she caught Ian glance up at her. Their eyes met for a moment and held there until Alex narrowed her gaze and motioned toward the crowd gathering to throw darts. *Gauntlet thrown. Game on, Ian.*

Once shrouded in the most dimly lit portion of the bar, she could observe Ian without being accused of staring. Although Alex hated to admit it, she couldn't deny that he was devastatingly handsome. Tonight, he was dressed in black jeans that hugged his backside, a black t-shirt, and a black leather jacket that completed the look of "devil-may-care" heir. She giggled at her own humor. His surname was literally the closest one could come to being named *devil.*

She watched him throw back the last remnants of his drink, most likely bourbon, and politely excuse himself from the small crowd of female admirers that flanked his table. Then, almost to her disbelief, he made his way toward her. A few thoughts raced through her head, one of which was the desperate hope that her sheer force of will and extreme competitiveness could win out over the fact that she had never thrown a dart in her life.

Luckily for Alex, a little liquid audacity blended well with her competitive spirit. Three rounds into the tournament, she had eliminated opponent after opponent with each missile-like strike of the bullseye. A small crowd had gathered to cheer her on with hands and voices rising with her every successful throw. Somewhere in her fuzzy brain, she had unlocked the key to winning at this game. Having nothing to lose had made her both reckless and unbeatable. Rox was standing in the second tier of onlookers waving proud encouragement from time to time when she wasn't being distracted by an attractive, olive-skinned guy with wavy hair that looked mildly familiar to Alex.

"Very impressive accuracy," said an all too familiar voice coming from behind her. He was so close that she could feel his warm breath on her hair and smell the distinct spice of bourbon.

"I'm just picturing your face on the dartboard." She sailed another dart through the air without turning around.

"Ouch," he said, feigning hurt and putting his hand over his heart.

"It looks like we are down to our final two opponents," boomed a voice over the speaker system, "Alex Wilde to represent the ladies and Ian Devall to represent the gentlemen."

Alex had been so focused on her own personal vendetta with the dartboard that she had failed to realize that Ian was actually good, and his skills had put him through to the final round of competition.

*Perfect.*

"For our final round, we will be doing a little around the world. Four darts to hit three spots on the board. The bullseye, number twenty, and number seven. Loser buys the winner a drink."

"Ladies first," said Ian, gesturing toward the board and dipping his head in a semi-bow.

For the first time that evening, Alex felt a creeping nervousness threaten her and not because she was afraid of losing at darts. She chewed her bottom lip like she did when trying to figure out what to do with a patient, took a deep breath, and let it out slowly, releasing her first dart. *Bullseye.*

Inwardly gleeful and unable to stop the smile forming on her face, she chose her next dart and aimed. The dart landed inside the twenty by a mere millimeter, and the entire bar erupted in a cheer. In her peripheral vision, she saw Ian toast her with his drink, a smoldering, unbelievably sexy look in his bluer than blue eyes. Her hand shook a little as she aimed dart number three and, subsequently, missed number seven entirely.

Missing only fueled her determination, and Alex blocked out the noise of the bar...the events of the day...and Ian...especially Ian...as she connected her fourth and final dart with number seven. Bar patrons she didn't even know hugged her, and someone shoved a shot of something pink toward her, which she downed greedily. She took a seat in the brown leather chair immediately facing the dart area, eager to watch Ian lose.

Amid a round of applause and a few whoops, he sauntered up to the dartboard and took a quick moment to flash a smile to his admiring set of female groupies. In quick succession, he sent three darts airborne. Alex couldn't even see where they had landed because everyone around her jumped to their feet excitedly. *Game over.* Alex pressed her temples between her palms.

"No time for a pity party, Annie Oakley. Now you owe me two drinks."

Alex looked up to see an extended hand in front of her face belonging to an expressionless yet impossibly sexy Ian, dark brows knit over still-smoldering blue eyes that studied Alex's face. As she met his gaze, her breath caught, and she hesitated for a moment, like whatever she did next might change her life forever. Her hand reached out of its own accord, and the next thing Alex knew, warm, strong fingers encased hers, pulling her to her feet.

"Annie Oakley shot rifles," she muttered, mostly to herself.

He led her to a semi-private area of Ex-Pats, a small room off the main bar where they held work parties and wine tastings. It was quite a bit nicer than the main seating area with traditional wooden chairs using stretched animal hides as seats placed artistically on a plush rug. Instead of a bar, there was a mini-kitchen with open shelves containing crystal flutes and wine glasses and an enormous floor to ceiling wine refrigerator. No one else occupied the space, and Alex was pretty sure this was a perk of being the heir to a fortune.

Suddenly her heart was pounding. She hadn't anticipated being alone with him or being this irresistibly drawn to him. Fortunately, what she lacked in poise and style, she made up for in will power and self-discipline. Although what it would be like to feel his strong arms lift her onto the counter and kiss every inch of her...

"Alexandra?" Her name sounded like a sonnet on his lips and hauled her out of her lascivious daydream. "Did you want a drink?"

"Sure," she responded, a bit too eagerly. "And you can call me Alex."

"All right, Alex." He narrowed his eyes and smiled seductively. "Anything in particular, or are you still deciding—what you want that is?"

Alex decided to ignore him for a moment in an attempt to rein in her imagination and let Rox's advice reverberate in her head. She perused the extensive options in the wine refrigerator and settled on a Chenin blanc from the Eastern Cape, something cold and crisp to calm her nerves and slow her pulse. She handed him the bottle, silently watching while he filled two glasses with the golden liquid. They sat down in matching zebra-hide chairs next to each other, not speaking, and Alex enjoyed how the wine drowned out the noise of their thoughts and relaxed the tension vibrating between them.

Alex's frontal lobe felt fuzzy and unhinged. Suddenly she realized her mouth was moving of its own accord without the beneficial censorship of a mental filter.

"I have a question for you, Ian Devall," she said with particular emphasis on his name.

"Okay," he said simply. "But fair's fair…if you get a question, then so do I."

Alex nodded assent, then took a deep breath and in a quiet voice asked, "why do you believe that people can't make a difference?"

He appeared taken aback by her question and furrowed his brows in concentration for a minute. His arrogance and egocentric mannerisms were replaced by thoughtfulness and a distant look in his eyes. "I never said people can't make a difference," he said carefully, "but in my experience, they usually don't. I don't like being disappointed. If my expectations are low enough, I won't be." He shrugged casually and put his wineglass to his lips.

"What a shame," said Alex defiantly, "that a person with your influence and resources can't open his eyes to see what is good in this world…what is worth fighting for." Alex continued as Ian stared at her, his mouth half-open. "Why are you even here?"

Ian took a swig of his drink, swishing it around in his mouth and swallowing audibly. "To see something good in the world…something worth fighting for." He smiled so sincerely that Alex was speechless for a moment and then shook her head dismissively.

"You are just mocking me now."

"No…no, I'm not. Cross my heart," he said with a grin and a hand placed over his flat, muscular chest.

"My turn for a question." Ian topped off their wine glasses. "What in the world were you doing the first night we met?"

Alex could feel the flush starting in her neck and spreading upward. She debated her options quickly and decided that there was too much circulating alcohol to invent a well-conceived lie. The truth it was then.

"My friend Roxanne and I play a game sometimes where each of us picks a random guy in the bar for the other," she said with a wince. "The winner is the one who can get the guy to kiss her in the least amount of time…without telling him about the game. And the loser has to pay for the drinks." Knowing this sounded completely ridiculous, Alex stole a glance at Ian to gauge his response.

"I can't imagine that you would ever lose," he said with a raise of one eyebrow.

Alex snorted in response. "I've never won. Rox is a tigress."

As she watched her wine swirl around her glass, mimicking her thoughts, she became acutely aware of a thumb gently tracing her cheekbone. The eyes that locked with her own were compelling, shining with admiration and a hint of disbelief. Reflexively, Alex closed her eyes and parted her lips just slightly. He was close enough that they were breathing the same air. She felt him exhale onto her bottom lip.

"Ian, there you are, man! You've got to help me with Rahul," said a voice from the doorway. Alex's eyes flew open and noticed the figure over Ian's shoulder. It was the handsome, olive-skinned guy she had seen talking to Rox earlier. Ian twisted around toward his friend.

"Be right there, Nic," he said in a clipped tone and then stood up with resignation. "I have to go."

Before Alex had time to respond, she was watching his black boots stride toward the door. Inexplicable panic rose in her chest, and she blurted out the first thing that came to mind.

"If you want to see something worth fighting for, meet me at the hospital in the morning."

# SIX

"So, he nearly kisses you and then just ups and walks away?" asked Rox the next morning as they watched the sun tint Alex's kitchen in a layer of rose gold. They were dissecting the night's previous events over mugs of steaming red bush tea and thick toast loaded with jam.

"Pretty much," quipped Alex, her mouth full of bread.

"Do you think he will show up today?" asked Rox carefully, her eyes flitting back and forth to her phone.

"I have no idea," said Alex, sighing and dipping her teabag deeper into her mug. "Maybe I don't even want him to."

"Mmm," murmured Rox distractedly, sipping her tea and checking her phone once more.

"Who was that guy I saw you ogling over last night?" inquired Alex, attempting to change the subject. "He looked familiar for some reason."

Before Rox could answer, Alex's phone rang, and Dr. K's name flashed up on the screen. Alex groaned inwardly. She still hadn't told him about the disastrous meeting with the foundation committee.

"Hi, Dr. K. What can I do for you?"

"Dr. Alex," he said in a booming voice. "I want to hear how everything went, but I am short on time. There is a dinner tonight at my house. I need you to come. Seven o'clock. Bring Roxanne if you like."

"Okay, that sounds…great." Halfway through her sentence, she noticed he had already disconnected.

Rox, utterly oblivious to anything outside the sphere of her current infatuation, grinned to herself and texted furiously on her phone, pink nails flying over the keypad.

Alex's own short excuses for fingernails drummed the table. "Rox...Rox!" She looked up then, a guilty, "cat-ate-the-canary" look on her face. Alex wondered why Rox was so enthralled with her phone this morning and was fairly certain it had something to do with a guy.

"I have to run over to PM and meet Mercy—we are going out in the field today. Can you go with me to some dinner party at Dr. K's tonight?"

"Of course, dear. Wouldn't miss it," she said slyly.

"And please plan on telling me why you are smiling like it's about to go out of style," Alex grinned, shaking her head at her friend as she grabbed the last of her toast and jogged out the door.


"Is that the last one?" She and Mercy were loading insulated ice coolers containing vaccines, a small selection of medications, and blood specimen vials into the back of the ancient white SUV used for hospital business.

"I hope so," exclaimed Mercy, whose breathing was coming quicker and heavier as she lifted the final container into the back of the truck. "Where are we going today, Dr. Alex?"

Alex barely heard her as she distractedly rearranged the supplies and threw her own emergency bag into the front seat. If she closed her eyes, she could still feel Ian's breath on her lower lip, and it filled her with an uneasy yearning that would not be ignored.

"Molepolole," she replied quietly. "We should probably get going." Alex let go of a breath she hadn't realized she was holding. He wasn't coming. I should lower my expectations, she thought ironically, as she climbed into the driver's seat and buckled in. He existed in an entirely different plane of the universe than everyone else. Visions of galas and supermodels and overflowing champagne glasses crowded her mind, and she started up the truck with a loud rev of the engine.

Mercy motioned for Alex to roll down the window. "What about him?" She pointed to a solitary figure visible in the side mirror, making room for a backpack amongst the medical supplies. He closed the tailgate with a bang and then his head and torso suddenly filled up the passenger side window. *Oh hell.*

Ian wrenched open the door and hopped nimbly into the passenger seat. "I call shotgun."

Five minutes later, they were pulling away from the front of PM with the wind gusting through the open truck windows, headed toward the village of Molepolole on the outskirts of Gaborone. Alex stole a glance at Ian, seated to her left, his head half out the window, aviators shading his eyes, arm holding onto the door frame as they whipped around Tlokweng circle. She smiled to herself as she deftly navigated the early morning Gaborone traffic to get them onto Molepolole road, recalling her first week in Botswana. It had been her first experience driving on the left side of the road, and she had driven painfully slowly amid a symphony of angry honks and undulating arms. She had tried to exit the roundabout but instead found herself in a throng of cars, unable to jostle for a position that would lead to her desired exit. Entirely stuck, she circled around and around at breakneck speed in a cluster of cars for several minutes until she could extract herself.

Now the whole death-defying experience seemed metaphorical. Alex had arrived in Botswana as a girl trapped in the proverbial hamster wheel of school and more school and internship and residency and then fellowship. She had let go of that girl while she was here and found the exit to her road—her path to happiness. Without any doubt, she knew she was meant to dedicate her life to helping kids survive and teaching others how to help kids survive. She had accepted the sacrifices it would entail long ago, mainly a work life imbalance that tipped heavily toward work. However, for something so worthwhile, personal sacrifice meant almost nothing.

So where did someone like Ian fit in? *Nowhere*, she thought, answering her own question. He would be gone soon, and life would be exactly as it should be. The only benefit to his presence would be the opportunity to persuade him to believe in these kids and possibly win that grant.

Alex cleared her throat and forced herself to make some conversation. "How was the rest of your night?"

"You mean after I whipped you at darts?" he taunted. She stole a glance at him, pieces of his hair ruffling in the wind like crow's wings. How could a man be so sarcastic and irresistibly sexy all at the same time? Narrowing her eyes, she returned her focus to the dust billowing up from the road rather than respond.

"Nic and I had to take a very drunk, very sloppy Rahul back to the hotel and convince him that even though his fiancé just cheated on him, broke his heart, and canceled their wedding…life is still worth living."

"Rahul?" Alex asked. "Quiet, polite Indian guy from the foundation committee?"

"The very one," said Ian with a smirk. "Whose existence reaffirms my plans to remain the eternal bachelor."

"Don't you believe in anything?" Alex scolded. "Love or charity or…good manners for that matter?"

"On the contrary, I believe in a lot of things…like self-preservation," he responded, scooting his aviators down his nose and giving her an exaggerated eye roll. "And excellent bourbon."

Alex grunted in response. "We're here." The gravel crunched under the tires as she threw the truck into park under a large acacia tree.

Without waiting for Ian, Alex hopped out and met Mercy around the back of the truck.

"Let's set up over there." She pointed to a grassy shaded area scattered with wooden benches. Mercy began pulling out a cooler, suppressing a smile as Ian, hands tucked in his jean pockets, edged around the side of the truck.

"Here," barked Alex as she thrust a heavy cooler into his mid-section, which he accepted with an audible grunt. "Follow Mercy."

Clusters of women dressed in colorful patterned skirts and headwraps with their children in tow were already making their way toward the park. This outreach program to the outlying communities and villages had been Dr. K's idea, and Alex had taken it over as her personal project. By expanding their catchment area, dangerous illnesses in children could be identified and treated before they became potentially fatal.

Alex and Mercy had honed the outreach process down to a science, which involved setting up an intake area to keep track of the children they saw and a testing station to collect blood samples to take back to the lab at PM. At the periphery of Alex's vision stood Ian, who, unlike his normal existence, was currently not the center of anyone's universe.

"Ian," she called, shielding her eyes from the sun's glare. "Do you think you can handle the snack table?"

Early on in their field adventures, she and Mercy had discovered how essential food and cool drinks were to the success of their mission.

"Your wish is my…" Ian's response drifted into the wind as he turned to unload the bags of crackers, cookies, and fresh fruit Alex had purchased at the grocery store earlier that week.

Being out in the open air on a sun-filled day surrounded by kids that needed examinations, vaccines, and treats for their bravery filled Alex with purpose and utter contentment. She thrived on the feeling of using her acquired gifts to serve others. Providing life-saving therapy in that critical moment of life versus death intoxicated her but today she was grateful for a break from the fast-paced hospital ward in favor of listening to little chests and handing out stickers.

"*Dumela ma! O tsogile jang?*" she said to her first patient of the day, a young mother with a baby wrapped close to her chest and a small boy of around eight holding tightly to her hand. The boy peered at her shyly with large milk chocolate eyes. He was small for his age but appeared healthy. Alex confirmed normal heart and lung sounds, providing a coveted *Superstar* sticker before sending them to see Mercy for blood sampling.

Alex dove into her work, asking the parents questions and examining each child before obtaining the appropriate vaccines or lab tests. A full hour later she finally looked up to check on Ian, who was diligently handing out packaged snacks to each family. A few of the kids, including her first little patient of the day, were kicking a soccer ball near the table and motioned for him to come and play.

With the unbridled enthusiasm of a young boy, he abandoned his snack post and jogged across the park, much to the elation of the children. After several minutes of hard play, his gray t-shirt hugged his lean, muscled back, and the edges of his hair were stuck to his temples with sweat. Finding it much more challenging to focus, Alex tore her eyes from the sight of a graceful Ian swiftly running across the park and doubled her efforts to get through the remaining families who had been waiting patiently in the sweltering heat.

While engrossed in listening to a baby's chest and, despite her ears being plugged up with the ends of her stethoscope, she suddenly heard a high-pitched scream. Grabbing her emergency bag, she and Mercy leaped up from their tables and sprinted toward the crowd gathering on the impromptu soccer field. The shy boy with the large brown eyes lay supine in the grass, his breath coming in quick, shallow gasps. Alex instinctively grabbed his wrist, palpating his pulse, which was strong but rapid, and feeling his skin, hot and dry to the touch.

"Heat exhaustion?" offered Mercy as she knelt down in the grass next to Alex.

"I think so. Probably dehydration and electrolyte abnormalities as well," responded Alex.

"Mercy, can you figure out how to call an ambulance? We should get him over to PM."

Ian cautiously observed from the crowd's edge, and Alex motioned for him to come over. "Ian, I need a second set of hands. Can you hold his head so that his airway stays clear—just like this." She demonstrated with her hands, and when his hands replaced hers on the boy's forehead and chin, she noticed they were visibly shaking. Alex filed this away for later and turned her attention to placing an IV and hooking it up to a bag of saline she happened to have in her bag. Once she had squeezed in most of the saline, the boy started to stir, his long-lashed eyes fluttering with wakefulness. The reassuring whine of an ambulance resounded up the street.

When the boy was safely loaded into the ambulance, Alex let herself breathe a little. After a bit of fluid and rest, he would be completely fine. Concern spiked for Ian, and she whipped her head around, searching and finding him sitting at the very edge of the park. Mercy had started organizing the coolers and cleaning up the scattered wrappers and banana peels buried in the grass.

"Can I join you in a moment?" asked Alex. "I need to go check on Ian." Mercy nodded, not bothering to hide her smile.

She found him sitting on a solitary patch of grass facing the street, elbows resting on his knees, his head pressed between his hands.

"Ian? Ian, are you okay?" Alex said softly as she laid a hesitant hand on his shoulder.

"I'm fine. I really need to get back though, if you are finished saving the world," he said with unbidden sarcasm.

Alex was too shocked by his response to reply immediately. "Mercy is waiting for us in the truck." She turned and did not wait for him to follow.

The drive back to the hospital in a truck filled with thick silence and unspoken questions sent Alex into an irritated state of despair. Every bump in the road made her adrenaline spike. By the time they pulled into the parking lot, she could not disentangle the various emotions coursing through her body—anger, compassion, distrust, and above all, a desperate need for resolution. Alex jumped out of the truck, leaving the door wide open in her haste, and strode around to the passenger side where Ian was knocking the dirt from his boots on the sidewalk.

"What was that back there?" she said, her voice thick with restraint.

"What was what?" he replied, still focused on his boots.

Alex folded her arms across her chest, partly to shield herself from his cruel indifference. "You were upset...and then you acted like a jerk."

"That's because I am a jerk, Alex." He turned his back to her then and walked away without a backward glance. For the second time that day, Alex stood, dumbfounded, with no words to describe the depth of hurt she felt. She had not felt that kind of hurt in a very long time.

When Alex entered her house, she could hear Roxanne rummaging through her closet and see several pieces of her clothing tossed haphazardly across her bed. Despite a terrible day, Alex had to smile at her friend's efforts to ensure it ended with a good night. McCartney was so excited to see her that he was circling the small bedroom, his tail not entirely clearing the bedside table where it was wreaking havoc on her photos and books.

"I'm so glad you're home!" sung Rox from the inside of the closet. "It's Friday! Time to get all dolled up." Two mismatched glasses next to a bottle of chilled sparkling wine lay in wait on her desk. With her propensity to generate fun, Rox was the human equivalent of Disney World, all packaged up in a shiny blonde Canadian.

"What's the occasion?" said Alex, bending down to let McCartney nuzzle his wet nose into her cheek.

"Two things," Rox called as a pair of shoes took flight. "One—I met the future love of my life and two—well—two is a surprise you'll find out later tonight." Her head popped out of the closet and took quick stock of Alex's constricted demeanor and grass-stained knees. "Whoa there, love."

Rox cleared a spot on the bed amidst the articles of clothing and patted it gently. McCartney, assuming this was meant for him, hurtled himself onto the open space before Alex could get there, whining and wriggling as he was forced to dismount. His antics brought a quick smile to Alex's face, a fleeting second before tears pricked her eyes. She allowed just one to spill over onto her cheek.

"I don't even know why I am crying," she said a few minutes later as Rox handed her a tissue. "I never cry."

She had revealed the detailed saga of her day—how Ian had indeed come on the field excursion and how he had transformed from kind and helpful to distant and spiteful. "The problem is," she continued, "that I started to care way too much about what he thought of me. It wasn't entirely about my work at the hospital. It was about me and my ridiculous ideas about love."

He had awoken something in her the first night they met—a rebirth of hope for irrevocable love, a love so powerful that it canceled out the burden of her pain.

Rox looked pensive as she wrapped Alex into a solid hug. "That kind of love does exist, my dear. You just have to be open to it, and unfortunately, being open to love means being open to hurt."

Alex sighed as her tears faded into nonexistence, and her emotions dialed back to neutral. "I can't handle any more hurt in my life, Rox. And I can't open my heart—not yet. Being vulnerable is terrifying for me and frankly, just not worth it." She picked at a piece of thread unraveling from her bedspread. "I have to close the door on this whole Ian situation."

"I'm sorry, my dear. I am here…always. Now—what can I do to help you through tonight?"

"Tonight?" Alex asked, puzzled.

"Ian and the foundation committee will be at Dr. K's party, Alex," Rox said gently. Alex's eyes widened for a second and then focused purposefully on her reflection in the full-length mirror hanging on her closet door.

"Do the thing you've always wanted to do," she said assertively, "make me into hot-Alex."

"How about 'I am a badass doctor who deserves better than you-Alex'?" Rox offered as a wicked smile spread over her features.

Two hours and a delicate glass of champagne later, Alex barely recognized herself in the mirror. She stood next to Rox, a bombshell on her worst day, who tonight was wearing a pale pink silk blouse with a few select buttons left undone tucked into a burgundy midi-length skirt. Rox had outdone herself doing Alex's makeup. Her ocean-blue eyes popped amid the dark eyeliner and swirling shades of lavender on her lids. Rox had loaned her a sheath dress the color of a rich pinotage that showed off the subtle curves of her thin figure and a pair of dove grey suede heels.

"You look sexy as hell. Now let's go." Rox grabbed her hand fiercely and shuttled them both out the door.

Several minutes later, they walked into Dr. K's home arm-in-arm to find a lively party already underway, complete with live music, tables lined with plates piled high with various local dishes, and guests holding glasses of wine milling about making conversation.

"Dr. K sure knows how to throw a dinner party," exclaimed Roxanne with a low whistle.

"Come on," said Alex boldly, surveying the room. "Let's get a drink, and you can spill the beans about the love of your life."

# SEVEN

They settled into glasses of a delectable pinotage under a canopy of stars as seen from Dr. K's courtyard, laughing and chatting until Alex felt her earlier misery lift a little. Her senses, although focused on Rox, disobeyed her periodically to scan the room for evidence of Ian. She desperately wanted to notice him first with the explicit purpose of mental preparation. However, when she spotted him in the distance, reaching out to shake hands with Dr. K, nothing could have properly prepared her. He looked intense and business-like with a discrete hint of melancholy but, as always, was impeccably dressed in a white button-down and a deep navy sportscoat over dark jeans. For the first time, she noticed how well defined his bone structure was in profile and how gracefully and purposefully his body moved.

"And then he just kissed me hard and pushed me against the wall…and my drink went flying!" Rox was talking through her chortling, doubled over with tears on her cheeks. Alex felt immediately guilty for sparing her attention from the story of Rox's post-Ex-Pats nightcap.

"You amaze me. It's a wonder you don't have men lined up around the block waiting to whip rings out of their pockets."

"Ah, well. Overachiever and all," Rox said with a bat of her lashes. "Listen, dear, there's something I need to tell you." Her tone switched from playful to serious.

Alex shifted her entire focus to Rox. "Sure. Everything okay?"

"The guy from Ex-Pats—he is the reason I have been so glued to my phone and I think he's the one, Alex. I know it in my soul."

"That's incredible, Rox," Alex gushed. "I am so happy for you!"

"He's Ian's best friend, Alex," she finished with an unreadable expression on her face as if preparing for any number of ways Alex could respond.

"Oh….oh." Alex swallowed past the obstruction in her throat and took a pause to process through panic, a smidge of envy, and then finally sincere excitement for her friend. "He is the absolute luckiest man in the universe then," she said and meant it.

"Oh definitely," said Rox, a seductive smile lighting up her features. "He just doesn't know it yet."

"I want to hear everything," said Alex. "But let me grab us some drinks first. This is a champagne kind of night."

As Alex strolled across the courtyard to the makeshift outdoor bar, she felt eyes on her back. She paused briefly to let Ian catch an eyeful of her hair falling in loose waves down her back and her rear-facing curves accentuated by the borrowed dress. *Door closing…*

"Two champagnes, please," Alex called to the uniform-clad young man tending bar and tried out her best smile. "Anything for you, Dr. Wilde," he replied, and she recognized Dr. K's oldest grandson, showing a full set of teeth as he grinned widely. "Leo," she whispered, "you are not old enough to be serving drinks." "I know," he said mischievously, "but *nkuku* promised me a small fortune."

Chuckling, she accepted her extra-full champagne glasses and turned around, her body connecting with something or rather someone steadfastly blocking her path.

"If you wanted to be closer to me, you just had to ask." Ian steadied her by the elbows to avoid a champagne catastrophe, his eyes narrowed and flirtatious.

"You are standing between me and everything that is fun about this night…so please move!"

"I would but I am seeing two of you, so I have no idea which way to go." He narrowed his eyes even further until they were slit-like.

"Are you drunk?" Alex asked, exasperated.

"Yep…as a skunk. I like that dress by the way. Very sexy…very not you." His eyes roved hungrily over her silhouette. Alex flinched a little in her uncertainty. Was he being insulting or complimentary? Then the liberation of not caring either way flashed through her.

"Ian! Ian, you promised to drink with us," whined an attractive redhead who snaked her arm around Ian's waist and stared at Alex like she was an alien lifeform.

"In one moment, dear. First, I want to introduce you to

Alexandra Wilde. She is a dedicated, talented doctor…but too afraid to be anything else." A delighted smirk spread across the redhead's face. "I guess you can't have everything," Ian said, shrugging and releasing his hold on Alex's elbows.

"You are an ass." Alex deliberately spat out each word as she skirted around them to rejoin Rox on the other side of the courtyard. *Door closed.*

Alex, freshly flushed and unhinged from her interaction with Ian, found Roxanne seated at a table with the hospital leadership executives and scooted in beside her. The table conversation centered around expanding the hospital teaching services, which both interested Alex and provided the distraction she needed. She sipped her champagne slowly and nibbled on some bread to settle her stomach. Although Roxanne kept passing her worried looks, Alex shrugged them off and tried to refocus the conversations around safe topics like work.

Halfway through dessert, which happened to be Alex's favorite, malva pudding, Dr. K stood up among the seated guests and cleared his throat loudly. "Thank you, my friends and colleagues, for joining us here on this beautiful evening." His rich baritone carried across the courtyard. "I have a very important announcement. Due to the commitment and dedication of our pediatrics department, especially Dr. Alex Wilde, we will be receiving a sizable grant from the Devall Foundation that will make our vision for this hospital a reality."

Alex sat in stunned silence as Rox tightly grabbed her hand. "I would like to give a special thanks to our new friends and partners at the foundation. Please join me in raising a glass." A symphony of clinking glassware and muttered toasts filled Alex's ears. "Let us continue our evening with dancing. Enjoy!" finished Dr. K as he swept forward into a sea of people ready to congratulate him.

Alex sat so still that she had to remind herself to breathe. Rox leaned over to whisper in her ear. "Sorry I couldn't tell you earlier. I was sworn to secrecy by Dr. K."

"No worries," said Alex, forcing a weak smile. "I think I need a little air. Be right back."

A few couples had filled up the courtyard and were swaying and weaving to the lilting music trickling from the outside speakers. Alex's heels sunk into the grass, slowing her to the pace of an awkward turtle, as she tried to sashay through the closely bound dancers. Drinking, high heels, and walking through soft sod did not mix. Proving her point, both shoe and foot failed to lift with her next step, and she hurtled forward into empty space with enough time to acknowledge her predicament but no time to react. A pair of steadfast arms broke her fall and tightened around her waist. She inhaled heavily—a spicy scent rich with bourbon.

"Alex," said Ian in an unexpectedly wistful tone.

*Damn.*

"Are you stalking me? You just want to keep the insults coming like I am your own personal dartboard?" Alex growled.

Ian ignored Alex and pressed forward with his agenda. "I was wondering if you would like to dance."

Alex said nothing but dangled her shoeless foot in front of her, at which point Ian bent to the ground to liberate her shoe and place it gently on her foot. Without speaking, he stood up and offered his hand to Alex. *Double damn.*

She placed her hand in his, and he quickly pulled her into a dancing embrace, his other hand precariously low on her back. As they swayed gently to the music, Alex kept a column of air between them and tried not to think. Not about the feel of his hand searing through the material of her dress. Not about how his sky-blue eyes never left her face, seeming to drink her in with every sidestep. Not about his body radiating with the need to be close to her. She tried only to focus on the disdain she felt. Her senses were heightened to a level of awareness that caused every nerve in her body to feel overstimulated.

When the music halted, and the dance ended, he stepped away from her, a half-smile briefly playing on his lips, and Alex discovered she was emotionally spent. In the spirit of resignation, she turned and hurried out of the courtyard into the open air of the night before she could change her mind.

She heard footsteps behind her, a musical accompaniment to her heels as they clattered along the sidewalk.

"Alex...wait."

She had no plans to slow down for him, but with her heels as a handicap, he quickly caught up with her. Gentle fingers encircled her wrist. Whirling around, she extracted her wrist from his grasp and folded her arms in a protective stance across her chest in one smooth motion.

"What?"

Ian inhaled a long slow breath and began to speak, "I wanted to apologize for earlier tonight...and for earlier today...and for yesterday." He looked sheepish as he rubbed the back of his head while recounting his crimes.

"Great. It's appreciated. I absolve you from all jerkish behavior. Now please feel free to let me go so that I can move past these ridiculous last few days." Even her ears burned with vehemence.

"I'm not finished." He spoke with such conviction that she stilled and raised an eyebrow in piqued interest.

"I am selfish, Alex. I am a self-serving idiot who makes decisions that benefit me above everyone else. Everything good and wonderful that you bring to the world was missing from my life—until recently."

She tried to interject then, but he held up a hand to silence her. "Please, just let me finish. I may have reasons for my behavior—my way of life—but I still own my past choices...and the consequences."

Alex stood in stunned silence, reveling in how right she had been. There was much more to Ian than she initially thought. This man was exceedingly self-aware and seemed to be on some precipice of change. Maybe she wasn't the only one plagued with an identity crisis as of late.

"What do you want from me?" Alex asked.

"I just want you to get to know me—the real me. I want this more than anything I have wanted in a very long time." He said these words with such desperation that she had to stop her arms from reaching out to him.

"Why me?" she breathed into the night air.

"Is it not obvious?" His gaze narrowed, and even in the dim patch of streetlight, she could see his blue eyes blazing. "I want you to come with me tomorrow. A few friends and I are spending a few nights in the Kalahari before we leave town. Will you come...please?"

"I...I don't know if that's the best idea." Alex undoubtedly knew her internal struggle was written all over her face.

"If you change your mind, we are leaving from the front of the Protea hotel at six tomorrow morning." He closed the distance between them and leaned down to place a chaste kiss on her cheek. "Good night, Alex," he whispered into her ear, then turned and quickly faded into the cover of night.

Minutes later, her face still vibrated where his lips had connected with her cheek. Her head spun like a whizzing top from today's events—the trip to Molepolole, Dr. K's surprise announcement at the party, Ian's mercurial behavior. She hadn't even thought to thank him for his part in choosing PM for the grant award. Rox found her there on the street bathed in moonlight, rooted to one spot with no idea where to go, both physically and metaphorically.

"He wants me to get to know him, Rox," Alex uttered, thinking the words were cryptic, but Rox was able to fast forward through the details and understand.

"And what do you want, Alex?"

"I don't know…"

"Yes, you do. You're just afraid to want it." Rox patted her arm affectionately.

"Interesting…" Alex said thoughtfully with her eyebrow cocked "that's what Ian told me earlier tonight except in a much ruder fashion." She sighed, heavy and deep, and let the burden of the unexpected sink to the pit of her stomach. "There are things you don't know, Rox. Things I never talk about."

"I don't have to know them until you are ready to talk about them. But I do know that I have seen you more alive in the last few days than I have ever seen you."

"What will this do to me?" Alex whispered.

"It will open your heart to possibility," Rox answered and linked her arm through Alex's, steering them both back toward the party.


Many hours later, the sun was just rising in the east, painting the promise of a new day, as Alex waited on the steps of the Protea, adjusting the strap of her navy canvas overnight bag. She huddled into her hunter green, flannel lined jacket to shake off the chill that seemed to emanate from her own skin. *Smile and breathe*, Roxanne had told her as she loaded into the awaiting cab this morning. She had stayed over last night, and they had stayed up until the wee hours of the morning, giggling and squealing like a pair of thirteen-year-olds as Rox texted with Nic. He seemed genuinely enthralled with her, at least by his late-night, sultry messages. Rox was unabashedly smitten.

Two shiny black Land Rovers pulled up to the circle drive, and uniformed men everywhere jumped into motion, loading a pile of duffle bags into the rear of each truck and shouting excited banter to each other in Setswana. Alex was blinded by the flash of a camera as Ian, and his entourage exited the front of the hotel, which she assumed was a local paparazzi trying to get a scoop. She waited precariously on the steps as her eyes readjusted, shifting her weight to the other hip when her bag became heavy. The first thing that came into view was Ian's face, as lit up as the flashbulb had been. His smile grew and grew until it extended to the corners of his eyes. He strode through the crowd of onlookers and lifted the bag off her shoulder.

"Thanks," she said, allowing a small smile to grace her lips.

"You came." He sounded utterly surprised.

"Don't make me regret it," she said teasingly but not entirely in jest.

She dissolved into the group, some of which she recognized as members of the foundation committee and piled in behind them into one of the waiting vehicles. Settling into a seat near the back window, Alex positioned herself so that she could see Ian in the front seat without being seen herself. She was suddenly thankful that she would have the entire drive to sublimate.

While Ian made animated conversation with the driver, she watched out the window as they left the city behind them, and the view opened up into endless savanna dotted with acacia trees and an occasional springbok. Dust clouds billowed around them as they left paved roads for unpaved ones. The earth, reddish-brown and arid, was dotted with scraggly bushes and gnarled trees that extended their limbs upward as if praying to an unseen god. Alex craned her head back and forth across the landscape, eager to catch a glimpse of frolicking wildlife.

Despite being in Botswana for nearly a year, Alex had not traveled much outside Gaborone. Her work schedule had just been too strenuous. When she wasn't on clinical duty at the hospital, she kept up with the latest medical publications or wrote research grants. McCartney and Rox filled in the remaining slice of her life's pie, which had always felt pretty complete—until lately. Inwardly, she frowned. She would be leaving in just six short weeks. Her return ticket flashed into her mind. *May 24 —Gaborone to Johannesburg to Atlanta then Atlanta back to Philadelphia.* She was suddenly inundated with a lengthy to-do list before her return stateside and back to her academic hospital and her tiny apartment containing everything she owned on the twenty-first floor of a building that overlooked the

Schuylkill river. Back to a life she felt very removed from at the moment.

"How long have you been in Botswana, Alex?" The question came from Rachel, who had twisted around in her seat to engage Alex with a friendly smile on her lightly freckled face. Alex smiled in recognition.

"Almost a year, but I'll be leaving soon. How long have you been with the Devall foundation?" Rachel ticked her fingers a few times. "Three years. Wow, where did the time go? This is my first job after college."

"Really? Where did you go?" Alex settled into easy conversation with this girl who exuded the carefree nature of youth.

"Duke. I'm a southern girl from North Carolina through and through and had never been anywhere. I majored in childhood development, applied for this job, and took the first flight out of there to London."

"London?" Alex asked.

"It's where the foundation's offices are located," Rachel confirmed.

Alex listened to her prattle on about living in London but, from time to time, let her attention drift to the front where Ian casually reclined in his seat. She couldn't see his eyes behind his aviators but noticed him casting a genuine smile periodically in her direction.

"We're here," announced the driver as he pulled into a clearing skirted by trees, a single rustic log-hewn dwelling in the center. With a much lighter heart and the type of exhilaration only brought about by the precipice of adventure, Alex jumped out of the truck.

# EIGHT

Alex had no idea what to expect on this trip but, luckily, was familiar with the required essentials for spending the night in the Kalahari. She was busily transferring items from her larger bag to a smaller day backpack when Ian knelt down beside her. His wind-blown hair made an appropriate frame for his wild-appearing countenance.

"Isn't this incredible?" he exclaimed, gesturing to the surrounding landscape. He practically exploded with exuberance, his antics even sexier than usual. Alex erupted in a smile, and her pulse quickened. In truth, she relished adventure and was intensely curious about what amazing outing Ian had planned for today. Before she had time to ask, Ian, with infectious enthusiasm, pulled her to her feet and grabbed her by the hand. "Time for a wild adventure, Alex Wilde."

The wild adventure turned out to be an epic hike through an area of the park dense with wildlife, most of which were elephants. They had divided the group between matching mokoro boats, which were canoes made from dug-out trees that the guides pushed through the water with a long pole. The boats entered a lazy river about a mile from the campsite, floating along through a sea of lily pads that sprouted beckoning, white flowers. The air buzzed with swarms of tiny insects, and the sun peeked out from behind the clouds to warm their backs. When the sun hung midway through the sky, they disembarked from the boats and started walking through the bushy landscape until the grass gradually changed from stubble to elegant slender blades.

Alex took a moment to recall everyone's names as they walked along, a jovial band of two guides, five friends, and her. Lydia, who she remembered as the petite, poised redhead from the foundation committee, led the group, along with Rachel, whose sunny disposition mirrored the current climate. Rahul was there, and Alex felt a twinge of compassion for him and his recent relationship sorrow. Ian trudged along beside a tall, olive-toned, extremely well-muscled man she now knew was Nic—Rox's Nic. She filed away a few questions for later, motivated by Rox's recent obsession with Ian's supposed best friend.

The day was turning hot as the sun reached its apex, and while they stopped for a quick break, Alex guzzled a bottle of water and removed her outer layer, a denim shirt that she tied around her waist. She was seated on a conveniently placed flat-topped rock when she spotted them—a regal herd of elephants comprised of mothers and their floppy-eared babies making their way slowly across the horizon, just at the edge of the tree line. They were exquisite as they lumbered across the savanna, trunks swinging and ears flapping. One of the babies broke away from the herd, her extra-large ears trying to keep up as she leaped and trotted.

The guide motioned for them to stay quiet and follow him into the wind to avoid scent detection. They crept carefully through the tall grass until they were positioned near the lead elephants, crouching down until they glommed low to the ground like an amoeba. Alex ended up next to Ian, shoulder to shoulder, their gazes trained on the elephant herd. Mesmerized by the sheer size and display of power, she had to stifle a cry when, out of nowhere, the enormous matriarch came striding from behind the herd, swinging her tusked head and flapping her ears.

"She knows we are here," whispered the guide. "Just stay calm and do not move." She trumpeted into the air, an ear-splitting sound that violently rang the tiny hair cells in Alex's cochlea. Ian reached for her hand, grasping it tightly as the matriarch elephant patrolled across the grass, positioning herself between the group of humans and the herd until the last stragglers had passed by.

"Elephants never forget being treated poorly by a human. It makes them hostile for the rest of their lives. And that one," the guide said, pointing a finger at the matriarch, "bears a hefty grudge."

"What happened to her?" breathed Alex.

"She was caught as a baby by bad men that used to profit from selling the Kalahari's elephants. She was abused and left with scars—and then she escaped, and we have protected her ever since." The guide rubbed the sweat collecting under his hat brim with his canvas sleeve.

Alex felt a startling kinship with this beautiful creature that had endured so much pain but emerged as a stronger, more impermeable being. Unbidden memories rose to the surface of her consciousness. *Screaming into a black void...the taste of blood in her mouth...paralyzing fear.* Her breath quickened as her sympathetic drive of fight or flight began to take over. She pushed the memories back down.

"Alex...are you okay?" Ian whispered in her ear. She realized she had a vicelike grip on his hand and dropped it immediately. The calm emerged once more as the memories sunk back into the ocean's abyss of her brain. "Sure," she smiled and wiped clammy palms down her thighs.


By the time they made it back, the sun hung low in the sky, and the campsite had been transformed into a more than comfortable space for spending the night. Where the clearing had once been, white canvas tents dotted the landscape, and a set of extra-large cushions on top of a blanket had been arranged on the ground in the center. A small fire was just starting to blaze, stoked to life by the second guide, who had stayed behind to set up this African dreamscape. "Welcome back," he boomed in a strong South African accent. "Dinner will be ready in about an hour."

Each tent bore the name of its intended occupant on a small sign posted near the canvas doorway, and Alex gleefully entered hers, throwing her backpack on the narrow, blanketed cot sitting in the corner and kicking off her grubby hiking boots. Like the rest of the group, she was eager to wash off the thick crust of dust accumulating on her skin and change into fresh clothes. She stripped off her outer layers until she was down to her underwear and used her water bottle and a cloth to wipe down her skin. It wasn't perfect, but she felt much fresher. Donning a clean white linen shirt and jeans, her thoughts meandered to Ian, followed closely by her eyes.

Through a small crack in her tent flap, she could see directly into his quarters. He had made no effort to conceal himself, allowing Alex easy access to the scene of his shirtless body, taut and lean, pacing around his tent while talking on the phone. His abdominal muscles were well defined, rippling as he walked, a subtle, graceful power emanating from his posture. Throwing back the tent flap, she stepped out into the forming dusk to find a much-needed drink.

The delectable aroma of Seswaa and pap led her to a wooden building with its door neatly propped open.

"Can I help?" Alex asked, poking her head inside.

"Hello, lovely," exclaimed the guide. "You can help yourself to one of those glasses of wine and take a seat outside." He winked at her, and she did exactly as she was told, choosing a glass of ruby red elixir and settling herself luxuriously into a body-hugging white cushion.

Minutes later, Ian, in a cream-colored sweater boasting a modest amount of stubble on his jawline, settled in beside her with his own wine glass.

"Is this what it's like being heir to the universe?" Alex said teasingly. "Last time I was here, Rox and I slept in a pop-up tent and ate crackers and a chocolate bar for dinner."

"It's one of the many fringe benefits." Ian gave her a quick half-smile before lifting his wine to hers. "Cheers."

The rest of the group began to fill into the cozy space. Soon, lively conversation between friends was happening around a roaring fire under an ebony blanket of southern stars.

"And then Ian acted like only spoke French, so the border patrol just gave up and let us on through." Between bursts of laughter, Nic regaled them with tales of his international adventures with Ian. Alex could see why Rox was taken with him. He seemed brazenly open and uncomplicated with a big personality, and he sure knew how to laugh. The nagging feeling resurfaced that she recognized him from somewhere. Then she realized—his picture was on the giant billboard in the Gaborone city center. Nic was Nicolau Brizido—the famous Portuguese footballer who played for Arsenal. *Nicely done, Rox, nicely done.*

Alex stifled an exhausted yawn. "Bored of me already?" teased Ian. The firelight highlighted the contours of his features and the artistry in his expressions. Alex could see why women were drawn to him like moths to a flame—just waiting for their turn to be incinerated.

"No...not at all. Just one of the curses of medicine—constant sleep deprivation. I can literally sleep anywhere in any position. In my car...in the hospital elevator." She rattled on mindlessly, hiding another yawn behind her hand.

Ian did not reply right away but raised his dark eyebrows as if considering other possibilities for those locations and the night luckily hid the furious blush rouging Alex's cheeks.

"I can walk you to your tent if you are tired," said Ian.

"I think I can make it." Alex stood up, stretching the kinks from her legs.

"I am not letting you go alone, Alex. There are all kinds of carnal beasts out here waiting to snatch you up."

*Including you.* The words settled inside her head, and she merely shrugged in admonishment.

They walked slowly, gazing upward from time to time to drink in the night sky, inky black and studded with stars. Alex noticed Ian opening and closing his left hand periodically, triggering something in her perceptive doctor-brain.

"What happened to your hand, Ian?" she asked in a no-argument fashion.

"Oh, it's nothing. One of those thorny trees attacked me," he said, balling his hand into a fist.

"Let me have a look at it," she said, gesturing inside her tent and, surprisingly, he didn't argue.

They sat, knees touching, on her cot, and she placed his hand, palm up, gingerly into her lap. The skin was inflamed and tender to the touch, and she could just make out a gray sliver underneath his skin, tracking upward toward his fingers.

"We've got to get this out, Ian," she started amid groans of protest. "You don't want an infection in your hand. Trust me— very messy and very high risk of amputation." He looked up at her, eyes wide with shock, and she chuckled. He didn't need to know she was only half-joking.

"I'm going to need more alcohol. I'll be right back," he grumbled. While he was gone, Alex rummaged around through her bag until she found the few first aid items she had brought—dry gauze, antibiotic ointment, and luckily a pair of thin forceps. Ian returned moments later with an unopened bottle of bourbon, which he dramatically plunked down on the ground beside them.

"I need you to do exactly what I say," said Alex solemnly. "First, open the bourbon." He furrowed his brows over skeptical eyes but did as he was told. "Now pour some over your hand and then over these forceps," she continued.

"What a waste of good bourbon." He took a long swig before obeying her requests.

"Fancy disinfectant for a fancy patient," she muttered as she got to work examining his hand and figuring out the tract the splinter had made. It was deep—really deep. She was probably going to have to do some minor dissection to reach the tip of it.

"Ian," she said, intending to prepare him for what was coming.

"Mmm," he said, eyes closed, the edge of the bourbon bottle near his lips.

"This next part is going to hurt, and I don't have anything to numb the pain. Keep drinking, and I'll talk you through it, okay?"

"I'm sure that whatever pain you inflict, I deserve it." About a quarter of the bourbon was already gone at this point.

Alex took the forceps and began gently probing into his palm, pulling off the top layer of skin as she went. Ian made no sound, but she could see the muscles in his jaw clench and hear his teeth grinding together. "Ian—tell me about your home. Where do you live?" Alex said quickly, using a distraction tactic that she frequently employed with her pediatric patients.

"London...near Hyde Park." His words came in staccato bursts.

"Do your parents live there?"

"My dad—the main offices for Devall are in London."

"And your mom?"

"She died a long time ago."

*Oh.* "I am so sorry." Alex felt a rush of sympathy for this man who was so much more complicated than he seemed. "You don't sound British. Did you grow up there?"

"I lived with my mom in California until she died when I was fifteen—mainly Los Angeles. She was an actress."

*Wow, what a family tree.* "Any brothers or sisters?"

"No...just me."

She noticed a slight hesitation before he answered and decided to change the subject. "What do you do for a living—besides being heir to a mining fortune, world's most wanted globe-trotting bachelor, and a giant pain in my ass?"

Ian laughed then and almost lost his current mouthful of bourbon to the dirt. Alex continued to work on the splinter, a broad smile overtaking her features.

"I work for the company, doing whatever my dad needs—visiting mining sites, meeting with our partner firms, being the social face of the company at soirées."

"I've noticed," Alex said with more than a hint of sarcasm.

"Did you google me, Dr. Wilde?"

"Maybe…once…but that's beside the point…I have a question," she blurted and sucked in a breath as Ian groaned heavily.

"Why was a self-proclaimed selfish jerk appointed the new chair of the Devall foundation, basically the most generous, philanthropic entity on the planet?"

Ian shrugged and lowered his eyes to the bourbon bottle, now half empty. "My dad was trying to teach me a lesson, I think."

"And what lesson was that?"

"That there are experiences….and people that could make me a better human." Alex could feel his eyes on her. She glanced up to see them smoldering with the rampant blue flame that was now comfortably familiar to her. She felt the heat emanating from them, and it scorched her.

"Got it," she said triumphantly as the thorn slid free from Ian's palm, and he emitted a painful yelp.

"Thank you," he breathed.

"Don't mention it," she said, a bit breathless, and then grabbed the bottle of bourbon to take a well-deserved, lengthy sip.

As Alex applied a dressing and some antibiotic ointment, Ian slumped onto her cot, the half-empty bottle of bourbon nestled in his lap like a child's treasured toy. "I think," he said with conviction, "that it's my turn to ask a few questions. It's only fair." He flashed her a sidelong grin that demonstrated his level of inebriation. Alex raised her hand in protest but then acquiesced.

"Fine. Be my guest."

"What are you doing in Botswana?"

"Pediatric ICU development, which is part of my fellowship training research project," she answered smoothly.

"Oh…where are you training?"

"Philadelphia—I've been there two years and have about a year left to go. I'll be going back at the end of May."

"Where is home?"

"Texas—a small town near the coast."

"Your family is there?"

"My mom lives there." Feeling nervous by the conversation's proximity to details she would not be willing to divulge, she hurriedly added, "I should probably go to bed. Doctors are taught sleep while they can…"

Alex rose from the cot, and Ian followed her example,

abandoning the bottle of bourbon and standing directly opposite her in the center of the tent. Her entire body tingled with awareness as she noticed every intimate detail of his physical form—his tongue tracing his bottom lip, the subtle V of his sweater showing off a few dark chest hairs, and mostly his incinerating gaze that radiated desire.

"I just have one more question." He enunciated each word individually, taking steps toward Alex until he had her backed up into a corner of the tent, arms limp at her sides and her heart pounding a frantic gallop. "What are you looking for, Alexandra?" His voice was low, seductive.

"You."

The word escaped her mouth before she could stop herself. In a microsecond, his lips were on hers, warm and definitive. He cupped her face at first, molding his lips to hers with the taste of bourbon and recklessness. Her lips moved of their own accord, catching fire as they explored one another. When their kiss deepened, he filled his hands full of her dark, silky hair, and Alex surged with an uncharted desire. She melded into his body, her hands reaching out to steady herself on his shoulders and pull her body even closer to his. He retreated from her mouth then and turned his attention to her face and neck, planting full luxurious kisses all the way from her jawline down her neck to her exposed collarbone. She could feel his heart pounding through his shirt...or maybe it was hers...and moved her hands around his neck to embed her fingers in his hair.

"Oh..." Alex exhaled a sigh and felt a low-frequency vibration begin in her chest until she was sure her entire body was shaking, somewhat from desire, but mostly from the deafening roar that seemed to be coming from right outside her tent. They both stilled into a single intertwined statue.

"What was that?" whispered Alex, and Ian shushed her with two fingers placed over her lips.

Another roar pierced the air, and Alex felt it reverberate through her chest again. "Lions?" she mouthed to Ian. He nodded and pulled her over to the cot, settling down beside her and placing a lantern in the center of the floor. The lantern's glow accentuated the shadows undulating around them, and Alex thought she was hallucinating when an outline of a lion glided across her tent wall. It was thrilling and frightening, and she had to remind herself that the pride was most likely passing through out of curiosity rather than looking for a meal.

Ian wrapped his arms protectively around her, and she leaned back into his lap. His breathing was rapid but steady as they counted four different lions cross the tiny sliver of moonlight outside the tent flap. It was one of the most wildly exhilarating experiences of Alex's life, and not all of it had to do with the lions. She wanted to stay guarded, to maintain some distance from him, but was quickly finding that to be impossible. The fire had melted the ice, and she had wanted it, even asked for it. Their bodies easily settled into each other until their heart rates slowed along with their breathing. Several minutes passed before they no longer heard the rustle of the lion pack exploring the campsite for some unfortunate prey.

Alex twisted around to face Ian. "What now?" she whispered. He dipped his head until his lips brushed her ear. "Get some sleep, Alex. I'll protect you from the carnal beasts."

*All the ones except you.* Bone tired, she quickly succumbed to the lead in her eyelids. As she relaxed into his lap, sleep came but along with it the deepest of dreams—dreams that she couldn't wake from.

Alex awoke with difficulty, like she was swimming upward from the bottom of an ocean abyss, breathless by the time she breached the surface of consciousness. She felt weighed down and weak and realized that long, muscle-bound arms stretched over her chest and wound around her waist. By the sound of Ian's deep, unhurried breathing, he was still asleep. Carefully, she slipped his arm off her chest and shifted her weight, intending to rise from the cot, freshen up, and process last night in the pre-dawn hours that remained.

Arms repositioned themselves like cables encircling her body, and Alex was pulled into Ian's warm frame. "Tired of me already?" he mumbled sleepily.

"No." She felt like a skittish lamb now that he had awoken. He rotated her around so that their faces were inches apart. She focused her eyes on his chin.

"You were dreaming about me," he said matter-of-factly.

"How could you tell?"

"There were moans…and a definite spot of drool on my shirt."

Alex felt a blush creeping into her cheeks. "You really are a narcissist," she said as she flicked her eyes to his. They were wide open, the smolder in their depths still present from the night before—a slow burn that gripped her insides and made him inescapable.

"Of course, I am...and reality," he said, dragging his thumb slowly across her bottom lip, "is so much better than a dream." He leaned down to replace his thumb with soft, roving lips that beckoned to a part of Alex she hadn't known existed—a region deep in her belly that throbbed with need. She returned his kiss, her insides igniting when he reached under her shirt to stroke the soft skin of her lower back.

"Ian!" A female voice that was not Alex shouted his name. "Ian!" The voice grew frantic.

Ian froze, a wicked smile growing across his face. "It sounds like they are making sure none of us were carried off by the lions last night." Before Alex could process her impending mortification, none other than Lydia poked her head into the tent.

# NINE

Her features gave nothing away. "Mr. Devall, the truck will be leaving soon for the safari." She exuded professionalism, and Alex buried her head into her arms, the heat of embarrassment spreading to her toes.

"Thank you, Lydia. I'll be right there," he said and then added "possibly" under his breath once her head had vacated the tent opening. Alex struggled out of his arms, clumsily rolling onto the ground in her haste and awkwardly making it to a sitting position while Ian watched in amusement.

"Get out of here," she hissed. "I have to get ready." He vaulted to his feet, chuckling, and grabbed the half-empty bottle of bourbon before vacating the tent, but not before sending Alex a carnal look that made her wish the complete opposite of her request.

Dawn had barely broken when their entire crew loaded up into two separate open-air jeeps driven by their khaki-clad guides. They rose and dipped through the terrain, encapsulated by a blanket of early morning fog. Alex squinted into the horizon, anxious to catch a glimpse of the lioness pride they were tracking through the bush. She had purposefully positioned herself in the back row of the jeep, immediately behind Ian, who couldn't provide her with fleeting touches or whispered thoughts without tremendous effort.

He seemed wholly unruffled this morning. He was clean-shaven with perfectly tousled hair without a hint of dark circles under his eyes—like he had not spent the entire night letting Alex doze while he waited for the lions to finish browsing the camp. Alex, on the other hand, pulsated with the caffeine high of a hasty early morning Diet Coke combined with the adrenaline rush of careening through the savanna.

A musty odor filled the air around them as they happened upon a herd of water buffalo, mooing and drooling over a small watering hole. The air buzzed with electricity and anticipation, the hairs on Alex's neck standing up attentively for a yet unknown reason. The dried grass on the other side of the water waved in the wind and then parted to reveal several pairs of bright yellow eyes.

Alex gripped the seat in front of her as the buffalo snorted and stamped anxiously, detecting a sinister scent brought by the gust. Some of the herd had already trotted in the opposite direction, and as the seconds ticked by, the others followed suit. Alex sucked in a breath as the first lioness stretched a deadly paw out of the camouflaging reeds, followed by her slinky body and her tail held low to the ground for balance. She watched Ian bring his hand to his mouth, and in that time, the lioness pride had all emerged from their hiding place, legs extended, sprinting at top speed to overtake the stragglers from the herd.

The guide threw the jeep into gear, and dirt showered Alex's hair as they burned off in pursuit of the lions and the thundering herd of buffalo. Alex had to grip the seatback to avoid being tossed either out of the jeep or onto Rachel's lap. In the distance, she could see that three big cats were in a coordinated predatory dance separating one of the largest animals from the herd. The struggling buffalo faltered, and in a fraction of a second, the lions had leaped onto its back. The jeep crept closer, pulling to a stop near a large rock where they had a sweeping view of the circle of life in its most brutal moment.

Alex detected the metallic, earthy odor of blood just as she heard the buffalo's distressed mewling as it stumbled weakly left then right. The lioness tribe panted in unison as they used brute force to pull it to its knees. A fourth lioness emerged from nowhere and fastened herself to the buffalo's neck, scrabbling to get her jaws clenched around the jugular, and with an earth-shaking thud, the buffalo was no more. Alex moved to withdraw her hand from the seatback and realized it was on Ian's shoulder, held in a vicelike grip by his own trembling fingers.

The morning mist cleared as the blazing sun popped over the horizon, officially welcoming the brand-new day. The jeep pulled off the road to a tree-lined clearing where a breakfast spread had been set up on contiguous rectangular tables covered in white linen tablecloths that fluttered in the subtle breeze. Alex, still shaken from their courtside view of the lion hunt, jumped out of the jeep, her knees buckling as her feet struck the ground. Strong fingers gripped her wrist.

"Need some help?" Ian appeared amused, but his eyes were unreadable behind his dark glasses.

"Thanks." She took back her arm from Ian and dusted off the seat of her pants with shaky hands as he sauntered in the direction of the delicious aroma.

"You are too beautiful and smart for your own good. No one expects you to be graceful too." She heard a light chuckle emanating from his vocal cords.

"Would you like a mimosa, Alex?" asked a bright-eyed Rachel who held two glasses of dilute appearing orange juice. "I'd love one," Alex replied, pulling out the chair next to her, which happened to be situated in front of a giant pile of fried pastries that resembled beignets.

"Wasn't that the most amazing thing you've ever seen in your life?" Rachel said, reaching over to pull one of the pastries from the bottom of the pile.

Alex nodded in agreement as she sipped her drink and cast her eyes down the table where Ian was enjoying his own libations and a pile of greasy eggs. He caught her spying on him and winked mid-sentence, a gesture that caused a few raised eyebrows from the rest of the group. Alex quickly averted her gaze elsewhere, pretending to be distracted by one of the waitstaff who offered to refill her glass, which she gladly accepted.

Rachel sat chewing thoughtfully on her sugary pastry. "You and Ian seem to be hitting it off."

"What?" Alex floundered for a moment. "No…it's not like that." *But it absolutely was.*

Rachel appraised her guilty face for a second and continued seamlessly. "He's a really special guy just…"

"One with a lot of baggage," Alex finished and received a vigorous nod in response.

"I don't mean to be intrusive, but you seem pretty special yourself and well…Ian never really finishes what he starts if you know what I mean." Rachel was picking her pastry into tiny little bits. Alex had already learned this from her internet homework, but her heart took a dive anyway.

"Well, I don't start things that I can't finish, so it looks like he is just out of luck." Alex smiled as brightly as she could manage, and Rachel observed her with sympathetic understanding.

"What did you all think of the action this morning?" boomed their hearty red-faced guide in a lovely South African accent. He lifted his hat a bit to reveal a shock of brown hair stuck to his forehead. Everyone started murmuring at once, and words like "spectacular" and "breathtaking" jumped out of the cacophony of voices. Alex remained quiet, lost in her own thoughts until she heard her name.

"Alex?"

"I'm sorry?"

"I said, how about you, dear?" The guide grinned at her with a set of perfectly straight teeth. The entire table shifted their eyes to her.

"It was brutal...but necessary. I've never seen anything like it before." She put her glass to her lips, hoping that would end her contribution.

In truth, she had found it thrilling and exotic, which seemed in opposition to the part of her that was the rescuer and the healer. She excused herself from Rachel, who had busied herself entertaining a moping Rahul, Ian's recently unengaged friend, and carried her drink over to the nearest acacia tree. She sat down under the twisting thorny branches in a precious little patch of shade, preferring the silence instead of the hearty conversation batted around at the table.

She had never felt so peaceful and unhinged all at once. *Speaking of unhinged.* She spied Ian wandering over, two freshly filled mimosa flutes in his hands. He sat down next to her, carefully avoiding any contact with the threatening spikes extending above them. "I thought for sure you wouldn't want to come and find me here." Alex glanced up at the clusters of thorns.

"I would probably come find you anywhere." His smile was so genuine that Alex's insides did a flip flop, and she tried to remind herself who he was—who he had always been.

"Mmm," she said, draining her current glass and reaching for the one he offered. *Nothing like a little liquid anxiolysis.*

"I'm surprised you didn't leap out of the jeep this morning with your little medical bag and try to save that poor buffalo." He seemed tipsy and cute, practically giggling at the visual he had created.

"Death is a part of life," Alex replied dryly. "I know that better than almost anyone."

"It is," he said, somber for a moment before continuing. "I can't help but wonder whether you are a buffalo—the necessary sacrifice for the wellbeing of another species—or the lioness—the queen at the top of the food chain?"

The question caught her off guard. It seemed too profound for a beautiful morning in the Kalahari when they were both mildly drunk. "A little bit of both...depends on the day," she replied with a raise of one eyebrow. He nodded, curling his lips as he weighed her answer.

"What about today?" The question was simple, but he said it so erotically that she had to staunch the desire flooding her veins.

"The thing is—being a doctor and all—I am a servant to humanity by nature." She took her index finger and traced it along his neck in the groove between his trachea and sternocleidomastoid muscle. "But I know exactly where your jugular is." She rose to her feet and headed back toward the jeep. She could feel him watching her the entire way.

"Sorry, everyone. This almost never happens." Their jeep had stalled out while rounding a corner, and they were still several miles from camp. The guide turned the key in the ignition, the engine repeatedly failing to turn over amid a cascade of groans from the jeep occupants. To make matters worse, a herd of zebra meandered about the dirt path, snorting and stamping with anxiety at the trespassers.

Alex was tipsy enough not to care in the least. From her perch in the rear of the jeep, she had been a content observer of the lively commentary from the rest of the group, laughing so hard that she had leaned on Rachel's shoulder at one point for support. Everyone else seemed thoroughly nonplussed by the delay, so when the guide suggested that perhaps a few of them get out and push while he popped the clutch, no one moved.

"I will," Alex said and hopped to the ground behind the jeep before anyone could change her mind. She snickered lightly and posed in a dramatic stance near one of the taillights. Another thud and then another met her ears as Ian and Nic joined her in the rear, causing a few zebras to scatter, blowing up a dust cloud with their hooves.

"All right. Here we go." The guide threw the jeep in neutral as the trio heaved into the metal frame.

"Alex—what are you doing?" Ian grunted.

"What does it look like?" she replied between gritted teeth as the jeep started to roll forward.

"Well, it looks sexy as hell," he tossed out casually just as the clutch popped, and the engine roared to life.

A giggle escaped from Alex's throat just as her foot made contact with a giant rock, sending her tumbling to the ground. She tasted grit between her teeth and could see the jeep plugging away down the road, Nic and Ian holding on to the back of it. For a moment, she considered staying there, casting her luck with the lions rather than hauling herself to her feet to face the teasing that awaited. A pair of brown hiking boots appeared in the crack between her forearms, and surprisingly gentle arms lifted her to her feet.

"I've got you, Alex. You okay?" Ian said, lifting her to her feet and inspecting her face.

"Pride took a little ding," she said, and his face relaxed from concern to amusement.

"Then, can you run?" He cocked his head toward the jeep that was gaining forward momentum and held out his hand. They ran, holding hands the entire way, legs pumping, bits of laughter bubbling up from each of them until jeep finally came into view. Ian picked her up by the waist and handed her to a waiting Nic and then nimbly leaped onto the running boards before climbing in himself.

"Head on over to your tents for a nice long break before dinner," shouted their stout, crimson-faced guide, as he dismounted from their transportation and popped its surly hood.

Alex, covered head to toe in grime, scrambled out the back and ducked underneath her tent flap without a backward glance to see if Ian had followed her. After a full day packed in a jeep with people she barely knew, it felt comforting to steal a moment to herself. Alone in her own space, she could refocus and recreate some mental boundaries—even though they seemed to fade at the first site of those ridiculously blue eyes.

She tossed her soiled garments to the side and used lavender wipes to clean every inch of her skin. She pulled on her last set of fresh clothes, a long-sleeved flannel shirt and her favorite broken-in jeans. Winding her long hair into a bun, she climbed onto her cot mattress, her body starting to ache from her earlier impact with the road. She felt clean and warm and groggy, but her brain would not obey and succumb to sleep despite closing her eyes. She wondered what Ian was doing and especially what he was thinking. She chastised herself and sat up quickly, swinging her feet over the ground as her thoughts raced. He was like an invasive disease, and she needed to be cured—she just didn't want to be.

The flap on her tent parted, and Ian slipped discreetly inside. "Don't you have any respect for people's boundaries?" Alex asked sternly but wasn't able to keep the smile from spreading across her face.

"Not usually," he said, flopping down next to her.

"What if I had been changing?" She folded her arms across her chest.

"I would have helped you," he said, leaning back on the tent wall and closing his eyes, a small smile playing on his lips.

"What are you doing here?" Alex asked, afraid she knew the answer...hoping she knew the answer.

His eyes popped open. "I'm no doctor but I am a connoisseur of anatomy."

He leaned closer and exhaled onto her exposed neck, making her back muscles tense around her spine and her lips part. She didn't move when he leaned closer and softly kissed the groove in her neck and then bent his head to kiss the soft spot above her clavicle in the exact trajectory of the jugular vein. She felt the tug of her shirt material before it parted and exposed the top of her cleavage. His lips continued their homage of her skin and moved down her sternum until meeting resistance from her next button, which he deftly released. He grabbed her behind the knee and pulled her down onto her back, his other arm cradling her head, and positioned himself next to her with ideal access to her entire midsection.

She felt an ecstatic lightness of being, and when their eyes met, she saw the desire in his irises along with something completely unforeseen—hesitation and humility. She reached out a hand and ran her index finger along his lower lip, and he groaned audibly and closed his eyes. She slid her hand behind his head and pulled his face near enough so she could take his lower lip between her own.

*I'm making all the wrong choices.* His tongue found the entrance to her welcoming mouth, and his fingers finished unbuttoning her blouse. She could feel the soft material of his t-shirt against her bare abdomen. He grabbed her leg and hiked it over his hip. They moved in unison with frantic lips and roving hands, every sensation magnified a thousand times. If this was the last kiss she ever had, Alex decided it would have been enough for a lifetime.

He buried his head between her breasts, tickling her with the ends of his glossy hair as black as crow's wings, and reinitiated his exploration of her southern hemisphere. Alex wound her fingers into his hair, a discomfort beginning to nag at her that competed with the blossoming of her own carnal desire. She exhaled a ragged breath as his lips snuck below the waistband of her jeans to the prominent point of her pelvis. Another sensation superseded the erotic feel of his tongue on her skin—a throbbing pain in her hip.

"Aah," she yelped, and his head snapped up.

"Are you okay?" he said with concern.

"I'm not sure." Alex palpated over her hip and felt a distinct puffy bulge. Without thinking, she undid the top button of her jeans to inspect it more closely. She could see a large purple bruise tracking down into her groin. "It must have happened when I fell," she said sheepishly. Ian was quiet as he stared at her exposed lower abdomen, the flare of lust evident in his gaze. He bent down and brushed the bruised skin with feather-light lips.

"All better?"

"Much better," she sighed. He propelled himself to his feet suddenly.

"I have an idea—be right back." He smiled wickedly and pulled back the tent flap. "You might want to put your shirt back on." He was gone in a flash, leaving Alex to wonder whether she was relieved or disappointed.


The sun hung low in the sky, like a yo-yo about to snap from its string, when they hiked over to a private spot under an overly large acacia tree where a blanket and a basket bursting with goodies waited for them. "I can see why you picked this one," Alex remarked, staring up at the giant tree whose branches cleared their heads by at least eight feet. Ian had already sat down and was busy unpacking the items from the basket, including a bottle of expensive-looking wine. He took his time pouring out a generous portion into two glasses and offered one to Alex.

"I am turning into quite a lush on this trip, which I think might not be a coincidence." She took a sip of the straw-colored liquid anyway.

"If I give you enough good wine, I might learn all of your well-kept secrets." He broke apart a hunk of thick bread and smeared it with a pale creamy cheese.

*Not all of them.* Her mind flitted to the lockbox in the most distant shadowy parts of her memory. "What do you want to know?"

"Everything," he said huskily, and she involuntarily gulped. "But I'll settle for what you like about being a doctor." She visibly relaxed and took another sip.

"I like the challenge and the ability to offer something that few people can. I like to be the heroine of a would-be disaster. I like to give kids their lives back—to give them a chance to grow up and do whatever they want." He listened attentively, sipping his own wine and letting her unwind her thoughts.

"Have you been a doctor in other places? Other than Botswana, I mean?" She nodded her head vigorously.

"I did a master's in public health and went to Haiti to do my thesis. I've also worked in Mongolia with a congenital heart surgery program."

"So, you like to travel?"

"I love it, but I haven't been many places for pleasure—only the places I've worked. I'm sure my passport has way fewer stamps than yours." She stared into her glass, lost in thought as she swirled her wine.

"Where would you go—purely for pleasure?"

She bit her lip in thought. "Paris for sure and maybe Greece? I've always wanted to eat my body weight in feta cheese." She giggled, the wine seeping into her bloodstream and flowing straight to her head. Ian laughed silently and refilled both of their glasses.

"How do you manage to be so...selfless?"

Alex rolled her eyes. "I'm nowhere near worthy of sainthood, but I believe if I have the power to make someone's life better, then I should. There's a certain freedom that comes with putting the needs of others before your own. It makes me happy."

"What do you think made you this way?"

*Extreme pain...terror...childhood trauma.* "I guess I was just born that way." She shrugged and bit into her bread, letting the rich cheese squeeze into her mouth as Ian sat casually next to her, elbows on his knees, staring at her with what could only be described as pure wonderment.

They talked until the southern sky had exposed the entirety of its constellations. When Ian walked her back to her tent, he left her there with a tender, lingering kiss that wasn't near enough to satisfy the yearning she felt deep in her bones.

# TEN

The ride back to Gaborone was quiet. The land rover's rhythmic vibrations were sedating, and most of its passengers had dozed off or were staring out the window at the landscape dotted with occasional animal sightings. Alex was seated directly behind Ian, afraid that sitting next to him would surely draw too much unwanted attention at this delicate stage of their relationship. *Was that what it was?* They hadn't even had time to talk this morning between the frenetic period of packing up the campsite and grabbing a quick breakfast before they had to be on the road. Instead of restfulness, Alex wrestled with a growing sea of fear and doubt.

In too short of time, the truck pulled into a private airstrip at Sir Seretse Khama airport, a Learjet of all things, waiting to sweep away the group—and Ian—and her current hold on a dream that might not evolve into reality. Alex panicked for a moment when the truck gears ground to a stop. She had no idea what to say to Ian or how to ask the questions that needed answers.

Everyone piled out and began toting their belongings up the mobile staircase to the awaiting comfort and luxury of the jet for the long flight back to London. Alex, uncomfortably stranded on the tarmac, returned the waves and good wishes sent her way by Rahul, Lydia, and Rachel. She watched Ian reappear from inside the plane and descend the stairs to pretend-grapple with a tall, broad-shouldered Nic who was waiting at the bottom.

"See you in a few days, brother," Nic said affectionately as he held Ian in a headlock.

For a moment, Alex prepared herself for the worst. Ian would reboard the plane, perhaps offer her a substantial wave, and return them both to their previous lives. Instead, while this unrealized scenario played out in her head, Ian covered the ground between them in three strides and swept her up in a full-frontal embrace. With her face against his chest, she inhaled sharply, the rich smell of his leather jacket filling her nostrils.

"I may be leaving, but I'm not going anywhere," he said with his head buried in her hair. He pulled back to cup her face between his palms and plant a lingering kiss on her parted lips.

Alex struggled to find words so instead, she let her eyes reveal the truth of what he had awakened in her.

"I'll see you soon." With a promise that she had no idea how he planned on keeping, he turned from her to board the plane—and didn't look back.

Nic offered to drive her home, and Alex gratefully accepted. "I've heard a lot about you from Roxanne," he started with his melted caramel voice. Luckily, Nic was a master of easy conversation.

"Same here," she replied, thinking of his late-night *sexting* with her friend. "I like your billboard."

Nic looked puzzled and then burst with laughter as Alex grew crimson from her social awkwardness. "Thanks," he said, glancing at her with such a curious expression that Alex started to feel self-conscious. The first time she had an actual conversation with the presumed love of Rox's life, she was an awkward mess.

"Rox seems really taken with you," she said, redirecting the course of their conversation to familiar ground for both of them.

"She is a singular woman," Nic said, eyes shining with admiration. "I'm certain we will be seeing more of each other, Alex. Give my best to Roxanne." He paused in front of her house to allow her to exit his car, waving as he sped into the distance.

Once Alex was inside, her house seemed too quiet and small to contain her stampeding thoughts. Her running shoes, thrown carelessly at the front door, beckoned to her with the promise of a much-needed catharsis and centering of her emotions. She took a familiar route down her street then through the main town thoroughfare before zigzagging over to her favorite dusty backroad. As she rounded the bend, a young zebra yearling galloped inside the fence alongside her, kicking up her heels in pure joy for the gift of a clear sky on a crisp day at the precipice of fall. Botswana had permeated Alex's being. The country and its people had written

79

poetry on her heart and stoked what Alex knew was a lifelong passion. Leaving here would be like leaving part of herself behind, waiting for the day she would return and reunite with it.

Alex ran and ran, kicking up mini-dust clouds, feeling the firm earth beneath her feet, pounding her emotions into the ground until they were more manageable. One by one, she let the memories of Ian surface, like a mental slide show of their brief time knowing each other. She allowed her body to re-experience his spiced breath on her face, his praise-worthy lips exploring her skin, and his palm pressed into her back, igniting her from the inside out. The daydream had kicked her speed up a notch, and her chest heaved, not entirely from exertion.

Slowing down, she bent her head to her knees for a second before continuing on at a more moderate, even pace. Her thoughts exited off hedonistic highway to a more rational, cerebral route and she wondered how deep she would be willing to go with Ian. How much of her carefully crafted wall would she be willing to disassemble? Was he really a narcissistic jerk pretending to care for his own benefit, or was it the other way around? How was she supposed to trust him enough to be more vulnerable than she had ever been with a man? Vulnerability required sacrifice—an emotional bloodletting—and through her twisted musings, an ancient scar reminded her of just how painful loving someone could be.

*The profanity resounded through the house as she pressed her knees into her chest. She did the rest of her homework by nightlight, and when she went to brush her teeth later that night, she was met with the stench of alcohol-infused vomit in the sink. Deprecating words echoed in her ears as she observed the telltale signs of struggle when she awoke the next morning to make herself a bowl of cereal—broken dishes, stuffed animal carcasses scattered about, fist-shaped holes in the wall.*

Not realizing she had stopped, she was jerked out of her daydream-turned-nightmare by a wetness that suddenly coated her upper arm. The donkey stood stock-still in his spot on the roadside, his muzzle covered in the same green slobber that now dripped from her bicep. She stopped in her tracks and looked directly into his long, tapered face. He didn't even blink.

"I'm crazy…you know it and so do I." Alex blew out a breath and his muzzle quivered. "But maybe I've found something I didn't think existed and I want to believe in it." An ear flicked in her direction, and she took that as a silent affirmation. With a quick pat on his muzzle, she turned toward home.

Rox, who had been dog sitting McCartney, found her at home a few hours later, furiously scrubbing the tile on her bathroom floor. Noticing the running clothes strewn on the bed, she pursed her lips and said, "I see running around with your problems didn't quite bring them to resolution. How is the cleaning therapy going?"

"Great." Alex was almost out of breath from scrubbing tiny streaks of grime from the grout. "I feel great."

"If by great you mean scared out of your mind," Rox countered. She folded her legs under her as she scooted onto Alex's bed. "I assume you can multi-task. Tell me about your trip." After half an hour more of scrubbing and giving an account of her activities over the last two days, her mind, as well as her bathroom, were nicely cleansed.

"I don't know why I care so much," Alex said as she rubbed her neck, aching from an hour of being bent over a tile floor. "He's my freaking kryptonite. I feel exposed and—" she floundered.

"Vulnerable," finished Rox, eyeing her patiently, almost empathetically. "I love you, Alex—like a sister. Just remember that your self-worth is not dependent on whether or not this man wants you."

How could Rox know her so well without even knowing her past? Her mind briefly settled on another man in another time that seemed like a lifetime ago. The first man who said he loved her but didn't. Her formidable wall had been constructed to protect her against him.

"I know," Alex said quietly, with more reassurance than she felt. "I met Nic." She saw Rox's eyes light up, her face emitting its own sunlight if that was possible.

Alex lounged on her bed pillows next to Rox and watched her friend gush over her new love interest. She listened to her talk and emote, not interrupting once, and loved getting caught up in the whirlwind of her best friend's happiness. Nic had originally come to Botswana with Ian but had decided to extend his trip for a week so that he and Rox could spend more time together. They were planning on taking an extended weekend into South Africa to some glamourous luxury resort. Rox sighed contentedly and propped herself up on her elbow.

"I've never felt like this, Alex. He is my MVP."

Alex laughed freely. "I suppose it's time for you to brush up on your soccer. Have you guys talked about the future? His plans? Your plans?"

"Too early," said Rox. "For now, we are just going to act like the wild animals we are."

"You are terrible," Alex said teasingly, but in truth, she felt more than a little envy for her friend's uncomplicated bliss.

McCartney let out a gentle whine, and Rox glanced at her watch. "Have to run, love. I'm meeting Nic for dinner. Keep me posted on Ian."

"Will do. Have fun."


Once alone, Alex paced around her tiny dwelling, McCartney close at her heels, and finally decided to eat dinner to pass the time. A boiling pot of spaghetti was soon sending puffs of steam into the air, warming Alex's face with wet heat. A few bites into her al dente pasta tossed with olive oil and parmesan, a shrill ring from her phone broke Alex's quiet dinner atmosphere, and she nervously flipped it over and hit answer.

"Hi, honey!" Janie Wilde's sugary voice echoed through the receiver, and Alex, though mildly disappointed, responded with exuberance.

"Hi mom!"

"I miss you! How are you? When are you coming home?"

"I miss you too, mom. I'll be back in Philly toward the end of May. How are things with you?"

One of the things Alex loved about her mom was the fact that she never pried. She accepted what Alex was willing to share without pressing her. Janie Wilde had barely left the small Texas town where she grew up and raised Alex as a single mom. Life there never became more complicated than a lack of parking spots in the church lot or a Friday night loss for the high school football team.

Janie both admired and ultimately failed to understand her only daughter's desire to travel to the most poverty-stricken places on the planet. Most of the conversations between Alex and her mother devolved into the latest town gossip—who had a baby, who died, who was getting divorced. Most of the time, Alex happily settled into the receiving end of her mom's need to be a storyteller. Like a free version of a soap opera, it had lots of entertainment value and required little mental investment. Before she was really ready, Alex found herself saying good-bye to her mom and promising to visit the first chance she had.

"Texas misses you, sweetie. I can't wait to see you. When can you come?"

"I'll look at my calendar for the fall. I should be getting my work schedule soon."

"Okay—I love you."

"I love you too, mom." Alex quickly disconnected before her mom detected the hint of melancholy in her voice.

As much as she loved living in Philadelphia, she was homesick for her small, one-stoplight Texas town where she had grown up. It wasn't as picturesque as most other places she had lived, but it was beautiful to her. Her town was situated between two slow-moving rivers that emptied into the Gulf, and the sun plus the ample water supply had produced some of the most fertile soil in the state. Everyone had a vegetable garden or livestock, and the townspeople freely traded among each other. Alex had known the same group of kids since kindergarten and still felt strong bonds to her friends that had shared adventures growing up in a small town—playing baseball in the summertime, jumping over fences to take a quick dip in someone's pool, driving backroads and sharing their latest teenage dramas. She smiled at the good memories, resolving to make a trip to see her mom as soon as she could.

After a long, cleansing shower in her immaculate bathroom, Alex nestled into her bed, exhausted in every way, and, for once, refrained from flipping open her laptop to work. Soon McCartney was snoring lightly, and Alex felt herself begin to drift into less than consciousness. A punctuated ding from her phone interrupted her slumber. Through one blurry eye, she saw Ian's name on the screen, glowing bright white on a little green rectangle, awaiting the swipe of a finger. Suddenly wide awake, her fingers trembled as she opened up the message.

*I hope you are sleeping and dreaming of me.*

Her entire body seemed to smile as she typed.

*I am.*

She fell asleep cradling her phone, a poor surrogate for Ian but currently the only connection she had. Her sleep was deep and dreamless, the sleep of someone who had cycled through a lifetime's worth of emotions and thoughts in a twenty-four-hour period. Which is why, several hours into the night, when her phone exploded with a violent barrage of ringing, Alex awoke startled and disoriented.

"Hello," she croaked.

"Dr. Alex," said an urgent female voice, "we need you at PM right away."

# ELEVEN

Alex leaped out of bed, throwing her hair into a hasty ponytail and pulling on her scrubs at lightning speed. In no time, she was striding down the corridor to the pediatric ward, running through a mental list of tasks that needed to happen as soon as she walked through the door. Several kids had already been admitted from a nearby village with fever, rashes, and devastating diarrhea, most likely from a typhoid outbreak. They had to work quickly to resuscitate the kids and contain the spread. Alex practically flew into the small conference room and noticed that Mercy and Lesedi were already there briefing the interns.

"Hi, everyone. Can I get an update on the situation?" Alex had transitioned into work mode, and she was operating at interstellar speed.

Mercy filled her in on the details. Five children had been admitted from the same village in the last three hours with symptoms consistent with typhoid—all severely dehydrated with high lactic acid levels and low blood pressure. Each patient had at least one symptomatic person in their immediate family, and the sources were yet to be identified.

"Okay," said Alex, already planning for the next seven days of turmoil. "Mercy—you and I will stay here at PM and take care of the kids in the hospital. I want the rest of you to head out to Mochudi to identify anyone with symptoms and quarantine them in one area of the village. Children need to be sent here to PM if they develop serious symptoms or can't stay hydrated. Take a bunch of extra water in jugs so that the people in the village have access to clean water…and try to figure out where this came from."

Alex tucked her hair behind her ear repeatedly, a nervous habit she practiced when her mind was on overdrive. She glanced over at Mercy. "Let's get over to the ward."

They entered the pediatric ward, where the stench of fever-induced sweat, excrement, and stained bedclothes hit her full force. Several children whimpered, writhing in their soaked sheets, frightened and parentless, their bodies wracked with fever. Alex felt her heart rate slow and her mind become precision-like. Physicians needed a certain level of arrogance to believe that medicine would prevail in the battle against a deadly disease. Right now, Alex had to believe without any doubt that they could save these kids.

"Lesedi," she called, "we need to separate the suspected cases from the other kids to prevent spread in the hospital."

"Of course, Dr. Alex." Lesedi, calm and utterly professional, instructed her cohort of white-uniformed nursing colleagues to separate out the four children that were not exhibiting symptoms. Soon they were stripping off bed sheets and sanitizing everything in sight.

Alex turned to Mercy, who carried a weighty clipboard. "Let's examine every single kid and take notes. Make sure they all have a working IV and adequate IV fluids on board and give everyone a dose of ceftriaxone."

Alongside the nursing staff, they went bedside to bedside to determine the level of illness in each child, rehang IV fluids, and change the children out of their soiled clothes and sheets. Alex brushed her hand over the forehead of one girl as she listened with her stethoscope. Her skin felt moist and warm with fever while her heart rate was inappropriately slow and periodically irregular, a telltale sign of typhoid.

Alex sent Mercy to document the supplies in the backroom. Once they ran out, they were unlikely to obtain additional IV solution and antibiotics. While she was gone, one of the interns texted Alex.

*Arrived in Mochudi—8 more kids—bringing them now*

That would make twelve kids total with only two remaining hospital beds. She did some mental math based on what the kids would need over the next few days and decided to call Dr. K for reinforcements.

Twenty-four hours into typhoid epidemic hell, Alex realized that she had not sat down to eat or drink anything, and she felt the typical anxiety that came with low blood sugar and dehydration. She and Mercy had worked through the night and the day and most of the next night admitting thirty children into what had become a very cramped pediatric ward. Thanks to Dr. K, they had borrowed from a partner hospital and at least had enough physical beds and linens for everyone. Unfortunately, this meant no room for parents to stay at the bedside, and with the risk of co-infection, it probably wasn't a good idea anyway. Most of the kids were too sick to notice, but a few of the toddlers had cried longingly to be held, and Alex had been unable to resist. She had taken turns with Lesedi, holding and rocking them through the night until they fell into a fitful sleep.

One of the infants, a little nine-month-old boy named Mmoloki, who had been wailing for hours, collapsed against her chest, his hands tightly fisting her hair, giving her a much-needed moment of humanity and compassion. The constant drive to function at high capacity, a basic requirement of her profession, sometimes led to the necessary compartmentalization of emotions, pushed down into some secret hole that may or may not be unearthed again. Moments like holding this little boy next to her chest—willing some of her life force into him and wishing that love was enough of a cure—were rare but so vital to her soul.

With the back of her hand, Alex wiped her eyes to revive herself, using the moment to block out her surroundings and think briefly of Ian. A precious banana and a bottle of water in her hands, she retreated to the supply room to enjoy a moment alone and lose herself in his mental image. Flinging open the window to let in the cool night air, Alex sat down in a patch of moonlight and evoked her mental box labeled *Ian*. Halfway into her banana and her memory of their first kiss, she practically threw her phone across the room when it rang and Ian's name flashed on the screen.

"Hello?" Alex said tentatively.

"I made it home to London, and I had to call you," said the deep, silky smooth voice she remembered so well.

"It's good to hear your voice," Alex said shakily. "I wasn't sure when we would talk again."

"Are you kidding? You are going to have to use a crowbar to pry me away from you," he said, and Alex could imagine the dark V-shaped brows and playful flirt in his eyes.

Alex laughed and relaxed a bit for the first time in two days. She was wound so tight that she could actually feel her shoulder muscles undergoing active relaxation as she slumped against a pile of IV fluid bags and settled into easy conversation. "So, what are you doing?" she asked.

"Nothing much—sitting here naked…having a bourbon… catching up on work."

Alex's laughter escaped her and grew into hysteria. Because one heightened emotion begets another, she was soon half laughing and half crying. The stress of the last few days had taken its toll, and the situational irony was simply too much.

Lesedi poked her head in right then and, giving Alex a puzzled look, said, "Can I speak with you, Dr. Alex?"

"Sure…sure," Alex said, calming the waves of emotion. "I'll be right there."

"Alex? Are you okay? Where are you?" Ian said evenly.

"Long story short—at the hospital in the middle of a raging typhoid epidemic. I have to go, Ian. Thanks for calling. I'll talk to you soon. Good-bye." Alex disconnected before he had a chance to respond, and she wasn't sure why she felt the need to be so abrupt. Maybe to protect him from the brutal trauma of medicine or maybe because sharing it made the horror too real.

She found Lesedi standing upright, displaying excellent posture even after close to thirty hours of being on her feet, a clipboard in her hand making notes. She met Alex's eyes and handed her the clipboard. "Thanks to Dr. K we have enough antibiotics, paracetamol, and IV fluids to last us two more days. But that's only if we don't get any more children."

"Okay," Alex said, her mind running through a few scenarios. "Let's try some of the kids on some nutrition by mouth. They might be ready. Also, do you think you can put one of the nurses in charge of supply distribution?"

"Sure, Dr. Alex. We can split the IV bags into smaller aliquots. I will have someone get started on that."

"Thank you, Lesedi. I don't know what everyone would do without you." They exchanged tired smiles, and Alex, for the first time, noticed her phone buzzing incessantly in her pocket.

*Alex—please tell me you are going to be okay.*

*I'll be fine—the benefit of being vaccinated.*

*Don't do anything crazy.*

*That ship sailed in the Kalahari…*

*Hilarious. Call me later Mother Teresa.*

Smiling the smile of a girl whose heart felt a smidge lighter, Alex stepped back into the frenetic atmosphere of the pediatric ward and took stock of the current situation. A few of the older kids were sitting up in bed, but several smaller children remained curled in a fetal position, their heads slick with fever sweat. Alex took a deep breath and transitioned back into work mode.

When dawn filled the open windows and dancing dust motes could be seen in the sun-drenched room, Alex could not have been more appreciative of the warmth on her chilled skin. There was always something hopeful about the sunrise. It represented the victory of making it through a disastrous night with no casualties and the promise of healing that a new day might bring. Hopefully, the worst was over and the interns had been able to quell the spread in the village.

Alex bent her head over little Mmoloki, her rocking chair pal from the night before, and placed her hands on his taut, tender abdomen. He was listless this morning, his skin cold and clammy to her touch. She pressed a finger over his nail bed and counted one…two…three…almost seven seconds for it to regain perfusion. *Damn.*

"Hey Mercy, can you help me get another IV started in this little one? He's still in shock and needs an adrenaline drip."

Alex opened up the saline drip until a steady stream of clear drops flowed into his arm like a tiny, life-giving river. While Mercy was working on the IV, she took a vial of antibiotic powder, mixed it with some saline, and injected it slowly into his IV tubing.

Typhoid was a veritable monster as far as epidemics were concerned. Many kids would survive the initial onslaught of fever and dehydration only to succumb to another infection as they became more and more malnourished from the inability to absorb food. Some kids would die from progressive shock as their organs shut down. Prevention certainly was the only way to ensure survival, and she wondered where this one had started—contaminated water or some feast with a shared dish where, unbeknownst to its guests, a sinister microscopic predator lurked.

The pediatric ward was divided into two large rooms with a partition running down half of the middle so that a pathway existed between sides. When Alex glanced up from her task, Lesedi was transferring some of the more well-appearing children to the other side of the partition. The rich aroma of warm pap wafted through the air. She sent out a silent prayer, fervently hoping that their bellies would be ready for food. They desperately needed the remaining IV solution for the sicker ones. Thinking of Mmoloki, Alex retreated to the medication cabinet to grab a pre-mixed bag of adrenaline that they could use to support his circulation as his body continued to rage against the infection. When she returned, Mercy was happily taping in the IV.

"I can get the adrenaline drip started, Dr. Alex," she said, swiping the back of her hand across tired eyes.

"Sounds good," said Alex proudly. She reached into her pocket for her phone to calculate the drip rate for the adrenaline, noticing several missed messages from Rox. She quickly swiped to view the content. The images filling her screen made her smile broadly—Rox and Nic posing with an enormous elephant, Rox seated by a luxurious pool at sunset while holding a glass of champagne, and a shirtless Nic standing in the doorway of an Afro-glam hut with a huge smile. Obviously proud of her new beau, Rox had probably already sent the pic out to the social media universe. She quickly typed a message and hit send.

*You look happy. Be safe and have a great time.*

Alex missed her friend and longed to hear her cheerful, encouraging voice, but she was honestly thankful that Rox had not called. She wanted Rox to savor this time with Nic, blissfully unaware of what was happening at PM. Being in medicine could be consuming to the point of self-martyrdom. Soaking in the good moments of life, like the unhurried bliss of a beautiful day in a vibrant world existing outside the hospital walls, was essential. Somehow the good had to balance out all the bad.

Some commotion was happening outside the ward doors, and Alex saw Khobi pushing along a gurney with two children. His face appeared strained, and his cheeks puffed as though out of breath. "Dr. Alex, some of the kids are getting sicker. We had to bring a few more."

Alex sucked in her breath and then let it out slowly. Just when she had thought they were getting ahead of this thing. "Put them over there and we can get their treatment started. How many more?" Alex wasn't sure she wanted to know the answer.

"At least ten more," Khobi said, not meeting Alex's blank expression.

"Okay," Alex said, trying to infuse more calm into the situation than she felt. "Can you head back there and get the rest of them?" Drawing from a source of fortitude that superseded her exhaustion, Alex filled in the others on the situation, and, as a team, they began to move beds around to make room.

The sun rose and dipped again, casting a muted orange glow onto the hospital wall, the only indication to Alex that the earth was actually continuing to spin. Days without a real shower had left a layer of grunge on her skin, and, despite catching a cat nap here and there, she had begun hallucinating from lack of sleep. Throughout the day, she had worked alongside Mercy and Lesedi, stabilizing all the new kids that got admitted and trying to separate out the ones who were worsening. Mmoloki had responded to the adrenaline drip and had even opened his eyes this afternoon, giving Alex a glazed-over but, nonetheless knowing, stare.

"Mercy—I have to go to the back and lie down for a little while. Can you wake me in an hour?" Worried that her exhaustion was affecting her judgment, Alex had given up trying to stay awake. Mercy nodded assent and then continued with her current task of adjusting IV drip rates.

Staggering into the supply room, Alex collapsed onto a small cot they kept in the back corner. She flung her arm over her eyes to block out the twilight and with it, the darkness that was literal as well as metaphorical. As the moon rose over her, she fell into a troubled sleep, barely submerged below consciousness. For no apparent reason, her eyelids fluttered open, her body poised for action, even though the supply room was quiet as a tomb. Glancing at her phone, she noticed only twenty minutes had passed and decided to try something else to assuage her anxiety. She dialed Ian's number.

"Hello—Alex?" She could barely hear him over lively jazz music and a symphony of voices in the background.

"Hi," she said slowly. "Where are you?"

"Charity event. Save the lions, I think," he joked. "A cause that I have become very passionate about." Alex could imagine the quirked smile on his face and that familiar, heart-wrenching smolder in his blue eyes. "How are you doing? Still at the hospital?" he asked, his voice sobering.

Alex sat up and folded her legs before answering. "Still here. This is one of the most challenging situations I've ever been in." She debated for a second and then, on a whim, decided to let him into her epicenter. "I am really worried, Ian," she started, her voice cracking from the strain of holding in her emotions.

She paused when she heard a female's voice in the background. "Ian...Ian, there you are, darling. It's your turn to take me out on the dance floor." She couldn't hear how Ian responded but listened to his low soothing murmur, placating his companion.

"I suppose I better go live up to my reputation," he said flippantly.

The hole in Alex's persona created by exhaustion and despair abruptly filled with an erupting vehemence. "Sure," she responded. "You should do exactly that."

"Don't worry, Alex. It's just a show for the company image. I drink...I dance...I donate."

Alex gripped the phone with a hand trembling from raw anger. "Worry? You are the last person on this planet I am worried about. I have thirty-two children dying of typhoid fever, twelve exhausted members of my team, and one ICU doctor who is losing it because she hasn't slept in days. So, no, I don't have the time or emotional energy to be worried about you right now."

"Alex...I...what can I do?"

"Absolutely nothing unless you can materialize IV fluids and antibiotics and medical supplies that I will most likely run out of in the next few hours." She did a quick survey of the room, realizing that what she had just said was actually true. A sick panic settled into her gut. She sighed, long and heavy. "I'm sorry, Ian. Just go back to your party. Have fun."

As she disconnected, she let the stubborn, irreverent tears spill over her eyes and cascade down her cheeks. Ian had not deserved this uncharacteristic outburst, which, in part, was due to her own insecurity. The distance she felt from him was not only geographic. His reality was a champagne-infused la-la land, and hers resembled a masochistic nightmare sometimes.

She wet her t-shirt with a splash of water from her bottle and scrubbed some life back into her grimy, tear stained face. Twisting her limp ponytail into a bun, she pushed open the door and stepped back into the ward.


In the witching hours of pre-dawn, Alex, Mercy, and Lesedi sat in a tight circle with faces that told the tale of the past forty-eight hours. The supplies had become scarce. Several children had to be disconnected from their lifeline of IV fluids and tried on oral rehydration solution before they were ready. No antibiotic doses remained. They were even low on soap since some of their supply had been sent to the village to clean people's homes. Dr. K had put calls out to several other hospitals, but it seemed that they were battling their own issues with resource utilization and could not help. Alex rubbed her throbbing temples, Mercy rubbed the tight mound in her lower abdomen where her baby was growing, and Lesedi, as always, was reserved and thoughtful. The women sat close together, drawing strength from one other, each lost in thought.

Soon they would have to start deciding how to triage the children into groups—from most to least likely to survive—and redistribute the supplies to the former. Alex's very soul rejected the idea. Brutal but necessary. She could not bear the thought of one single child dying from a totally preventable disease. The dawn came and bathed them in its golden glow, and today, instead of feeling renewed with hope, Alex felt disheartened and dreaded every coming second of the rest of this day.

"I guess we should get started figuring this out," she said, her voice little more than a hoarse whisper. As they pulled out their complicated scribbled spreadsheets of patient vitals, morning lab values, and remaining supplies, they heard a diesel engine thunder into the parking lot. A huge bright yellow truck eased in to park outside the open window. A man jumped out of the cab and raised the rear door to reveal the treasures inside—bunches of water bottles encased in plastic wrap, cardboard boxes labeled *IV solution,* crates of medical supplies, pharmaceuticals, hand sanitizer, and even bananas.

Alex was speechless as she stared at box after box being unloaded from the truck like manna from heaven incarnate.

"Dr. K must have come through for us after all," said an awestruck Mercy.

"Not Dr. K," said Alex, still searching for words as she noticed the writing on the side of the truck that read *Devall Mining Cooperative* in large black letters.

# TWELVE

Alex had not heard from Ian despite several early morning text messages consisting of an apology, a heartfelt thank you, and one rare selfie holding little Mmoloki, who had made a miraculous recovery in the last several hours and now clung to Alex with fervor. She knew he was probably sleeping after his late-night demonstration of widespread charity—both at his event and, apparently, at her feet. Later in the morning, while tucking Mmoloki back into a crib, her phone buzzed, and a single message flashed on her phone.

*You requested. I delivered.*

Alex began to type a speedy reply, erased it, and then retyped it. She couldn't quite think of how to respond. *Thank you for saving the day. You are not the self-centered, womanizing jerk I thought you were* flashed through her mind. She decided on something simpler.

*Thank you for everything.*

Alex sent a thoroughly exhausted Mercy home after the supplies arrived, insisting that she rest for the baby's sake and promising to give her an update later in the day. She and Lesedi spent a frenetic afternoon making good use of the newly delivered supplies and transitioning about half of the kids to the "improving" side of the ward. By the time dusk settled, the kids were tucked in for the night in beds with clean sheets, IV fluids hanging, and dosed up with antibiotics. With strict instructions to the overnight interns to call her if anything changed, Alex decided to go home for a few hours for a hot shower and a stretch of sleep in her own bed.

The last thing she remembered was how amazing it felt to be horizontal between the layers of a firm mattress and a heavy duvet. She awoke to a pitch-black room lit only by starlight and the soft whine of a dog who needed letting out. Her limbs felt achy and heavy as she unbundled herself from the bedcovers and padded behind McCartney to the backdoor. While he was sniffing around the yard, she checked her phone—three messages from Ian and one missed call from Rox, but none from the hospital. Alex let out a sigh of utter relief and decided to relax at home for a few hours before heading in to relieve the night team. Back in bed with McCartney snuggled at her feet, she took an indulgent moment to open Ian's messages.

*Close your eyes, and I'll kiss you*
*tomorrow I'll miss you*
*Remember I'll always be true*

Her heart beat erratically. Had she mentioned her love of the Beatles? The name of her dog, maybe? She was sure she hadn't, but there in black letters on a white screen were the lyrics from *All My Loving* by McCartney and Lennon. If there existed ways to win her affection, this man was hitting home runs.

In her crazed internet examination of Ian's life, she hadn't found anything personal. She really didn't know much about him except for the fact that he had as many layers as an English trifle and the few details she had learned while camping. Every interaction had been completely mutually exclusive—the flirt, the jerk, the self-centered, independently wealthy heir, the emotive, the master of seduction, the generous benefactor. Which versions of Ian would end up being real? She decided to text him back.

*And then while I'm away, I'll write home every day*

*And send all my loving to you.* She refrained from writing that last line. She was absolutely not falling in love with him. Was she? It was too soon and they barely knew each other, and between the two of them, they had enough baggage for a five-piece set. He replied almost immediately.

*Awake?*

*Very.*

In the next nanosecond, her phone rang and connected her with Ian across time and space. She briefly wondered what he was doing up at one in the morning London time.

"Hi," she breathed, and despite feeling drained from the ordeal of the last few days, she couldn't keep the joy out of her voice.

"How are you?" he asked, concern coating his words.

"Tired but managing. Much better now that the kids are better," she trailed off. He remained silent, and she continued. "Ian, I...I can't thank you enough. The kids are going to make it through this because of you."

"What am I good for without my worldly influence? A lot of people owe me favors," he said casually and then in a deeper, more reverent tone, "The kids will make it because of you, Alex...not me." A brief pause ensued, thick with emotion from both sides that caused Alex to swallow hard.

"So, what are you wearing right now?" Ian said wickedly. "Something hot, or are you completely naked?"

If embarrassment could travel long distance, Alex's would have landed in a heap on Ian's head.

"Is that all you ever think about?" she chided while inside a secret thrill bloomed.

"Pretty much. I didn't get the title of world's most eligible bachelor just lying around."

"Maybe that's exactly how you got it," countered Alex pointedly.

"Touché, my dear." He snickered into the phone.

"How did you know I liked the Beatles?" Alex asked, abruptly changing the subject. Ian's many late-night trysts were not something she wanted to analyze right now.

"I know more about you than you think, Alex."

"I don't even want to think about how," Alex said, imagining all sorts of hired ex-MI6 agents combing through her browser history and her credit card purchases.

He sighed dramatically. "Nic met McCartney at Rox's place. I just put two and two together. I happen to love animals, by the way." Alex knew this was her chance.

"Speaking of which, I will add that to the extremely short list of things I know about you."

"If you want to know anything, Alex, all you have to do is ask."

"I don't even know where to start." Alex had a brief mental debate about what she actually did and did not want to know about Ian.

"It's a good thing I am full of extremely brilliant ideas lately. Every time you think of a question, text it to me, and I will do the same."

"And this will help me get to know you?"

"Just think of it as a game of I'll show you mine if you show me yours."

Her ears burned with trepidation. "Quid pro quo then?"

"I prefer the term foreplay, Alex."

As she hung up the phone that evening, she detected the pulsing glow of something deep within her—a part of her where the thrill of Ian had started to outweigh her fear.

The next two days passed in a blur for Alex. She spent most of the time at the hospital except for a few sacred hours in her horizontal haven, also known as her bed. All of the children were improving daily with the careful ministrations from the hospital staff. Not a single child was lost to typhoid. Little Mmoloki had started eating his meals that consisted of porridge diluted with milk on a spoon and subsequently had a notable bump in his energy level that threatened the nurses' ability to keep him in his crib. Their Herculean efforts had not gone unnoticed by Dr. K, who had personally visited the ward and offered his encouragement and praise.

"We must talk about your future here, Alex," he said while walking through the various bed spaces.

"I'd like that very much," she replied, in awe of the potential opportunities that awaited her.

"Good—before you leave Gaborone then," he called over his shoulder, already striding toward his next task of the day.

Alex stayed late that night, long after the night team had arrived and received their assignments. She often had trouble separating at the end of the day, sometimes out of fear of what might happen overnight or the need to see things to completion or possibly a combination of the two. She lingered over each child, reviewing their vitals and mentally charting their progress. Finally satisfied with her synopsis, she headed home for a much-needed respite.

The lights were on in her kitchen as she trudged up her driveway. She hadn't left them on, or had she? McCartney was unusually quiet, so she was confident nothing sinister awaited her inside the house. Opening the door, she was met with an elated shriek and the concomitant pop of a champagne cork, which caused her adrenal glands to squeeze out any remaining drops of adrenaline she had left. She reflexively fell to her knees in the entryway.

"Oh, honey! We didn't mean to scare you!" Rox said, both concerned and giddy at the same time. Sporting a nice golden tan from her recent outdoor adventures, she looked amazing in a leopard print halter and white jeans. Nic and his stellar reflexes had grabbed Alex by the elbows before she puddled onto the floor. She glanced up at him with a grateful expression.

"I'm okay. Just tired," Alex said, trying to muster enough energy to enjoy her company.

"You look like a truck hit you." Rox bit her lip in anguish and then brandished her champagne in Alex's direction. "Cheers! We are so proud of you."

"Cheers," said Alex, taking a mouthful of elegant bubbles into her parched mouth. "I want to hear all about the trip," she continued, trying to refocus the attention from the hellscape of the last few days.

"Tomorrow love. When you have had rest. In one word, it was glorious. Nic's just leaving, and I'll stay with you tonight if that's okay."

Alex didn't know whether to cry, laugh, or just wrap her friend in a giant hug of appreciation. Roxanne had a gift of knowing exactly what she needed, and Alex knew how sacrificial it was to give up a precious night with Nic. Rox and Nic bid a prolonged goodnight on her front porch, long enough for Alex to shower, change into pajamas, and climb into bed.

"You are so into him," Alex said as her friend jumped in next to her.

"He is just...so..." For once, Roxanne failed to find a proper adjective to describe her favorite mammal. "How are things with you and Ian?" Rox asked cautiously, and her eyes widened a bit as Alex told her the tale of the last several days.

"Who knew this man was a complete genius." When Alex looked puzzled, she continued, "No flowers and chocolate for you, love.

He found the only way to your heart—boxes and boxes of medical supplies."

Laughter exploded from both of them and threatened never to stop. Finally, with tears in her eyes, Rox said, "Now, let's have a look at these questions, shall we?" Eagerly curious but also nervous, Alex flipped over her phone and clicked on the messages from Ian she had been ignoring.

*What is your middle name?*
*Who is your favorite author?*
*What one thing do you want in life more than any other?*

Rox snatched the phone from her hand, probably expecting Alex to dodge the questions tonight, and said brightly, "I'll be your scribe. Go on then…wax poetic and the like."

Alex groaned aloud. "Fine. Jean is my middle name. My favorite author is Dominique LaPierre, and I want to spend my life improving childhood survival."

Rox paused in her keystrokes long enough to cast Alex a dirty look. "He's asking what you want, Alex—not what you can do or will do because you are talented and philanthropic. Give me something better."

Alex bit her bottom lip in concentration. Her identity had intertwined with her profession, and it had been a long time since she had thought much about creating a life for herself outside of work. She did want one, and if she was honest with herself, there were many things she wanted in life that had always seemed unreachable. Ian's callous but honest assessment of her was accurate—she was afraid to want more.

"I want a life full of joy that tips the scales on all the pain I've experienced." She blew out a breath and cast a sidelong glance at Rox. Who knew soul searching could be so energy depleting? Rox's fingers scurried over the screen, a look of empathy in her eyes and a satisfied set to her lips. Not too long after Rox pressed send on Alex's soul-baring replies, Ian answered.

*No middle name. James Herriot. To find my soul mate*
*Where is your favorite place?*
*Breakfast-sweet or savory?*
*Your greatest fear?*

"Does this man ever sleep?" grumbled Alex at the same time Rox was scrolling through his messages. "I'm glad there is nothing private about this moment."

"What's a few shared secrets between best friends?" said Rox, the gold flecks in her irises practically glowing with excitement. "It would seem that I am just as excited to know the answers as Ian." She was poised over the phone screen like a cat ready to pounce.

"Okay, but then I have to sleep before I turn into a pumpkin." Alex sunk her head into her pillow and let her arm flop over her face. "My mom's house in Texas. I like both for breakfast—some of each—and my greatest fear is living a life without meaning." *And rejection...loving extravagantly without being loved in return.* She shut her eyes tightly, not concerned that Rox continued to type God-knew-what to Ian and let her insatiable need for sleep overtake her.

When Alex returned to PM to check on things the following day, she was swept up in the escalating confidence and morale that had magnified over the last few days. Only a few scattered cases that needed hospital admission had shown up, and almost every single kid from the first week had returned home, including Mmoloki, to whom she bid a bittersweet goodbye as she handed him off to his doting mother.

For the next several weeks, between patient care and closing up loose ends with her research projects, Alex found little time to reflect on the future, except for the stolen moments she spent answering Ian's questions. She had resolved herself to honesty, as much as she could muster it, and apparently, he had done the same. She now knew his favorite place was Necker Island, his greatest fear was dying alone, he had wanted to be a veterinarian when he was growing up, and he had a Jack Russell terrier named Clementine. Ian had been right. Every tiny tidbit of information offered about herself had made her feel more exposed. It was equally thrilling and terrifying. She frequently stole private moments in the PM courtyard to address his questions, soaking up the final rays of fall sunshine. Today a single text message patiently sat unopened on her screen. She performed a deliberate swipe with her thumb as she chugged a Diet Coke.

*Can you meet me in Paris on your way home from Botswana?*

*Wow. Paris?* She had never been, and it was at the top of her list of dream destinations. And Paris with Ian. A tingling sensation started in her toes and spread warmly upward until her hands shook and her face felt numb. He had been right about the foreplay, and he was a master at it. Her fingers strained at the ends of her arms, wanting to type a huge *YES* and leave it at that. She paused as her mental gymnastics kicked in. Logistically, she wasn't confident that she could make any promises. Another text pinged her phone as she vacillated.

*Just say yes*

Another ping.

*I will take care of the details.*

Smiling and shaking her head, she felt her emotions peak into soft waves that carried her impulses into her fingertips as she typed and hit enter.

*Yes*

Days piled up into weeks as Alex spent her daylight hours taking care of kids in the pediatric ward and holding her last few teaching sessions. She spent nearly every evening cradling her phone while she and Ian traded their texted queries for verbal ones, and McCartney thumped his tail in encouragement.

As the air in Botswana continued to chill, the days grew shorter and so did Alex's time there. In two days, she would be leaving on a flight to Paris before heading home to Philadelphia. Loose ends abounded, and Alex spent the entire day making phone calls, packing, and letting tears spill over periodically. She had met with Dr. K and gone over the plan for her continued involvement with the PM pediatrics program while finishing her fellowship. At the end, she had embraced him in a solid hug that spoke volumes.

McCartney would be living it up at Roxanne's while she figured out how to get him approved for a transcontinental transition. She was headed there now, her lanky puppy trotting along beside her, sniffing the delectable scents he detected along the way. Rox stood on her porch waving them both over when Alex rounded the corner. McCartney broke free from his leash to place his paws on her chest and plant a kiss right in the middle of her perfectly made-up face.

"Are you all packed up, then love?" Rox said, laughing as McCartney continued to barrage her with wet doggy lips.

"Yes," said Alex, a twist of emotion catching her by surprise. "I'm not ready, Rox."

Her friend smiled up at her broadly. "You are, Alex. You are ready for so many things."

They pulled each other in for a magnetic hug, like two opposite charges clinging to each other. "No tears yet," said Rox as she dabbed her eyes on her shirt sleeve. "First, we have a goodbye dinner, and then I will take you to the airport where you can feel free to bawl like a baby."

Alex's friends and colleagues from the hospital had arranged a going away dinner for her at, where else, the patio of Ex-Pats. The atmosphere was lively as food was passed and drinks were poured under the starlit ceiling. Alex felt herself continuously oscillating between her current reality and quick jaunts down memory lane of the evenings that she and Rox had spent forming a lifetime bond, becoming more like sisters than friends.

As the partygoers thinned out one by one, Alex had been offered hands and hugs and promises to keep in touch. She had patted Mercy's belly and vowed to see the baby as soon as she could. Soon only she and Rox remained, seated in the same alcove that she and Ian had shared not too many weeks ago. Her mind drifted to the very real fact that she would be seeing him in a little over twenty-four hours.

"Rox," she said, a question burning through her mind, "am I ready for this?" Once again, her sister in spirit knew exactly what she meant and took her time before answering with well-chosen words.

"I believe that you are, my dear. I think that you will be shocked at just how ready you are. In relationships, timing is everything, so the question remains—is he ready for you?"

Assuming that the question was rhetorical, Alex continued to listen, soaking in the last bit of Rox-isms she would get for a while, hoping they would be enough for Paris. "You are wonderful, Alex, but you are not a filler." Alex frowned in confusion, and Rox explained, "A girl who fills in the empty space on your dance card while you are waiting for *the* girl. You are *the* girl, Alex, and soon you'll know whether Ian thinks so too."

"Do you think he…?" Alex trailed off, and Rox interrupted her with a question.

"The most important thing is, do you?"


Alex hesitated before opening the door to the cab once they arrived at Sir Seretse Khama airport. Her throat felt tight, and tears pricked her eyes with their salt. "I can't say goodbye, Rox. I can't do it."

"It's not goodbye unless we don't have a plan to see each other again—so let's make one," Rox said hurriedly, her words trying to outrun her own tears. Rox's eyes lit up with excitement, and Alex could tell she was pleased with her own brilliance. "New Year's," she said firmly. "Every year, no matter what, we celebrate together."

"Every year," repeated Alex as she lost herself in Rox's loving embrace.

# THIRTEEN

The inside of the hotel was the grandest, most opulent structure Alex had ever set foot in. Even her taxi driver had reverence in his voice when he turned to her and said, "Mademoiselle, we have arrived at Le Meurice Hotel." Alex stood, dumbfounded and jet-lagged, in the hotel lobby, mesmerized by every detail—the wall frescos in muted colors depicting cherubic ladies in rustling dresses, the light particles refracted by dangling crystal, and the hexagonal floor tiles polished to perfection. A compact Frenchwoman with a tight brown bun interrupted her gawking.

"Pardon me, Mademoiselle. May I help you?"

"Yes...*oui*...please." Alex took a breath and smiled. "I am here to check-in. The reservation is under...Luke Skywalker?" Whispering the last part, Alex halfway thought the hotel management would toss her out once she supplied the fake name Ian used to check into a hotel. He said that it cut down on the "riffraff" trying to connect with him. Aspiring journalists or ambitious ex-girlfriends—Alex was sure it was a bit of both.

"Of course," replied the Frenchwoman, a crinkle developing near her clear blue eyes. "We have been expecting you."

Several staircases later, Alex stood in front of a gilded dove-gray door with a gold plate that read *La Belle Etoile*. The Frenchwoman, whose name badge read *Marguerite*, smiled sweetly as she directed Alex inside what could only be summed up as a mini-palace. Decorated in a color palette of muted gold and grayish-blue and cream, the suite boasted impeccable furnishings that were modern but also promised comfort. A giant crystal chandelier that resembled an upside-down Christmas tree illuminated the entrance to a golden spiral staircase that led to a lower level.

"There are two floors, an upper and a lower. Please make use of any of the rooms. They are all part of the suite," informed Marguerite as she caught Alex's gaze sweeping over the expansive space. "I would like to show you the highlight of *La Belle Etoile*, and then I will leave you to enjoy everything."

The highlight turned out to be an outside terrace with luscious potted plants separated by clusters of outdoor seating that wrapped around almost the entire upper level, offering a 270-degree view of the Paris skyline. Transfixed by the phenomenal view, Alex was unaware that Marguerite had discreetly left her side, and she was now alone to imprint this picturesque cityscape into her mind. Each side of the terrace depicted a new visual treasure to behold—the Eiffel tower boldly soaring above the city streets, the dome of the Sacré-Cœur in the distance, the verdant Tuileries garden bordering the familiar boxy architecture of the Louvre.

In the early morning, not long after the start of a workday, she could almost hear the increase in footfalls as patrons flocked to their favorite cafés for a latte and a soft, buttery croissant. Despite the sun comfortably above the horizon, the May air in Paris blew cold and damp, and Alex snuggled into her sweatshirt embroidered with the University of Pennsylvania logo.

Once back inside the suite, she noticed her bags awaited her in the foyer. As the adrenaline rush from arriving in Paris waned, a foreboding sense of exhaustion crept over her and she could think of nothing besides a hot shower and a nice mattress. She halted in front of the master suite, and then, shaking her head, descended the spiral staircase to the lower level to claim one of the guest rooms.

After a scalding hot shower in the marble bathroom, she luxuriated in the fluffy cotton hotel robe, her hair still damp and creating a growing wet spot on the cream-colored satin duvet. Her phone buzzed, and she held it up to her freshly washed face.

*Hope the hotel is up to your standards Dr. Wilde*

*I guess it will do*

*Picking you up for dinner. See you soon but not soon enough.*

Alex closed her eyes and fell into an exquisite sleep before she could come up with a reply.

Several hours later, she awoke amid a cascade of wet hair, her knees tucked into her robe for warmth, and glanced at the time on her phone—2:14 p.m. She had a few precious hours until Ian arrived. The reality of seeing him again cascaded over her, and she vibrated with nervous energy, thoroughly unsure of Ian's expectations and partly unsure of her own. Fortunately, exceeding expectations had always been her way of life, and Alex did not intend to change that now. Summoning a newfound boldness, she picked up the phone on the bedside table and dialed the concierge.

"Bonjour, I need a dress for dinner tonight. Can you direct me to the nearest shop?"

An hour and a hefty charge on her credit card later, Alex proudly reentered the *Belle Etoile* suite with a chiffon halter dress of deepest azure blue that nicely displayed her back and complimented her eyes. Settling down in front of the vanity mirror in the lower level bathroom, she dumped her entire collection of cosmetics on the countertop, which consisted of mostly hand-me-downs from Roxanne. The few choice items of her own included her favorite lip stain in a delicate pink that made her lips feel lusciously moist.

Alex had never put beauty products as a priority, but what girl didn't want to look pretty when it mattered most? Not one to disappoint, Alex peered at her reflection, her efforts come to fruition, and thought Rox would be proud of her protégé.

With the hair tools supplied by the hotel, she transformed her long, wet tresses into soft waves that ended in the middle of her back, realizing it had been nearly a year since her last trim. Slipping on the dress and her trusty nude heels, she stopped for a glance in the hallway mirror before heading up the spiral staircase to the upper level and barely recognized herself. Inside, she grappled with fear and uncertainty, but outwardly, she had donned a layer of beautiful that definitely helped to even the balance.

The first thing she noticed when she ascended the staircase and reentered what she had deemed the "posh parlor" was a bottle of champagne on ice, two crystal flutes, and a card with her name on it. She shakily opened the card and read,

*I hope you don't mind*
*that I put down in words*
*How wonderful life is while you're in the world.*
*Ian*

Recognizing the lyrics from *Your Song* by Elton John, Alex's chest fluttered like a pair of hummingbirds. The man sure knew how to make an entrance without even physically being there. She took the liberty of popping the cork to the bottle of Veuve Clicquot, and to her delight, a pink effervescent liquid bubbled into her glass. Rosé champagne—her favorite.

Feeling entirely indulgent in her new dress, dolled up to perfection, and holding a glass of pink champagne, Alex stepped out onto the expansive terrace to watch the sun settle over Paris and wait for Ian. Toward the end of her first glass, her entire body vibrated with excitement and possibility. The tiny surge of alcohol through her bloodstream, combined with the romantic atmosphere of this city, made all of this seem like a very good idea. The nagging self-doubt and the constant evaluation of the intactness of her protective layer gradually slipped away. In their place, she felt an unexpected surge of power coupled with the actualization of what she could offer, not as someone's doctor or friend, but as a woman—a woman who could be bold yet tender...strong yet feminine...and authentic yet desirable.

Partway through her second glass of champagne, the insidious thoughts caught up with her and forced themselves into her consciousness. What if Africa had been a fantasy or a fluke or an escape from reality for both of them? Her champagne-infused brain longed for magical, romantic perfection. Anything less seemed unacceptable. What if, after spending time with her, Ian lost interest and she became just another girl with whom he was briefly enamored—like a good book or a savory bottle of wine? Or what if she fell for him but couldn't bring herself to trust him inside the well-conceived, forbidden fortress of her heart? She couldn't offer him all of the good without all of the bad.

As she teetered on this emotional precipice, she heard the glass door behind her slide open. Alex turned to see Ian standing in the opening, bathed in fading sunlight, fashionably dressed in a white button-down under a charcoal blazer, phone to his ear, and dark hair tousled over the now-familiar eyes, bright and smoldering as they focused only on her.

"That all sounds good," he said, his eyes never wavering, "I'll follow up with you tomorrow."

In the next breath, he had pocketed his phone and closed the distance between them. Without speaking, he tipped up her chin with his fingertips and waited a microsecond for unspoken permission before he met her lips with his—gentle but hungry. As they both lost themselves in their reunion moment, their kiss deepened, tongues intertwining, filling her mouth with an exquisite spice. His hands wound into Alex's hair, and she reached up to run her palms over his flat, muscled chest, then around his neck and up through his already-mussed hair. He groaned into her mouth and pulled her in close enough so that she felt the erratic pace of his heart through his shirt. After too brief a moment, he grabbed both of her hands and separated his mouth from hers. Her eyes fluttered open to the sight of his sky-blue irises, shining halos around the black abyss of his dilated pupils.

"Paris suits you," he said, appraising her with an up and down motion of his head. "You look stunning." A tiny flick of his tongue dampened his lower lip before he grazed it with his teeth. The blood thundered into Alex's most intimate crevices, and her breath caught.

"Thank you."

He was still grasping both of her hands, holding her near enough that their bodies touched each time either one of them exhaled. "So, what now?" she asked.

"Well, I'm starving, and I'm ready to treat my girl to an amazing night in Paris," Ian said casually as the wind began to play with his hair. He leaned down close so that his mouth just grazed her earlobe and whispered, "Are you ready for your life to change?"

Alex didn't have the capacity to ascertain precisely what he meant. A delicate shiver had started at the nape of her neck and gathered force as it reached the tips of her toes. "It already has," she responded, taking his proffered arm and allowing him to lead her toward the elevator to the hotel lobby.

Once downstairs, his words from the terrace sunk in as they were met with light sources from every angle, mostly flashes from camera bulbs and suspended smartphones held aloft by a variety of women. Ian tucked Alex next to him as they were hustled through the crowd by a giant of a man wearing black aviators and a leather holster. They were practically shoved into a waiting black SUV as the "man in black" slid into the driver's seat and pulled away from the curb. Still giddy from her earlier bubbly indulgence, Alex fanned herself dramatically and then pretend-swooned at Ian, who was busy buckling his seatbelt.

He chuckled and said, "It's not always like this, but I have spent a bit of time here, so people recognize me."

"What did you do when you were here?" Alex asked.

"This and that. Nothing important," Ian quipped. Although not thrilled with his evasiveness, Alex decided to file it away for now and focus on their evening.

"Where are we going?" she asked, but Ian was too engrossed in running his fingertips up the back of her calf to answer. Alex felt a bloom of desire start between her legs as he lightly traced her kneecap and then pushed her dress up a tiny fraction to caress the inside of her thigh. She held her breath so long that she had to remind herself to exhale as the car pulled to a stop, and her door was ceremoniously swung open.

The restaurant, situated on the bank of the river Seine, epitomized French history, culture, art, and literature. Reinvented a number of times in its several hundred-year history, *Laperouse* remained a Paris staple as well as Ian's favorite. Decadent entered Alex's mind when they stepped into the softly lit bar area decorated with muted red silk tapestries in swirling feminine patterns that contrasted with the marble floors and chestnut wood ceilings.

"Monsieur Devall," said a kindly gentleman dressed in a black dinner jacket. "Please follow me to your table."

As they were led deeper into the building, Alex noticed that it was divided into separate dining areas that would provide patrons with the opportunity for intimacy and privacy during their dinner. She and Ian were taken to one of the smaller salons overlooking the Seine. The salon contained a single table flanked by two red velvet chairs underneath a glorious chandelier hanging from a blue marbled ceiling that resembled the night sky. Ian pulled out her chair and then sat next to her, so they both faced an enormous window with a view of the Seine. The sommelier stopped by the table to pour each of them a glass of wine, a blood-colored Bordeaux with a sharp but pleasing aftertaste. After a few sips, they settled into the evening and each other.

"Favorite girl band?" Ian said between succulent bites of lobster soaked in some type of *beurre blanc* sauce. Alex was so lost in conversation that she had barely registered the wine that kept getting poured and the elegant dishes placed before them then whisked away.

"Dixie Chicks, of course," Alex answered. "I am from Texas after all."

"Yes—I can really tell once you've started drinking and your accent comes out," Ian teased.

Alex rolled her eyes. "It's a curse that I use to my advantage from time to time."

"I'd like to be on the other end of that," said Ian seductively.

Alex blushed and redirected the conversation. "You have really good taste in music."

"I have good taste in general," he said, taking a lengthy sip of wine and swirling it around his mouth. If he was going to throw down the witty foreplay gauntlet, then she might as well pick it up.

"Me too," she replied evenly, a smile hinting at the corner of her mouth, strangely satisfied by the choking sound from the other side of the table.

Once recovered, he began tracing a tiny circle over the soft skin of her inner wrist. "Tell me about your little town where you grew up."

Finding it quite difficult to concentrate, Alex closed her eyes and launched into a narrative about the remote Texas town with one stoplight and more cows than people. Her words flowed as well as the wine that evening as she talked more than she ever had with another human, even Roxanne. She found herself describing the beauty in the miles and miles of green pastures dotted with shady cedars and frolicking calves, the white stone church in the middle of town where she was baptized, and the summers of driving back country roads when the air was so humid that it felt heavy to breathe. Ian continued to ply her with a flight of French wines and listen attentively, watching her with curiosity.

Halfway through the after-dinner cheese and chocolate course, a midnight blue sky scattered with stars filled the window opposite their table, and Alex realized that she had been dominating the conversation. "I'm sorry," she said, cutting the rest of her thoughts short. "I never talk this much. It must be the wine."

"Or the company," Ian said, narrowing his gaze and shooting her a sexy half grin. "Come on," he said, with a nod of his head toward the outside, "let's go. Are you okay walking back?" Alex nodded affirmatively and reminded herself to pepper him with questions on the walk back to the hotel.

She never got the chance, however, because after walking a short distance, he pulled her into a cozy, dim-lit bar called *La Lune* where they were met with a chorus of cheers from the bar staff.

"I take it you've been here before," Alex said.

"Once or twice," said Ian, winking and grabbing her hand firmly as he navigated them to a couple of open barstools. "Jack," he called to a thin, middle-aged guy with black hair streaked with gray.

"Ian! It's been too long, mate," he said with a noticeable Australian accent. Alex raised an eyebrow in piqued curiosity and decided to bide her time until the right moment to ask about Ian's Parisian period.

"I'm here for pleasure this time." His eyes cut toward Alex.

"And how is that so different than last time?" Jack wheezed as he plunked a bourbon down in front of Ian. Ian covered his discomfort by taking a long swig of his drink and avoiding Alex's narrowed stare.

"I'll have one too," she proclaimed.

Jack, it turned out, was an excellent resource once he had imbibed a few drinks. With Alex's encouragement, he shared the bulk of Ian's shenanigans during his time in Paris when he had first joined the Devall corporation, including his generous patronage to *La Lune* and the list of ladies that had accompanied him along the way.

"Actresses, models, singers, heiresses….and never the same one two nights in a row," confirmed Jack as he shook his head in apparent admiration. "He put my bar on the map. I'm a rich man thanks to this dog." He slapped Ian on the shoulder as Ian cringed deeper into his drink. Alex had known who Ian was, but it stung to hear it broadcast over the bar even if Jack's accent did make everything sound lovely.

The walk back to the hotel was painfully slow thanks to Alex's inefficiency in heels. They had plenty of time for the stimulation of the clamorous bar to wane into an easy quietude. Alex let the crisp air rolling off the Seine clear her thoughts and reinvigorate her inquisition into Ian's person. Her voice filled the quiet void around them, silent except for the clattering of her shoes.

"It sounds like you have a lot of memories here."

"Yeah, I guess I do," he said with uncertainty, "but it was a while ago, Alex."

"I'm not upset," she said. "If it's part of you then I want to know about it."

"Okay," he said, letting out a long slow breath. "I lived here for about two years after I finished graduate school and told everyone that I was working for my dad in our Paris office, but my life was really one big party. Socializing...spending money...indulging in life's finest enjoyments. I think I showed up to the office a total of five times. Not one of my finest periods."

Alex sunk her teeth into her lower lip and tried to not focus on the incredible ache in her feet. "Everyone has things in life they aren't proud of, Ian. The important part is how it changed you and how you can use it for some type of good."

"Maybe," he murmured, staring into the distance at something only he could see.

"Well, Jack certainly benefited from your late night trolloping," Alex said sternly and then, unable to hold it in, burst into a fit of laughter. Ian joined in, seeming a bit lighter after his confession. Still laughing and somewhat disinhibited from the alcohol, Alex reached down and removed her heels.

"Ah," she groaned, stretching her toes out onto the pavement. "I was never going to make it in these shoes." She could feel Rox's annoyance spiking back in Botswana.

"As luck would have it, we are here," Ian said as he scooped her into his arms, marching boldly through the mostly empty hotel foyer and depositing her into the waiting elevator.

Without pausing for the doors to close, he pressed his body into hers until her back was flush against the mirrored rear doors and distractedly tucked a silky strand of her dark brown hair behind her ear. "I love to hear you laugh," he said, his eyes transfixed on her mouth.

Alex reached up one hand behind his head and pulled him into her waiting lips. Kissing him was pure ecstasy. Driven by the woven fabric of their newfound intimacy, she kissed him slowly, savoring his bottom lip, and as the elevator rose, so did her level of desire. Her fingers intertwined in his hair as she delighted in the spice of bourbon on his lips, and she felt his hands run down the length of her body. He reached under her dress and cupped her bottom firmly, lifting her until they were eye level and she was forced to wrap her legs around his waist for support. The elevator doors slid open and, while clutching her, he backed into the suite, deepening their kiss with every step. Alex could feel the tense muscles of his forearms as he shifted her upward so that he could bury his lips into the tender skin below her ear. She could hear his breath, ragged and wanton.

An alarm sounded, somewhere deep in her subconscious, and she stilled, frozen by a sudden desperate urge to extinguish the moment.

"I'll be right back," she whispered and planted a kiss on his lips as her feet hit the ground. He didn't say anything while he watched her descend the stairs.

Taking the day off her face and shedding her evening clothes for a t-shirt and flannel pants helped Alex regain some control over her tumultuous emotions. Staring at her clean face in the mirror somehow helped to return her to reality—one where she did not become a girl on a list of actresses and heiresses. She wasn't ready. Not yet. Not until she knew for sure.

When she padded out of the bathroom, pulling her hair into a high ponytail, Ian was reclining on her bed, hands behind his head and somewhat decent. He had unbuttoned his shirt completely so that she had a provocative view of his entire chest, bare except for the sprinkling of a few dark hairs, his well-defined rectus abdominis rising with every breath. She stifled a moan, surprised by her own carnal nature, and then recalibrated quickly by offering him the book on the nightstand.

"The Coming Plague," he read aloud as he flipped through the pages.

"Checking to see if there is a chapter about you?" Alex said sweetly.

With a devious expression, he tossed the book aside, grabbing her by the waist and pulling her down next to him. They laughed while the bed jiggled, and then Ian propped himself up on his elbow to face her. His face had morphed into seriousness. "I never quite get what I expect from you, Alex." Assuming he was disappointed, Alex wilted a little inside as he confirmed the truth of her long-standing ineptitude with men.

"It's a good thing I like surprises." She startled at the words, suspended in a moment of disbelief, but his smile was so genuine that she couldn't help but trust him.

"Still want me to get to know you?" Alex said, feeling her timidity on the rise.

"More than anything," he whispered, a distinct yearning in his voice. "Well, maybe not more than anything." He stroked her side with fingers as light as feathers, a wanton look emanating from his blue eyes.

Alex snuggled into her pillow, positioning herself nose to nose with Ian, and said, "Tell me about your dad."

Ian rolled onto his back, staring at the ceiling, a look of consternation crossing his sculpted face.

"My dad is a saint and impossible to live up to. He and I couldn't be more different." Ian told her about how his dad let his mom stay in Los Angeles to pursue her acting dreams, but as the company expanded, he visited less and less often. "I think he loved her so much that he wanted her dreams to come true...even though it hurt him."

"That seems really selfless," Alex said.

"That's my dad." Alex stayed silent, hoping it would encourage Ian to continue. He told her how he moved to London when he was fifteen after his mom died and his dad had provided him with every opportunity imaginable—private school at St. Edwards then Cambridge, travel to stoke his interest in worldly affairs, and introductions to people with influence.

"I spent a lot of time indulging myself and not taking advantage of opportunities."

"How is it being chairman of the foundation?" Alex asked. Ian closed his eyes tightly as if in deep thought.

"I'm surrounded by righteous do-gooders all day that try to infect me with their sense of purpose."

"Is it working?" Alex said in a faux serious tone, but Ian didn't answer. His breathing had become deep and regular and his face had relaxed into a still work of art. Planting a soft kiss on his cheek, she nestled into his chest, interlocking her fingers with his, and closed her eyes.

# FOURTEEN

Alex awoke many hours later, in the same position from which she had fallen asleep, her hand still grasping Ian's, her cheek overly warm from its position on his chest. The sun was barely making its debut over the horizon and the clock on the bedside table read 6:09 a.m. Ever so stealthily, she extracted herself from the bed and crept upstairs to watch the sunrise on the terrace. Ian found her there about an hour later, tucked into a ball on one of the cushioned lounge chairs, clutching a mug of hot tea.

"You look cozy," he said and ruffled her hair before sitting beside her on the chaise. He had changed out of his dinner clothes into a loose-fitting pair of black track pants and a long sleeve t-shirt.

"This view is breathtaking," Alex said, still in complete awe of where she had woken up this morning.

"Do you always get up so early?" Ian complained.

"This isn't even close to early. I'm usually halfway through rounds at this point."

"Overachiever...morning person...loves tea and expensive wine." She took the liberty of nudging him playfully with her elbow.

"If you are making notes, I hate tea." After an odd look from Ian, she continued, "I just like holding something hot when I'm cold."

"Say no more," he said, flashing her a flirtatious grin, as he placed her cup on the table and pressed both of her hands to his chest. She palpated his heartbeat with her palms—slow and steady—and felt her own pulse skyrocket. Her blazing desire from last night resurfaced and would not be kept at bay much longer.

"The world is quite literally at your feet," he said, glancing over the terrace railing. "What can I interest you in?"

"I want to see the city," Alex said shyly, not moving her hands from the warmth of his lean chest. "Do you like to run?"

Although it took some cajoling, a breakfast pastry, and a shot of espresso, Alex convinced Ian to take her on a running tour of Paris with stops at all of the nearby sights. Running had always been her refuge, and, today, she hoped it would bring her the clarity she needed regarding Ian. They pounded along in comfortable silence for a while, each lost in thought, while their skin temperature adjusted to the cool, damp Parisian morning.

Alex ran ahead, craning her head down every cobblestone alleyway and stopping to photograph the quaint cafés covered in cascading flowers. She sensed the soul of this city in the air she breathed and in the ground beneath her feet. Paris was elegance itself—history and culture realized. They stopped for a moment at the famous Louvre pyramid to admire the sky's reflection in the light refracting panels and then turned north headed toward the white dome of the Sacré-Cœur.

Every pulsating strike of her shoes on the sidewalk offered a lightness of being that she rarely allowed to happen. Was it the romance of this city or the seduction of adventure? Or was there a burning ember inside her glowing inexplicably brighter every day that she spent with Ian? Was it simple chemical attraction, an insane infatuation, or something even more? He felt more real than fantasy at this point—more real than her internet research and more real than the sexy stranger from the bar in Gaborone. He had dimension now, creatively constructed by a flawed past and a depth to his troubled, beautiful soul. There was an earnest tenderness about him that captivated her.

Alex shook her head back and forth like a paddocked horse, trying to clear her mind. She picked up her speed, allowing the exchange of air in her lungs to purify her thoughts and leave a condensate of actual truth there instead. Heart pounding and chest heaving, she puffed out a gust of air as she paused at a crosswalk as realization dawned. He had infiltrated her very bloodstream, and no matter how many times she breathed in and out, she could not exhale Ian.

Ian caught up with her shortly. "There it is Flo-Jo," he said, wheezing as he spoke. "The entrance to the Sacré-Cœur."

Alex peered across the street at the upsloping green hillside divided by a staircase that led to a stark white domed basilica, a symbol of love and purity lording over the Montmartre. Disconcerted by the tsunami of feelings that surged through her chest, she opted with the stress response of flight.

"Race you up to the top," she said, breaking away to start the steep climb to the dome.

The view from the top of the steps of the Sacré-Cœur, the second highest point in all of Paris, was truly divine. The soft outlines of Parisian homes muted by the gray clouds rolling in, quieting the sun, resembled an impressionist painting in progress. Alex tilted back her head to fully appreciate the large marble dome that blanched white with every rain shower due to the calcium deposits in the stone. She felt warm breath near her ear.

"Want to see the view from the dome?" Alex nodded in excitement, and, like an overeager child, let him lead her to the side of the building where a woman was collecting tickets.

Ian squeezed her hand, a silent request to stay put, then made his way over to the stern-faced woman standing at the entrance. Alex watched in amusement while the lady's countenance changed from disdained to flustered as Ian smiled crookedly and half closed his lids over the flaming blues. The lady's hand flew to her neck to finger a strand of pearls that hung there, giving Ian a tight-lipped smile and a confirmatory nod. He sauntered back over to Alex, smiling broadly and immensely pleased with himself.

"You and your methods of persuasion. That lady didn't stand a chance," she said, teasingly.

"Neither do you," he replied huskily, almost predatorily. Alex's skin erupted into gooseflesh and she shivered inside her sweatshirt.

They climbed the dark winding staircase to the top of the dome, the tension between them palpable and cloaking them like the surrounding air, heavy with moisture. After what seemed like a short eternity, the air seemed to lighten and they entered a light-filled circular space, the underbelly of the famous dome directly above them.

"I want a picture with the city in the background," Alex said, excited by a potential addition to her treasure trove of framed memories.

"Anything you want," Ian said, winking. "Marie said we had ten minutes to ourselves before she lets everyone else in."

"The best angle is if I," Alex said, throwing one leg between the columned structure, "lean just a little bit…"

She could feel the wind hit her face full force as the upper half of her body was suspended over a spectacular aerial view of Paris. "I can see the Eiffel tower," she called to Ian. The elevation of her senses as well as her physical self, perched above the slowly moving world below, made Alex feel ethereal. For one moment, she was an angel, suspended from the heavens, then she was unexpectedly falling through space as a pair of arms pulled her back inside the cloister. Ian's face appeared strained and his sculpted features wore the hard lines of worry and fear.

"Be careful, Alex. That's dangerous," he whispered, holding her firmly by the shoulders.

"I...I'm fine, Ian" she replied, a bit dazed. Out of nowhere he pulled her close. The lengths of their bodies collided, and he kissed her deeply before relaxing his hold, leaving her breathless and stunned. The tight muscles of his jaw relaxed, and he smiled down at her.

"Come on—I'll help you get your photos."


Alex admired the artistic shots she had managed to snap from her iPhone as they slowly made their way down the multi-level staircase to the street level. She remained curious about Ian's reaction in the dome, but he seemed fine now, having returned to his overconfident, sexier-than-thou state of mind. A cold drop of water hit her nose and dripped off the end, landing in the middle of her screen and then another and another until tiny pellets of rain turned her photo into a digital watercolor.

"I think we better duck inside somewhere," called Ian as his speed picked up to a slow jog.

"No," Alex replied, "it's not bad yet. I bet we can make it back."

She gave him her most winning smile, knowing that he would give in, and they headed into the drizzle. At first, the rain felt refreshing, but as they picked up their tempo, the drops followed suit until they were splashing down the city streets. Somehow running wildly through the streets of Paris with Ian beside her, both of them soaking wet from exposure to nature's elements, seemed to bring him down to her level. She could see him laughing quietly out of her peripheral vision, his dark hair plastered to his skull, arms pumping to the rhythm of their strides, and for the first time, she acknowledged the growing kinship between them.

As the front of Le Meurice came into view, they simultaneously sped up their pace and entered the elegant doorway, breathless and dripping. Two horrified bellmen immediately fetched white embroidered towels and ushered them into the nearest elevator. Alex looked at Ian, the heir to the universe, a bedraggled mess of hair and sloppy running clothes, creating a puddle in the middle of the gilded lift and erupted in laughter.

When the elevator door dinged open, they stayed bent over laughing until tears ran down their faces already wet with rain. Alex laughed deliriously, shaking until her sides hurt. Rather than from humor, she realized the shivering had initiated from a wet cold creeping into her bones. Ian had quieted when her teeth started to chatter, and he looked at her through wide eyes.

"Alex—your lips are actually blue. Come with me."

He grabbed her hand and hustled her through the posh parlor into the master bedroom and then into the most extravagant bathroom that Alex had ever seen. The floors, walls, and ceiling were white marble with swirling brushstrokes of black. A giant white soaking tub with a gold faucet sat in front of a window to the outside terrace, and the opposite wall contained floor to ceiling panes of glass, housing a shower with various sized gold fixtures. Ian reached in and started turning various knobs to allow water to stream from all directions. He reached in to test the water, turning to flick some in Alex's direction.

"Be my guest," he said, kicking off his shoes.

Alex stilled from an internal surge of panic. Ian, keeping his gaze trained on her expressionless face, bent down and removed her running shoes and socks, then picked her up over his shoulder, plunging both of them fully clothed into the beckoning steam. Alex felt the cold leave her body immediately, replaced by a delicious radiant warmth. She tipped her face upward into the rain shower and pulled out her hairband, letting her hair lengthen down to her lower back.

She watched Ian through the rivulets of water in her visual field as he removed his shirt. He stood facing her, lean and muscled, eyes closed under the luxurious pressurized water streaming past his cheekbones and lips. Without thinking, Alex impulsively reached out with her hands to palm his face and stood on tiptoe to capture his bottom lip between hers. His eyes flew open, and she briefly felt the singe of their heat before she was lost in the devouring nature of their kiss. Her mouth beckoned his tongue to enter it, and she felt as fluid as the streaming water—shapeless and freeform.

Once his mouth locked with hers, he seemed intent and purposeful, kissing her deeply and then taking her lips section by section and ravaging them with his. She felt her shirt being tugged over her head before she could protest, and he bent down to do the same with her shorts, planting wet, succulent kisses all the way to her navel. Once Alex was undressed to her underwear and sports bra, she felt a tinge of discomfort creeping in and tried to shoo it aside like a pesky fly. Her desire was real and unthwartable, and to prove it to herself, she ran her hands down Ian's etched abdominal muscles and slipped her fingers into the waistband of his shorts, intending to return the favor of undressing him.

She could feel the tensile strength of his lower abs and hear his gasp when her fingers tickled the upper border of his pubic hair. Alex froze. Without any muscle memory for this situation, she couldn't will herself to keep going. As the rain shower struck her face, so did the realization of just how out of her league she was. She backed away from him slowly until her back was flush with the formidable cold of marble. Wishing she could be anywhere except for this moment, she enviously watched the swirl of water happily exiting through the drain. Ian said nothing. He ran his hand through his thick hair, slicking it back into place as water streamed over eyes that, for once, revealed nothing. Grabbing a fluffy white towel from the stack outside the shower, he exited into the master bedroom.

Once alone, Alex finally exhaled. Feeling hot and a little faint, she turned off all the shower heads and stepped out onto the frigid marble floor. She took a moment and then another just to breathe and settle into a decision she had avoided for half a lifetime. It wasn't as terrifying as she thought it would be.

Several minutes later, with freshly scrubbed skin and her wet hair brushed out, she slipped on the only thing she could find in the luxe bathroom—a black silk kimono-style robe that was probably intended for royalty. She opened the door and went to find Ian.


Rejection did not suit him well. He was seated on the plushest of the cream-colored sofas and was two fingers deep into a bottle of bourbon that had apparated from nowhere. The sight of him deep in thought, swirling the bourbon in the glass slowly in front of his face, dressed in a black cashmere sweater and soft, broken-in jeans made Alex's heart leap into her throat. A familiar flame ignited in his eyes when he saw her. It was brief, but she saw it and knew that all was not lost. He patted the cushion next to him and, heart pounding furiously, Alex sat down, tucking her knees into the folds of black satin. He studied the etched crystal of his glass and took another swallow, not yet meeting her eyes.

"Ian," she said softly and scooted over so that her knees abutted his side. He tucked his arm around her like a mother duck would envelop a duckling.

"It's okay," he said equally softly. "Granted, that's never happened to me before...but it's okay."

"Ian," Alex tried again.

"I feel something profound for you, Alex. It has shocked me...changed me...and I thought you might..." he faltered, "but if you don't..."

"Ian!" Alex yelped, and he looked up at her, searching her face for answers, his mouth finally unmoving. She used the silence to take a breath and begin. "A very long time ago, someone who should have loved me caused me a lot of pain. It made me strong but unreachable, so I never let anyone in—figuratively and...literally." She gave a quick wry laugh at her own humor. He continued in silence, eyebrows furrowing as he followed along the path to her conclusion.

She inhaled a shaky breath, her voice barely audible over her pounding heart. "Ian, I'm a v—"

"Vampire?" he blurted. "I knew it. You are always cold. Your job gives you easy access to your food source..." His mouth twitched with humor, and Alex had never been so appreciative of his ability to alleviate her anxiety. She smiled without laughing and said the word that seemed so much less scary now that he had accused her of being a supernatural creature.

"A virgin," she said clearly and slowly while regarding his expression that softened into a look of tenderness.

"How?" he said, cringing at his own stupidity. "I mean—you are beautiful. Surely guys have wanted to..."

Alex shrugged. "They have. It was always me. You were right about me the first night I met you. I was always searching for the epic love story. It's the only thing that could have broken through the walls I live behind. I just never found anyone worth being vulnerable for."

He had taken her hand at some point and held it tightly over his chest, and she could feel the rapid pace of his heart that belied the cool, unmovable look in his eyes.

"Until now." Her voice was quiet but steady. He bent his head and put his lips to her hand as if in prayer, his eyes shining in stunned disbelief. When he spoke, his voice was raw, all traces of glib humor gone.

"Are you sure?"

"I've never been more sure, Ian." At the sound of his name on her lips, he kissed her palm and then grazed the inside of her wrist with the tip of his tongue. Desire spread through Alex's inner thighs like a raging wildfire, and she clenched them together to stop herself from shaking.

"I want to give you the most unforgettable night of your life," he said raggedly, continuing to pay homage to the soft skin of her inner wrist.

"I'm nervous," she said shyly, pulling her hand from his grasp and clutching the silk edge of her garment.

"Don't be. I'll do everything," he said gently. "When you imagined this happening, did you have specifics about the details?" He raised his eyebrows and peered at her scrunched-up face.

"I'm too embarrassed."

"Come on—I'll make it happen if I can, and you can return the favor someday."

*Someday.* The word hung in the air, and her heart took a giant leap off the cliff of reason. Alex focused on her knees.

"There was one. Imagine *Top Gun* circa 1986."

He nodded with earnest approval. "The arrogant flyboy and the smart, sexy professor. Say no more," he said as he jumped to his feet. "Meet me in the bedroom in five minutes."

It was a long five minutes, and Alex passed the time alternating between running her hands through her damp locks and taking small sips of bourbon straight from the bottle. When the time was almost up, she took a cleansing breath and pushed open the master bedroom door.

Ian was waiting for her, standing in a pool of flickering candlelight, the epitome of sex appeal in his worn jeans and shirtless under his black leather jacket. The shadows accentuated his features—his sculpted cheekbones and jaw, his etched abdominal muscles, and the jeans hanging so low on his hips that Alex could make out the carved V of his lower pelvis. Like a moth into the flame, she went, perfectly willing to be incinerated.

"Wait—I forgot one thing," he said excitedly and pressed a button on his phone. The sensual first bars of "Take My Breath Away" filled the air, and Alex threw back her head in laughter.

Ian was so close that she could feel the heat emanating from his body, much like the first night they met in Gaborone, only this time, she could touch him if she wanted to—and she wanted to do that and much more. He cupped her face and kissed her gently as if asking for permission, and Alex answered him by sliding her hands under the leather jacket to reach the skin of his lower back. He continued kissing her, using his lips to worship her face and neck and the soft spot above each collarbone. The music filling her ears combined with the smell of leather made her heady, and she boldly pushed the jacket from Ian's shoulders, planting a few delicate kisses in the middle of his chest. His chest heaved with desire, and she was certain that if she could see his eyes that they would be burning with flames of bright blue.

He stepped back from her then and reached out to grasp the sash binding her robe together. In one fluid pull, the black satin parted, revealing her naked body underneath. Seeming to sense her impending timidity, Ian turned her around so that her exposed front faced the other direction and set his lips to her shoulders as his hands pushed the silk into a shapeless puddle on the floor.

Alex had thought being naked in front of a man for the first time would be horrifying, but instead, she felt liberated and filled with power from the effect she was having on Ian. His breath coated her ear as he pressed his thorax into her back like a warm pillar and reached around to cup her breasts with his hands. With his thumbs, he drew circles on her nipples, and they responded by hardening under his practiced touch. Alex felt one hand leave her breast and travel south to her navel and then between her legs. He sucked on her earlobe, tugging it gently while his fingers explored her most sensitive region. Alex's knees weakened, and as they trembled, she found herself leaning harder into Ian for support, magnifying the pleasure his hand was creating down below.

In one motion, his arm scooted underneath her knees, and he cradled her in his arms, depositing her carefully on the bed. Propped on one elbow, her hair cascading over her shoulder, she watched him finish undressing. Undoing the buttons of his jeans, he let them fall unceremoniously to the floor and then shed his boxer briefs to reveal the object of her immediate desire. The big reveal. She had seen plenty of penises, just not ones intended for her, and she allowed a nervous laugh to escape.

He smirked and slid next to her, the soft coolness of the white cotton sheet settling over their bodies. She had never felt more feminine.

"You are exquisite," he said, pulling her so close that she could feel his skin from her chin down to her toes.

Alex felt an ache grow in her heart as actual tears pricked her eyes. This was perfect—more than she had ever hoped for. The pang in her heart disappeared and was replaced by a much deeper ache as Ian resumed trailing kisses down her naked body—first her neck then her cleavage, then a quick dart of his tongue onto her still raised nipple. He rolled on top of her, pinning her supine and buried his head into her abdomen, kissing first her navel, then dragging his tongue to each point of her pelvis before bringing his lips to the precious spot between her legs.

Alex should have been more self-conscious, but she was too consumed with the surges of pleasure rippling up through her back like tidal waves. She gripped the sheets, crumpling them into her fists and let out an inadvertent cry. Ian's face appeared near hers immediately, and he rubbed his nose on her cheek.

"Are you okay?"

"I don't know what I am, but if you stop, I'll never forgive you," she said breathily with eyes closed.

She could feel his smile as his body shifted over hers, and he covered her mouth with his own. She could taste herself on his lips, and it was thrilling. Deepening their kiss, he plunged his tongue into her mouth and simultaneously slid one, then two fingers inside. It felt unimaginably good, and the tingling sensation grew. She wanted more—wanted every inch of her being to be filled up with him. She could feel herself starting to convulse around his fingers as he gently explored, stretching her boundaries just a little at a time. Suddenly the tingling that had originated in her lower back spread upward to her ears and downward to her toes. She felt high, and Ian was her drug.

She opened her eyes, immediately swept up into the intensity of his gaze. "What do you want, Alexandra?"

"I want you…"

She barely got the words out before his face broke into a sultry grin, and he removed his fingers slowly, replacing them with something quite a bit larger. A moan escaped his lips as he paused very briefly before he pushed against her, and she felt a sharp, swift pain. She must have gasped because his face paused with concern. "I'm okay," she whispered as she moved one hand to the back of his head to draw him into her parted lips.

They began to move slowly together, the pain all but forgotten as her body burst into an electrical frenzy. He moved in and out of her, slowly, gently then with more fervor, unable to stop the tempo from escalating. Alex thought she heard someone shouting, but Ian's name was coming from her own lips. She arched her back, and the now violent convulsions spread from her pelvis up her spine as she felt him come inside her with a groan of exquisite pleasure. The last thing she remembered was her nose next to Ian's, closing her eyes with him still inside her.

# FIFTEEN

When she opened her eyes, the room was pitch black. Her back was nestled into Ian's stomach, and she could feel his light snores huffing across her hair. A protective arm curved between her breasts, and she leaned down to lightly kiss his fingertips before ducking out from under him. He stirred but didn't wake.

Alex searched around in the dark and her fingers connected with the rumpled black silk robe, her only current option for clothing. She quietly pulled back the drapes to reveal a gorgeous Paris skyline, complete with a glittering *Tour Eiffel* in the distance. Pressing her forehead to the cold glass of the window, she took in the spectacular scene and allowed yesterday's memories to flash in and out like scenes of a movie. It had been as romantic as a movie—as perfect a fantasy she could have imagined. It still seemed like a dream. A dream that had left her delightfully sore in her most private places with an ache that could only be treated with one type of therapy.

Ian remained still except for the regular excursion of his chest with each breath. Alex took a moment to memorize his perfect features in their relaxed state. Nagging bits of fear about what the future held threatened to manifest themselves in Alex's mind, but she pushed them down for now and decided to drown them out with distraction. Her body was drawn into Ian's warmth, and she started gently kissing the tender spot under his jaw. As she worked her way down his throat, her lips devolved into a dance of sensual foreplay, and she lightly nipped his deltoid with her teeth. His eyes flew open.

"I thought I was dreaming," he said as he pressed the length of his body into hers.

"You are," Alex said as she continued her trajectory of kisses down his flat, muscled pecs to his chiseled abs and then on to the final area of his most sensitive skin stretched taut between his pelvic bones. Alex paused for a singular moment, and she sensed Ian's breath catch. Her mind had emptied itself of all thought—only passionate tension remained. She licked her lips and reached out her tongue to gently guide him into her mouth.

"Alex!" he exclaimed, giving her the encouragement she needed to continue her exploration of his contours with her mouth. When she paused, Ian pulled her face to his, immediately ravaging her with his lips. She could feel him everywhere—his lips on her lips, his chest hairs tickling her nipples, his legs wrapped around her own, and his manhood begging for entry through the curtain of her throbbing core. His voice was in her ear.

"Tell me you want me."

"I want you."

The dueling enemies of pain and pleasure dominated her senses. The more she ached, the more Ian massaged the ache into ecstasy, until she felt as taut as a bowstring. Ian buried his face in her hair, his rhythmic movements creating a spreading warmth into her lower back. She heard her name, a sonnet on his lips, before he collapsed next to her.

"I've created a monster," Ian said playfully as he languished on his back between rumpled white sheets, bathed in the glow of morning sunlight and post-coital bliss. "A beautiful one," he continued as he tenderly looked down at Alex, lying naked on her stomach, and ran his knuckles across her cheek.

"You just opened the cage," she said coyly, and his eyes widened in mock horror.

"I know. I hope I don't regret it," he groaned.

"What in the world are you talking about?"

"You'll see…the beautiful, sex-hungry femme fatale will have to beat men away from her bed."

"The only man I want near my bed is you," she said, pushing up to her elbows to plant a sweet kiss on his mouth. "I never wanted this with anyone…only you," Alex said solemnly. "Besides, I am still a completely unreformed ice queen."

"It's a good thing I love snow-cones," he said with that flirty half-smile Alex was growing to love, and she couldn't help but laugh.

"Come on, Frosty. It's time to get you into the shower—this

time without your clothes."


Alex felt different. Her reflection even looked different as she wiped away the condensation from the bathroom mirror. The dark circles that trademarked her as a sleep-deprived doctor had lightened and her complexion was flushed a feminine shade of pink. She was dressed in dark jeans and a navy cashmere hoodie for the plane ride back to Philadelphia, her hair swept up into a messy bun.

Sex Goddess came to mind, followed shortly by Negative Nancy. Doubt and anxiety had finally pushed themselves to the forefront of her mind despite her best efforts at ignoring them. Alex needed reassurance but didn't know how to ask for it. She and Ian hadn't talked about a plan to see each other again. She didn't even know what he was doing after she left Paris.

"Almost ready?" he said, poking his head into the bathroom, looking every bit magazine-worthy in a tight pair of dark jeans, gray t-shirt, and the black leather jacket. "I took your bags downstairs. There's a car waiting for us."

"Thanks," she said softly and took his hand.


The hotel lobby was a repeat of their first night in Paris—a barrage of synchronized camera flashes as they were hustled into a waiting black SUV.

"How do you ever get used to this?" Alex asked as they sped away from the front of Le Meurice and the boisterous crowd.

"Bourbon," he said matter-of-factly and produced two tiny plastic cups and a mini-sized bourbon bottle.

"I've pushed you to day drinking. Fabulous," Alex said, watching him pour aliquots into each cup.

"This is a celebration drink," he replied. "Cheers." He tapped the two cups together.

"What are we celebrating? My deflowering?" asked Alex innocently, to which Ian choked lightly on his shot of bourbon.

Recovering quickly, he downed Alex's portion as well, his face curiously set in consternation as he began twirling the empty cups around in his hand.

"What's on your mind?" Alex asked with some concern.

His eyes darkened as he stared into the scenery flying by outside the window before he began.

"For the first time in a very, very long time...I feel happy...and it's you, Alex. It's who I am when I am with you...and I don't want to ruin it...or lose it."

"You won't. Hey—" Alex whispered, placing her palm on his face and turning his head toward her. "You won't," she said more firmly, her heart welcoming the extra weight of connecting her life with someone else's. She knew this was different. She felt terrified and reckless, but Ian wasn't the only one clinging to a life-altering happiness. Alex was too.

Charles de Gaulle was a madhouse of honking taxis and scurrying passengers. Fortunately, as a member of the topmost echelon, Ian could gain entry to the private lounge where celebrities and notoriety waited for their flights away from the frenetic atmosphere of the regular airport. Alex checked her flight information and her phone clock one last time before packing her items carefully in her light blue leather carry-on for the long flight back to Philadelphia. Her chai tea latte sat in front of her untouched as her stomach roiled with the anticipation of saying goodbye to Ian. She felt erratic, and the ectopy generated by her heart agreed. She mentally scolded herself. Everything was going to be fine—she had told Ian as much.

In truth, her life had already careened out of her careful control with the potential for a major crash and burn. The girl that Ian had met in a bar in Gaborone seemed like a lifetime ago. She wasn't just a workaholic humanitarian physician with a dog and a predilection for running. Her time in Paris with Ian had opened up a part of her that she only suspected existed. Alex didn't want to let it go...as much as she didn't want to let Ian go. The two were intertwined— the woman she was morphing into and the man who had opened her chrysalis.

She felt warm, strong fingers on her shoulders. "The car is here to take you to the plane," he said, leaning down to kiss her cheek and pick up her carry-on. The black sedan with engine running sent wisps of exhaust into the bitterly cold French evening, and Ian opened the rear door to place her bag inside.

"Let's see if you have everything," he said, rifling through her contents. "Water bottle, passport, steamy romance novel." He held up *The Coming Plague* as she laughed. "And a little something so you won't forget all about me by the time you land." He slipped a small blue box deep into her bag.

"Ian, you don't need to give me anything," she chided but inside felt a secret thrill.

"You mean...anything else," he said, winking at her, and she blushed. "But don't open it until you get home. Think of it as gift foreplay." She laughed freely, girlishly, and reached up to wind her arms around his neck and bury her nose in the pungent scent of leather and bourbon.

"Now kiss me," he said in a deep, low voice that weakened her core.

They kissed deeply, passionately, saying goodbye with lips instead of words. When they separated and caught their breath, Ian brought Alex's fingertips to his lips, brushing them lightly and directing her into the waiting car. With one final squeeze of her hand and a depth of emotion in his eyes she had never witnessed before, he closed the car door.


The flight home was eerily peaceful as the plane was plunged into darkness and traveled into an eternal night as the earth turned opposite its course. Ian had upgraded her to first class and she hadn't put up a fuss. She was grateful for the extra comfort as a physical and emotional fatigue settled over her. She plugged in her earbuds and tried not to think about how every second put an increasing distance between her and Ian. He had told her that he would be in Paris for a few days at the Devall offices before heading to Namibia to meet with the development team of a new mining cooperative. His lifestyle certainly was anything but boring between the travel and high-profile events and learning to run one of the world's wealthiest companies. She knew very little about his actual life, and he knew very little about hers.

Although brief, the time they had spent together had been profoundly real—full of passion and adventure. Giant voids still existed in her knowledge of Ian's life, but she had traversed his outer layer and discovered the riches within. He was arrogant and entitled but capable of incredible kindness, authenticity, and generosity. Could their fantasy romance handle a downshift to reality?

Alex settled into the sultry voice of Howie Day for reassurance.

Soon she succumbed to a light slumber that provided a much-needed respite from her own doubt.

Standing on the covered sidewalk, bags in tow and covered in a light spatter of rain, Alex felt overstimulated by the bustle and noise of the City of Brotherly Love. From the window of her cab, she watched sheets of rain mix with the dusk settling over the buildings in center city. Everything here was a shade of gray—gray skies giving rise to a gray skyline rising up from gray sidewalks. Even the air looked gray most of the time. Alex would be thankful when she could trade her current home for a perhaps more colorful, more permanent one when she graduated from fellowship next year. For the first time ever, the future seemed unpredictable.

The inside of her tiny one-room apartment held a familiarity that she didn't realize how desperately she needed. It was filled with a cozy collection of furnishings—a warm brown couch that she could stretch out on for a nap, a yellow upholstered chair for reading, her desk piled high with mail and medical journals, and her lovely four-poster bed with the floral Anthropologie bedding, a splurge after her first year of fellowship.

Tossing her bags in an unused corner, she hopped onto the bed, reclining into a mountain of various sized pillows and let the kinks of airplane travel start to work themselves free. Alex's bed was a precious sanctuary in which she spent precious little time. Curling up under her blue Mongolian cashmere blanket, she assumed her usual position of sleeping on the bed rather than in it.

Although that might change with Ian in the picture. A devious vision of him naked, swathed only by a white cotton sheet filled her mind. She wondered if he was right about her newly discovered self as a woman who had had sex. Not just any sex either—spectacular sex. Would it be evident to men like some barely perceptible pheromone? She laughed at her own precociousness. Not likely, and if so, too bad for those that would come calling. She was taken—body and soul.

Even now, when he was thousands of miles away, her body responded to the mere thought of him, aching for his touch, her pulse beating a sensual rhythm in her most private parts. She felt needy and uncomfortable and emotionally strung out, and she had absolutely no idea what to do about it. Luckily, she knew someone that would. It was three in the morning Gaborone time and Alex dialed Rox's number, taking a chance that she might be awake waiting on a delivery. She answered on the third ring.

"Alex! For some reason, I knew you were going to call. I've been up for hours—just finished delivering a set of twins. Cute little things. Mom is going to have her hands full." She was breathing heavily into the phone like she had personally given birth to these babies.

"What in the world are you doing?" Alex asked.

"Yoga," Rox grunted into the phone receiver.

"Yoga? From the woman whose idea of exercise is shopping in heels?" Alex teased.

"I need," she paused for breath, "to improve my flexibility."

"I can only imagine this has something to do with your world-class athlete boyfriend."

"Life's too short not to try everything once," Rox replied wickedly. "Enough about me. How was Paris, my dear?"

Alex described her two days with Ian in bits and pieces, faltering from time to time. She started with the safe material like the beautiful hotel, the exquisite dinner the first night, and the Sacré-Cœur. Eventually the empty pauses between her words grew longer, filled with omitted details that Rox immediately noticed.

"Sounds fun," Rox said, biding her time. "Did you make it to the Eiffel tower?"

"No."

"The Louvre?"

"No."

"Shopping on the Champ-Élysées?"

"No..."

"So, you flew to Paris and didn't see any of Paris?" Rox chided. "How was it?" she said in a low, conspiring tone, and Alex could hear her colossal smile through the phone.

"Perfect," Alex said dreamily, letting a whoosh of breath leave her chest.

"I knew it!" said Rox triumphantly. "Best you've ever had?"

"The only...I've ever had," Alex murmured into the silence.

"Seriously? Wow, Alex. I always suspected, but I never wanted to pry. Are you okay? It can be...pretty emotional."

"I don't know, Rox. Part of me feels completely terrified and naked. I literally feel like I am walking around buck naked and everyone can tell that I just had sex for the first time or…times," Alex said, blushing a deep shade of pink. "But the rest of me feels empowered. Different but good different."

"Uh-huh," encouraged Rox. "Go on, my dear."

"And I miss him. My heart actually aches…but that's not the only part of me hurting. I physically miss him—like my body needs something, and I feel restless and irritated."

"Sweetie, your libido just went into overdrive. The Ferrari is all revved up with no one in the driver's seat."

"Since when do you know anything about cars?" Alex asked.

"Since never, but I do know a thing or two about being sexually frustrated."

They talked for the better part of an hour, and Rox filled Alex in on all the latest gossip at PM as well as her steamy trysts with Nic, who had, incidentally, decided to extend his stay until he was due back for training at the end of June. Alex was reluctant to hang up the phone and separate from this connection to a life that she already missed, but Rox was called to another delivery.

"Give McCartney some love for me," said Alex.

"I will. I miss you. Kisses and hugs," she replied, and the phone disconnected.

The phone call to Rox had merely provided a temporary distraction for the stabbing twinge of an Ian-less evening. She wondered if he felt the same, if his reality was just as lackluster as hers at this moment. Reaching into her blue leather carry-on, she fished around for her emergency bottle of ibuprofen. Dehydration and jet lag had caught up with her, and a dull ache had started behind her left eye.

Instead of a medication bottle, her hands closed around a small box—the one Ian had slipped into her bag at the airport. Forgetting everything else for the moment, she sat cross-legged on the bed, staring at the robin's egg blue box in her lap. Nervously, she slipped off the white ribbon and opened the lid. Alex pulled out a delicate gold chain from which hung an intricately designed lion charm. It was breathtaking.

A folded sheet of paper rested at the bottom of the box. She opened it to reveal Ian's neat cursive.

*Alexandra,*
*Something to remember where it all started.*
*Ian*

# SIXTEEN

Her lion necklace was tucked securely beneath her scrub top as Alex strode through the welcoming glass doors of the Children's Hospital of Philadelphia, only marginally jet-lagged and ready to re-immerse herself in the perpetual maelstrom that was ICU medicine. Ian had called yesterday before he boarded his flight to Namibia, and her heart grew wings thinking about it. With every conversation, she felt closer to him and wondered why she had ever worried about the kink that physical distance would put in their burgeoning relationship. He charmed her, even from a completely different continent.

Breezing through the double doors labeled Pediatric Intensive Care Unit, Alex was inundated by the sounds of chirping monitors in a symphony of pitches, a din of voices immersed in morning sign-out, and a few squalling babies, unhappy with their sleeping accommodations. *Home away from sweet home.* She rolled a chair over to the nearest computer to start combing through morning labs. Each patient came with about a thousand pieces of generated data that wove a unique tapestry of illness—vital signs and physical exam findings, lab values and urine output, ventilator settings and blood gases. Her entire profession revolved around assimilating these various pieces of data, discarding the ones that were outliers, and deciphering the message encoded by the others. What was the diagnosis? How was the patient responding to the treatment? What needed to change that day to improve the patient's condition?

In many ways, she preferred the simplicity of working in Botswana. Less available data meant more reliance on her intuition and experience to reach conclusions. As an ICU doctor in training, she stuffed her mind full of trends and values, prepared to report them to the attending physician during rounds and provide her interpretation of what they meant for the patient. In her time training to become an ICU specialist, she had learned that the numbers did not necessarily reflect the severity of a kid's illness or predict her prognosis. One of her favorite mentors had shared an adage with her: "Kids make their own rules, and we simply follow along." She tried her best to practice medicine that way. Her phone vibrated her out of waxing philosophic.

*Rounds are starting in 5. Bed 28*

It was the type of terse message she had come to expect from Dr. Gibson. Mona Gibson was a brilliant, renowned senior-level critical care attending who had made it her life's mission to torture Alex at every opportunity.

"Fabulous," Alex muttered as she gathered her stack of papers and shoved them into the pocket of her white coat.

Her first morning back flew by as she threw herself into a flurry of activities that included presenting her patient plans to Dr. Gibson, being reamed by Dr. Gibson for her lack of attention to esoteric details and accepting the many "welcome back" hugs that irritated Dr. Gibson to no end.

By the time rounds concluded in the early afternoon, Alex's head pounded with an impending migraine. She sought a temporary refuge in the office she shared with the two other critical care trainees. Slumping down into her office chair, she pushed aside the milieu of papers and Post-it notes in her cubicle to rest her head on the desktop. Still on Africa time, she wearily closed her eyelids for a few minutes of battery recharging. Out of nowhere, someone plunked an ice-cold bottle of Diet Coke in front of her face, and she startled into complete wakefulness.

"Do they take naps after rounds in Africa?" said a familiar voice in a teasing tone.

"Hi Tim," Alex said, smiling up at her extremely tall, blonde-haired friend and co-fellow. Tim erupted into a megawatt smile that lit up his American golden boy features and crushed Alex into a hug.

"It's good to have you back," he said. "Beth was tainting the office with her crap taste in music."

He motioned his head to the third desk in the room, which held various sized bins for organizing papers and a sleek laptop on top of a pink silicone desktop protector. It was quite different from Alex's harried pile of to-do lists and controlled chaos. Beth Hanson took her position as chief ICU fellow very seriously. She literally had a placard in her cubicle in decisive cursive that read "Queen B". Their mutual disdain for Beth's antics had cemented Alex and Tim's friendship during their first year of training, and Alex had missed the unassuming camaraderie they shared.

"What's her Royal Highness been up to?" said Alex, legitimately curious.

"Biting off nurses' heads…sucking up to Gibson…the usual," Tim replied, swiping an apple out of a woven basket and taking a huge bite.

"It's good to know that some things don't change," Alex said, standing up to stretch before checking her phone for messages.

"And some things do," said Tim thoughtfully.

Alex could feel his eyes on her from across the room. Before she could mount a response, she discovered two missed messages from Dr. Gibson on her phone.

"Crap. I have to go. Let's catch up later, okay?" she called, already dashing down the hallway.


"Can we get a portable chest X-ray?" Alex said, stethoscope in her ears, bent over a distressed ten-year-old girl clutching a stuffed rabbit. Very little air moved inside her chest, likely from an asthma attack considering her history. While she listened, Alex had rapidly mapped out a treatment plan. After starting the young girl on continuous breathing treatments and ordering a few additional IV medications, Alex listened to the girl's heaving chest once again and heard the telltale noises of wheezing.

"She is better with the treatments but not out of the woods," she said, turning to the girl's mom. "You need to stay with us tonight so we can make you all better," she said, giving the solemn girl with thick braids a quick squeeze. "I'll be back to check on you later." She glanced at her phone to check a message and then rushed to the next child requiring attention—a tiny baby who had developed pneumonia and needed a breathing tube.

Well after sunset, after adjusting ventilator knobs, titrating IV drips, and checking on her patient with the asthma attack, Alex finally made it back to her apartment where she finished logging patient notes and passed out for a few hours to do it all again.

Each day continued much the same for a while. Leave in the dark, shove a million pieces of data into her brain, work tirelessly to make kids better, get home in the dark, and repeat. She had little time in her first few weeks back at work to pine over Ian. Life had mostly picked up where she left off, except that her endless days and nights were now punctuated with Ian's sexually charged inquiries. She fiercely enjoyed the stolen moments sharing flirtatious banter with Ian and often found herself smiling uncontrollably.

*Good morning sunshine*

Alex glanced down at her phone. It was just after midnight which meant, in London, Ian was either awake really early or just now going to bed. She sent a quick reply, pleased with her wit at this hour.

*Hard day's night?*

A minute later, her phone burst into song, and she quickly fished it out of her white coat pocket.

"On the contrary, I'm just starting the day with a morning run. Someone has recently inspired me," said a smooth voice that reached out like a hand and clutched Alex's heart.

"Maybe you'll be able to keep up with me someday," she said, fingering her lion pendant fondly.

"Please," he scoffed, "I am the king of endurance."

"So I've heard," she said wryly.

"Ouch. How about the next time I see you, I never let you leave that shoebox you call home."

"Well, you're in luck because we can actually watch the fireworks from my bed."

Ian had rearranged his schedule to stopover in Philadelphia on his way to New York and planned to spend July 4th weekend with Alex enjoying the massive festivities in the city where independence was born.

"They will be nothing compared to the ones in your bed," Ian replied.

"I can't wait," she murmured. "I have to go, but I'll see you in two days." She smiled to herself all the way to the elevator.

Alex still wore a stupid grin on her face later that morning when signing out her patients to a sullen Beth.

"Last patient Alex. Hurry up so I can get coffee before Gibson gets here."

"Sure thing. She is a six-month-old previously healthy baby girl who has had three days of cough and one day of increased work of breathing and throwing up everything she eats."

"Get to the point. Pneumonia, antibiotics, blah blah," said Beth as she made a few notes on her clipboard.

"I don't think so," said Alex. "She has a dry cough and a really high heart rate. Her pulse feels…fluttery."

"Fluttery?" said Beth with narrowed lids, her tone dripping in disdain.

Alex reached back in her memory, her mind traveling to several months before and a boy with a fast heart rate, an enlarged liver, and a pulse that felt like butterfly wings.

"I think you should get an echocardiogram," said Alex. "It could be heart failure."

"Africa didn't make you any smarter, Alex," Beth said tartly and huffed off to get her beverage.

The girl's mom, barely above drinking age and dressed in a Coldplay t-shirt, came to the sliding glass door of the hospital room. "Is my baby going to be okay?"

"I don't know yet," said Alex. "We are still trying to figure out why she is sick, but I promise that we will take excellent care of her."

The young mother looked up at Alex quizzically. "You look really familiar. Have you been Adeline's doctor before?"

"No…I don't think so," said Alex. "I'll be back tonight, though, and I bet she'll be much better by then."


After a fitful sleep under the comfort of her cashmere blanket, Alex returned to the hospital for her last night shift before Ian arrived, feeling like she had barely left. She yawned and closed her eyes, using the minute between the ground and the seventh floor to rest. Her phone buzzed as she rose in the elevator.

*I miss you*

Alex grinned, typing as she walked quickly down the corridor to the ICU.

*Not for long*

This was just the stimulus she needed to get her through the night.

As she walked up to the long orange desk that divided the unit into two sections, she noticed a group of young nurses gathered there, whispering as they looked down at something. They simultaneously glanced up at Alex when she approached. Some of them had secretive smiles while others tittered nervously in the background. One of the senior nurses appraised Alex and held up a copy of *Us Weekly*, her long bony finger tapping a small picture in the lower right corner of the cover. "Is this you, Dr. Wilde?"

"What?" said Alex in disbelief, taking the glossy magazine out of her hand and staring at the front.

Although the photo was slightly grainy, she could make out a pair of ducked heads stepping off the sidewalk of a grand hotel, the soft waves of an azure blue dress fluttering in an imaginary breeze. It was her...but it wasn't. That girl looked stunning—her face upturned toward her companion and lit up like the Eiffel Tower itself. In the photo, Ian's eyes focused on their clasped hands as he smiled broadly, looking every bit the confident billionaire heir. "Trouble in Paris-dise?" read the caption. Alex frowned and rifled through the magazine until her eyes landed on the article.

*"Ian Devall, renowned bachelor and international heartbreaker, heir to the Devall mining fortune and newly named chairman of the company's philanthropic organization, was seen stepping out in Paris with a new lady friend last month. They reportedly dined on lobster at Laperouse before they were seen cuddling up to each other at La Lune later that evening for an aperitif. Ian is rumored to have been secretly engaged to well-known American actress Rebekah Matheson, whom he has been seeing on and off for the past three years. Matheson's representatives report that she is devastated and spending time refocusing her energies on her career from her base home in L.A. The Devall foundation publicist failed to comment."*

Alex scanned the page for additional information. A few additional photographs bordered the bottom page—Ian and a blonde bombshell of a woman at the red-carpet premiere of some movie, Ian and the same woman exiting a swanky restaurant, and an additional picture of Ian with Alex in tow, walking down the steps of the Sacré-Cœur.

Alex's fingers were glued to the paper. She kept staring at the images hoping for them to morph into someone else. The nurses stared at her expectantly, and in her distress she couldn't formulate a believable denial, so she nodded twice, hoping that would be enough to placate them. Romantic sighs erupted along with a few squeals, and then she was peppered with questions. "Where did you meet?" "What is he like?" "Are you together?"

Before Alex could respond, a manicured hand reached over and plucked the magazine out of Alex's hands. Beth's face remained carefully composed while she perused the article and, with a cocked brow, let the magazine flutter to the floor. "I have a research meeting I need to get to," she said indignantly and beckoned Alex to follow her into the unit for sign-out.

Halfway through examining patients for night rounds, Alex's rationale finally outweighed her emotional response. In truth, she had experienced a massive shock wave rip through her body at the sight of the photos, and she couldn't begin to separate the various surging emotions. Jealousy? Anger? Disappointment? All three wrapped up into one big ugly monstrosity? Mostly she felt betrayed. Ian had not necessarily lied, but he had not considered her important enough for the truth either. A part of her, albeit small, believed that the entire drama must be a lie, but the photos revealed that some element of truth existed. She pulled out her phone to text Ian.

*Can we talk for a minute?*

Three patients and two more text messages later, he still hadn't answered, and her annoyance grew exponentially. She managed to push it down under the surface as she quietly stepped through a curtained alcove into Adeline's room, the baby with breathing difficulty from the night before.

"Hi, sweet girl. Feeling better?" she said to the supine baby who reached up for Alex's badge. Her breathing had become much easier, but when Alex felt her pulse, it was weak and erratic at times—like it was desperately trying to tell her something. She placed a hand on the child's abdomen and palpated gently until she felt the firm edge of an enlarged liver. *Damn.* Her frustration with

Beth flared. This baby needed her heart evaluated...now. The child's mother, exhausted from the day's events, snored lightly from the upholstered pullout couch, and Alex didn't have the heart to wake her just yet. As she was washing her hands in the sink, she noticed a stack of magazines scattered on the bedside table, the picture of her and Ian jumping to the forefront of her vision.

Impulsively, she grabbed the magazine and angrily stuffed it in the pocket of her white coat.

The night was steady with three admissions from the emergency room and one from the inpatient floor, which turned out to be a sweet boy with leukemia who needed a blood transfusion for severe anemia. Sometime around midnight, she had tried calling Ian and reached his voicemail. It was now almost noon in London, and he was probably already at the airport. She plopped down onto one of the plush chairs in the glass-enclosed corridor that separated the two halves of the ICU. Watching the sun peek out from behind the Center City skyline, she gave herself a moment to stew. She would see him in less than twelve hours and still had no idea how to handle this. Distractedly, she put her lion charm to her lips, hoping to establish some metaphysical connection to Ian through the cold metal.

"Penny for your thoughts?" said a warm, friendly voice over her head. Alex looked up to see Tim peering down at her, a quirky smile on his face and nothing but kindness in his eyes.

"It's going to take more than a penny," grumbled Alex.

"How about a penny and a tequila shot?"

"Now, you're talking." Alex flashed him a smile.

"Seriously, what's up?"

Alex screwed up her face and opened her mouth, delivering a stream of unfiltered speech that typically happens with sleep deprivation. "I met a guy, and it turns out that maybe he isn't who I thought he was...and now I feel really dumb." Her heart squeezed tightly as she said the words aloud, a fresh heat filling her face.

"Oh," said Tim and, in an uncharacteristic move, placed his hand on Alex's knee. "The only dumb one here is him." Alex smiled nervously, fretting a little at Tim's casual touch, and rubbed the heel of her hand across her damp lashes.

"I'm a hot mess when I'm post-call," she said dismissively and shifted slightly so that his hand dropped down to his side. The semi-awkward silence lasted for a quick second before Alex's phone rang violently. "It's Dr. Wilde."

"We need you now in bed twenty-seven," said a frantic voice.

"On my way," she said, sprinting down the hallway without waiting to see if Tim was following her.

"What's her blood pressure?" Alex calmly sent the question into the flurry of activity around Adeline's bed.

"We can't get the cuff to read, but we still feel a pulse."

Alex, with Tim now over her shoulder, pulled up Adeline's echocardiogram at their workstation. They simultaneously groaned as the grayscale video clips flashed up on the screen.

"Her heart is barely functioning," said Tim in a low voice.

"I should have followed up on this earlier," Alex whispered mostly to herself, annoyed that she had been so distracted by her Ian drama. Alex reached out and picked up Adeline's pale chubby wrist, feeling only the slightest affirmative tap against her fingers. "Let's call the ECMO team," she said aloud to the room of waiting nurses.

Activating the ECMO team opened up a floodgate of activity as carts were wheeled into the hallway, a slew of medications was drawn up into labeled syringes, and every available monitoring device was attached to the baby. Alex had sent her tearful mother to the waiting room, promising an update when they were finished.

"We are going to use a special machine to support her heart and lungs for now, which gives her body time to heal without causing harm to her other organs," Alex had told her.

ECMO could be a lifesaver in circumstances where no other options existed…except for death. As the team set up the ECMO machine outside the room, Alex delivered orders to the nurses and tried to stabilize Adeline until they could place the large cannula in her neck—one in her jugular vein to drain blood from her heart and another in her carotid artery to pump it back in.

"Tim," she called, searching the crowded room, "I'll put her to sleep. Can you put in her breathing tube?"

He nodded and gave her a confident thumbs-up. Alex was grateful he was here as the activity frenzy heightened into a subsequent blur. Tim easily placed the breathing tube, but Adeline's heart didn't tolerate the medication needed to put her to sleep. Alex had to give her multiple doses of epinephrine and shock her heart a few times while the surgery team put in the ECMO cannulas. The sight of the bright red blood bridge between baby and machine was a beautiful one. The massive contraption on wheels, basically a heart-lung bypass machine, could pump well-oxygenated life-giving blood to Adeline's entire body while they waited for her heart to recover.

Alex stepped outside the room to remove her sterile gown where Tim waited with a Styrofoam cup of ice water. She downed it greedily, spilling half of it down the front of her scrubs, her hands shaking from adrenaline and probably hypoglycemia.

"You did a great job in there," said Tim.

"We did a great job," Alex said, her hand poised for a high five. "Seriously though, thank you, I couldn't have done it without you."

"Dicey resuscitation…high chance of disaster…low chance of success…potential for all the glory…count me in," Tim said, grinning widely.

Alex giggled, a punch-drunk kind of laugh that persisted, and pulled her phone out of her back pocket. Several texts from Ian and a missed call filled her screen. *It served him right.* She glanced over at Tim who was fishing around in his pocket.

A minute later, he triumphantly held up a shiny penny. "Now, let's go get your tequila shot."

# SEVENTEEN

Two identical shot glasses clinked in midair, and Alex tipped her head back, letting the liquid burn a trail down her esophagus. Her freshly washed and blown out waves tumbled down her bare back. Summer in Philadelphia was sweltering, and she had chosen a simple white halter dress with a low back and above the knee skirt that showed just enough leg to be exciting.

"This stuff is smoother than silk," she said, wiping the excess from her lips and taking a squeeze of lime between her teeth.

"Only the best." Tim downed his own shot in one fell swoop.

Alex glanced at Beth, perched on the barstool next to them, sipping something rose-colored from a martini glass. She and Tim had invited her as an act of goodwill, hoping a night drinking would soften her spiky personality.

"When do we get to meet the mystery guy?" asked Tim, holding up two fingers to the bartender.

"Soon." Alex felt a sudden rush of panic that not even the alcohol could attenuate. She rechecked her phone. Ian had made it through the airport and was headed into the city.

*Where should I meet you?*

Alex had forgone meeting him at the airport, instead suggesting that he drop his luggage with her doorman and then meet up with her. She was stalling, and she knew it, clinging to a desperate hope that the anxiolysis from the tequila would facilitate their reunion. She hadn't mentioned the magazine article to him yet.

*Bob and Barbara's on South Street*

146

Beth tossed her ebony locks. "Yes, Alex, do tell about your debut in *Us weekly*."

Alex scowled into her beer, gripping the chilled glass and letting it permeate the heat of embarrassment generated by Beth's comment. Bob and Barbara's, a dive bar in South Philly, served the absolute best Pabst Blue Ribbon on tap—so cold that it could quench a dragon's thirst.

"Beth, I have no idea what you're gassing about and what's more—nobody cares," retorted Tim, who was busy massaging his own frosty beverage. Alex flashed a look of gratitude his way, which was returned by a definitive "I've got your back" wink. Beth shrugged and rolled her eyes, crossing her legs and becoming increasingly interested in the napkin under her martini glass.

Alex sipped her beer in silence, mentally counting down the moments until Ian arrived, and she had to address his deception. She had emotionally prepared for all scenarios—the most likely being that he really was a girl-hopping gigolo, and she could thoroughly freeze him out of her life. The least likely was that the entire thing was a lie, and she could continue riding the momentum of this wild journey. Then there was door number three—the story was part lie/part truth, and she was left with a tough decision. How could she continue to trust him, be vulnerable with him, and resolve her hurt at the same time?

She was prepared for everything—except for the rush of rapturous desire she would feel when his silhouette moved slowly toward her through the crowd. Graceful and confident, he wore a marled gray t-shirt and dark jeans, a black fedora shading the light stubble he had let accumulate on his jawline. His searching eyes found hers and alighted with a familiar burn. Before she was ready, he stood right in front of her. Every single cell in her body burned with longing but the cumulative stress of the day's events weighted down her joints. Filled with a tormenting river of hurt, she felt paralyzed when he wrapped his arms around her.

"Hi," Ian said, peering quizzically into her face, clearly not expecting this type of reunion.

"Hi," Alex said, shaking off her conflicting emotions. "These are my friends Tim and Beth."

Despite his wary countenance, Tim held out a hand to Ian. "Nice to meet you, Ian."

Beth's eyes, glossy from her drink, were glued to Ian in phenomenal disbelief. Utterly flummoxed as Ian gave her a wave, she responded as most women did to his overt charm.

"We're drinking tequila," Alex announced to Ian and made room for him between her and Beth at the bar.

An hour later, Alex was drunk, not yet sloppy but definitely enjoying the gift of disinhibition and the lightening of her dread. She wasn't entirely ignoring Ian, but she hadn't warmed to him yet either. He had proceeded with caution, knowing something was bothering her. The more tequila she imbibed, the more she had focused her energy on laughing loudly with Tim about inside jokes from the hospital.

Ian had matched her shot for shot but, as a much more durable drinker, he continued long after Alex had quit. She glanced over at his beautiful form. He had stopped trying to engage her with barely audible whispers and secret touches, as if he could sense that she had become impermeable. Instead, he had focused on getting as drunk as possible, and, at the moment, was trying to teach Beth how to take a proper tequila shot, much to her exquisite delight.

"You have to lick the back of your hand before you shake out the salt...like this," he said and demonstrated with his own tongue, to which Beth erupted in a fit of girlish laughter.

"Salt...shot...suck," he said, putting a lime wedge between his teeth. Somehow that seemed like the most erotic thing Alex had ever seen, and for a second, she imagined leaning over and taking out the wedge with her own teeth.

Her temper flared as a tiny squirt from Beth's lime landed on her nose. She felt ridiculous and volatile—ridiculous for every second she had ever spent with Ian or pining over Ian or getting distracted because of Ian. Abruptly, she hopped down from the barstool and practically stomped to the back of the bar to a dark alcove decorated in tattered advertisements, stepping into one of the concrete-floored bathrooms. The door had nearly closed when a hand appeared in the doorjamb and pushed it open. Without an invitation, Ian forced his way into the small room and locked the door behind them.

"Alex, what are you doing?" he challenged.

"Trying to go to the bathroom," she said, arms folded across her chest.

"That's not what I was referring to," he said, one eyebrow cocked. "You've barely said a word to me, refused to touch me, and

148

tried to make me jealous by flirting with your friend Tim—who you should really stop leading on by the way."

Temper flaring, Alex opened her mouth to protest, but nothing came out, and she ended up just glaring at Ian.

"What is wrong with you?" asked Ian in a measured tone.

"Nothing is wrong with me," she said, her voice as cold as permafrost.

Ian hung his head in defeat and moved closer to her, right inside the sphere of her personal space, so close that she got a whiff of tequila when he exhaled. Although she knew he would never hurt her, she felt threatened anyway, her knees shaking under her dress. He reached a hand out toward her face. She automatically winced but then settled into the warm fingers caressing her cheek, calming her flighty nerves.

"What's wrong, baby?" he asked.

His words were so unexpectedly tender, that the dam holding back her emotions burst loose and a few unbidden tears came, slipping over each other in a race to make it to her chin. Ian pulled her close, and she buried her face into his chest, partly relieved and partly embarrassed at her display of emotion. A hand stroked her hair, and he shushed into her ear, much like someone would calm a frightened horse. Summoning all her available willpower, she pushed back on his chest with her palms and reached into her purse for the rolled-up magazine lying at the bottom.

Alex watched Ian's face transform from confusion to anger to annoyance in the span of a few minutes while he flipped through the copy of *Us weekly*, rolling his eyes periodically.

"This stuff is garbage," he said, dramatically launching the crumpled magazine through the air where it landed neatly in the trash can.

"Sometimes so is reality," she said, calmer now. "I just want to know the truth."

"Here is the truth," he started, grabbing both her hands and intertwining them in his. "Rebekah and I dated off and on for a few years, but I haven't even seen her in over a year. Publicists use this crap all the time to push their clients back into the spotlight and elevate their career. I know Rebekah, and she wouldn't think twice about lying to get something she wants. As for being engaged, I've never tied myself down to a single woman my entire life…but I do plan on changing that."

Alex glanced up at him sharply and noticed his eyes shone with sincerity. Every piece of her wanted to believe him, and she didn't push him away when he bent his head to find her lips. The kiss was soft and gentle, like a balm to her wounds—a tequila-infused balm with a trace of salt and lime.

"Okay," she said, coming up for air after a few delightful minutes of being reminded what an incredible kisser he was. "Okay," she repeated, taking a deep breath. "I believe you, but Ian, I can't handle this type of drama. I'm not wired for it."

"Unfortunately, I tend to come with just a little bit of drama," he said, squinting his eyes and trying to pull her back into his embrace.

"I'm serious! I have to focus at work—on the kids—not my personal life. One of my patients even had a copy of that magazine," she said severely as she tried to resist melting from the kisses trailing down her neck. "And you can't fix everything with…sex."

"I can try," he said, his breath infusing her with a desire that reached her very toes.

Suddenly the wall behind them shook with the deep bass tones of a popular tune, and Alex ducked out from where Ian had pinned her against the wall. "Come on. We're missing the best part of the night."

Exiting the bathroom, Alex noted the free space in the bar had dramatically diminished and filled up with a cadre of outlandish crossdressers. Some wore gowns and feather boas with perfectly made-up faces, and some were ready for the runway in the trendiest of outfits.

"Did I mention Bob and Barbara's has the most fabulous drag show in the city?" Alex said excitedly.

The dance floor was packed with writhing bodies, and Alex spotted a very drunk Tim holding his beer aloft as he swayed to the beat from the safety of the bar. His eyes immediately sought Alex's, and she gave him a confident thumbs up. He nodded, but she couldn't read anything else from his expression. As her arm was pulled toward the middle of the throng by an eager Ian, she smiled and motioned for Tim to join them on the dance floor.

Ian could move, which wasn't surprising considering his innate sex appeal, and soon they had a cluster of admirers belonging to both genders. Plenty tipsy enough to keep up with him, Alex tilted her head back and let the music and Ian's hands guide her. She discovered that dancing actually wasn't that much different than having sex, just clothed and upright, and soon they found a smooth rhythm between their gyrating pelvises. It was hot, literally and metaphorically. Alex was melting from Ian's rhythmic foreplay, and she had a sheen of sweat on her cleavage to prove it.

"I'm going to grab us some water," she said in Ian's ear when the song ended. He gave her a quick nod, looking practically edible with his gray t-shirt that outlined his chiseled midsection and dark pieces of hair plastered to his forehead.

As Alex waited to order a few bottles of water at the bar, Beth sidled up to her, composed even after a few drinks.

"Sure, you know what you are doing out there?"

Alex couldn't tell if she was being smug or concerned, most likely the former.

"I don't know what you're talking about," responded Alex. "But even if I did, it would be none of your concern."

Beth shrugged and fanned out her fingers to admire her manicure. "I'm just trying to say that some men prefer sports cars...and you seem more like a Honda."

Alex bristled internally but kept staring ahead. Beth's attempt to rile her up was unfortunately working, mostly because she knew her statement, although unkind, held truth. She frowned, unsure if she was more disturbed that Ian was a sports car kind of guy or that she was definitely not a sports car.

"I'm not judging, Alex. Enjoy it for what it is."

"And what do you think it is?" challenged Alex.

"Just look at him, Alex. He is quite literally God's gift to women...and men for that matter."

Ian was immersed in a throng of admirers all vying for his attention, his radiant smile bouncing among them, coating them with his charisma.

"You are his distraction—his foray into the world of the normal and mundane. Like the prince who disguises himself as a pauper and gallivants around his kingdom. But one day, he'll be expected to return to the castle." Alex swallowed and realized that despite the overly warm room, she felt a shivery cold creeping into her skin. "We all know that you don't belong in a castle."

Alex snatched up her water bottles and fled toward the dance floor before Beth could dish up any more abuse. She was snarky and petty but also brutally honest, and Alex let the weight of her words settle into the pit of her stomach as she went to find Ian.

Instead of Ian, she found a thoroughly inebriated Tim chatting it up with two sorority girls with miniskirts and obvious agendas. Alex felt only a tiny bit of guilt as she interrupted. "Have you seen Ian?"

"No, not in a while," said Tim, turning all of his attention to Alex, much to the disappointment of Tim's potential late-night liaisons. "Everything okay?"

Alex didn't answer as she scanned the crowd again for any sign of him.

"Don't let Beth get under your skin," Tim continued as if he could read her mind. Alex looked up into his concerned face. "I saw her giving you an earful at the bar. She sure is a piece of work."

"She's a piece of something..." Alex responded absentmindedly, and Tim laughed and threw one arm around Alex's shoulders.

"Let's move to the front. It's time for the show to start."

The show was a combination drag pageant and karaoke contest, where the contestants walked a short lit-up runway while members of the audience serenaded them. Alex had witnessed some pretty incredible costumes and vocals during their frequent visits to this bar.

"Here is our first contestant of the night—Sheila!" boomed a loud voice over the P.A. system and the crowd, along with Alex and Tim, erupted in whoops. "Sheila" was dressed in a floor-length, green taffeta ball gown with a waist and décolletage that would be enviable to any woman. She tossed her platinum hair and sashayed down the runway as the pianist let loose with the first few bars of a classic tune.

"It's a little bit funny...this feeling inside..." sang a very familiar tenor, and the spotlight focused in on the silhouette of none other than Ian, his fedora pulled low over his face and a microphone held to his lips.

Alex felt a dramatic shift in pretty much all of her internal organs as he belted the words to "Your Song" in a rich voice that was saturated with emotion. She had no idea he could even carry a tune. The crowd was in an uproar as he commanded the stage, kissing Sheila on the cheek at one point and gesturing to his groupies.

"Yours are the sweetest eyes I've ever seen!" he sang, sweeping his gaze through the swooning audience until he found Alex. Still singing, he walked toward her and knelt at the end of the runway. Bathed in the glow of the spotlight, Alex, still frozen in some degree of shock, let him take her hand and finish the last few lines of the song.

"I hope you don't mind that I put down in words...how wonderful life is while you're in the world." He leaned in to kiss her as the piano faded. Cheers erupted, and his lips found her ear. "Let's get out of here."

In silence, they walked arm in arm, zigzagging across the quiet residential streets of Center City as they made their way to Alex's apartment building.

"I had no idea you could sing like that," she exclaimed.

"Four years of high school glee club." Ian grinned.

"You don't seem like the glee club type."

"The girls were hot." He shrugged as Alex nodded intently.

"Totally makes sense now."

He tightened his grip on her arm as they walked as a unit past Rittenhouse Square, where a few stragglers still enjoyed the sultry summer evening with hula hoops and glow-sticks. As the street lights from the park faded and they stepped down a poorly lit street of brownstones, Alex's courage emerged.

"What kind of car do you drive?" she blurted awkwardly.

"Do you like cars? We have a few...but mostly we have drivers. I have one that I take out on weekends sometimes—a vintage blue corvette stingray convertible," he said enthusiastically.

"She has soul," he continued. "A few dings here and there, but it only elevates her character."

Unexpectedly, Alex was plunged into darkness as Ian pulled her into the covered doorway of a trilogy brownstone. Even with her pupils dilated, it was so dark that she couldn't see a thing, including Ian. She could hear him though, breathing rapidly, and feel the heat radiating from his chest. He pressed his body against hers, the polarized sensations of cold stone on her bare back and Ian's heat on her front.

"She's beautiful," he whispered into her ear. "Hard, cold steel on the outside that can withstand anything, but on the inside..." His fingers drifted up her inner thigh, beyond the hem of her dress closing in on the apex of her thighs. "She's soft and supple—fast when you ask her for it and slow when you need it."

His fingers found their mark, pushing her panties to the side and exploring her most sensitive region. She dug her fingers into the impermeable stone as she exploded under Ian's touch, his fingers tracing the pathway to a destination that felt both painful and intensely pleasurable at the same time. Her back arched, her body as responsive as she imagined his car would be as it zipped around a curve, and she moaned a quick "Ian" as he slipped his fingers inside her. They retreated farther into the shadowy corner, their secretive rendezvous unknown to anyone else awake at this hour. His mouth found hers, kissing her hungrily, refusing to separate even for a quick breath. He gripped Alex in every way, with his hands, his mouth, his soul, and she accelerated until she launched into oblivion.

# EIGHTEEN

"I just have to run up to the ICU and grab something I forgot," Alex said, as she pulled into the hospital on her way to drop Ian at the airport.

"No problem. I'll just wait in the car."

"I can show you where I work..." Alex trailed off, trying to entice him.

"No, I'll just catch up on my reading," he said, tapping an additional copy of *Us weekly* sitting in Alex's car. She had scoured the hospital and collected every last one of them for proper disposal.

"You are incorrigible." She leaned over to give him a swift kiss.

"I try to be," he sang, as she closed the door on him flipping through the pages of the magazine.


Later, when driving home from the airport after many tender goodbye kisses and quiet promises, Alex reminisced over the celebratory weekend. True to his word, they had barely left her apartment and had a spectacular view of the fireworks, which had paled in comparison to the fireworks between the two of them. She couldn't deny their chemistry and, what was more, she was starting to trust him and to believe in the concept of a *them*.

His avoidance of her doctor life seemed odd, and she recalled his response when the boy collapsed on the soccer field. Maybe sick kids made him uncomfortable, or maybe he was in denial about how her lifestyle would affect their future. Because of geography, their relationship still existed in a proverbial fantasy bubble rather than a day to day reality. But it was a fantasy to end all others. Her skin still felt electrified from where his hands and mouth had paid homage to her body last night. She didn't mind living fantasy to fantasy...for now.

Several weeks later, as Alex typed furiously on her laptop, she realized nearly three months had passed since Rox had dropped her at the Gaborone airport. The nights would be cold there now, a distinct contrast from Philly, where the sun seemed to be squeezing out all of its excess heat in the remaining weeks of summer. A trickle of sweat dripped lazily down her back into the waistband of her shorts. Alex was seated outside at her favorite outdoor café during a rare administrative day where she could work anywhere, catching up on emails and reading the latest journal articles. As she lifted the straw of her soda to her lips, a bright blue bubble popped up on her laptop screen. She quickly clicked the bubble, and Roxanne's beautiful, flushed face appeared in pixels.

"Alex! Mercy had her baby! We would like to introduce you to Naledi." She held up a sleeping bundle wrapped in pink. The baby's face was angelic as she peacefully stretched one arm upward and then opened her mouth like a tiny baby bird waiting for its meal.

"Tell Mercy congratulations. She is absolutely beautiful."

"I will. Better take baby back to mama before she realizes I have no appropriate food source. Be back in a flash." Rox disappeared for a few moments before returning and flopping into a chair opposite her computer. "Like my new office?"

The walls, painted spa blue, were decorated with traditional embroidered Botswana hangings and woven baskets. Rox flipped her laptop around to display the corner of her desk where a framed photograph of her and Alex sat proudly.

"I remember that day," Alex laughed. "We got lost on the way back from the Okavango and had to stop at that little gas station for directions."

Rox's lilting laughter floated through her speakers. "And the guy thought we wanted to buy a chicken, and he kept trying to put a hen in my car. She flapped her wings so hard that feathers went everywhere, and we had to chase her around the parking lot to get her back in the crate."

Alex doubled over and laughed freely, not caring who was

listening. "Oh Rox—I miss you," said Alex when their giggles subsided. "How's PM? How's Nic? I want to hear everything?" "Things are good here. Dr. K is making plans for how to use the foundation grant. Oh, he told me he needs to talk to you soon. We've been sort of slow on the baby front, so I've had some time to set up a surgical skills lab."

"Rox—that's incredible!"

"I know. We have our first set of residents coming through next week. Let's see what else—McCartney misses you. He whines and I wine in misery together. Nic is busy with football things right now, but we talk every night, and I am going to stay with him in London for the holidays. Put this on your calendar, sweetie—me and you— New Year's in London. Doesn't that sound amazing?"

"It sounds spectacular." Alex's heart leaped at the possibility of spending New Year's with her best friend. "Should I invite Ian?"

"He already lives there, dear, and besides, it was his idea. Apparently, he and Nic throw this amazing party every year on his rooftop."

"Wow. I guess I'm not surprised."

"Well, please act surprised because I'm pretty sure he wanted to ask you himself. How are things with you? How does being in love suit you?" Rox added with a gleam in her eye.

"I don't know the first thing about being in love, Rox. Ian is...well...let's just say he's exceeding my expectations."

"In every way imaginable, I bet. When are you going to see him again?"

"Not until October. He invited me to this fancy Save the Children charity gala in L.A."

"Didn't he grow up there?"

"Yeah, until he was fifteen and then moved to London to live with his dad."

"Home tends to be a place that stirs up memories. I bet you'll have a chance to ask him all those burning questions that you just can't quite get to."

Alex stared at her, genuinely flabbergasted. *How did she always know?*

"How do you know these things, Rox?"

"You guys haven't spent that much time together, and I doubt you have been spending it combing through each other's childhoods. At least I hope you're not."

Alex flushed with embarrassment before answering, "No, we absolutely are not..."

With September came cooler mornings and evenings, bookending each day with the perfect temperature for being outdoors. Alex hustled to the hospital before the sun rose each morning, anxious to see all of her patients and know their data backward and forward before rounds. She had two weeks left out of a grueling six weeks in the cardiac ICU before her long weekend with Ian in California, which would be her first days off in what seemed like forever.

The cardiac ICU housed all newborns, infants, and kids with congenital heart disease or some type of heart failure. She had a wide variety of patients on her team, including a newborn baby awaiting heart surgery and a teenager who had just received a heart transplant. It had been the most stressful few weeks of her training so far. Because these kids were extremely fragile, the level of intolerance for errors in judgment was the highest she had ever experienced. Dr. Gibson was Glinda the Good Witch compared to her current attending—Dr. Susan St. John. Highly specialized, impossible to please, and always in heels, she intimidated even the most senior level staff. Her attention to detail and demands during rounds had prompted Alex to extend her day in both directions, arriving earlier and earlier each day and, unfortunately, staying late into the night studying the complex surgeries performed on her patients.

"Good morning Adeline." The round-faced infant with sprigs of red hair was already awake, trying to pull up on her crib.

Alex put the stethoscope to her chest, hearing her heart heave with each contraction and detecting the faintest crackles in her lungs. While on ECMO, her heart had improved enough to support her body but not quite enough that she could go home yet. Alex had helped transfer her to the cardiac unit so that she could get evaluated for a transplant. Adeline reached up and grabbed a fistful of Alex's hair, jerking it toward her mouth.

"Strength is intact," Alex said laughingly as she untangled her hair from the squealing baby's fist. "And I'm about to be late for rounds!"

Alex stood, poised and ready for rounds, when she heard the clickety-clack of heels approaching, and Dr. St. John, in her typical red lipstick and pearls, swept toward her. Never looking anyone in the eye, Dr. St. John began poring over the coveted nursing flowsheet where all the events, vitals, and medication changes in the last twenty-four hours were recorded.

"Begin please," she said in a tone that was not meant to be ignored. Alex cleared her throat.

"This is a six-month-old female with dilated cardiomyopathy being evaluated for a heart transplant."

"What is her indication for transplantation?"

"Progressive heart failure that requires IV medications."

"And what information supports her need for these medications?"

Luckily, Alex was highly invested in Adeline's care and could spout her entire history like the back of her hand. She got an affirmative nod as they moved on to the next patient, and Alex released a breath she hadn't realized she was holding.

Rounds continued painfully for hours as she was asked to recall, evaluate, and interpret the details of every single patient on their service. She had received a few nods and just as many disgruntled snorts from Dr. St. John but nothing painfully chastising yet. Feeling quite proud of herself, she pulled her incessantly vibrating phone out of her pocket to check for updates from the nurses. Instead, she encountered a barrage of texts from Ian.

*You are so sexy*
*I can't wait to get you naked*
*When I see you, I am going to rip off all your clothes and—*

Alex felt a pair of eyes on her as she frantically shoved the phone back into her pocket as it continued to vibrate with a stream of consciousness from a sexually deprived Ian.

"Please. Take your time Dr. Wilde. The patients and I don't want to interrupt."

Eyes the color of sandstone dissected her like she was a frog in science class. Every single cell of her body felt hot like her metabolism was on overdrive, and she inwardly cursed herself and Ian for his timing.

"It's not important," she mumbled and tried to step toward the next bed space. Dr. St. John blocked her path.

"When you are here," she said, pointing a jeweled finger at the floor, "your personal life does not exist." Then she turned and walked away, heels clicking with every stride.

"I am such an idiot," Alex wheezed as she and Tim jogged along the well-manicured trail that ran alongside the Schuylkill River.

"Pretty much," confirmed Tim as he sped ahead of Alex to avoid the attempted punch to his arm. "What made you pull your phone out anyway?"

"I thought it might be patient-related."

"No one is going to send you that many texts. How many was it?"

"By the time it was finished, a total of thirteen. We kept rounding, and my phone just kept vibrating every time I started to talk."

Tim gave a low whistle. "I bet St. John was about to have an aneurysm."

"You think?" Alex stopped and collapsed on the grass, letting the cool blades massage her temples.

"Did you text him back yet?"

"No. I don't know what to say—thanks, but your sexting put me on the chopping block."

Tim crouched next to her on the grass and started twirling a slender blade between his fingers. "I'm probably the wrong person to be saying anything."

"What?" said Alex, intrigued, and she propped herself onto her elbow.

"Does Ian really get it?"

"Get what?"

"Our profession...our life...the terrible things we see and how we deal with them..."

The breeze ruffled Alex's hair and made her sweat turn cold.

"No, and he probably never will. He absolutely avoids anything to do with sick kids." Feeling a little defensive, she added, "but I've never wanted to share my grief with anyone anyway."

"I know," Tim said thoughtfully, "but it doesn't mean you don't need to."

Tim's words frequently percolated through Alex's mind as she finished her last week of work before her weekend break. Death had seemed epidemic at one point in August—eleven kids total. All had died for different reasons—drowning or cancer or, the absolute worst, child abuse.

When was there even time to process it or to grieve or to heal? One minute Alex was telling a family how incredibly sorry she was that their precious child was going to die, and the next minute she was called to put a breathing tube in a kid having seizures. She carried the burden of this grief—a grief born of other people's tragedies—and stuffed it away deep inside a keyless compartment.

The night before her highly anticipated trip, she sat in bewilderment among the strewn-out contents of her closet, picking up each item in turn and then discarding it. It was late evening in Los Angeles, and she dialed Ian.

"Hello there," he murmured. If voices were food items, his was definitely melted drippy dark chocolate.

"I'm in the middle of a clothes crisis. What in the world am I supposed to wear to this thing?"

"I am so glad you asked." Sounding very pleased with himself, he explained further. "I have your dress covered. All you need to do is bring what goes underneath. Maybe something...I don't know...in the black lace category."

"Oh—you like black." Alex smiled coquettishly.

"It's my favorite color."

*How did he make everything sound so seductive?*

"Now that I don't have to dress shop when I get there, I can focus my energy elsewhere."

"I have an entire agenda for you."

"I can't wait." Her heart pounded into the silence of the phone.

"I have to go meet some friends, but I'll pick you up at LAX tomorrow night."

"Okay. Have fun."

"Bye, beautiful."

"Bye." Alex sighed like an unrequited lover and surveyed the mounds of clothes surrounding an unpacked suitcase.

She paced another loop around the cardiac unit. With fewer

windows on this side of the hospital, she felt stuck in a time warp. She glanced at her phone for confirmation—4:30 p.m. Luckily, she was signing out her patients to Tim and could snatch a cab at the hospital with plenty of time to get to her 7:30 p.m. flight. She tucked a piece of stray hair behind her ear and jotted a few notes to herself in earnest. She was looking forward to this well-deserved break and had the premonition that waves of change were about to crash onto her shore. A shrill ring from her phone interrupted her thoughts— Dr. St. John incoming.

"Hello—it's Alex."

"Adeline Davis just got a heart. Go tell the family and make sure she is ready to go to the operating room." *Click.*

Alex had never been given the responsibility of telling a family the good news before, and despite her professionally cool façade, she practically burst with joy. Adeline's mom hugged her tightly. She had continued to refer to Alex as her "Hollywood doctor" since that scandalous edition of *Us weekly*, and Alex didn't have the heart to set her straight. Alex leaned over the side of Adeline's crib to personally share the news and did not like what she observed. Adeline looked pale, and each breath came with a noticeable forced grunt.

"She's been like that for the past few hours and not wanting to eat at all," said her mom.

Alex took the tiny hand in her own. It was limp and very cool to the touch, not the hand of the vivacious baby that had grabbed her hair.

"Her heart is getting worse," Alex said gently to Adeline's mom.

"This transplant could not have come at a better time. We just need to get her stabilized for the operating room."

"What does that mean?" Adeline's mom covered her mouth with a freckled hand.

"I am going to put her to sleep like we did before when she first got sick and put in a breathing tube. We can start some medicines that will help her heart make it through the surgery," Alex explained.

"Please save my baby…she's everything to me." Adeline's mom stared at her through an ocean of tears. "I know if anyone can do it, you can." She grazed her baby's forehead with trembling lips and left the room.

Alex thrived on this kind of challenge, maybe because she was confident enough to know that she could pull this baby out of the proverbial drain and get her safely to the OR. However, she could not deny the sense of security she felt when Tim's tall frame filled up Adeline's doorway.

"Round two? In it to win it, I hope?" Tim shot a pair of gloves into the trash can with a smack.

"Absolutely. Now get in here and help me. We have a heart on its way, and we need to get this young lady ready for surgery."

They worked in parallel, providing the staff with instructions and asking for various medications to be administered. Like a well-executed military objective, they coaxed Adeline's heart into service while she underwent sedation, placement of a breathing tube, and insertion of catheters into her blood vessels. Now all they needed was the heart to show up.

Alex glanced at the clock—6:12 p.m. If traffic was heavy, she would just barely make her flight. Tim saw her eyes darting between the clock and Adeline.

"Go, Alex. I've got this."

"Are you sure? The heart's not here yet."

"Go," he said in a commanding voice. "I'll do everything you would do…only better."

"You are my hero."

Tim dropped his head to his chest. "Just have fun."

"Okay—text me with updates," Alex called as she raced toward the elevator. She pushed the down button and hopped from one foot to the other. Nothing could happen fast enough right now. After what seemed like a short eternity, the elevator dinged, and the doors slid open, revealing the cardiothoracic team carrying Adeline's heart in an Igloo cooler. She stepped on the elevator and said a quick prayer of thanks.

*Ian's status would be a godsend right now.* She stood in the serpentine security line of an airport that was more congested than usual for a Friday night. She hadn't even taken the time to check luggage and was pretty sure the flight attendants would give her hell about her overstuffed carry-on. Her flight was boarding now, and she hadn't even made it to the identification checkpoint. Nothing caused her anxiety quite like being late, especially being late for a flight. She would rather walk down a runway of glass shards than miss this flight. She blew out a breath and reached in her purse to text Ian.

"Ma'am?" A tough-looking TSA officer lightly touched her on

the shoulder. *Now what?*

"Yes?"

"We noticed your attire. Are you a nurse by any chance?"

Alex glanced down at the rumpled scrubs stamped with the Children's Hospital of Philadelphia logo. In her haste, she hadn't had time to change.

"I'm a physician," she said warmly. "Can I help you?"

"We have a situation with a passenger. Can you come with me?"

Alex realized that by offering her services, she would definitely miss her flight to L.A. She wavered for a moment then two before her professional duty won out. "Of course."

The officer hoisted her bag onto his shoulder and led her straight through security to one of the metal benches on the other side where a frail appearing lady clutched a quilted Chanel bag. Alex sat next to the lady and took her hand, reassured by the presence of a strong regular pulse.

"My name is Dr. Wilde. Can you tell me what happened?"

The lady described a sudden onset of chest pain and a frantic feeling in her chest after passing through security. Alex didn't actually need a history to diagnose her. She could feel the distinct irregularity in her pulse consistent with atrial fibrillation.

"Everything is going to be okay. We just need to get you to the hospital. Your heartbeat is very irregular, and you will probably need some medicine to fix it, but you will be okay in the meantime. Security makes me nervous, too," she whispered and received a tiny smile in return.

Inside her own chest, Alex's heart shattered with disappointment. The flight crew would most likely be closing the cabin door on her airplane right about now. A staticky buzz filled the air around them while the TSA officer conversed with someone over his radio.

"The ambulance is here, and the paramedics are on their way."

Alex stood, uncertain of what to do now, heavyhearted and disoriented by the rushing travelers dodging their little trio. The officer, brimming with authority, picked up his radio. "I'll be escorting Dr. Wilde to her flight—please hold the plane until we arrive."

The stiff fake airplane-seat leather had never felt so good against her skin. She pressed send on her message to Ian.

*On my way*

# NINETEEN

It was the middle of the night, but L.A. buzzed with activity. The warm air felt like a nice lightweight blanket on Alex's body, and the smell of car exhaust and potential filled her nostrils. Ian belonged here. He smoothly guided the rented BMW convertible through the glittering city streets lined with welcoming palm trees, a smile playing on his lips, his dark hair rippling into the night.

She fingered the soft petaled flowers in her lap, recalling how she had broken into a run to collide into the arms of the beautiful man in dark sunglasses holding a giant bouquet of pink camellias. Their fragrance wafted through the car, picked up by the wind whipping through her hair. The sweet longing of Sara Bareilles played at low volume over the radio. Ian's fingers found her hand, and they began lightly stroking her knuckles. That was the last thing Alex remembered before sleep claimed her.

Something was chasing her. Her legs wouldn't move, and all of her screams were whipped away by the wind—a blowing, terrible wind that howled into her ears. Whatever was coming was getting closer. Her dream-self shouted at her to wake up...*wake up!* Her eyes flew open, barely able to focus on the scene from the unfamiliar bed.

Muted morning light, a fresco of palm trees, and rolling hills blanketed lightly in smog were framed by a giant window. The last thing she remembered was being in the car with Ian. He exhaled heavily and rolled over toward her. They were sandwiched between a soft, body-hugging mattress and a heavy white duvet that smelled of jasmine. Alex shifted slowly but pointlessly because Ian threw a heavy arm over her.

"No…no…no," he murmured sleepily, "don't even think about it."

Alex giggled. "I am disgusting. My hospital grime is covered in airport yuck. I need a shower."

"Okay, Sleeping Beauty, but you're going to have to settle for a bath."

The master bathroom of the Beverly Hilton Presidential suite boasted a black and white checkerboard tile floor, floor to ceiling windows along one wall depicting the famous L.A. hills, and the most enormous white marble tub Alex had ever seen. Alex shed her clothes and slid luxuriously into the warm water frosted by effervescent bubbles. She leaned her head back and closed her eyes and felt the first nudges of relaxation start in her shoulders.

"I hope you saved me some room." Ian's face was directly above hers, and he gave her a quick upside-down kiss before stepping into the opposite side of the tub.

"Aah…I could get used to this," he murmured.

"You *are* used to it." Alex batted some water in his direction.

"I have been in bathtubs all over the world, but none of them had you."

He made a kissy face in her direction and then picked up her foot and pulled it into his chest, encasing it in both of his hands. The tactile pressure he applied to the sole of her foot made the remaining tension seep right out of her skin. She moaned lightly and let her head loll to one side. His lips joined his hands in silent worship of her foot, and Alex felt the spectacular bloom of desire in her core as his teeth grazed the arch of her foot. Jerking her foot from his grasp, she floated through the water so that she was straddling him. Dripping and coated in a fine layer of bubbles, she pressed her breasts into his chest and felt immense pleasure when he moaned in gratification.

"I want you," she said timidly, shyness creeping over her.

"You have me."

For an entire minute, Alex surrendered to his mouth, unable to kiss him deep enough or connect more of her bare skin with his warmth. For the first time, she was positioned above him, and it was intoxicating.

166

A sharp rap occurred on the hotel door, and she froze in the middle of running her tongue up Ian's neck.

"Are we expecting company?"

"Arghh. It's the lady from the dress shop."

"Now?"

"Tragically, yes," he said, resigning himself to stepping out of the bath. "Come on out when you get dressed and, by the way, I knew you'd like being on top," he said with his signature cocky half-smile and narrowed eyes.

Alex had nothing to throw, so instead, she sank underneath the bubbles letting the water dilute some of her embarrassment.


"These are exquisite. I don't know how I'm ever going to pick one." Alex rifled through a portable rack of evening gowns of every fabric and color—some so elaborate that they sparkled like a Tiffany diamond. "How do the celebrity ladies do it?" She turned to the tall, elegant lady next to her whose gray hair was cut in a trendy bob and who was wearing a pink pantsuit the color of Alex's camellias.

"They have their own stylists, my dear."

"Oh," Alex replied forlornly.

"Do not despair *mon Cherie*. I happen to be very good at dressing people. Now tell me about yourself, so I can make sure we capture your style."

Alex wasn't sure she had a style that involved much more than scrubs and running attire, but she wasn't about to turn down the talents of this real-life Fairy Godmother.

"I am a doctor. I work with children...really sick ones."

As Alex talked, the lady listened attentively, nodding in encouragement but rarely speaking. Alex found herself sharing more with this woman than she intended—how she had a simple upbringing in a small town, how she was a natural introvert and a devoted friend, how much she loved what she did despite the heartache. She stopped mid-sentence when Ian poked his head around the corner of the living room, where she and Fairy Godmother were seated on an elegant blue couch.

"Don't mind me. I just have a few errands to run. Be back soon," he announced, and with a swift kiss on Alex's lips and a lingering look of longing from the doorway, he left.

"Well, isn't he a dish?" the dress lady remarked after Ian had cruised through the quarters displaying his typical delightfully sexy self.

"He is," said Alex, smiling and thinking how Ian's appeal extended across generations.

"I have just the dress for you," she announced, a smile crossing her red lips as her hands deftly separated the garments hanging on the rack. She pulled out a white floor-length gown made of layers of thin gauzy material the color of suffused candlelight. "Let's try it on, shall we?"

The dress had a fitted bodice that gathered at one shoulder and was decorated with delicate white flowers. The skirt, full and multi-layered, rippled beautifully every time she moved.

"Never forget Dr. Wilde that the accessories make the outfit glorious." She produced a pair of glittering diamond and pearl drop earrings, which she fastened in Alex's ears as well as a pair of Jimmy Choo heels embellished with a silver and blue glitter dégradé. Alex observed herself in the mirror. The real-life Fairy Godmother had transformed her into a real-life Cinderella.

With the borrowed dress and shoes stored safely in the closet, Alex, back in her comfortable sweats, crawled back onto the bed and tucked her legs under the duvet. Hoping Tim was still awake, she dialed him quickly before she could change her mind.

"Alex?"

"Did I wake you?"

"No, I'm still here at the hospital?"

"Geez—you *are* better than me," she said playfully. "How did the transplant go?"

"Not so great, Alex. The new heart is a real dud. Nobody knows why."

Alex felt like someone had punched her in the gut. "Oh." A million questions coursed through her. "Have you thought about treating more aggressively for rejection? Or supporting her with ECMO for now? Or relisting?"

"Yes, times three. We got this, Alex—just have fun. I'll keep you posted, okay. I have to go."

"Okay." She disconnected and immediately felt the weight of despair. *I should be there. I am part of this fight...and I don't know how not to be.*

"Alex?"

Hearing her name on Ian's lips, Alex consciously transitioned into the girl enjoying her weekend with a wonderful guy.

"In here."

He sauntered over and crawled up next to her on the bed, collapsing onto the mountain of pillows. "Everything okay?"

He took her hand, and his eyes searched her expression for something she hoped he couldn't see.

"Sure. Absolutely. I found a dress." His smile was so ecstatic that Alex's heart lightened just a fraction. "What a face—why so happy?"

"I can't wait to show off my sexy doctor girlfriend."

*Girlfriend?* Alex bit her lip to keep from revealing how amazing that sounded. "Did you get your errands done?"

He put his hands behind his head and looked up at the ceiling. "Mostly—one of which you are going to love."

"Please say a one-way ticket to Barbados."

"No, but that could be arranged in the near future." He flashed her a sultry smile. "I arranged for some lady sprucing for you—hair and stuff like that. I figured one less thing for you to stress out about."

"How long until they get here?" Alex asked, still chewing on her bottom lip.

"Long enough." He eyed her with a ravenous look—one that she equally returned.


Alex truly felt transformed as she twirled in front of the bedroom mirror, enjoying her singular Cinderella moment. The light reflected off her shoes, her earrings, and the white crystal-embellished clutch that Fairy Godmother had thought to leave for her. Her long chocolate brown hair had been pinned in an elegant updo so that her lovely neck and collarbones were on display. Although she had never worn this much makeup in her life, her face bore a natural quality per her request, just completely flawless. A pair of smoldering blue eyes appeared in the mirror. She rotated a full circle, a bit awkwardly with a full skirt in tow.

"What? Do I look okay?"

Ian was abnormally silent for a moment. "You look absolutely breathtaking."

Alex paused and simply lived in this exhilarating moment for a second before replying. "I saved the black for later."

"Alex," he replied in a low husky tone, "if we don't leave right this second, I am going to strip you of everything except for your shoes and those earrings and make you see stars."

An immediate rush of heated desire and desperate longing filled her every blood vessel. She loved how he delighted in arousing her, how it seemed like an art to him—an art he had perfected. She tucked a shaky hand under his arm, and off they went.


"You didn't tell me there was an actual red carpet," Alex whispered, through clenched teeth.

"Just breathe and smile."

"Easy for you to say," she murmured as flashbulbs exploded in her face, temporarily distorting her vision and causing her to wobble in her heels.

Fortunately, they made it into the reception area without incident. Ian, clean-shaven and ridiculously debonair in his black tux, was in his element in the spotlight, smoothly guiding them past the throng of photographers to the glitz and glamour awaiting them inside the ballroom of the Beverly Hilton. Everything in sight seemed to sparkle, from the champagne being transported on gilded trays to the jewelry clad celebrities. Alex was suddenly grateful for the investment into her appearance. At least outwardly, she fit in.

"I'll get us some drinks," Ian whispered into her ear, and then he was gone, whisked up by the momentum of the colorful, active scene in front of her. She pulled her phone out of her clutch and fired a quick text to Tim.

*Any news?*

He replied almost immediately.

*No better no worse. Will call you later.*

Unsatisfying though it was, at least it wasn't bad news. Putting away the phone, she surveyed the crowd for anyone she might recognize, and her eyes riveted toward a tall blonde with perfect bone structure dressed in a fuchsia satin gown. As she conversed with her friends, her long stick-straight hair rippled like a cornfield in the wind, reminding Alex of her childhood Barbie doll.

"Did I forget to mention that Rebekah would be here?" said a smooth voice and Alex cut her eyes to Ian's sheepish face.

Unsettled, she sighed heavily and accepted his peace offering in the form of a crystal flute filled to the brim with expensive champagne.

They worked the crowd as a unit for almost an hour, sampling intricate hors d'oeuvres, chatting with Ian's celebrity connections, and imbibing champagne. Never leaving her side for a moment, Ian offered reassurance in the form of gentle touches on her bare skin, and flirty glances meant just for her. After a second glass of effervescent liquid, Alex was noticeably less tense, and her words began to flow much easier. She also discovered that she easily dove into the evening conversation, which centered around the activities of children's non-profits around the world.

As Ian admirably watched, she debated the various solutions for the high infant mortality rate in Tanzania with one of the U.S. Goodwill Ambassadors.

"You are quite a lady, Dr. Wilde. Give me a call if you are ever interested in working with us." Alex took the simple white card and was busy stuffing it in her tiny clutch when a high-pitched voice reminiscent of a hand bell choir rang out.

"I don't believe we have been properly introduced."

Raising an eyebrow at the white silk gloved forearm extended toward her face, many thoughts vied for position in her brain, not one of which was kind, but the high road of her upbringing won out.

"I'm Alex," she said and accepted the white gloved hand into her own.

"Rebekah Matheson." The green eyes that stared into her blue ones were guarded and wary and flitted from her to Ian like a cat watching a mouse. Apparently deciding that Alex was not in the least bit threatening, she turned her attention to Ian. "Ian, darling," she cooed and leaned in to plant a pouty pink kiss on both his cheeks.

"Rebekah, you look stunning," Ian said, grabbing both of her hands and pushing her back to examine her silhouette. "Not at all like someone who just had her heart broken."

171

"What?" Confusion crossed her face. "Oh...that. Publicity is everything. You know how it is. It was harmless."

"Not for Alex."

Alex had never seen Ian angry. Although he maintained composure, she noticed the tension in his jaw and the collected cold stare he directed at Rebekah. The actress appeared taken aback but recovered in the next instant.

"Tonight is about the children, Ian. Alex, I hear the silent auction has some lovely items." At this party, the guests were either a "somebody" or attached to a "somebody" and Rebekah had accurately put her in the latter category.

"I'll be sure to take a look," she replied evenly, knowing that everything would be out of her price range. She probably couldn't even afford the silverware she was about to use during dinner. Once Rebekah was out of earshot, Ian relaxed and muttered something under his breath that rhymed with witch—just a lot more accurate.

Cocktail hour ended, and the clusters of celebrities, dignitaries, and deep-pocketed business leaders were ushered to their tables by a cadre of white-coated serving staff. Alex slid into the gilded dining chair next to Ian, maintaining a poised countenance that revealed nothing when Rebekah was seated opposite them. The person in charge of the seating chart must have had a tremendous sense of humor.

The trio that took the remaining seats at the table were two women and a man dressed in traditional garb that Alex recognized as Malawian. Alex struck up an easy conversation with them over the salad course and learned they were indeed here representing the tiny country of Malawi and the immunization program funded by Save the Children.

"When I worked in Botswana, we had similar struggles with access to healthcare. We started an outreach program where we set up vaccine distribution in village squares, parks, fields. In fact, Ian even went with me one day." They shared a smile at the mutual memory.

"We are extremely passionate about our cause as well and hope that the generosity tonight will support us in the future," remarked one of the ladies, dressed head to toe in an exotic gold print.

Rebekah, who had been abnormally quiet during most of dinner, used this break in the conversation to pipe up. "Isn't this organization just wonderful? I personally plan on making a substantial contribution to the cause tonight. The life of even one child is priceless. Alex, dear, how do you plan to contribute?"

While Alex struggled with a response, Ian broke the ice-like tension. "Dr. Alexandra Wilde is here tonight as an example of what we all should strive to be. Her existence is her contribution...since she actually saves children's lives every single day. All before you have even put on your makeup and had your morning coconut water."

Rebekah narrowed her gaze, seething in silence as a pink flush spread over her porcelain face. Glancing between the two of them, Alex mentally retreated to the periphery of this feud as she detected the uncomfortable chuckling of her table companions.

"Well, you stopped by so early this morning, I barely had time to look decent, Ian darling." A stormy expression crossed Ian's face, and Rebekah glowed with victory. "Oh...I'm sorry. Was that not common knowledge?"

Emotional entanglements and melodrama were not in Alex's repertoire. She rose stiffly, clutching her purse to her chest and feeling the snowball of emotions grow larger as they rolled downhill. "I just need a minute."

She fled the scene leaving a concerned Ian calling her name, a gloating Rebekah, and an untouched plate of buttery lobster tail. Leaving the lobster was the most regretful.


The ladies' room of the Beverly Hilton was more spacious than her apartment and significantly more posh. She sunk into the deep blue velvet chaise in the anteroom, letting her dress billow around her like a parachute. Why wouldn't Ian just tell her that his "errands" had included a trip to Rebekah's? Unless he was being surreptitious for a reason. After everything with the magazine, Alex couldn't believe that Ian would betray her, but his dishonesty had caused her public ridicule...again...and forced more unnecessary drama in her life. Her anger dissipated into a dull ache. Craving a distraction that reconnected her with her real life, she dialed Tim. She heard him answer with a strangely quiet tone.

"Hello."

"Tim, I'm sorry—I know it's late there—I just wanted to check on Adeline."

"I was just about to call you." Alex didn't like his somber tone. "She died, Alex. We tried everything. It just wasn't enough." "Okay. Thanks for letting me know. Please tell her mom that I'm so sorry."

Alex hung up and let the unshed tears spill over onto her cheeks, a wound ripping open inside her, and instead of trying to patch it up, she just let it bleed. An ocean of well-contained grief swelled up inside of her like a tsunami wave right before it pummels the shoreline. She had to get out of there before it struck. Dabbing her red-rimmed eyes with a balled-up tissue, she opened the door and broke into a wobbly run, opposite the direction of the party.

Once outside, the warm breeze surrounded her like a gentle embrace, and she slowed her pace, weaving between the potted trees and flower bushes with no true direction. Without fully realizing it, Alex had been following the pink glow she could see above the swaying palm trees, like a west coast Aurora Borealis. An expansive freeform shaped pool came into view, and she gratefully sank down onto an outdoor sofa with aqua cushions and slid off the glittering torture devices on her feet.

"Alex?"

Hearing her name on Ian's lips was so unexpected that she startled. He approached her cautiously, like she was a gazelle ready to leap at the first sign of danger. There was nowhere to go, and no matter how fast she ran, she wouldn't be able to outrun her feelings.

"You can sit down, Ian."

Her voice sounded alien and distant. He lowered himself onto the cushion next to her and reached out for her hand, like he was fearful that she would try to escape.

"You are really fast in those shoes."

"Not fast enough it seems."

"Alex, I'm sorry about Rebekah. She is lashing out and—"

"This isn't just about Rebekah."

Alex could feel the tsunami cresting. She let Ian's arms surround her, her cheek flush with the silk lapel of his tuxedo, as the tsunami finally crashed into land. Alex cried and kept crying, silently and then huge hiccupping sobs, until she was certain that she was close to dehydration from the fluid loss. She was crying a trilogy of hurt— today's loss of Adeline, the children who had already been lost, and the ones who would be.

"I can't save anyone, Ian. I feel like a living, breathing example of irony tonight. Do you know how many children I have to watch die from unimaginable things that I can't change? There is a little baby that I have taken care of for months. She was so strong despite everything she went through. She used to grab my hair every morning."

Alex paused and smiled through her tears at the vision of Adeline clutching the end of her ponytail. "She finally got a heart transplant...but it didn't work, and she died tonight. And I wasn't there. I was here playing Cinderella...and I don't even know why. So that you can show me off to your ex-girlfriend and she can feel threatened and then embarrass me during dinner to one-up me. None of your Hollywood drama even matters. It's such bullshit compared to real tragedy...and I need someone in my life that understands that."

She paused for breath. "I am so full of pain and grief, and I can't even remember where it all came from."

Ian held her tighter, which only made her cry harder. He said nothing while her body trembled, and her face became streaked with tears carrying with it the colors of her cosmetics that eventually bled onto his white shirt. A classic doctor dictum popped into her mind: *All bleeding stops eventually.* As does crying, she thought, as her tears abruptly ceased. The tsunami had ended and left behind only wreckage in its wake—the wreckage of extreme vulnerability.

# TWENTY

Alex awoke with a pounding headache that throbbed behind her right eye. Apparently, emotional catharsis gave her a hangover. She preferred the alcohol-induced kind. She was grateful to be alone at the moment.

After her outburst, Ian had said little and simply steered her back to their suite, which fortunately had a second bedroom. He had tried to console her and then seduce her, but she hadn't wanted any connection with him whatsoever. She felt too exposed and feared using him as a poultice for her wounds. Instead, she closed the door in his face and found solace in her solitude, where she could regroup, sift through her emotions, and decide how to proceed. The secondary bedroom luckily had its own bathroom complete with shower, and after she dug through her bag for some ibuprofen, she decided to start there.

Once she had scrubbed her face clean of any traces of yesterday's beauty products, she disrobed from her sweats and stared at her own reflection. Outwardly, she looked like the same thin, brunette girl with large blue eyes and pale skin from too many hours in the hospital. Inside, she felt strangely different, similar to her first experience of real physical intimacy with Ian.

In Paris, the excitement had far outweighed her fright. This new level of intimacy, a loss of emotional virginity, was deeper somehow and left her feeling raw and edgy. She had no idea how Ian would respond after last night. All kinds of things came to mind like awkwardly pretending that it never happened, outright shunning, or Ian's favorite—physical distraction. Whatever was going to happen, she needed a shower first.

The pressurized water scalded her skin, and she hoped last night's outer layer was being burned off. Her hair had gotten so long that it extended down to her lower back, and she slicked it back from her face. Closing her eyes, she pretended she was in some exotic location under a cascading waterfall with nothing but the sound and sensation of rushing water. This escapist fantasy usually thrilled her but not today. She startlingly realized why. Right now, she wanted to be with Ian more than she desired her solitude, even in a fantasy world. Inspired with a new-found resolve, she twisted the shower to off and tucked herself in a fluffy white towel.

Ian was waiting for her, leaning casually in the doorjamb, already dressed in jeans and a Decemberists t-shirt, hair still damp, and a sly smile across his beautiful face.

"Have you been here this entire time?" Alex yelped.

"Unfortunately, no. I missed you getting undressed." He held up her discarded panties, which were thankfully a no-fuss plain cotton.

"I suppose I could schedule a repeat performance," Alex said in an uncharacteristic moment of coy.

"As much as I want to tear you out of that towel and fling you on the bed, I need a raincheck."

Disappointment abounded, but Alex felt a tremendous sense of relief when she caught the familiar burn of his gaze and a quick flick of his tongue across his lower lip.

"Ian…about last night…"

He held up a hand. "We'll talk about it again when you're ready, but today I want to take you somewhere."


Alex threw her mostly dried hair up into a messy bun and observed her options for clothing. She chose a pair of denim shorts and a long-sleeved linen button-down that would suffice in the California sun. On a whim, she pulled out a simple but matching bra and panty set made of light pink silk and slipped them on. Her trousseau had expanded as of late. At least if the moment arose, she would be prepared. And she wanted it to. She smiled as she slid her arms through her shirt and pulled on her shorts, enjoying the sensuality of wearing dainty lingerie underneath her day attire.

*Today was a day for joy.* She and Ian sped down the Pacific Coast Highway, radio blaring, and the wind whipping through the car like a mini-tornado. The sun took center stage in a cloudless sky, and Alex was grateful for the classic black sunglasses allowing her to drink in the scenery. Once they had escaped the hustle of Beverly Hills and entered the highway, Alex was sandwiched between the ocean on her left and expanses of trees interspersed with whitewashed stucco homes on her right. Her nose even caught the faint scent of oranges as they rounded a curve.

"Where are we going?" Alex asked when they were several miles down the Pacific Coast.

"Malibu," Ian called above the instrumental genius of Coldplay.

Soon he exited the highway into a residential neighborhood along the coast and made a few well-calculated turns before pulling into the driveway of a beautiful two-story home with a Mediterranean tiled roof and a small fountain in the front circle drive.

"Wow. Who lives here?" Alex asked, craning her neck to see the terraced second floor.

"I do," said Ian quietly, hands gripping the steering wheel. "Or I did. This was my mother's house."

Alex followed him up to a heavy wooden double door that looked like it had belonged to a Medieval church, complete with iron hardware and intricate carvings along the border. He thrust a thick key into the lock and twisted.

"This is why I had to go to Rebekah's," he said, grunting with the weight of the door. "Her housekeeper takes care of the place when I'm not around and she had my extra set of keys."

Alex was too enamored with the scene before her to respond. A quiet awe crept over her as she observed the light-filled home with wide-planked floor stained a beautiful natural oak, a winding spiral staircase, a crystal chandelier as a welcome beacon in the entryway. Ian grabbed her hand.

"Come on—I'll give you the tour."

There were just a few furnishings in the downstairs area—an oversized white leather couch, a few occasional tables and a cowhide print rug. The kitchen was all white with open shelving containing a stack of white porcelain dishes and a friendly island that Alex could imagine using for homework or having friends over for Friday night snacks.

"Do you have good memories of this place?" Alex asked,

running her hand along the granite countertop.

"Some," Ian said as he led her out of the kitchen and over to the stairs. "My mother threw some pretty raging parties here, and I used to sneak a hooch here and there when people abandoned their drinks." His smile was mischievous but overpowered by the distant sorrow in his eyes.

"Sounds like she was a lot of fun."

They crested the stairs, which emptied them onto the threshold of the master suite, guarded by a pair of beautifully paneled French doors and concealed from view by a fluttering white linen swag. Ian opened the door into a bedroom filled with suffused light from a floor to ceiling panel of windows that lined one wall. The windows portrayed a breathtaking view of the ocean, midnight blue and depthless, juxtaposed to a brilliant blue sky. The room's only furniture was an antique French four-poster bed painted white with a simple white duvet and blush-colored velvet pillows.

"This is the best part."

Ian pulled on the handles of the window wall, and they collapsed into a single pane, effectively making the bedroom contiguous with the terrace. The heat and salt-infused breeze caressed Alex's face and beckoned her outside.

"This is incredible. I would spend every second right here," Alex said, motioning to an oversized corner chaise lounge.

"Try it out."

Like a thrilled child, she settled into the chaise and tipped her head upward, listening for the waves crashing on the rocky beach down below. Eyes tightly shut, she reached for Ian's hand. "You must miss this when you're in London."

"Are you kidding? This old shack? I can smell bus exhaust and the Queen's perfume from the rooftop of my London pad." He flashed a sardonic smile. "Which reminds me—how does New Year's in London sound...with me?" He seemed shy like he wasn't sure of her answer.

"I'd love that, but I have to confess that Rox already spilled the beans."

"Roxanne—she is a nonstop party bus. She reminds me a little of my mom...vivacious...loved by all."

Alex sat up and patted the spot next to her on the chaise. "Tell me about your mom."

He hung back for a minute as if weighing a decision and then let out a subtle but detectable breath. "I'll be right back."

When he returned a few minutes later, he held a small stack of Polaroids, two orange juice glasses with faded Star Wars characters, and a bottle of bourbon.

"Do you have bourbon hidden all over the world for yourself?" Alex joked.

"Storytime," he began, "deserves appropriate refreshments."

He poured each of them a hefty amount in the Star Wars glasses. Alex wrinkled her nose at the initial burn but took a sip. Ian drained his glass, then set it gently on the weathered teak side table and sat down next to her, displaying the Polaroids like they were a hand of cards.

"My parents met here in L.A. My mom moved here at nineteen dreaming of becoming an actress, and my dad, a brand-new executive for the Devall company, was here scoping out potential mining sites."

He showed her a picture of a beautiful girl with long, dark hair framing a heart-shaped face wearing a sundress. She looked like a tiny doll next to the lanky, bearded man in a casual suit holding her hand as they strolled down a nondescript street. The next photograph showed the couple hoisting a naked toddler between them as they stood in the churning surf.

"That's you," Alex exclaimed as she peered closer at the chubby dark-haired little boy, his face erupting in glee.

"In all my glory."

Alex greedily snatched the stack of pictures and began sifting through them—the same dark-haired boy in a cowboy outfit during Halloween, Ian's mother in a red dress and headscarf sitting on the hood of a convertible, and Ian as a young boy, his arm lovingly tossed around the shoulders of a much younger sandy-haired boy who was smiling as he held up a dripping ice cream cone.

"Who is this cute guy?" Alex asked, flipping over the picture to inspect it for a date.

"That's my brother."

Alex froze, mentally repeating Ian's response before she reacted. He had never mentioned having a brother, and Alex wondered why he did so now. "Your brother?" she swallowed.

"My brother," he confirmed, slowly, as if the words were foreign on his tongue, having not been spoken in quite some time.

"Benjamin Ryan Devall—but he went by Ryan." He smiled as

he fingered the picture. "I was five when he was born, and it took a few years, but we became really close—especially after my dad moved back to London, and it was just me, him, and my mom."

"Why did your dad leave all of you here?"

Ian poured himself another splash of bourbon and settled back into the chaise. "He had to go back for the company—duty called I guess—and my mom wouldn't even consider leaving her acting career or her friends. She was getting a lot of small parts and felt like her big break was coming any time. My dad came back as much as he could, but it wasn't a lot. He loved her too much to ask her to give up on her dream—even if it meant he suffered for it."

"Why didn't you and Ryan move to London?"

Ian closed his eyes and tensed his jaw with the stress of dredging up memories. "When Ryan was six, he collapsed on the playground at school. We rushed him to the hospital, and the doctors told us that he had contracted some virus, and the aftereffects of the virus had caused his heart to fail. He was in the hospital for a month while he was poked and monitored and switched around on medicines until eventually, he was well enough to come home. I stayed with him a lot—reading books to him or helping him play tricks on the nurses. It sounds easy when I say it, but it was actually pretty terrible. I still can't make myself go into a hospital."

Feeling a surge of empathy, Alex grabbed his hand and held it to her quivering lips.

"In the end, we didn't go to London because my mom was acting selfish. She wouldn't leave her career, and she didn't want us to leave her, especially after Ryan got sick. That was the only time I can remember my parents fighting. Ryan had come home by then and was actually doing really well, and my dad begged my mom to come to London. She wouldn't do it."

"What happened then?" The sun had gone behind a cloud as if foreshadowing the next segment of the story, and Alex felt a hovering chill despite the warm day.

"Life went on for a while. Ryan got tired more easily, but he was still the same happy kid who loved ice cream and Star Wars. We probably watched *Empire Strikes Back* about a hundred times one summer."

Ian glanced down at his glass, and Alex could see the tiniest teardrop leak out onto his cheek.

"One day in the middle of summer when he was eight and I was thirteen, he wanted a chocolate chip cone from this place down the street. So, we jumped on our bikes and raced over there. We were eating our cones outside on a bench when a group of girls from my school showed up. They happened to be the coolest, prettiest girls in school, and I had heard that one of them had a crush on me—Nora Phelps."

"Imagine that." Alex gave his hand another squeeze, and he flashed her a half-smile.

"Long blonde ponytail...even longer tan legs...cute smile. You get the picture. Anyway, I wanted to stick around and—"

"Flirt?"

"Yeah." He raised his dark brows over vacant eyes. "But Ryan got bored and wanted to go home. I told him to go—he was a big boy, and he knew the way and I would be home in a few minutes."

Ian's voice sounded raw like he was scraping the bottom of something.

"So I stayed and felt pretty awesome that these girls wanted to talk to me. Then I rode my bike home like I was king of the universe...and I saw Ryan. He had made it up the driveway and chucked his bike in the grass. He never made it inside and was lying on our doorstep. I don't remember much about the rest—apparently, I dragged him inside and called 911. I remember sirens and uniforms and then he was whisked off to the hospital. I never saw him again."

Alex counted the tears gliding down his cheek. One then two then three. She used her thumb to brush them off. She wanted to hold him tight enough so that her arms bore some of this burden. She wanted to be the salve that anesthetized this wound and the thread that could sew it closed with neat, punctate stitches.

"This was not your fault, Ian."

He acted like he hadn't heard her—his eyes still far away, seeing a place and a time that she could not.

"The doctors told us it was probably a fatal heart rhythm or something—that it can happen when the heart is frail for so long. Everyone told me it wasn't my fault, but no one understood that I wasn't arrogant enough to think I could have saved him. I blamed myself because I wasn't there when it happened. He died alone...without his big brother to tell him it was going to be okay."

His eyes still pooled with tears, but they remained unshed. He cleared his voice and took another solid swig of bourbon from his glass. Alex remained quiet, anticipating that this was not the end of the story.

"My mother never recovered. She became distant...reclusive. We never talked about what happened to Ryan. We never talked period. It was like in her mind, we both had died that day. Anyway, a few years later, when I was fifteen, I came home from school one day, and she was gone—completely vanished. She took a suitcase full of clothes but nothing else. She didn't leave a letter. Not even a Post-it note."

"She just abandoned you?" Alex was flabbergasted and angry as she imagined Ian as a vulnerable teenager trying to live with his little brother's death and then being terminally shunned by his own mother. No wonder he had attachment issues with women.

"I started telling everyone that she died," he said with an eye roll. "It helps avoid the awkward questions that usually come after."

"Where was your dad this whole time?"

"Still in London. He was dealing with Ryan's death in his own way—perfecting his work ethic and starting the Devall foundation. About two weeks after my mother left, he was waiting for me in the kitchen one day when I got home from school. He had my things packed, and we hopped on a plane to London, and I never looked back."

"You don't talk about him much." Alex rubbed Ian's knee protectively.

"He is the most generous, kind person you will ever meet, and he's always let me find my own way without harsh judgment—even when I deserved it."

Ian fiddled with the glass in his hand, tracing the blue outline that was once Luke's lightsaber. "Moving to London marked the beginning of a fifteen year bender for me."

"You were a teenage boy who lost his brother and then his mother and then moved away from everything you had ever known. Your dad was right to not pass judgment."

"He tried a few times to rein me back into my responsibilities, but I was childish and felt like the world owed me, so I indulged in whatever it would give me—whatever money could buy and whatever I could obtain with my...uh...charm."

"Women?"

"Especially women. I loved women...and I loved that they loved me. There was no one that wasn't attainable, and they offered a lot of...distraction."

He paused to drain the last of the bourbon from his glass. "Luckily, I pulled myself together enough to finish graduate school, but wherever the party went, I followed. London, Paris, Barcelona, Greece. I couldn't even remember where I was waking up most mornings." He frowned and furrowed his dark brows even further.

"What changed?"

Ian stretched out his long legs and swung them over the chaise. "I matured over the years and realized that I had inherited some of my father's work ethic. I never grew out of living a fast-paced bachelor life, but I wanted to be a part of something that mattered, so I started working for the foundation." He pushed up to a stand and held an outstretched hand out to Alex. "And then I met a girl."

Alex followed Ian out of the house to the car noticing, as he opened the passenger door, that his tears had vanished, evaporated into the breeze.

"I want to show you one more thing."

His burden seemed lighter as they drove a twisted path along the coastline and entered a small dirt lot secluded from the road by towering trees and grotesquely shaped bushes. The sun was sinking lower in the sky as the afternoon waned, and Alex could hear waves crashing in the distance as they hiked along a well-marked path toward Ian's destination. Once the tree line broke, they were suddenly standing on a rocky outcropping suspended above the ocean.

"What is this place?"

"Just somewhere I used to come and emote as a kid."

He smiled at the fond memories that seemed to be surfacing. The scenery was metaphorically tumultuous—waves crashing onto a stationary rocky shore, a realm of dark clouds cloaking the sun and a wild wind whipping its way through everything stationary. Alex couldn't help but let out a small laugh.

"What? Are you laughing at me?"

"I was just thinking how this place is perfect for the soul-searching turmoil of an emotionally immature teenager."

"It is." He picked a small delicate purple flower from a nearby bush and tucked it behind her ear, brushing back the strands of hair from her face.

"I need to tell you something." He locked his gaze on her face, and Alex stilled immediately. "I am not a good person, Alex. I am rude and vain and selfish—especially when it comes to women. I know I don't deserve to have someone like you."

Alex's heart pounded so violently inside her chest that she was certain Ian could hear it. His fingers traced her cheekbone down to the corner of her trembling mouth.

"The difference between us, Alex, is that I have used the tragedy in my life as an excuse to do whatever I want—even at other people's expense. You have been hurt too—I don't know how—maybe someday you'll tell me. The point is that you took everything that happened to you and turned it into a life of such good. You give so much of yourself to everyone else—even if it sometimes hurts you in the process."

He cupped her face in a pair of warm palms. "I don't deserve you, but I need you because I am a better person with you in my life…a person I never thought I could be."

The look in those limitless blue eyes was so earnest—so desperately tender and genuine. Alex lost herself in their depths and reconciled the pull on her heart by whispering, "You have me."

# TWENTY-ONE

"The etiology of bleeding during ECMO is multifactorial" read the sentence in her bulky critical care textbook that weighed almost as much as a small child.

*Ian's fingers roamed up her leg inside her cutoffs, exploring the crest of her inner thighs.*

She reread the sentence and began reviewing "Table 1: Most common causes of bleeding".

*His mouth torched her bare skin with its wet heat.*

"Thrombocytopenia, therapeutic anticoagulation, tissue injury".

It had been six weeks since their rendezvous in the sunshine state, and her skin still felt electrically charged where his hands had been. She shifted in the formidable library chair as her back involuntarily arched and the page in front of her faded from black and white into shades of cloudy gray.

The raw display of emotion on a Malibu cliffside had demanded a physical manifestation, and Alex felt herself being swept up in a current of passion. Ian's face, alight with joyful disbelief, had bent down to kiss her just as the first spatter of raindrops landed on their noses. The sky had become overcast without them even realizing it. They joined hands and ran like wild ponies to the car, jumping in as the spatter turned into a downpour. Their cackling laughter filled the car, the humidity from their breath creating a sheen of fog on the windows.

Alex paused for a moment to drink in Ian—face blissful and boyish, glistening with raindrops. One drop, in particular, had taken up residence on the precipice of his upper lip. An unstoppable force catapulted her into his lap so that she sat astride him. He stilled while she lowered her face to his and sampled the fresh cool rain on his lips.

With the steady thrum of rain all around them, they dove into one another—mindlessly, recklessly—the cumulative grief and tragedy of the last day drowned out by their torrential desire. Sensation ruled over thought pushing everything out of Alex's mind except for a mouth, hot with desire, diving into her own, and hands grappling for bare skin. Deft fingers unbuttoned her shirt, and she shrugged it off carelessly as he buried his damp hair into her chest, pushing aside her silky pink bra with his teeth and finding her nipples.

A ding on her phone interrupted her salacious daydream, jerking her back to the present and the cramped corner of the medical school library where she was wedged, studying for her in-training exam. It was Tim.

*Don't be late for fellowship meeting.*

Alex glanced at the clock, scooped up her study materials, and bolted to the door in a cadence that rivaled an Olympic athlete—all to avoid the wrath of one terrifying Dr. Gibson.

The monthly meeting between the critical care trainees and Dr. Gibson, who was in charge of the fellowship program, usually devolved into a painful dissection of their performance. Beth typically sat with hands clasped and gave tight nods in response to her feedback while Tim made colorful, witty comments that substantially lightened the mood. Afterward, they traditionally drowned their cumulative sorrows in a beer at the bar within closest range to the hospital—Baby Blue's—the irony of which was not lost on any of them.

After the meeting, they all rose as a unit, preparing to trek down the street together. An expressionless Dr. Gibson remained in place.

"Alexandra, can I speak with you?" It was far from a request.

"I'll catch up with you," Alex called to Tim and Beth, waving them down the hallway. She took the chair opposite Dr. Gibson's throne and decided it was best to remain quiet until spoken to.

"What are your plans?"

Alex was taken aback with the vagueness of the question. *Today, next year, with her career, life, all the above?*

"I'm not sure what you mean."

"Where do you see yourself in five years?" She clasped her hands and settled her elbows on the table.

"Oh. Probably working in a large children's hospital that gives me opportunities to also work internationally."

"So, you want to devote your life to this profession?"

Alex paused before she spoke. "That was always my plan."

The eyes fixed on Alex remained emotionless, muddy brown pools. "You have been different lately. Less invested. Distracted."

An uncomfortable flush started in Alex's cheeks. "I'm sorry," she stammered. "I will get back on track."

A pause ensued, pregnant with some sort of pre-epiphany.

"Some people," Gibson articulated, "will tell you that you can have it all—successful career, marriage, children, social life. That's a lie. You can't. There is always a sacrifice. Only you can decide what that sacrifice will be."

Alex swallowed hard. "Do you wish you had chosen differently?"

Dr. Gibson sat back into her chair, pressing her hands into the table, eyes distant, focused on her own life's path.

"You can love this job all you want, but it will not love you back. There will be days of immense suffering, no gratitude, exhaustion in every possible way. But very few people in the world can save a child from the brink of death, and that feeling is irreplaceable. So, no, I wouldn't change a thing."

Tim's hand flew into the air when Alex entered Baby Blue's, and she made her way to the three-person high-top table, squeezing in between him and Beth.

"I hope you ordered me an obnoxiously large beer and a plate of something that goes with ranch dressing," she grumbled, dropping her bag underneath the table.

Tim winked and took a swig of his Shiner. "Ray is all over it."

Ray owned Baby Blue's and had intended to give the east coast something special when he opened an authentic Texas honky-tonk right in the middle of West Philadelphia, complete with neon signs and nightly live music. Once Ray had discovered Alex was a real live

Texan, he elevated her to VIP status, meaning that she and her friends always had a table and served as the official taste testers of all new dishes on the menu.

"What was that all about?" Tim asked as soon as Alex's mouth was full of fried pickle slice dipped in a copious amount of ranch.

Taking a long pull of her beer, she shrugged. "I think in her own way, she was trying to give me life advice."

Although subtle, Alex noticed a look pass between Beth and Tim. *When had those two become chummy?* Beth eyed her sharply.

"What kind of advice?"

Alex swallowed the delectable fried concoction before she answered, "That I can't have everything, and I need to decide which direction my life is going."

"How did she come up with that?" Tim asked.

"She said I have been distracted...which is ridiculous. I've been working my ass off."

Alex picked at the breading on her next pickle target as Beth piped up. "You have...on both accounts."

"What are you talking about?" Alex challenged.

"You're not...*present* like you used to be. Your head is somewhere else, and when it's not, you are glued to your phone."

Ian had been texting her a lot at work lately.

"So, I'm not allowed to have a life outside the hospital—to be happy about something that has nothing to do with which kid left the ICU." Alex curled her hand into a defensive fist and flicked her gaze over at Tim, who was spinning his beer bottle in his hand.

He sighed. "Sure you do, Alex."

"And am I just as good a doctor?"

"Well " Beth started, but Tim cut her off

"Of course you are," he said resolutely. "You just haven't been the Alex we know."

A wave of emotion vaulted her off the stool. "Maybe you don't know me as well as you thought," she said coolly before marching straight out the door into the autumn chill.

She stalked into the night, fueled by a variety of emotions that flashed between anger and a finite dread that there was truth to what Beth had said. Soon she was bathed in the soft glow of Rittenhouse Square, having passed her apartment building some time ago. Her anger subsided, and, in its place, an uncomfortable disconcertment settled like a stone into the pit of her stomach. Absentmindedly, she walked on, turning down a familiar street with an even more familiar shadowy corner that probably still had the imprint of her posterior. She fumbled in her purse for her phone and called Ian.

"Hi," he mumbled sleepily, unaccustomed to such an early rousing.

"Hi," Alex stammered. "I'm sorry for waking you."

"I was," he yawned loudly, "just about to get up. Lydia has every minute of my life scheduled right now."

"No rest for the deviant turned humanitarian." Alex joked.

"Mmmhhmm…how was your day?"

"Awful."

"Want to talk about it?"

"Not really."

"If I was there, I could make you forget all about it."

"Oh really? And how would you do that?"

"Undress you agonizingly slowly while I kissed every bare patch of skin until you screamed so loud your little patients would need earmuffs." She could hear him chuckling into his pillow, and she smiled, the travails of her day all but forgotten.

"I'm standing in front of your favorite place in Philadelphia," she murmured into the receiver.

"Ooh…the secret corner of east coast erotica."

"You are terrible."

"I know. I can't wait to show you the ones in London."

"I miss you. New Year's seems so far away."

"I'll make it worth the wait," he said seductively.

"I know you will."


That night Alex snuggled into her bed pillows underneath her favorite quilt. It was bitingly cold in her apartment despite the heat being on full blast. She tucked herself in up to her chin and, before sleep claimed her, she let her mind wander back in time to a solitary car on a rainy cliffside on the west coast.

At one point in their conquest of each other's bodies, they had paused, eyes meeting, the blue hues of sky and ocean, allowing access to the epicenter of each other's souls. They had made love in the driver's seat of Ian's rental in the middle of a tumultuous rainstorm—slowly and deliberately—like one would massage an aching muscle or tend to a wound.

Alex fell asleep with the sound of pattering rain in her ears and the imprint of Ian's hands searing her lower back. The freezing room didn't quite bother her that night.

The holiday season had officially begun, and with it, a sense of renewal for everyone at the hospital who was promised a short but restorative vacation. Alex had been home to celebrate Thanksgiving with her mom every single year, except for this year, when she had switched her schedule with Tim so she could go to London for New Year's. Instead of tender bits turkey and creamy mashed potatoes decorated with a side of chunky homemade cranberry sauce, she was perched in front of her laptop with a pile of salad topped with hunks of feta and grilled chicken from Greek Lady takeout.

"I can't believe you have to work so much. No chance of coming home for Christmas, either?" lamented Janie Wilde.

Alex watched the lines in her mother's face deepen on her laptop screen as she dangled a fork over her cornbread stuffing.

"You know frowning is bad for you. I'm going to have to get you a gift card for Botox this Christmas," teased Alex. Her mom squinted and wrinkled her nose.

"Peter doesn't seem to mind my beauty lines," she retorted.

"How is Peter?"

Her mom had been seeing a gentleman from a nearby small town, a technician for the local power company who she had coincidentally known casually during her high school years.

"Just peachy. He's coming over later after he finishes getting Mrs. Robbins' porchlight working. Then we may go out dancing tomorrow." Country dancing at the local legitimate honky-tonk establishment was one of their favorite pastimes.

"Sounds fun, mom. I really wish I was there."

"After you sent me a picture of Ian, I understand why you aren't. When do I get to meet this guy, by the way?"

"Soon. I promise."

Alex took a large bite of feta cheese and let the tang spread through her taste buds. While she was chewing, her mom then launched into a detailed review of the latest town scandals, including who was seen joyriding together down Main street and which businesses were likely going to close. Nothing lasted long in Cole's Church. Alex had seen one tiny building on a corner of the only thoroughfare morph from a noodle restaurant to a laundromat to a pizza parlor. The pizza parlor had thrived so far, thanks to the patronage of the teenagers in town.

Alex heard frantic barking in the background as two Labrador retrievers burst through the screen door off the kitchen leading to the back yard, tails wagging so hard that their ears were shaking. A pair of black noses immediately shot to the ground in search of discarded tidbits.

"Hank and Delilah look enormous."

Janie laughed in her typical high pitched tinkly fashion. "They better stop growing soon, or else I am going to need a bigger house."

The pups, one jet black and the other a silvery blonde, had been rescued by Alex's mom from the side of the highway where someone had abandoned them. Their method of obtaining pets was apparently familial.

Janie, thinking similarly, asked, "How's McCartney? I bet you miss him. When can you bring him over?"

A vision of her gangly rust-colored companion tugged Alex's heart. "I do miss him, but I want to figure out what I'm doing after graduation first. He's happy with Rox right now."

She was intentionally vague regarding her plans. By the end of next May, she would be a free woman, and then what? For the first time in her life, there were external variables to consider, and she actually didn't know. She had boarded a train of academia that had started in kindergarten and continued to chug along until she was practically thirty—which she would be in a few short weeks. It was impossible to imagine a life that didn't involve waiting for the next station of training to come along. Now that she was about to disembark for good, she felt terrified.

"I should probably go, mom. I need to get ready for work." She was working the next several night shifts, the last of which extended into a reverse twenty-four where she worked all night then stayed all day in the hospital. It was going to be brutal.

"Bye, sweetie. Call me soon. I love y—" The screen froze, filled with her mom's face mouthing "you."

The one great thing about working overnight was the reward of calling Ian first thing in the morning while both of them were decently awake. After a haphazard night hopping from bedside to bedside, making adjustments in ventilator settings and titrating sedative drips, putting her stethoscope on little chests and palpating tiny abdomens, Alex gratefully flopped onto her bed still fully clothed in her scrubs and scrolled down her contact list to Ian. He answered on the third ring.

"Good day sunshine. How's nocturnality treating you?"

"Oh…terrible," Alex groaned dramatically. "My body rejects working nights, and how do you even know that word?"

"Nocturnality? I might just have a minor in English. From Cambridge."

"Bravo. What was your major? Women's studies?" Alex stifled a laugh into her pillow.

"No—I taught that course."

She could just imagine his narrowed gaze and sideways grin through the phone. "You know what they say—those that can't do…."

"Okay punchy, I actually majored in land economy. It's a very sexy subject."

"Ooh…tell me more. Did you know that discussions of local resource utilization really turn me on?"

"Somehow, I actually think they do," teased Ian.

He launched into a monologue about his day so far—how Lydia was cracking the proverbial whip over his head to finish reviewing grant proposals and how Rahul, recovered from his broken heart and disengagement, had started dating bubbly, happy-go-lucky Rachel, even though no one was supposed to know about it.

"They text each other constantly and then look up to make sure no one is watching them share googly eyes, which everyone is, of course," he said with mock exasperation. "Nic is in the throes of football right now—either football or Roxanne—I can't decide which one takes more of his time."

"You sound lonely."

"I just wish you were here. In my bed, mostly." He tried to play it off as a casual comment, but Alex could sense the wistfulness in his tone.

"I will be soon, but I have to go, Ian." She glanced at her clock—

it was already midmorning. "I have a twenty-four-hour shift starting tonight."

"I have a twenty-four-hour shift waiting for you in London, but I promise mine will be a lot more fun."

She giggled, and they exchanged flirty phone foreplay for a few more minutes before Alex glanced at the clock again.

"Ian, I have to get some sleep. I am literally going to keel over tonight!"

"Okay. Dream of me."

"I always do."


That evening, Alex schlepped to work in the dark amidst the biting cold of an invading east coast winter and was busy unwrapping herself from her outer layers when she heard a soft, timid knock on the office door.

"Oh, hello," said a surprised voice when Alex opened the door. It was one of the new nurses who had just started working ICU. She was petite and slim with short dark hair and large brown doe-like eyes framed by elegant black lashes. Alex thought she remembered her name as Kim.

"Did you need me?" Alex asked, confused.

"No...I...uh..." she fidgeted uncomfortably. "I was just hoping Tim was here."

"Oh," said Alex, driving some clarity from the situation. "He is home with his family in Georgia, but he'll be back Monday."

She looked mildly defeated, so Alex continued her explanation. "He was supposed to be here, but he was kind enough to switch holidays with me."

"Okay. I'll see you later, Dr. Wilde."

She scurried down in the hall in her pink scrub pants and clingy black t-shirt, leaving Alex no doubt about the purpose of her late-night visit to their office. *How scandalous.* She would have to give Tim the third degree when he was back from vacation. Although the situation slightly vexed her, she really was happy for her friend. He deserved something fun in his life.

Although their relationship had always been platonic, she knew deep down that Tim had taken opportunities to test the waters, fishing for something more, but Alex had never bitten. Alex knew that she had previously been the "something fun", but lately, between the hospital and Ian, she hadn't had time or energy for anything else—even Tim. No wonder he had seemed distant lately. She made a one-sided promise to spend some time with him once things settled down.

Holiday weekends were always hectic times in the ICU, and this one was no exception. Alex had little time to ponder anything at all while answering what seemed like an endless string of phone calls from nurses, the emergency room staff, and various outside hospitals trying to transfer sick children in the middle of the night.

When the weather turned cold, and families lit up their fireplaces for warmth, the asthmatic kids came in struggling to breathe. When Thanksgiving feasts were being consumed all over the city, the diabetic kids came in with a metabolic crisis. When families were traveling to and from their loved one's homes, car accidents ensued, and injured children had to be admitted to the ICU.

Alex had expected their ICU census to increase over the weekend, but they were nearing capacity. By the time the sun rose the next morning, she had admitted twelve kids to their thirty-six bed ICU, and all twelve had required quite a bit of attention to achieve stabilization. Her fatigue sunk deep into her bones until she felt like her muscles were straining against a titanium skeleton with each motion.

Her eyes were blurry from staring at various computer screens and patient monitors, and every few minutes, she felt the telltale flutter in her chest of a premature ventricular contraction—the consequence of adrenaline and massive amounts of caffeine. Splashing some cold water over her face helped revive her, and she momentarily glanced at her string of unanswered texts from Ian and Rox that would have to wait until after rounds.

"Dr. Wilde?" Kim practically collided with her as she was leaving the ladies' room.

"Hi, what's going on?" She could already feel the dread gnawing at her probably macerated intestinal lining.

"I already gave sign-out to dayshift, but my patient isn't looking very good. Can you go check on him?"

Her patient, if Alex remembered correctly, was a teenage male who was sent to the ICU for continuous breathing treatments because of out of control asthma.

"I'd be happy to," said Alex as she willed her body in the direction of his room with all of her remaining self-discipline.

Her brain immediately switched back into high gear as she stepped into the doorway and saw that he was bent over, hands atop his knees, chest heaving with each forced exhalation.

"I need epinephrine now…in a syringe…in anything…I don't care."

Alex pulled her hair up into a sloppy bun and put her stethoscope on his almost silent chest. No air movement whatsoever.

"I also need a bi-pap machine and mask, and someone help me get him back into bed."

She knew that she was barking orders at the bedside staff, but she didn't have the time or emotional bandwidth for niceties at the moment. The respiratory therapist transitioned his oxygen delivery to bi-pap so that he received added airway pressure with each breath. Someone palmed Alex a syringe of epinephrine like a baton in a relay race, and she screwed it into his IV.

Epinephrine, given straight into an IV, was an excellent bronchodilator and, if it worked, would substantially improve his breathing. She pushed a small amount into his bloodstream and listened attentively to his chest. She depressed the plunger a little more and then just a micrometer more, and finally, she could hear life-giving air moving in and out of his lungs. Eyes that were once tightly closed fluttered open and stared at Alex, small brown almonds that manifested a subsiding fear now that he could breathe again.

"Let's start a drip," she said curtly. "I'll grab a kit to place a central line."

Central lines were basically obnoxiously large catheters placed in the body's largest vessels so that necessary medications could be administered, and labs could be taken at any time. Alex turned to the frightened teenager.

"I'm going to give you some medicine to make you sleepy and then put a special catheter in your groin, okay?"

He nodded solemnly in understanding.

"And can someone find his parents?" she called out into the crowd.

Donned in her sterile attire, Alex leaned over the boy's outstretched leg and expertly popped a needle into his femoral vein. A gush of violaceous venous blood filled the syringe, and she twisted it off and slid the guidewire into the vessel and the needle out. The wire served as a placeholder for where the catheter would go. She passed the dilator over the wire to make a tract through the skin and then loaded the catheter onto the wire. It took a few attempts since her hands were trembling from the six Diet Cokes she had consumed throughout the night. Fitting the wire into the tiny end hole of the catheter was like threading a needle.

"Finally," she muttered to herself and slid the catheter onto the wire. Excited at her success, Alex continued pushing the catheter in until it was buried to the hub in the boy's groin. Then she realized that, in her haste, she had forgotten to pull out the wire as she was pushing in the catheter, and the glinting silvery piece of spaghetti was gone.

# TWENTY-TWO

"I know better. It's one of the first things you learn when you are putting in central lines."

Alex paced around the office like a wild animal while Tim listened, patiently stationed at his desk. He tried to soothe her.

"Alex, it happens. I'm surprised it hasn't happened to me."

"I have never ever not controlled the end of the wire. You know I had to call interventional cardiology to come and take him to the cath lab to remove it and thank God it hadn't gotten very far—only his right atrium," she said sarcastically, flopping down into a chair and putting her head in her hands.

"You are just human, Alex. Mistakes happen."

"Well, they're not supposed to...not now...not ever."

She felt a warm, steady arm around her, and when it was removed, it had a large wet spot on the sleeve.


Over the next few weeks, Philadelphia's skyline turned gray and overcast, like a living, moving black and white photograph that contrasted with the suspended strands of twinkly lights and cheerful jewel-toned decorations filling the hospital hallways. The holiday spirit spread like sugary frosting on a warm cookie and was gobbled up by all, including the staff, who, in addition to their regular duties, tried to make every day extra-special for the little ones who could not go home for Christmas.

This was Alex's favorite time of year, but she had spent little time reveling in the frivolity. A renewed sense of purposeful perfection had grown from the guilt of her mishap with the central line wire and had magnified her work ethic. As Ian had once joked, she truly felt like a vampire. Not one drop of sun had touched her face since early fall.

Every conversation with Ian had been cut short these days as she scurried to and from the hospital and her text replies became even shorter—*I will* or *I am* or *Me too*. And so here she sat, head reclined onto the back of her office chair, unable to muster enough momentum to push herself up to a stand much less trudge home in the freshly fallen snow.

She hadn't even told Ian that today was her birthday. Her mom had called earlier, and she listened to the voicemail again.

"Happy birthday, honey! December 13 is my favorite day of the year because it brought me you!" Then a rendition of "Happy Birthday" ensued in her mom's high-pitched voice amid a symphony of barking in the background.

A sigh escaped her lips. She was officially thirty. Did that mean it was time to figure out what to do with the rest of her life? Ironically, her friends back home had been living the "rest of their lives" for a while now. Medicine seemed to put all doctors in a state of arrested development. They cycled through the subsequent phases of training like high school on a repetitive loop—only they worked exponentially harder in a high stakes game of patient care, setting aside conventional pursuits like kids and mortgages and book clubs.

Her musings in the deathly quiet were interrupted by Tim pushing open the door of the office and scaring her half to death.

Without moving, Alex chastised him. "You almost killed me from fright...really...I think I just had a run of V-tach."

"At least I brought you an excellent final meal." He held up a champagne bottle, the gold foil already peeled away from the top, and a small brown box with a transparent lid revealing a large mound covered in dark chocolate ganache.

"Is that what I think it is?" Alex straightened abruptly and reached for the box.

Tim clutched it to his chest. "No way, birthday girl. If you want the goods, you have to follow me."

He led her through an unlit portion of the hospital converted to offices when the new wing was built. They entered a door labeled "maintenance", revealing a staircase that rose into blackness.

"It would have been easier just to off me quickly," she joked.

"You seem to be doing a good enough job of that yourself," he replied, using his giraffe legs to take the stairs two at a time.

Alex didn't have the will to argue. He had set up a blanket on the roof of the old wing of the hospital lit by the neon glow of the mega-sized Children's Hospital of Philadelphia sign and a view of the downtown cityscape. She collapsed onto the blanket and even the rock-hard surface supporting her backside was preferable to being upright.

"What makes you think I have suicidal ideations?" she muttered.

"You are exhausted, Alex. When is the last time you went home for more than just a few hours of sleep?"

"I'm just taking everyone's advice. Avoid distractions. Put my entire self into our job. I am practicing selfless commitment."

"Well, tonight, you are officially off the clock."

She heard the satisfying pop of a champagne cork and watched Tim frown in bewilderment before handing her the champagne bottle.

"I forgot the cups," he said sheepishly.

Alex laughed, her first authentic one in a few weeks, and they passed the bottle back and forth, sharing bits of gossip and venting about work between swigs. Alex dove into the decadence in the brown box, licking every bit from her fork before diving in again.

"I am so glad you remembered forks. Otherwise, I might have had to go face first into this thing."

It was her favorite dessert—a peanut butter mousse concoction dipped in dark chocolate ganache served with toasted bananas and whipped cream. Every bit of her felt lighter, like her burdens of granite had temporarily transformed into feathers. She laughed louder than she had in weeks and let the champagne fizz through her bloodstream.

"So, Tim, what's up with you and Kim?"

The dark couldn't hide the surprise crossing his face. "How did you hear about that?"

"She came to the office one night looking for you when I was on call."

He screwed up his face as he emptied the last drops from the bottle into his mouth.

"Hey, I'm not judging. She's cute and seems nice. I'm happy for you."

"We've been out a few times. She's a nice girl just—"

"Just what?"

He sighed, "Not tonight, Alex. How's Ian?"

She slapped herself on the forehead in response. "I was supposed to call him today, and I totally forgot," she squeaked and then began to laugh hysterically, reaching the point of intoxication where everything was suddenly funny.

Between the alcohol and the sugar rush mixed with a generous amount of chronic fatigue, Alex's emotions waxed into various extremes on the walk back to her apartment with Tim guiding her elbow.

"I don't know what I'm doing with Ian or after graduation or with my life? Do I have to decide everything right now?"

She clutched his arm dramatically and felt his fingers tighten over hers.

"You do...just not tonight." He paused on the sidewalk. They were at her apartment building. "Goodnight, Alex," he said, unwinding his arm from around her.

She took one shaky step up the short concrete flight of steps to her building then another until she and Tim were eye level.

"Thank you for an excellent birthday."

"My pleasure, Alex."

She heard him muttering to himself as she turned and trudged up the remaining steps.

Upon entering her apartment, she was immediately overwhelmed by an exquisite fragrance permeating her space and discovered a giant bouquet of blush pink, burgundy, and cream peonies in a crystal vase. Artfully arranged on her coffee table, the bouquet supported a pink envelope labeled *Alex*. Her heart squeezed as if caught in a vise as she opened the card.

*I forgive you for not telling me it was your birthday. Ian*

She glanced at her phone. It was early for Ian, but she dialed anyway.

"Hi," he murmured.

"Hi. I love the flowers. They're lovely."

"I missed your birthday." He sounded forlorn.

"Luckily, it's my birthday for—" She glanced at her phone. "One more minute. Happy birthday to me!" The words came out unintentionally shrill.

"Are you drunk?"

"Technically…yes. That would be my official diagnosis."

"Good for you. I just wish I was there to take advantage of drunk Alex. I bet she's great in bed."

Alex snickered into the phone. "I'll make sure I bring her to London."

"What did you do tonight?"

"I was practically falling asleep in the office, and Tim dragged me up to the hospital roof for dessert and champagne. I think I drank way more than my half of the bottle."

There was a palpable silence over the phone.

"Oh."

"He's just a friend, Ian. There is zero reason you need to be jealous."

"I don't do jealous Alex, but next time you see him, make sure you tell Casanova I said well-played."


Alex slept in luxuriously late the next day. Visible through one half-open lid, the clock by her bed read 7:30 a.m. She awoke with only a minor headache and a slightly more than minor heartache after last night's birthday shenanigans. She hadn't meant to hurt Ian, but she had really needed some fun and some time to reconnect with her friend. Tim was right. She was utterly exhausted in every way and not all of it was because of work.

Trying to maintain a transcontinental relationship, finish up her research from Botswana, and figure out her next steps in life, not to mention be a decent daughter and friend, had squeezed every ounce of physical and emotional energy she possessed. At the end of the day, it felt like a chore to even brush her own teeth. She threw back her quilt and rolled out of bed on her one day free from hospital duties until she left for New Year's in London. Making a spontaneous decision, she dressed warmly in layers and her heaviest down coat and just made the 9 a.m. bullet train to New York City.

Alex loved the lively bustle of NYC, and she jostled for a tiny spot on the sidewalk in front of the Macy's window to catch a glimpse of the mechanized dolls playacting various Christmas scenes. Actual physical separation from the tiny microcosm she usually inhabited felt indulgent and intensely therapeutic. She purchased a paper cone of warm sugared nuts in Central Park and then wandered the trails like a typical tourist, admiring the horse-drawn carriages and sketch artists furiously working despite the cold. While watching the bumbling ice skaters careen around the tree at Rockefeller center, she tried Ian but disappointingly got his voicemail. She sent a text instead.

*Quick trip to NYC for the day. I wish you were here. Miss you.*

A few minutes later, her phone buzzed, and Alex answered, breathless and excited, "Hello!"

"Dr. Alex," crooned a familiar, rich-sounding voice.

"Dr. K, it's wonderful to hear your voice! How are things at PM?"

"The same but not the same…you know how it goes." He laughed quickly and deeply. "I will not take much of your time. I know you must be a very busy woman these days."

"I'm actually off today, so this is a great time." She smiled and took a seat on a nearby bench.

"The grant money from the Devall foundation will be coming to us starting in the spring."

"That's absolutely wonderful," Alex gushed.

"It is. It is. The amount is much more than we ever anticipated—enough to pay the salary of a top-notch ICU doctor to work in our midst."

Alex scooted to the edge of the bench, dangling on its precipice in anticipation.

"We would be honored if you would consider taking a position here with us at Princess Marina," he concluded. "After your graduation, of course."

Alex licked her lips with the cotton swab that was her tongue. "I want to say yes today, but I should probably take some time to think about it. Would that be acceptable?"

"Of course," he boomed, "take all the time you need. We will talk again soon." Then he was gone, like a panther fading into the inky darkness of an African night.

Armed with shopping bags full of treasures, Alex entered her frigid apartment, puffing out breath that crystallized in the air and cranked up her heat to high—not that it would make a difference. She collapsed on the couch and tried Ian again with no answer, but a text did flash across her screen.

*At a charity event. Will call you later. Hope you had fun today*

*I did. Have fun donating.*

She fell asleep on her couch, wrapped in her heavy down coat with the scent of peonies wafting through her dreams. She awoke much later and checked her phone for missed calls before she transferred to her bed. There were none.

The week of Christmas at a children's hospital was filled to capacity with musical acts and celebrity visits and finally, the biggest celebrity of them all—Santa Claus, who *ho ho ho'ed* his way through all of the wards on Christmas eve to hand out presents to every single child and a few of the luckier staff. Alex pushed a headband of blinking Christmas lights across her hairline and stood with a group of nurses watching the kids bounce up and down in their beds and extend greedy hands that were rewarded with toys. Alex ticked her fingers. Three twenty-four-hour shifts until she boarded her British Airways flight. She knew exactly what she wanted for Christmas, and it was definitely not in Santa's plush red bag.

If she allowed a moment for her submerged emotions to surface, she entered a state of yearning for any kind of connection with Ian. After her birthday, he had let the distance between them widen and dialed back his previous dogged pursuit of her. They continued to talk every few days and send "checking in" texts, but the tone had changed to one that was looser and more superficial as he tread more carefully. Alex knew it was mostly her fault. She only had time for one boyfriend, and right now, that boyfriend's name was critical care medicine.

Gibson's words of wisdom, if one could call them that, played on a constant loop in her head like the little train chugging around the tree in the hospital foyer. She needed to make some decisions but putting them off until after the holidays was her Christmas gift to herself this year.

Ian traditionally spent Christmas day at his father's house. It was just the two of them this year since his grandfather had passed last February, and Alex had promised to Skype during dinner and officially meet Mr. Devall senior, albeit virtually.

Alex made another round through the ICU where the children were unusually quiet and stopped by the nurses' break room to share in a cranberry juice toast when the clock struck midnight. They had only one admission during the night, and thankfully none of the kids dramatically worsened. She had even made enough progress to prepare a few of them for removal of their breathing tubes.

By the time she signed out to Beth, who was alternating shifts with her, she felt the first glimpses of hope for the end of her holiday stretch and even hummed a few bars of "Have yourself a Merry Little Christmas" on the walk back to her apartment. With freshly washed hair and her body wrapped in softest blue cashmere, Alex nestled into her bed, visions of a shirtless Ian dancing in her head.

Trying to awake from the depths of slumber was like swimming up from the bottom of a dark ocean. Alex kept kicking toward the surface, away from something dark and sinister that threatened to pull her down toward the murky bottom. She kicked furiously, her head breaking the surface, and her eyes popping open to complete disorientation. Everything was dark. *Was this a dream?*

She grappled for her phone that read 7:30 p.m. in large white numerals. She was late—really late. As she pulled on her scrubs with superhero-like speed, she scrolled through her gargantuan list of missed calls—her mom, Rox, four from Ian, and a snarky text from Beth.

*Are you planning on letting me go home at all on Christmas?*

Alex audibly groaned and raced out the door in nothing but a sweatshirt over her scrubs.

Once a disgruntled Beth had been relieved, and Alex's adrenaline rush had peaked and then dipped, she settled into the office to review labs and call Ian. As it rang, she silently pleaded with him to answer.

"Merry Christmas," he mumbled sleepily.

"Merry Christmas," she said softly. "I'm sorry I missed dinner. I overslept and was really late to work, and I am definitely on Beth's naughty list now if I wasn't before."

She knew she was prattling out of guilt and stopped in mid-thought, waiting on a response.

"I have a list with your name right at the top."

"Nice or naughty?"

He paused before answering, his characteristic wit blunted at the moment.

"I haven't decided yet."

She could hear the disappointment in his exhaled breath.

"But I prefer you on the naughty list." And he was back to the perpetual flirt that she knew.

"How was dinner with your dad?"

"Traditional with the most terrible British dishes you've ever heard of. Did you know Yorkshire pudding isn't even pudding?"

"Did Santa bring you anything good this year?"

"Not yet."

Her phone vibrated three times in quick succession.

"I have to go Ian. The emergency room is calling."

"Goodnight, Alex." He ended the call before she could reply.

The night passed quickly, and as Alex checked in with nurses and followed up on labs, she formulated a plan that was spontaneous and out of character and wildly exciting. Ian needed reaffirmation of her feelings. She needed a bold experience that separated her from work, both physically and mentally, and allowed her some time to transition into just a girlfriend. As soon as the time was halfway reasonable for a London wake up call, she tapped Rox's picture on her phone.

"Hello dear, just a moment." She could imagine her friend untangling herself from one very long-legged Arsenal footballer.

"Rox, I have a crazy idea, and I need your help."

"We will be landing at London Heathrow in approximately thirty minutes. Please fasten your seatbelts and place your tray tables upright."

Alex clutched her carry-on excitedly and fussed with the lion pendant that had become a wardrobe staple. As luck and Christmas wishes would have it, she had snagged the last flight to London out of Philadelphia, taking the red-eye over the Atlantic and planning to arrive a full day earlier than expected.

When she spied Rox's curvy frame leaning over the guardrail into the arrival zone, she broke into a semi-jog until she had collided straight into her best friend's bosom.

"I can't breathe, Rox," she squeaked, her voice muffled by the silky fabric covering her face.

Not one to waste a second of precious time, Rox grabbed her suitcase in one hand and interlocked Alex's fingers in her other.

"Come on—phase one starts now."


"I want to look glamourous hot…not slutty American hot," said Alex as she rotated in front of the trifold glass mirror in the Harrod's dressing room. "You can practically see my underwear when I lean over."

"Rule number one—no leaning over. Rule number two—no one can see your underwear if you aren't wearing any." Rox snickered and took a delicate swallow of her rosé champagne.

Alex rolled her eyes, and then emotion gripped her.

"I've missed you. Things haven't been easy lately," she volunteered.

"Nothing worthwhile is ever easy, my dear."

"Speaking of worthwhile, how's Nic?"

"Dreamy…complicated. We are figuring it out." Her eyes still sparkled when she spoke of him, which Alex took as a good sign.

"What about you? Five more months and the timer goes *ding*. Time to pop out of the oven and into the real world."

Alex wrinkled her nose. "I know I have to get a real job and be in charge like a responsible, contributing adult."

"Any thoughts?"

"Dr. K offered me a job at PM."

Rox nodded, unsurprised by the news.

"And?" She took another sip from her disposable flute.

"I told him I would think about it, but I would love to work there. It's always been my dream."

Rox said nothing, just eyed her friend speculatively and passed her another dress to try. "This is the one," she said reassuringly.

It turned out that it was—a long-sleeved black mini dress with every square inch covered in sequins. Ian was going to love it.

The sun weighed down the western sky, and Alex yawned with each step, her purchases banging her legs as they walked.

"If I don't make it to Ian's soon, I'm going to lie down on a park bench and wake up covered in newspapers."

"Just one more stop. We have time. Nic took him out to dinner at a pub."

They strolled through a glitzy part of London with outdoor shops along a cobblestone street with potted trees and white holiday lights marking their path. Rox pulled Alex's hand into a gold-framed glass door, the entryway to a shop with a plush burgundy carpet and velvet curtained alcoves held closed by gold tassels. Every wall, floor to ceiling, was lined with a selection of lingerie that would surely make her worthy of the naughty list.

"Welcome to Agent Provocateur," said a petite girl with a French accent dressed in a pink buttoned up lab coat.

Alex's mouth opened and then closed as her eyes drifted over the silk straps and intricate French lace in a myriad of colors from blush to ebony to fuchsia.

"I'm Roxanne Clarke. I have an order to pick up." The young girl handed Rox a pink box secured with a black ribbon, which Rox thrust into Alex's arms. "Merry Christmas, dear."


An hour later, Alex was showered and draped in a clean towel, excruciatingly tired but refreshed nonetheless. Rox had let her into Ian's house in Queen's gate across from Hyde Park, an architecturally classic four-story stone building bordered by a little black wrought iron gate. The interior was spotlessly clean with rich oak floors and upholstered leather furniture that looked like it had been purchased in Africa. There was even a full zebra hide rug stretched out in front of a giant limestone fireplace.

Feeling very much like an intruder, Alex had climbed the stairs to Ian's bedroom—a massive room with one wall of oversized windows partially covered with heavy silk drapes and a king-sized bed with an elegantly carved mahogany headboard. Rox lounged in a stretched animal hide chair in the corner flipping through a magazine, her feet on a leather ottoman while Alex rifled through the contents of her pink box—a sultry black lingerie set that would make a burlesque troupe blush. She lifted out each item one by one, rubbing the delicate French lace between her fingers, noting the purposeful windows in the fabric where her bare lady parts might peep through.

"What does this do, Rox?" she asked, holding up two bits of lace held together by satin straps.

"Those are the panties," Rox said, avoiding Alex's stare and biting her lip to stifle a laugh.

"But there's no…there's no bottom." She looked at Rox quizzically through the oval-shaped space in the fabric.

"I know. It's called the *ouvert*—French for open. Make sure Ian sends me a thank you card."

Alex, bubbling over with embarrassment and with absolutely no words whatsoever, stuffed the outfit back into the box. Rox abruptly stood and grabbed her handbag to check her phone.

"I better get going. Nic is going to drop Ian off soon. See you tomorrow, love."

Alex hugged her fiercely and watched her scamper down the stairs. She quickly shrugged on the white button-down Rox had snagged for her from Ian's closet and a pair of red silk panties she had picked up at Victoria's Secret in New York. Alex crawled into the chair that Rox had just vacated, crossing her legs suggestively on the ottoman and letting her still damp hair tumble in messy layers over her chest and shoulders. And then she waited.

# TWENTY-THREE

The first thing Alex felt when she awoke next to Ian in his giant-sized bed was a genuine soreness in her inner thighs that was strangely comforting. It reminded her that last night had not been a dream and instead was the consequence of their raucous lovemaking and intimate reconnection on every level. She could feel a warm blush christening her features as she lay on her stomach, dressed in nothing but morning sunshine. Her eyelids, as heavy as lead weights, fell closed, reviving visions from the night before.

Reclined in the corner armchair, she had heard the front door close, followed by heavy steps on the stairs before his face appeared in the doorway. An entire plotline happened across his features—consternation, disbelief, the dawn of realization, and unadulterated elation. Ian had said nothing, with words at least. He simply walked into the middle of the room and stared longingly at her bare legs and his white dress shirt barely covering her torso. She watched the flames ignite for a split second before his arms scooped her out of the chair. Her bare legs wound around his waist, and he kissed her as if the world was literally ending.

Alex swept the room, her gaze parallel to the floor, observing the carnage of their discarded garments, specifically her red underwear that had been ripped in half at some point, possibly with Ian's upper incisors. They had oscillated between murmuring quietly to each other and making love not so quietly until the streetlights outside snapped off in anticipation of the day to come.

Strong fingers traced her vertebrae, fingers that had explored every section of her body last night in glorious detail.

"Don't move," Ian whispered, and she felt the bed creak as he pushed up to a sitting position.

"What are you doing over there?"

"Imprinting this visual in my memory for all eternity," he said simply.

"What?" she flipped her head around and saw that he was reclined on a pile of fluffy white pillows, eyes narrowed but notably wanton and naked except for the flannel sheet barely covering his manhood.

"You," he breathed, extending one hand to brush the hair from her face, "are the most beautiful creature I've ever seen."

Alex said nothing, unwilling to break the trance-like bubble shimmering in the air around them.

"An angel...my angel."

He rubbed his thumb over her bottom lip. She opened her mouth and bit his thumb playfully.

"I'm pretty sure angels don't scream sexually charged profanity."

"I'm pretty sure mine does."

They laughed, and suddenly she wasn't near close enough to him. She sat up quickly and used her momentum to pounce on top of him like a lioness, draping the sheet over herself like a hooded cape. She was a nanosecond from kissing him when a violent knock on the front door caused the magical bubble to make a nearly audible pop.

"Who is that?"

"Pamela...the party planner...ughhh."

He manifested his bottom lip in a massive pout as he rushed to throw on some jeans and a black t-shirt. "She's here to start setting up for tonight."

"What should I do?"

He gave her a lingering kiss. "As much I would love for you to be naked in my bed all day—all tousled and sexy," he sighed and ruffled her hair. "The bathroom is right through there. Take your time getting ready and then meet me on the roof."


The London wind cut right through her as she emerged from the winding iron staircase onto Ian's rooftop terrace, and she was thankful for the aubergine wool coat hugging her from neck to knees. Not surprisingly, the view was spectacular, and the muted gray overcast sky added an element of British authenticity. In every direction, neat rows of homes with brick faces and kind windows were separated by curvilinear streets. A solitary cluster of trees met the horizon in the distance, marking the entrance to Hyde Park.

The terrace floor was planked in rich honey-colored hardwood and contained a menagerie of well-manicured potted trees situated along an iron railing. A woman with flawless coffee skin and a coiffed up-do busily jotted notes on a clipboard while simultaneously barking orders at two bewildered men stringing lights between trees. Each corner of the terrace was flanked by a pair of white tufted couches with matching tufted cubes for extra seating, clustered around a rectangular stone coffee table upon which a giant bouquet of white peonies emerged from a gold vase. Ian knew how to throw a party.

"What do you think?"

Alex felt arms encasing her from behind and warm breath on her neck.

"Not near fancy enough, but I guess it will do." She turned to let him kiss her. "Really, Ian, it's beautiful. I can't believe I'm actually here."

"Wait until you see it all shined up for tonight. Pamela is an artist."

He sent a blown kiss over to the stern-faced party planner who gesticulated while she shouted into her phone via an earpiece and received a thumbs up in return.

"I think things here are under control. Do you want to see the rest of the house?"

"I'd love to." He grabbed her hand, and she skipped joyfully down the stairs.

In her nervous haste to arrange the surprise rendezvous last night, she hadn't paid much attention to the layout and details of the house.

"We'll start in here since you've already received the grand tour of my bedroom. I've always wondered how my wall feels against a naked backside." He ducked away as her punch connected with his bicep.

The third floor contained the master bedroom and bath as well as a sparsely furnished guestroom with only a simple wooden bed and dresser. She picked up a solitary framed photograph—it was the one of Ian with his arm slung around Ryan that she had seen in

California. She held it gingerly and looked up at Ian, an unspoken question dangling in the air. He shrugged and plucked it out of her hands.

"You're the only person I've ever told about Ryan. After I got home from our trip, it seemed like he was real again. You knowing about him made him real."

She touched his cheek with her palm, coaxing his face toward hers. "You need to start healing."

"I have. I'm practically turning over a new leaf."

He smiled briefly and bit her thumb playfully as he replaced the photograph on the dresser.

The middle level comprised an open concept living room and kitchen. The living room was decked out in warm neutral tones that reminded her of Africa and contained a cognac leather sofa and chunky rough-hewn coffee table and the zebra hide rug. Alex ran her foot over it, biting her lip and wondering how zebra hair would feel on her bare backside. The walls were covered in large stretched canvases with abstract animal silhouettes that bore the signature of an artist she didn't recognize. Alex moved into the kitchen where a butcher block island sat in the center, surrounded by updated appliances that barely looked used.

"Do you cook much?" she asked, running her hand over the spotless stainless-steel refrigerator.

"I don't, but I can."

"Really?"

"I may have learned a thing or two from living in France."

"Mmm...what can you make?" Her stomach decided to growl obnoxiously right then at the mention of food.

He bowed dramatically and pulled out a barstool for her. "Welcome to *chez* Devall, mademoiselle."

While he whipped eggs and cream in a bowl, Alex sipped on a glass of orange juice, admiring the view of his backside that did not quite hold up his jeans. Every time he bent over, she caught a glimpse of the bare skin along his waistband and felt a spasm rock her lady bits.

A familiar rock tune came over the speaker system, and soon Ian was flipping omelets in a pan and crooning, "you're my angel...come and save me tonight."

"That song is a million years old," Alex teased. "But you really are doing it justice."

He slid a warm plate of cheesy omelet in her direction. "I'm an old soul." he remarked, winking and sitting down next to her.

"Mmmm…this is amazing. Like heaven on a plate."

She stuffed bite after bite of fluffy egg mixed with melted gruyere into her mouth. She scrolled through his iTunes playlists as they ate.

"Impressive taste."

She chose Revolver and hit play, and they were engulfed in the enthusiastic chords of "Good Day Sunshine".

"I love music. Ryan and I grew up with my mom blasting Beatles and Beach Boys and the Eagles on our stereo system. Once we got old enough, we claimed it and went through our various phases—the Cure, Guns N' Roses, U2. I guess listening to music always made me feel close to him even though I didn't always realize it."

Alex twirled her fork over the mostly consumed breakfast. "I know what you mean. It's like a soundtrack to your life that you keep adding to."

His eyes met hers in solidarity. "I have something else I want to show you."


The street level, where Alex had entered the night prior, boasted an elegant foyer with more art and an occasional table carved from the lower half of a tree. She hadn't realized that the foyer provided entrance to an additional room behind the stairwell.

Her breath caught when she entered the arched doorway. Every wall from floor to ceiling was filled with volumes of books. Matching leather armchairs separated by an industrial floor lamp sat in the corner of the room, and, taking center stage was a shiny black Baby Grand piano. Like a child in a toy store, she didn't know where to go first. She ran her hands along the book spines on one shelf and then touched the smooth lacquered surface of the piano.

"Do you play?" she asked Ian, mesmerized by the black beauty.

"Not well but I can get by. You?"

She was already pulling out the bench and stretching her fingers over the ivory keys.

"Let's hear it, Beethoven."

She smirked and played the first few bars of the "Moonlight

Sonata" and then switched to "Yesterday" by the Beatles and then finally, a complex rendition of "Auld Lang Syne".

Ian had settled onto the bench next to her, elbow resting on the music stand, eyes following the rhythm of Alex's fingers skating over the keys. Stopping her in mid finger flurry, he brought her left hand to his lips, tasting each fingertip before running his tongue over the inside of her wrist. Alex immediately flooded with the heat of lustful desire, warm and achingly good. Ian reached behind her knee and rotated her around to sit astride the bench facing him. Her hands that had been flying over the piano now flew over Ian—up his lean midsection and over his straining pectorals and into his hair. He pulled her onto his lap and ran his lips up her neck as his hands tightened on her bottom. She could feel the pulsing heat through his jeans and, as she tilted her head back in complete ecstasy, she heard nearby murmurings and foot shuffling.

Out of her peripheral vision, a familiar set of eyes darted her way.

"Don't stop on our account," projected a rich caramel voice coming from a certain tall footballer followed closely by Roxanne.

Ian dropped his head to his chest in defeat. "Foiled again," he whispered to her as he rose and gave her one final lingering sear to her lips.

The activity in the house grew to a solid hum over the next several hours as party preparations shifted into high gear. Rox had volunteered to supervise the food and beverage set up, and she had elicited Alex's help, mostly as an excuse for them to girl chat away from the boys.

In the time that Alex and Ian had been downstairs, clear acrylic tables and chairs for seating had been added, as well as a rolling wooden monstrosity that would serve as the bar. Alex and Rox were seated cross-legged on the ground, unpacking boxes of various libations to artfully display on the bar shelves. She watched Ian across the roof, waving to someone on the street below to come up. The entire afternoon, an endless stream of visitors and delivery men, dropping off everything from party furniture to heat lamps to an ice sculpture, had entered and exited the house like a line of marching ants with Pamela as their queen.

"Alex...Alex!"

Rox's urging snapped her attention away from Ian. She bit her lip with chagrin.

"Sorry—I am a little distracted."

"It sweeps you along like a rushing river, doesn't it?"

Alex knew she wasn't talking about her and Ian.

"You and Nic seem happy. Do you think you can make it work when you go back to Botswana?"

Rox averted her eyes and concentrated on the bottle of pinot noir in her hand. "I don't think I'm going back."

Alex involuntarily gasped. "Really? At all? What will you do?"

Alex knew her questions came as a rapid-fire and did not quite encompass what she was feeling. She had always assumed the Rox would be there if she took Dr. K's offer and moved to Gaborone full time. The concept of being there without her best friend caused a dull ache to spread down her throat.

"It's not official yet, but..." She reached down the front of her shirt and extracted a gold chain on the end of which was a sparkling diamond the size of a small egg supported by a thick metal band.

"Oh, Rox," Alex exhaled. "I have so many questions, but mostly I'm just happy for you."

Roxanne fondly caressed the ring. "We don't want the media to know yet. You are the only one that knows, other than Ian, of course, but you and I will have a proper chat soon. I am going to need you, Alex."

Alex, who had always known that she was the needier friend, felt an intense pleasure at the tide turning. "You have me," she said, reaching out to clasp hands with her kindred spirit.

As she and Rox divided and conquered to finish plying each table with a selection of wines and various glassware, Alex kept stealing glances in Nic and Ian's direction. They were chatting it up with a tall statuesque man boasting a vibrant blue overcoat, overly large sunglasses, and even larger headphones, who Alex assumed was tonight's DJ.

Nic certainly seemed perfect for Rox. He was ambitious, charismatic, easy to love, and his fame had not seemed to distort him in the least, Alex noted, as she caught him running over to help one of Pamela's workmen balance an obnoxiously large set of speakers. Ian looked over, and she gave a timid wave. He motioned for her to come over. Once she was within arms distance, he pulled her close to him and nuzzled her ear.

"It's about time to get ready. I'll meet you downstairs."

As her stomach performed a somersault, she and her immense libido descended the stairs.

Alex was towel drying her hair when Ian finally entered the master bathroom that consisted of an open shower resembling a rocky cavern complete with waterfall and a black marble vanity. Without pausing, he walked straight over and lifted her, towel and all, onto the frigid counter, shocking her skin that was still toasty warm from the shower. He put his arms around her in a relaxed embrace.

"Alone…finally. When did you learn to play piano by the way?" he asked.

"As a kid. The lady who played piano at our church taught lessons."

"You're good. Really good."

"Thanks. It was a nice escape. It still is, I guess." She studied the buttons on his shirt as if they would somehow give her a clue how to redirect the conversation.

"Any other hidden talents I don't know about?"

He moved within a breath's distance of her, eyes roving everywhere but her face.

"I," she whispered, her lips millimeters from his ear, "am a spectacular…. speller."

His shoulders shook for a moment, and then desire overtook them both, and he gave her towel a forceful tug. Her naked, still-damp skin sizzled with the smolder from those blue eyes.

"Ian!"

Nic sounded like he was right outside the bedroom door. "Ian, they need you up top for a minute."

"You…have…got…to be kidding me."

He hung his head in defeat once again, the frolicking ends of his hair tickling Alex's nipples.

"T-h-w-a-r-t-e-d," Alex muttered as he reluctantly trudged out into the hallway.


"You look gorgeous. Turn around."

Rox pushed her away, and they had a sisterly moment of reciprocal admiration in the full-length mirror in Ian's apartment-sized closet.

"You think so?" Alex rotated and examined herself from the rearview.

The dress was more risqué than she usually wore. It was covered in tiny black sequins and stopped mid-thigh but with a modest top of full-length sleeves and a high neck. It hugged her subtle curves nicely.

Rox definitely looked the part of glamourous celebrity, decked out in a gold lamé dress with a flirty skirt and deep V neck that boasted her signature jewelry. Tonight, it was a pendant dripping with diamonds resting between her visible cleavage.

"You look like a starlet. Who would guess you are a badass doctor by day? Aren't you going to be cold though?" Alex asked.

"Thank you and not in the slightest. The question is, my dear, are you?"

Alex frowned in puzzlement.

"Please tell me that my Christmas present is getting proper use underneath that fabulous dress."

"I'll never tell," she replied coquettishly, puckering her red lips in a faux kiss.

Ian's roof had transformed into a magazine-worthy New Year's Eve bash while Rox and Alex had fussed over each other's appearances downstairs. Twinkling fairy lights accented each tree and were suspended overhead, creating a canopy of stars. Accent tables and seating options surrounded a central clearing where a few couples were already jiving to the beats generated by the handsome DJ who had changed into a sparkling blue tuxedo jacket.

In every direction, bouquets of flowers seemed to grow out of the accent tables, and clusters of guests engrossed in conversation tipped back their glasses of potent elixirs. The concentration of beautiful people on the rooftop was truly impressive. Immaculately made-up ladies shone like diamonds and strutted provocatively through the rookery of gentlemen.

"Is that...?" Alex's eyes widened in shock.

"Chris Martin from Coldplay—yes, I think so," finished Rox as she tightly clasped Alex's hand.

"Ouch! I see you decided to wear the ring tonight."

Rox twisted it around so that the oval-shaped yellow diamond was kissing her palm. "I don't think anyone will notice."

"Hopefully, you are still able to lift your champagne glass. That thing must weigh as much as an actual rock."

"I'll make do," she said and made a face.

Alex noticed a hand waving at them above the crowd and connected it to Nic's colossal frame.

"Come on, bride-to-be!" Alex grabbed her arm, and they hustled over to join the fray.

Alex and Rox took up residence on one of the white tufted sofas brought in for the party and settled into glasses of Cristal that felt like a party in Alex's mouth. Nic became their official drink fetcher, and, as the night progressed and more empty glasses appeared around them, Alex alternated between laughing at Rox's dramatized stories and cuddling suggestively with a very touchy-feely Ian. As the party host, he had the duties of managing the waitstaff and greeting guests as well as catching up with friends. Alex didn't mind sitting back and letting him make the rounds. He appeared several times an hour with a new piece of gossip or a tasty hors d'oeuvre for them to try.

"Look—there's Rahul and Rachel," he said, his speech starting to slur a bit. "I guess they're out of the "inappropriate work relationship" closet." He snickered and squeezed Alex's knee. "Come on. Let's dance." He stood up in a ceremonious bow and offered her his arm.

Alex had enough rhythm to blend in and had imbibed enough alcohol to have fun doing it. She and Ian hit the dance floor during an upbeat mash up of popular club hits, and they soon were moving in sync to the music. Ian's arms rested atop her shoulders, his fingers starting to wind themselves into her hair as he moved his body side to side and ever closer to Alex. There were barely any molecules of air between them as they "dirty danced" in their corner of the dance floor, forgetting the rest of the partygoers entirely.

Ian's stark white shirt was damp with sweat, and he had relinquished his silk-lined jacket and bowtie some time ago. His inhibitions were running on low, and, just like Alex remembered him the first night they met, he was dripping sex. His face was upturned to the sky, eyes closed, as he melded with the beat of the current song. Alex put her lips next to his ear and let her words travel through her exhaled breath.

"I want you."

Sky blue eyes snapped open and were the only clue that he had heard her. Without a break in rhythm, he danced them to the periphery of the crowd so they could descend the stairs.

"Mr. Devall!"

Party planner Pamela, earpiece and all, held a steady hand up to Ian's sweaty chest. "We are going to need a few more bottles of champagne for the midnight toast."

As Alex's lascivious fantasy was thrust into limbo, she felt a soaking wave of disappointment. She observed Ian's mouth moving in response, and then they were striding purposefully once more.

"The champagne is in the cellar," Ian said as soon as they were out of earshot of the party. It was the sexiest thing Alex had ever heard.

The cellar was the most modern room in the entire house with three walls of floor-to-ceiling climate-controlled refrigerators housing Ian's extensive wine collection. Off to the side of the main room was a remnant of the original cellar housing a few wooden crates and an iron chandelier with actual candles. The walls were a smooth planked wood, and a rich, spicy aroma wafted through the small space. Alex sensed Ian standing behind her.

"This is where I keep the special occasion bourbon," he said.

"Why here?" asked Alex.

"No one would ever look in here," he whispered.

He closed what little distance existed between them and buried his face in her hair all the way to the back of her neck. Every tiny sensory nerve in Alex's skin responded with rapt attention. The heat building between her thighs became an inferno as Ian ran his fingers up the back of her black stockings underneath her sequined hem and found the embroidered French lace of her panties. His fingers trailed the silk border until the material disappeared, and they met with something warm and wanting. He froze.

"Alex?"

She heard the unspoken question carried forward by his ragged breath and quietly responded, "Happy New Year...and Happy Birthday."

He removed his hand from under her dress and pulled down the entire zipper with one motion, the dress ending up a glinting shadow on the ground and spun her around to face him. Even Alex had to admit that the entire outfit was sensational—a silk strapped bra with barely enough see-through lace to cover her breasts and a garter belt with satin trappings holding up her stockings and, of course, the *ouvert* panties, which seemed suddenly like a hilarious oxymoron.

If the flame blue eyes smoldered before, they now spontaneously combusted. He turned her back around so that she faced the wall.

"What are you doing?" she giggled.

"Checking for wings. I am now absolutely positive that you are some kind of angel."

She heard his pants drop to the floor and then felt his hands cupping her breasts and the moist heat of his midsection, warming her back. After an entire day's worth of foreplay, neither of them could wait, and it wasn't long before Alex professed her ecstasy to the wood paneling of the secret room of stashed bourbon.

They made it back to the roof just in time for the fireworks.

# TWENTY-FOUR

"How did you know it was my birthday?" Ian sat cross-legged on the bed the next morning while Alex brushed her teeth. Alex rinsed her mouth and then bit her lip. "I googled it."

"You are kidding me."

"I felt bad after mine and I didn't want to miss celebrating yours." She gave him a genuine smile. "There's a lot of information on you out there."

He smirked in his characteristic way.

"New Year's Eve is either the best or worst day to have a birthday—except maybe Christmas—and I have always tried to make it the best."

"Hence the gigantic party every year." Alex wound her hair up into a bun.

"Not every year. A few times, Nic and I traveled instead. Maybe next year, you and I could..." He let the sentence float out into mid-air.

*Next year?* Alex pondered that for a moment and nodded.

"Deal...and I get to pick where."

She was within reaching distance, and he pulled her onto the bed next to him.

"Anywhere you want—as long as I'm with you."


The lightly falling snow kept crusting up her window, making the scenic drive through London out to Heathrow seem like the inside of a snow globe.

"I've never been more grateful that this drive is so long," he said, and she felt a pang for what was to come.

Anxious to change the subject, she asked, "So how did you and

Nic meet?"

He settled back into his seat as the driver twisted through the London streets.

"College, actually."

"Nic went to Cambridge?" Alex asked, impressed.

"Only for a year before he got snatched up by Arsenal. I don't know if it counts if you never went to a single lecture." He scanned the car absentmindedly as if dredging up memories.

"You seem close—like you've shared a lot."

"We have. Too much sometimes." He gave her an enigmatic grin.

"I imagine there is a story there that I do not want to know about."

"Probably best to keep that hatchet buried."

"Rox told me about the—"

"Engagement?" he finished. "Yep. I thought we would be bacheloring around for life, but it looks like we both might be destined for a happy ending after all."

"Is that so?"

"It is."

He looked like he wanted to say more, like the words were clamoring for a way to exit his lips but instead, he reached into the pocket of his down Barbour jacket and pulled out a small blue velvet box.

"I got you a little something. Merry Christmas, Alex."

She opened it, heart fluttering like it needed cardioversion, and felt a sense of exhilarated relief as her trembling fingers touched the diamond earrings inside.

"Now, don't worry," he said, smoothing her hair behind her ear. "They are fair trade guaranteed from our site in Botswana."

He really did know her well at this point. *But not well enough.* She pushed the mute button on the irritating voice in her head and admired the light particles refracting in the facets.

"These are so beautiful, Ian. Thank you. I got you something too." She reached down into her blue leather shoulder bag and extracted a parcel tied with a red ribbon. "People who own their own airplanes are incredibly hard to buy for. It's not much."

He slipped off the ribbon and opened the box to reveal a pair of silver cufflinks in the shape of the Millennium Falcon from Star Wars. Alex suddenly felt embarrassed by the very geeky gift.

"I remember you telling me how Ryan liked *Empire Strikes Back*, and I thought this would be a way to keep him with you sometimes."

Ian still said nothing and continued to stare down into the box— a single glistening tear like a tiny melted snowflake wetting his dark lashes.

"It's perfect—just like you," he said and kissed her so long and deep that she was breathless at the end.

Alex's work schedule did not care about her jet lag. She had literally jumped off the plane and gone straight to the hospital to begin a several week stint of clinical service. She had worked nonstop right until her trip to London, and although she had had the time of her life, it was far from restful. Now she was right back at work in the thick of respiratory viral season and the highest ICU census all year.

Her forearms made a teepee to support her head as she scrolled through yet another set of blood gasses so that she could walk around for the fourteenth time making adjustments to the tiny knobs giving tiny lungs air in and air out. She reached out for her warm mug of tea to combat the cold that had settled deep into her tissues. The temperature was freezing both inside the hospital walls and outside, where the winter had deposited a hefty dusting of snow on the ground for the better part of January. Lately, she had actually taken to drinking the tea instead of just holding it for extra warmth, her caffeine binges becoming the checkpoints of her busy days in the hospital. Her jaw-breaking yawn broke her concentration, and she noticed a presence behind her.

"It seems like you need something to do, Dr. Wilde," informed a voice that could cut granite.

Alex turned in her chair slowly like one would turn toward a rabid dog or a crocodile. "What can I do for you, Dr. St. John?"

She wasted no oxygen molecules with her request. "I have a sick cardiac baby at some outside emergency room that has probably never taken care of a child, much less one with congenital heart disease. Go up to the roof and get on the helicopter and plan on bringing me this baby better than you found it."

Heels disappeared into the distance by the time Alex collected herself enough to start moving.

A snowstorm was blowing in, and every few seconds, the helicopter swerved unexpectedly to one side. Entirely focused on the child, Alex didn't have time to contemplate the very real possibility of not making it back to the hospital.

They had raced through the air to reach the baby before the storm hit and had all agreed that the he would be unlikely to survive if they got stuck and couldn't fly back. Profoundly cyanotic, he needed an operation as soon as possible to restore life-giving oxygen delivery to his body. Alex had band-aided what she could by placing a breathing tube and starting an epinephrine drip to support the heart. When she had called Dr. St John to give her an update, she instructed Alex to land and transport the baby straight to the operating room.

The helicopter made contact with the roof with a deliberate thud and relief flooded through Alex. She checked the monitor before they unloaded—the oxygen saturation was barely fifty percent. With no time to spare, they rolled to the waiting elevator, chilled wind striking them in the face until the silver doors securely closed, and they descended.

A prepped and ready OR team, already dressed in blue surgical gear, eagerly listened to the handoff as Alex smoothly described the baby's anatomy and how she had mitigated the impending crisis. She stepped out of the double doors as the team swarmed around the baby, the adrenaline rush still flowing through her arteries, and even received a confirmatory nod from Dr. St. John as she exited the OR suite.

Unzipping her flight suit, she reached for the incessantly buzzing phone in her scrub pocket, expecting to have a list of calls missed while in flight. The first name on her missed call list was Dr. James Stark, the chief of the critical care section and her bosses' boss. Panic arose as she pressed his name and mentally recounted all of her transgressions that might be the impetus for this phone call.

"Dr. Wilde," he said in his mild southern twang, "how good is your Haitian creole?"

"Better than it should be," Alex answered warily. It was common knowledge that she had spent time in Haiti for her master's thesis; in fact, it was in Arial twelve-point font on her curriculum vitae situated between medical school and residency.

"I thought so," he replied, sounding extremely satisfied. "There's been an earthquake near Port au Prince. Pack a bag. You are leaving in the morning with our CHOP response team."

Apparently, being drafted for a disaster mission in the Caribbean counted for something because Alex was relieved of her clinical duties for the rest of the day. She paced around her apartment as a continuous output from CNN, offering updates on the earthquake damage played across her television. Various scenes flashed across the screen—the crumbled façade of the capitol building, the devastation outside the Hotel Montana, people wandering the streets covered in drywall dust.

She was allowed one small duffel, and it was already brimming with supplies that included a few changes of clothes but mostly medical equipment and a water sterilization device that used UV light. The earthquake would have magnified the already dismal issues with sanitation and water availability in the city of Port au Prince. She was nervous, but it was an excited nervousness that stemmed from the thrill of possessing skills that could save children's lives.

She made a quick call to Janie to let her know she'd be leaving in the morning. After a few shocking tears, her sentimental mother had told her how proud she was of her and to call when she returned. Now the call she dreaded most. She dialed Ian. He texted in response.

*In a board meeting for foundation. Call you soon.*

She knew he would answer if she called again…so she did…and he did.

"Alex, are you okay?" he said in a worrisome tone.

"I'm fine. I just…something's happened. I don't know if you've seen the news, but there's been an earthquake in Haiti."

"I haven't seen it myself, but Lydia was just telling me what happened."

He paused, and she let the words rush out before she changed her mind. "My department wants to send me there with a disaster response team from our hospital." She heard his quick intake of breath.

"Does it have to be you?"

"I am the best candidate. I know how to work with few resources, and I speak the language. I want you to support me on this."

He exhaled heavily, and she could imagine the furrows deepening on his forehead.

"I do. I think you are amazing, but it's going to be dangerous and...I don't want you to go."

He had actually said it, and she had heard it, but her resolve was unshakable.

"I have to Ian. This is what I am on this planet to do. This is who I am."

"Even if what you do hurts the people that care about you?" His voice had become deathly quiet with a hint of desperation.

"I'll be fine," she replied firmly.

"I love you, Alex...and I can't lose you."

The words settled into her like lobbed grenades, ready to explode with emotions that didn't have time to be processed.

"I know you do...and you won't, I promise."


They finally landed in Port au Prince, welcomed by air that was heavy with ash and humidity. From the inside of the truck, on the drive to the only hospital that still stood, Alex peered into the darkness, the streets lit only by the occasional cigarette or trashcan fire. She tried to emotionally prepare herself for the trauma of what she was about to delve into. The city looked like some hellish monster had tried to devour it and then spit it back out. These people, who had historically undergone tremendous suffering, now had to rise from the ashes of their own city.

Once at the hospital tucked into a corner cot, amid the continuous buzz of mosquitoes seeking a meal, she retreated into the depths of her mind and let herself think of Ian. She had ended their monumental phone call and hadn't spoken to him again. She was afraid that hearing his voice again and hearing the sweet, beautiful words he uttered would be the catalyst that made her jump from her airplane seat and bolt down the jetway. *He loved her.* Did she love him? She was dreaming before she even fully closed her lids—of glowing blue eyes beckoning to her in the darkness.

Even in the middle of winter, the sun rose early here, chasing away the terrors of the night but also heating up the air around them to a feverish level by mid-morning. Grime and sweat trickled down Alex's back, plastering down her cotton t-shirt and dripping into the waistband of her jeans. She and a few medical students from the university were occupied unpacking and sorting boxes of medical supplies in the makeshift tent hospital that would accommodate the overflow from the main hospital. Every few minutes, their work was interrupted by harried shouts from the street as the injured were carried up the hill on roughly-made stretchers, in a cluster of arms, or simply drug along the ground.

Venel, one of the medical students, had been tasked with helping to transport incoming patients to the neat rows of cots in the tent and place a tag for triage—green for minor injuries, red for those that needed immediate attention, and black for those who were already deceased. So far, the red and black tags were outpacing the green ones.

Alex was collaborating with Dr. Josephine Adrien, the head of pediatrics at University Hospital, to run point on the evaluation and management of any children that were brought in. Only a few had arrived today—a school-aged child with a broken leg and a baby with severe dehydration. Alex knew the actual traumatic injuries from the earthquake were only the beginning. The second wave would be infectious disease outbreaks like cholera and typhoid from the contaminated water supply or just simple dehydration from the disadvantaged populations like children who couldn't find water at all.

"Hey Venel, what do you have over there?" she called to the tall, lanky young man still wearing his white coat despite the heat.

"It looks like long bone injuries—broken arm and leg—and many abrasions."

Alex walked over, wiping her sweat-stained face on her shirt. "I can help you get him into temporary splints if you want."

He smiled down at her with a mouthful of white teeth, amazingly enthusiastic despite the circumstances. "Okay. That box over there has the supplies."

Alex brought over the green container that resembled a large fishing tackle box and started drawing up a hefty dose of morphine to give the man before they started. The man was old with a face weathered by seasons of rain and sun and what little hair he remained was stark white. He grabbed Alex's hand before she entered his vein with the needle and shook his head vehemently. Alex gently placed her hand on his shaking arm.

"We need to give you pain medicine to set your fractures," she said in English and, correcting herself, tried again in Haitian creole.

She entered the vein and depressed the plunger. The man's face became slack, but his lips continued to move, and a brightness burned deep in the abyss of his pupils. She repositioned his head on the cot and put her ear close to his lips, where a string of words was being uttered at remarkable speed.

"What is he saying, Venel?"

Venel walked over from where he was preparing the fiberglass splints and closed his eyes.

"Inside...more inside...my granddaughter."

"Where is your granddaughter...where is she inside?"

The morphine overtook him, and his eyes closed. "Who brought this man in Venel?"

"I see them," he said, "the two men in the orange vests." He took off in a run down the hill with Alex close on his heels.

"I'm glad people are still willing to drive us around," shouted Alex to Venel as they were tossed around the back of the tap-tap like sailors on a rough sea, bumping along the road leading out of the city.

"I suppose so," said Venel, tight-lipped and just a slight shade of green as he clutched the edge of the truck bed.

"Where are you from, Venel?" Alex asked, trying to take his mind off the ensuing nausea.

"Petite Goave."

"Isn't that on the coast?"

"Yes—and wonderfully flat."

They shared a laugh, bonded by both witty humor and the purposeful resolve they shared to find this man's granddaughter. They were headed to Petionville, the next biggest town immediately inland of Port au Prince, to the grounds of a small elementary school. The old man had been found there slumped in a doorway, muttering what they now knew to be his granddaughter's name—Margarethe.

When Alex and Venel arrived at the correct street, rubble filled the road, and they climbed out of the truck to walk the rest of the way. A fine mist of dust particles hung in the air creating an ethereal appearing curtain as they picked their way over large chunks of building plaster and stone. A few rescue workers still dotted the landscape, knocking on doors of the buildings that were still standing and shouting to each other when they found someone inside. The schoolhouse was one of these. Its sturdy wood and stone A-frame had withstood the initial 7.0 magnitude earthquake, but there was no way to know how stable the structure was or how it would hold up in an aftershock.

"*Bonjou, como ye?*" Alex yelled to a rescue worker, denoted by his bright orange vest.

The gentleman motioned them over, and Venel started talking quickly and pointing toward the school, receiving a few shrugs and shakes of the head in response.

"He says all the children were evacuated from the school right after the earthquake."

"Ask him if we can take a look—just in case. Maybe she was scared and is hiding or something," Alex offered.

In response, the man gestured toward the building, giving them a thumbs up.

Alex and Venel pushed back the door gingerly as if this tiny motion might eradicate any remaining sturdiness to the upright structure. They stepped inside a small central room with eight different hallways leading off it like legs of an arachnid. Dust motes danced in the air from what little sunlight was still able to squeeze through the caked window panes, and the sense of fear still lingered in the air. A few backpacks, their contents spewing out, remained discarded on the floor as if thrown off in haste.

Alex's spirits plummeted. "She could be down any of these hallways."

"Margarethe," Venel shouted, his baritone voice reverberating off the walls. "We can go together, take one passage at a time," he said.

"It will be faster if we split up," Alex argued. "She could be unconscious." *Or worse.*

With reluctance, he gave a quick nod, and they each headed into the jaws of one of the dimly lit hallways.

Alex ducked her head past a piece of wall plaster suspended by rebar and took careful steps, peering into each gaping opening in the wall, searching for any tiny appendages or flashes of material that might belong to Margarethe. She could hear Venel calling the girl's name in the adjacent hallway and sent a silent prayer over to him.

Along with Christianity, Vudu was actively practiced in parts of Haiti, and unlike its American connotation, it could either bring good or bad spiritual energy. She hoped the good Vudu spirits were on their side today.

She wished she had thought to strap on a headlight because the further she explored, the darker it became until she had to pause for a moment to allow her pupils to dilate.

"Alex!"

She started as her name echoed around her.

"Venel?"

The voice seemed to be coming from somewhere ahead of her. She reached out, and her hand met a pile of sharp wood layered with broken brick.

"I found her outside behind the school. She's okay. Can you get out the back door?"

"I don't think so," Alex called. "Part of this hallway is collapsed. Take her to the truck, and I'll backtrack and meet you in the front."

"Okay. Sounds good," Venel replied, and he was gone.

Alex let herself breathe a sigh of pure relief, imagining the beautiful reunion between grandfather and grandchild that would ensue once they returned to the hospital with an uninjured Margarethe. They desperately needed moments like these—a tragedy that turned into joy. A win in a sea of loss. She could feel the air receding around her as she picked her way closer to the front of the school with a few shafts of light marking her path.

A bone deep tired weighed down her steps. She hadn't had any water in a while and felt suddenly dizzy and nauseous like the earth around her was in motion. The cracking of wood above her head and the chalky taste of drywall on her tongue were her last sensations before everything was black.

Her eyes were open, but they only saw a black void, and her mouth was cotton dry, a metallic, salty liquid taste on her lips as her only source of moisture. Everything was quiet. Still. Like waking up in a tomb. She placed a panicked hand on her chest and was reassured by a steady rise and fall and a rapid but regular pounding of her heart. Her eyes detected a glimmer of light, and with pure force of will, she pushed up to her knees and started dragging herself toward it.

# TWENTY-FIVE

Alex awoke, eyes unfocused but able to detect snippets of conversation around her.

"In front of the school…"

"Aftershock…"

"Lucky she got out…"

"Concussion…probably internal bleeding…fractured ribs."

It was hard to breathe—like drowning with a brick sitting on her chest. She closed her eyes again and willed herself to be calm. Everything hurt from the hair on her head to her chest wall to the bottoms of her feet, and she felt grimy, her face sticky with blood mixed with dirt and sweat.

Systematically, she assessed every part of herself for injuries starting with her toes. Everything moved, and nothing was grossly damaged until she reached her hand up to her right thorax and palpated the sinking portion of her ribcage every time she inhaled—broken ribs and probably blood in her chest too. She moved her head from side to side then tucked her chin to her chest. No neck pain.

Reaching a shaky hand to her head, she palpated a tender swelling along her right scalp crusted over with a healthy eschar. Opening her eyes wider, she could only make out a graying haze. Nightfall. A playful breeze stroked her skin as she fell once again into the abyss of sleep.

The next time she awoke, a bright sun lorded over the sky, threatening to burn a hole in the tent canopy draped above her. She shielded her eyes, and even that insignificant movement made her almost vomit from the pain. She felt cold despite the surrounding warmth of the day and had the conscious but calm realization that she was probably in shock. A lovely warm hand reached out and took her cool one.

"Dr. Wilde? Alex?"

"Venel?" His name came out garbled from her thick tongue that moved over dry, cracked lips.

"I am here. What do you need?"

She tried to push up on her elbows, but her vision narrowed down to tiny dots before she collapsed back on the cot. She squeezed her lids shut and focused on breathing. "IV fluids."

Venel returned within moments with a few bags of normal saline. She held out her left arm, and he expertly placed an IV in the crook of her elbow. Alex watched the continuous drip of clear fluid entering her venous system, promising to fix her fluid deficit problem. Venel took a syringe and inserted it into her IV tubing and began to depress the plunger.

"What's that?"

"Morphine," he replied smoothly.

Fear surged through her chest. Losing consciousness and, with it, the little control she possessed, terrified her. She thought back to the resistant old man with the lost granddaughter. "Just a little to take the edge off. I want to stay awake. How is Margarethe?"

He removed the syringe and capped it, smiling broadly as he did so. "She is fine and happy to be with her *grand-pere*."

Alex's lips split apart grotesquely as she smiled. "We did a good thing."

"Sleep now, Dr. Wilde. I will make sure you get a few liters of fluid."

"Thanks, Venel," she sighed and let the drugs ease her breathing and quiet her mind.


Lips were roving over her skin. Lips belonging to a beautiful face. She had never felt anything so good. She spasmed with desire. *The ocean's skies were in his eyes. A sunshine smile...a promise to beguile...even the stars.* Words tumbled across the backs of her eyelids, and then a crash sounded and roused her from her drug-induced dreamscape.


"Sorry, Dr. Wilde," whispered Venel as he picked up a large suitcase containing surgical instruments.

Fully awake now, Alex's senses were heightened since the IV fluids had returned her to a state of adequate circulation. The world had spun while she had slept and cycled back to nighttime. She heard the backfire of a truck and, for the first time in two days, picked up her head to survey her surroundings. She was on a cot in one corner of the medical tent isolated from the other patients by a perimeter made of boxes. The rows of cots were about half full of patients in various stages of healing—and some that never would.

"Venel," she croaked.

He was at her side in moments. "What can I do?"

"Why am I over here in the corner?"

"Dr. Adrien assigned your care to me. I did not want anyone messing up my graduation project."

Alex tried to hold in her laughter, which only made her feel like someone was stabbing her through the right chest. Her breath caught, and she coughed involuntarily, "I could use some tequila."

Venel laughed heartily and pushed some additional morphine into her IV.

Having slept the better part of two days, Alex could not convince her body that she needed more rest. Even the morphine hadn't lulled her back into dreamland, so she huddled on her side following the crystal droplets of IV saline slipping into her veins and thought of Ian...of her mom...of Rox...but mostly Ian. She had not let herself cry—not from panic or desperation or even from physical pain, but the thought of breaking her promise to him, of allowing him to lose another person in his life, was too much to bear.

The unfurling of her emotions gripped her in a vice, and she felt paralyzed for a moment before calm rationale during crisis superseded. She ticked off the injuries in her head: mild concussion, broken ribs, some lacerations, and bruises. There was nothing too terrible; otherwise, she would probably be much worse by this point. When she had improved enough to travel, she would get checked out stateside and let Ian know she was okay.

Convinced she would heal under Venel's careful supervision, she focused her energy on distraction as a form of pain management. She could think of nothing more distracting than Ian. She spent the starless night replaying in her mind every interaction—every conversation, every expression, every kiss, the narrowed flirty gaze and half-smiles, the glib humor, the explosions of passion, the exquisite intimacy. The words that meant everything.

Sleep came eventually, but it was disturbed—deep enough so that she couldn't wake up but light enough so that her senses stayed attuned to her surroundings. She had willed herself into dreaming about Ian and had disciplined her subconscious into a constant loop of his face. Her head broke the churning surface of slumber, her eyes peering upward into the bluest of skies. Was she dreaming or awake or dreaming that she was awake? Sleep faded, and in the early morning light, still dark enough for a halo of stars, her brain registered the image of Ian's face mere inches from her own.

He leaned closer to her and brought her slack hand to his lips, closing his eyes as if in prayer.

"Talk to me, Alex."

"You're here" was all she could manage from her bone-dry throat. He brushed his knuckles across bloodstained cheeks, eyes hardening with resolve as he did so.

"I'm taking you home."

"I'm okay. Venel is taking excellent care of me," she slurred and gestured to her white-coated friend.

He hushed her. "Shhh. It's going to be okay."

He slid strong arms underneath her and picked her up from the cot, cradling her to his chest while Venel unhooked the tubing from her IV. Even the small movement of transitioning to Ian's arms rocked her body with waves of pain, and she nearly lost the contents of her stomach.

"Hold her tightly to your chest," she heard Venel instruct Ian. "Her ribs are broken, and she needs stability."

"What she needs is to get the hell out of here," snapped Ian as he readjusted Alex's position.

Venel remained nonplussed. "I can give her more morphine for the trip to the airport."

"No," Alex grunted. "No more morphine." She turned to Ian. "How did you get here?"

"My airplane," he replied tartly, "which is waiting for us as we speak. Just hold on."

Alex picked up her head and swept the rest of the tent. "Venel, how many patients are here that need surgery?"

"Probably ten or so."

Her face peered up at Ian, who was concentrating on treading lightly toward the mouth of the tent. "Ian, if there's room on the plane, we could take them..."

"There's not," he said curtly.

"Why not?" Her voice was not her own. It was shrill and soaked in adrenaline. "We can take them with us. They need help. Everyone is overwhelmed here, and they deserve a chance. They need us, Ian."

She struggled against him, but the pain of her injuries and the dreadful weakness made her struggle completely ineffective. He folded her into him like a child and began striding through the tent.

"No!" She was screaming now, and as her words landed on deaf ears, something inside her would not let her stop. "No….no…we can help them."

Ian halted abruptly and turned to Venel. "Give her the morphine," he said in a strained tone.

"No! I don't want—"

Alex's tongue stopped working in mid-sentence as Venel put a calming hand on her arm and emptied the rest of the syringe into her vein.


She felt clean—so very clean—and warmed by a small patch of kind sunshine striking her in the face. She reached a tentative hand toward her face that was no longer caked with layers of bodily fluids and dirt. A neat row of pokey stitches ran along her right temple, and someone had pulled her hair off her face into a braid. Her clothing had been changed out for a starched hospital gown that billowed over her body like a sail. She tested her lung compliance with a deep breath. Her chest still ached, but the binding dressing around her middle took the edge off. Ian slept crookedly on a nearby chair, his feet propped on a stool, shadows under his eyes and a light growth of stubble along his jawline. For the first time ever, he appeared far removed from the glossy heir with the world at his fingertips.

Alex didn't remember anything from the last several hours—not the flight or being admitted to the hospital. She didn't even know what city they were in. The earthquake and the accident all seemed like a dream. If she didn't hold onto the pieces and commit them to memory, they would disappear. With most of the drugs out of her system, she felt shaky but mentally more stable and able to deal with her internal conflicts.

Ian had rescued her. He had flown in on his silver winged aluminum Pegasus and scooped her up like a damsel in distress, which she supposed she had been. She was grateful and in awe of his courage and the bold display of love, but she struggled with his complete disdain for the rest of the people. He had lacked compassion, not even considering what she had requested. She wanted to know why.

Ian stirred and leaned forward in a massive stretch like a sleek cat waking from a nap. Noticing Alex's wakeful state, he came over to the bed and sat down gingerly. Searching, worried eyes found her face. "How are you feeling?" he said in a husky voice.

"Better...much better." Her voice was raw, and each word scraped her throat as she talked. She sipped ice water from the pink plastic pitcher on the bedside table.

"The doctor said you were really lucky." He rubbed his thumb over the back of her hand. "You have some broken ribs and cuts and bruises. Everything should heal up okay except for this..." He tapped a finger gently on her forehead. "The damage here is permanent."

He grinned then, just slightly, revealing a glimmer of his typical persona. She grabbed his hand instinctively.

"Thank you...for coming for me. It was very superhero-like."

"I could dress up in a cape and tights next time if you like." He gave her a wry smile.

"How did you even know what happened?"

"A very interesting game of telephone—somebody called your hospital, and Tim found out. Then Tim called Rox, Rox called me, and here I am."

"I'm sorry. You must have been worried."

"Worried doesn't even begin to describe it." He stared out the window and fiddled with the edge of her sheet. "You could have died, Alex."

"I know. But I didn't, and I'm okay."

"I'm not okay."

"I'm sorry. I knew that it was going to be dangerous, but..."

"But you didn't care."

"Wait a minute! I do care...I was just doing what I needed to do. I helped the people that needed me."

"I need you."

Alex stilled into a stunned quiet. "Don't make me choose between you and my career choice...or the way I choose to live my life."

"Choose? Let me tell you about choosing. In any situation in any part of this entire world, I will always choose you. Over myself. Over anyone else. Even when you are not choosing yourself."

"Then you don't understand anything about being supportive …or love for that matter," she fired back. She could tell that her words wounded him, and he cringed momentarily before taking her face in his hands.

"I love you, Alex, and if choosing you makes me selfish, if leaving a tentful of injured people to make sure I can get you home in one piece makes me selfish, then that is who I am and who I will always be."

Alex said nothing. She felt a small piece of her reality crumble, revealing a basic understanding she knew to the depths of her soul. She could not live life as she imagined and make Ian happy.

Ian and the nursing staff fussed over her for two days straight until she was discharged from Miami General. Her hair was washed and brushed out, and Ian went shopping and bought her several sets of silk pajamas, yoga pants, and a random Miami Heat sweatshirt.

Alex took her first shower in almost a week, and despite the sub-par water pressure, the temperature was scalding hot, and she scrubbed herself voraciously until she had exfoliated an entire layer of skin.

Her mom had called the night before and sobbed for almost ten minutes before telling Alex that her room was ready, and she would see her soon. She had pivoted to Ian, the phone next to her ear. "You are taking me to my mom's house?"

"Yep," he said, stuffing their belongings in a newly purchased duffel bag.

"What about work?"

"Consider this a medical leave of absence," he quipped, pulling the zipper closed.

He had been kind and amazingly sweet the last few days but also more reserved, and Alex could tell something was bothering him. They had never revisited their conversation about Haiti. He had put all his energy into providing her with pillows and beverages, magazines when she was bored, and holding her tightly in the narrow hospital bed when every breath wracked her chest wall with spasms of pain. Most of the time, she was grateful for the physical manifestation of pain. It made the hurt on the inside feel real.

Once discharged, Ian gathered all of her things, intently read every word of her discharge instructions, and piled them in a taxi to a private airstrip where he insisted on carrying her up the rollaway stairs.

"I promised your mom I would deliver you better than I found you," he joked.

"So, you and my mom are besties now?"

"Janie and I happen to share common interests."

Alex rolled her eyes in the most exasperated way possible and settled into her oversized and incredibly soft airplane seat.

Unlike the most recent few weeks of her life, the flight was downright boring and uneventful. Ian stayed busy click-clacking on his laptop, catching up on foundation affairs, and Alex alternated browsing a National Geographic magazine about whale sharks and nodding off to sleep. As the plane wheels touched down, she gasped at the mini-view of the landscape through her oval window depicting tall blades of emerald grass as far as she could see. The wheels kicked up clouds of rust-colored dirt as the airplane rolled to a stop right outside a metal-roofed shed that glinted in the afternoon sun.

"This isn't even an airport," she exclaimed. Ian continued typing.

"Nope."

"Where are we?"

"In a field about ten miles from your house."

"I didn't even know this was here." Alex glued her face to the window, desperately trying to catch a glimpse of something familiar and spied a glossy red truck with a pair of yapping Labradors craning over the truck bed.

"Mom," she breathed, fogging up the glass of the oval window. She anxiously fumbled with her safety belt as the door to the plane swept open.

Despite being the middle of winter, it was generously warm in the land of her youth, kept temperate by its short distance to the Gulf of Mexico and the warm Caribbean winds carried throughout coastal Texas. With Ian supporting her, she descended the stairs onto the loose red dirt runway, dancing sunshine playing on her skin and welcoming her home. She inhaled deeply, a cleansing breath of freshly mown grass and simplicity.

When she was a young girl, she would run through fields just like this one, pretending to be a wild horse as she covered ground in her bare feet, head held high into the wind. Although she ambled rather than galloped on this day, the effect on her psyche was the same. She broke away from Ian when she was near enough to her mom to hop from him to her like a skipping stone and let herself be wrapped in the blanket of a tender hug by her petite mother whose head barely grazed Alex's chin.

Ian hung back until her Janie, tears glistening on her cheeks, motioned for him to join them in their reunion embrace. Much taller than either of them, he awkwardly settled his arms on their shoulders, maintaining some distance until Janie slid her arm around his waist, pulling him into what could only be described as a down-home Texas style hug.

"I'm so glad you're here. Both of you," she said, smiling so vibrantly at Ian that it took him off-guard and disturbed his careful composure. Alex wondered if he was thinking of his own mother.

Janie expertly navigated through the winding country roads bordered by endless fields dotted with cows or a square of tilled earth with tender sprouting shoots. Alex had not realized how truly exhausted she felt until her head hit the pillow of her old bedroom and her bones settled into the decades-old mattress that maintained an imprint of her body in the middle of the flowery bedspread. She watched Ian set down her bag and attentively peruse her collection of childhood belongings.

"This is a blast from the past." He held up a photo of her as a skinny, awkward teenager in glasses, hair down to her waist, hand firmly entwined through the mane of a chestnut mare and then another of her at senior prom, posing with her date in front of giant white numerals.

"Who is that?" he asked, genuinely interested

"Um…that's Justin."

"Oooh...Justin." He waggled his brows suggestively.

"Hush—he was just a friend."

"I bet he wanted to be more than your friend." He replaced the photograph and continued his curiosity tour. "Student of the Year, first place spelling bee 1988, second place district math meet...what happened there?" He cringed and set the ribbon back down on the shelf.

"I would throw something, but it would set back my recovery," Alex grumbled and stuffed her head into the pillow.

That night after a solid dinner of roasted new potatoes dripping in melted butter and tender shreds of roast beef and even a freshly baked pie for dessert, Alex yawned and pushed back from the table on the precipice of a food coma.

"Thanks for dinner, Mom. I'll see you in the morning."

"Good night, honey," her mom said as she started clearing up the dishes.

She changed into the silk pajamas that Ian had bought her and was arranging the pillows on her bed when he walked in with a tall glass of ice water and a handful of ibuprofen. "I thought you might need something to help you sleep."

She hadn't been able to sleep through the night since her incident in Haiti. Every position was associated with some kind of dull throbbing ache.

"Thanks."

"I'll take my stuff over to the guestroom."

Alex chuckled lightly. "We don't have a guestroom. You can stay with me."

"Are you sure? I don't want to be disrespectful."

"We may be country, but we're not prude." Alex made a face. "Besides, my mom knows I wouldn't be able to...you know...in my condition."

His eyes blazed and then quieted. "I'll make sure to keep the walking around naked to a minimum then. Wouldn't want to tempt you."

He held her that night, and she intermittently woke to the presence of strong protective arms, creating a corporeal sanctuary. She let herself meld into it, willing her biorhythms to sync with Ian— her heart rate, her breathing, her temperature—until she felt like they were one organism. She was desperate to imprint every sensation into her memory, just in case she never again felt this way.

# TWENTY-SIX

Keys sailed through the air and landed on the painted kitchen table where Ian was glued to his laptop screen. "Let's go," said Alex impatiently. "I am going stir crazy, and I need a designated driver." She flashed him a smile and pointed to her ribs. They had been holed up for a few days at her mom's house, and Alex was going to need therapy if she watched one more rerun of *Friends*.

"Are Ross and Rachel still on a break?" he asked, not looking up from the computer screen.

"I'll meet you in the truck," she said, letting the screen door slam behind her.

Ian, never one to turn down a road trip, gunned the truck engine and smiled at the sound like a boy with a brand-new toy. "Where to—let's see, what was it? Miss Cole's Church 1997?"

"Don't remind me. Wait until we start dredging up your past," she grumbled and clicked her seatbelt with satisfaction. "Take a right at the end of the driveway."

Tires crunched on gravel as Ian accelerated onto the two-lane highway. Soon they were speeding along a gently curving road past ranch homes on expansive acreage, over a set of railroad tracks, and then popped out onto the main thoroughfare of Cole's Church. Ian slowed to accommodate the abrupt change in speed limit and crept past a small park with a gazebo, a strip of businesses including a Family Dollar, and a gas station that moonlighted as a pizza joint.

They blew through a stoplight, and Alex rolled down her window to let the breeze float through the truck, mixing with the music softly playing on the radio. Ian drove on while the sunshine voice of Taylor Swift told a story of heartache and redemption.

"Count to three," Alex said as they drove past a family-owned diner.

"One...two...three," Ian complied.

"And that's it."

"What do mean that's it?"

Alex giggled uncontrollably. "That was my town. All of it."

"You're kidding me."

"I wish I was. Take a left at the light."

The neighborhoods faded as they crossed another set of railroad tracks and the road twisted in a serpentine fashion through miles of pastureland.

"There was nothing to do here growing up, so my friends and I used to drive this road at night, windows down, music turned up..." Alex reminisced.

"Sounds fun."

"This is literally my memory lane."

She opened the lid to her mental memory box of high school—the obsessions, the drama, the crushes, the heartache. A lifetime of change in such a finite amount of time.

"Slow down...here it is."

She pointed to a gravel road between two fields of tall corn that was easily missed by someone not familiar with the landscape. Ian expertly guided the truck onto the narrow strip until they reached a clearing where the road ended, and a handmade wooden bridge extended across a creek toward the entrance to a simple white A-frame church.

"This looks like something out of a teenage horror movie," Ian muttered.

Alex was already sliding out of the truck and heading toward the wooden bridge. Ian crept over the creaking structure to join her, sitting down carefully and then swinging his legs off the side.

"My friends and I used to come here to have dramatic, life-changing conversations." Alex tucked her chin and smiled. "This bridge has seen its share of break-ups and make-ups. I decided to go to medical school, right in this very spot."

"What about over there?" Ian cocked his head to the church, surrounded by gray headstones peeping out of the overgrown grass.

"The church? It's old, and no one uses it anymore. People say it's haunted...that they used to bury people in its cemetery who had unforgivable sins and now their restless spirits roam around the cornfields at night." Alex sat down next to him and glanced at his face.

Ian had visibly paled and averted his eyes from the church building and over to Alex. "Remind me to avoid this place at night."

"It's just a small-town ghost story." She laughed freely and squinted into the sunlight, letting its glow warm her cheeks. "Being here suits you."

"It does. It's home…but unfortunately, I didn't choose a job that would ever let me come back to this life."

A silence settled over them like a thick blanket of anticipation for what was to come. Unspoken words shimmered in the winter air until Ian blew on them with his exhaled breath and made them materialize.

"What is it that you want for your life, Alex? Because I know exactly what I want."

Alex hesitated on the edge of a metaphysical cliffside and then closed her eyes, stepping off into a freefall and then landing feetfirst into the water below—a deep cold filling up the space around her.

"I want…"

She hesitated as the words grew wings and exited her mouth. "Freedom," she said simply. "Freedom to choose how I live…where I go…what I sacrifice. I want what we have, but I don't want to give up anything else." She paused and then continued slowly, carefully. "I know I can't have everything."

"No—you can't, baby."

"I can't have you and everything else—not without making you incredibly unhappy. But I am meant to live my life in a certain way."

"And how is that? By martyring yourself to the entire world?"

"Maybe. Maybe that's the plan. Maybe that's who I am supposed to be."

Alex looked down at the creek water, stagnant and murky, and wondered if she believed what she had just said. Out of the corner of her eye, she could see Ian pinching the bridge of his nose between his forefingers.

"Do you even know who you are, Alex?"

"I know I'm not someone who wants to be the reason you are motivated to do good things. You don't need me to be happy with who you are."

"You aren't the only reason. And I don't need you to be happy…but I do need you."

"Don't you understand? You can't need me so much because

other people need me too—sick babies and scared mothers. People who have no one else to believe in. I can't live up to that kind of expectation because I'm always disappointing someone—my patients, my colleagues, my friends...you. I refuse to be someone who disappoints you."

They faced one another on the bridge, their voices rising and filling the deathly quiet of the cemetery. Ian stood, tall and statuesque, arms to his sides, a line of visible tension extending from his jaw to the ends of his fingers.

"What about you? What do you need, Alex? Do you need me?"

His string of questions started as a challenge but ended as a prayerful plea. Alex internally winced. A battle raged within her. She wanted to say yes—to have the perfect happy ending to this otherwise disastrous conversation. She wanted to gather him in her arms and never let him go. Lies were so much easier than the truth, but she had never made anything easy on herself.

"I don't know how to need anyone. I never have," she whispered.

Her eyes widened, and she steeled herself for his response, for some emotional display of unrequited love. It didn't come. When he looked at her, searching for understanding, it was with eyes whose perpetual flames had burned out. They both stood there in wordless tension—an absolute juxtaposition to the twittering birds and elegant rays beaming through the clouds to coat them in sunlight. Alex swallowed the massive ball in her throat and finally spoke.

"I can't be the girl you need...and I think you should let me go."


Alex told herself that she did this for him as an act of pure selflessness. She had offered him a chance to be happier. He could have a life that he had imagined, without sharing her with an insane career that made her both physically and emotionally unavailable. It felt like the right thing to do at the time.

However, the next morning, when she awoke and he was gone, whisked away into the early morning mist by an unknown entity, she only felt an agonizing emptiness like a bottomless crater that kept expanding. She lay on her side on top of her bedcovers and clutched a ratty stuffed dog, a childhood object of permanence through many long nights.

Alex had transitioned beyond a place that brought tears. No amount of waterworks could reflect the depth of her pain. During her trauma rotation in residency, she had worked in a pediatric burn unit. The searing pain from progressive levels of tissue damage was extreme—until the fire had burned through every single layer all the way to the bone. Which was why third-degree burns, although the most detrimental, didn't hurt.

Her mom's doll-like silhouette filled the doorway. "You have to eat something, honey. I'll bring it to your room."

Alex had spent one entire day and night prostrate in her bed. "I'm not hungry."

"I didn't ask."

Janie was on a mission, and in a few minutes, she sat gingerly on the edge of her bed with a tray of steaming tomato soup and a grilled cheese sandwich, gooey melted cheddar oozing out of the middle. Alex obliged her and sat up, suddenly dizzy with the acute change in position and gripped her side as pain shot through her middle.

"Thanks, mom." She started tearing the sandwich into tiny dippable pieces.

"Have you talked to him?"

Alex shook her head.

"Do you want to tell me what happened?"

Alex shrugged and stuffed a bite into her mouth. She didn't want to say the words out loud. The reality of what she had done had set in, and she was on the verge of frantically calling him and changing her mind. Ever the emotional masochist, she decided to rip off the band-aid.

"I...told him he needed to let me go."

Her mom said nothing, just reached over and squeezed her knee. "Did he not make you happy?"

"No...no. He did...he does," Alex floundered. "He's incredible. It's me. I can't devote myself to medicine and make him happy too."

"Why not?"

"He needs someone that can always be there for him...who doesn't fall asleep at the drop of hat...who doesn't go to a devastated country and get hit in the head with part of a school." Alex gave a wry smile that Janie did not return.

"Don't you think he knows what he needs?"

Alex contemplated this for a moment like she was turning over an object for the first time. "He thinks he does...for now...but I can't imagine how I could make him happy long term."

"You don't love him?"

"I never said I didn't love him."

Her breath caught in her throat with this bold revelation, the crater expanding to a canyon with greater width and depth than she thought possible.

Tears glistened on her mom's near translucent lashes, and she drew a deep inhale before speaking.

"We didn't have much when you were growing up—you remember—and what we did have was always in danger of being taken away. One time we were in the supermarket, and you saw a set of colored pencils and a Hello Kitty coloring book—nothing extravagant—but I could tell you wanted it. Your little fingers reached out to trace the pencil box, and your eyes shone as you flipped through the pages of the book. I decided I had to buy it for you, and I tried, but you wouldn't take it to the register. One of the only times you pitched a tantrum. I never could understand why you didn't want it. And then later...much later...probably years later...I finally understood that you did want it. You were just afraid that you didn't deserve it. That you would take this precious gift and something terrible would happen to it. You would rather not have it at all than be responsible for losing it or damaging it."

Alex's heart pounded violently at the vision of herself expertly created by the person who loved her the most in the world. A tiny rivulet of tears streamed from the corner of her mother's eye and down her cheeks, flushed from remembrance.

"You lost so much as a child. And I know it's easier for you to live tragically...but it's time that you start learning how to live joyfully."

Janie stood, rubbing a hand through her ginger hair, cropped to her chin, and then lifted the collar of her shirt to dab her eyes. Alex watched her mother, in awe of her insight and wisdom. For better or for worse, she had never meddled in Alex's life. She had never even enforced a curfew or told her which boys to avoid or made suggestions about her appearance. Having an early recognition of Alex's predilection for self-discipline and ambition, she had provided support and encouragement but very little guidance. Alex never blamed her mom for her tragic upbringing. They had both been victims of terrible circumstances and had risen together like a pair of phoenixes.

Alex hugged scruffy dog close to her chest, at that moment feeling very small and childlike. "I'll try, Mom."

Janie smiled down at her daughter, an expression plump with unconditional love. "I know you will."

For the next week, Alex developed a comforting routine. She woke at dawn, threw on some running clothes, and set off on a several hour walk through the winding country roads bordering her mom's property. Although her body was still too broken to run, she tolerated more mileage every day. While the snail's pace bothered her, the sights and scents she picked up on the way did not. Walking past fields of frolicking baby calves and freshly tilled earth was a chance to refocus her energy after a typical restless night—a night filled with distressing dreams, sometimes of Ian.

Every morning when she huffed back up the driveway to her mom's front porch, she dialed him, and every morning, she had gotten his voicemail. She hadn't left any messages. She didn't know what to say, but she thought hearing his voice would bring some clarity to the tumult surging inside her.

Alex plopped down at the kitchen table amid the delectable scent of homemade pancakes browning on the griddle. Janie had spoiled her with every southern delicacy that she could whip up in the last few days, hoping to tempt her into dealing with this Ian situation by eating her feelings. A plate of pancakes with an obnoxious amount of butter appeared in front of her, and she watched it melt and drip decadent little puddles on the side of her plate.

"No answer?"

"No," she replied. "Maybe he hates me or he changed his phone number. It doesn't matter." She poked a piece of fluffy pancake with her fork, swirling it around a lake of butter and syrup, lacking the motivation to actually put it in her mouth.

"Maybe tomorrow?" her mom said encouragingly.

"I think it's over, Mom." Tears threatened and then retreated, and she felt warm, calloused hands on her shoulders.

"It's not over," she whispered and kissed her lightly on the top of her head. "And it's okay to cry."

"I just can't, Mom. If I start, I'll never stop."

There wasn't much to pack. Alex only had the few clothes that Ian had purchased for her and a few belongings that he had thought to retrieve from Haiti. On a whim, she tossed scruffy dog into the duffel and felt interestingly comforted seeing his little sandy brown head poking out of the zipper.

Tim had called earlier today to check on her and offered to pick her up at the airport this evening. His voice had sounded foreign, having adopted a tone of timidity and worry that wasn't typical. She had reassured him that she was fine and actually anxious to get back to Philadelphia and to her regular life—a life that held the keys to her complete recovery. A life where she could drown herself in work until her scars were entirely healed—the physical ones and the non-physical ones. She felt as broken as a doll, but it was time to pick up the shards and put Humpty Dumpty back on the wall.

"Are you ready, honey?" Janie called from the living room.

"Coming," Alex called and noticed a neatly packed roller bag blocking her path. She grasped the handle and began to push it toward the door, eyeing her mom quizzically.

"Well, surely you didn't think I was going to let you go back alone, did you?"


Tim's oversized hand waved at them from the open window of his silver Honda and Alex, with Janie in tow, piled into the backseat.

"Hi, Mrs. Wilde. It's good to see you again."

"Hello, Tim." Janie had a magnetic smile on her face that mirrored Tim's.

His eyes widened at the sight of Alex.

Although the bruises and swelling on her face had begun to heal, her appearance remained shocking. Tim crept at a slug's pace over the speedbumps in the passenger arrival lane, and Alex reached up to put a reassuring hand on his shoulder. "You don't have to drive me around like Miss Daisy. I'm not going to break."

He glanced at her in the rearview mirror. "I'll be the judge of that since I am completely over-qualified to be your chauffeur." His demeanor had started to ease up, and the tight lines on his face relaxed.

"What did I miss?" Alex asked.

"Well, I accepted a job."

"Tim, that's amazing! Where? I didn't even know you were interviewing yet."

"Graduation is in five months, Alex," he chided.

"Don't remind me."

She had been so engrossed with clinical work and Ian that she hadn't even pursued the available job opportunities.

"I'm going home actually...to Georgia. I accepted an attending spot at Children's in Atlanta."

"I am so happy for you." She reached up to grab his arm between the seats, and the familiarity of it was so warm and comforting that it sent a pang through her chest. "What about Beth?" Alex inquired.

"Everyone is recruiting her, of course. I think she is deciding between Seattle and Boston."

"Wow—those couldn't be more polar opposites."

"I know, but that's our Beth. She lives by extremes."

Alex nodded in agreement, thinking of her usual nemesis sometimes friend.

As they pulled into the circle drive of her building, Janie squeezed her hand reassuringly, and soon they entered her box-sized apartment, dropping their bags in an empty corner of the living room space. Alex fretted for a moment. Her apartment was toasty warm despite knowing that she had turned off the heat before she left, and several bags of groceries sat lined up on her kitchen counter. She opened her refrigerator—full of Diet Coke and sparkling water. Looking guilty, Tim shuffled toward the doorway and gave her a wink.

"I'll see you at work Monday."

"Thank you, Tim," Alex whispered and surprised them both by wrapping her arms around his waist and letting him envelop her in a sweet embrace.

Meanwhile, Janie, who was the epitome of efficiency and hyperactivity, had plumped up the couch cushions and created a corner for Alex to lounge, complete with the cashmere throw blanket. She patted the space on the couch and glanced expectantly at Alex.

"Mom, I'm not an invalid. I can help you unpack."

"Don't be ridiculous, Alex. Take advantage of being lazy for once." She handed her the TV remote.

With a massive snort of complaint, Alex did as she was told and flopped onto the couch, flipping on her television perhaps for the first time in six months. As her mom scurried around the apartment unpacking groceries, wiping down counters, and folding clothes neatly into drawers, Alex scrolled through channels and settled on the mind-numbing *Entertainment Tonight.*

"The Golden Globes are on," Alex called to her mom, as she

watched the upper echelon of Hollywood glamour parade down the red carpet. In the next moment, there was a sweeping shot of the Beverly Hilton with sleek black limousines lined up on the street.

The flood of memories hit her like a tidal wave. She heard the lapping of pool water as she sobbed into Ian's tux jacket and smelled the fresh rain on Ian's skin as they kissed on a Malibu cliffside. He had told her he needed her and she had responded with "you have me" followed by rain-soaked car sex that still made her shudder in all the right places. She dug her phone out of her purse. She had downgraded from calling to texting and saw that her two from this morning were still unanswered. She tried again with one final plea.

*I need to talk to you. Please.*

Several minutes went by, and then her phone dinged a promising tone. Just one line.

*I'm sorry Alex. I can't.*

"What should I do with these?" Her mom panted from the exertion of organizing and wiped the hair from her forehead. The vase of peonies from her birthday, now dried up and brown, extended from Janie's arms.

"Just toss them," Alex whispered, her throat constricting around the words.

# TWENTY-SEVEN

Donned in powder blue scrubs, sneakers, and a wonderfully warm puffer jacket she had purchased with her mom over the weekend, Alex crept silently through the apartment to avoid waking a mildly snoring Janie. Because she was still healing from her injuries, especially the broken ribs, Alex had been put on two weeks of "light duty" by Gibson. She would be giving lectures to the pediatric residents and rotating medical students and catching up on administrative tasks but nothing else. Alex was both relieved and disgruntled by her assignment. She had hoped that the distraction of a fast-paced ICU full of sick children could take her mind off Ian.

Last night after her mom fell asleep, her eyes refused to close, and she pulled out her phone and typed his name in the google search engine. With held breath, she hit enter, merely to ensure he had moved on and re-assimilated back into his life. She clicked the images tab, a surefire way to see the most recent paparazzi photos of his activities. Being strikingly handsome, wealthy, and always up to his elbows in drama, Ian had been a constant source of gossip fodder for the media for the last decade.

Strangely, Alex could not find a single photograph of him after January 13—the day she had left for Haiti. That day he had been dressed in a navy suit, looking tense and dramatically sexy, one hand on the ajar door of a massive orange bricked Edwardian style building. Alex read the caption "Devall trades his dalliances for the office" and assumed that the building in the background housed the main offices for the Devall corporation. She traced his face on her screen. Somehow just seeing him had rubbed a salve on her inner ache, and she fell asleep with the phone clutched tightly to her chest.

Alex was entirely unprepared for the hoopla that collided with her as she entered the flat gray double doors to the ICU. A quiet murmuring began that spread like wildfire and culminated in an ear-splitting cheer complete with clapping and shouting. Alex ducked her head in overwhelming shyness, unsure at first of the reasons behind the welcome and significantly uncomfortable being the center of attention. The charge nurse, a tall fearsome hexagenerian with short spiky black hair and a wide red-lipped smile, took her elbow and led her into the breakroom where a spread of breakfast foods awaited along with a giant cookie cake that read "Welcome back, Dr. Wilde."

Still numb from shock and overstimulation, she peered around the room at the masses that had gathered—her attendings, Tim and Beth, the nurses and respiratory therapists, even the coffee barista from the cafeteria. Her heart swelled with gratitude for her work family. She cleared the obstruction in her throat.

"Thank you…thank you all. Wow, this is too much."

She wanted to say more. She wanted to express the depth of her appreciation for this demonstration of love. She wanted to tell them about Margarethe and how she would make the same decision if faced with the choice again. The words in her mind wouldn't obey and exit her lips. Tim saved her from further discomfort by wrapping a protective arm around her shoulders and steering her toward a steaming pile of bagels.

"She's been out of Philly for a while. We think she forgot what a real bagel tastes like." Everyone laughed light-heartedly and began filling their plates with the menagerie of baked goods.

"Thanks," she said under her breath. "I am not cut out for the limelight."

"I know," he said in a deep-throated voice, so dangerously close that his breath tickled the tiny hairs in her ear.

Alex stiffened and extracted herself from his arm. "I've got to take mine to go. I'm giving the resident lecture this morning."

"No worries. I'll see you later." He ruffled her hair as she left, thankfully on the opposite side of her healing scalp laceration.


"Shock is a state of inadequate tissue perfusion," she said, using the mouse to scroll over her PowerPoint bullets like a sniper trying to find a target. "The key to treating shock is anticipating it…getting ahead of it…not waiting to react to it."

The pediatric residents sat in silence, furiously scribbling notes and periodically glancing up at the large screen displaying Alex's slide presentation. She remembered what it had been like learning how to really take care of kids—memorizing every disease process and methodically examining hundreds of normal children so the abnormal stood out. Her experience as a resident in the ICU had been the most difficult. The hours were brutally long caring for the sickest patients in the entire hospital, but she had never been more exhilarated. Rather than choosing this career path, it had chosen her and continued to push her to a level of excellence that she hadn't known existed. It demanded excellence from every single facet of her education—book knowledge, clinical acumen, emotional intelligence, and spiritual maturity. Every child was singular with a unique set of challenges, even if Alex had seen the diagnosis hundreds of times before.

She continued flashing up slide after slide, explaining the various causes of shock in children and how to recognize and treat them. It felt good to be contributing something again, flexing her brain cells after weeks of watching re-runs and staring out the window. It also took her mind off Ian, which she needed...desperately.

"What questions do you have so far?" she asked the group, hoping that at least someone was formulating a thought or two. A dark-headed girl in thick glasses flashed her palm. "Yes—Keira, is it?"

"I was wondering..." She paused, casting a sideways glance at her friend across the room. "Is it true a school collapsed on you in Haiti?"

"Um...yes, I guess so," Alex fumbled.

"We heard you rescued like ten kids from the building," said another voice from the back of the room.

"And you almost died in a M.A.S.H. tent."

"And you were rescued by your famous boyfriend," crowed Keira, who clasped her hands under her chin like she was revealing the end of a romance novel.

Alex sighed heavily. Even with Ian out of the picture, he was still able to dominate her life.

When she arrived home that day, her mom was stirring something incredibly fragrant on the stove that turned out to be her famous turkey chili. "How was your first day back, honey?" she said, slurping as she sampled the dinner fare.

"It was fine." She knew this phrase, once uttered, would close the door on that particular topic of conversation.

"I reorganized your kitchen today and made you some freezer meals. I talked to Peter—he's taking care of things at home, so I can stay as long as you like."

Alex smiled to herself at her mom's ingenious way of not prying.

"Also, Roxanne sent you something. I signed for it downstairs and brought it up. It was heavy."

Alex felt a flash of guilt. She had not returned any of Rox's phone calls and had barely replied to her text messages since returning to Philadelphia. The breakup with Ian had left her scantily equipped for emotional responses, and she knew that, in addition to reliving the last few weeks, she would need to revel in the wedding plans.

She found a spare scalpel that she had nicked from the hospital and expertly sliced the tape holding the box closed. The top layer was stuffed with pink tissue paper and rose gold glitter that cascaded onto Alex's carpet. A card lay on the top of several bulky shapes filling up the rest of the box. She opened it and could swear she detected a minuscule waft of Rox's perfume. The card was shaped like a high-heeled shoe and simply read, "Will you be my maid of honor?"

Alex pulled out the rest of the contents—two bridal magazines the size of medical textbooks with Post-it notes marking the pages of final contenders for bridal gowns and a selection of self-care items including scented candles, a lavender foaming bath soak, and a pair of fuzzy spa socks depicting jumping lambs.

Despite the time difference, Alex desperately wanted to talk to her friend, to fill any role other than a broken-bodied, broken-hearted invalid trying to pull the pieces of her life together. Wearing the lamb socks, she hopped onto her bed, laptop open, and hoped that Rox was up late waiting on someone's baby to crown. The little blue Skype cloud dinged and expanded into an entire screen of her best friend's face shadowed by the meager glow of a tiny desk lamp.

"Where are you?" Alex said laughingly. "You look like the first scene of a scary movie."

"My new office. It's brilliant but not very well lit—not one single window."

Alex gasped. "You got a new job!"

"I did—started last week. It's in a less than desirable part of London, and I love it. Lots of single mums having babies who need a bit of guidance."

"That's fabulous, Rox. Everyone around me is getting a real job lately. It's probably time that I tackle that road."

"I can't imagine you've had time with all your heroism and near-death experiences."

"I did not have a near-death experience." Alex laughed deeply for the first time in weeks.

"Tomato *tomato*," Rox said, shrugging nonchalantly.

"Thanks for the care package, by the way. I assume that I am supposed to peruse the bridal magazines in my lavender bath under flickering candlelight."

"Add some rose petals to the bath as well—it really enhances the experience." Rox sent her a wink.

"I would be honored to be your maid of honor. When is the wedding?"

"We are thinking June. Somewhere in Provence. Something elegant and exclusive." Her eyes lit up with excitement. "I'm sure Ian will be best man, and you guys will look absolutely smashing walking down the aisle together."

Alex's facial expression must have functioned as a visual synopsis of the downfall of her relationship with Ian because Rox startled in surprise, putting her hand up to her lips.

"He didn't tell me…" she whispered.

"You've seen him?" Alex said.

"Just yesterday. He came by to give Nic something. He didn't say much, and he looked stressed, but I just figured he was worried about you."

"He won't return my calls or texts."

"What happened?" Rox asked.

As Alex filled her in on the tragic details and their final conversation, Rox remained silent, thoughtful, her full lips in a set line and furrows developing in her forehead. "How are you dealing with this?"

"I'm okay, Rox…really. It would have never worked. I would never have made him happy. It's better that we go back to our normal lives and move on."

Rox drummed her fingers on the desk solidly. "Alex—I love you, but your denial is the size of Nic's—"

"Okay! No more! I get it," Alex yelped.

"I was about to say ego," Rox said through pursed pink lips.

By the next weekend, Janie had to head home, and although Alex regretted losing the company, she also knew her mom was behind on gardening not to mention with her job as a secretary in a small-town law office. She was left with the essence of Janie Wilde everywhere. Her apartment had never been cleaner, her freezer had never been fuller, and even her sock drawer had been forcibly reorganized. For the first time in a month, she was alone, a state of being that she had never minded. Tonight, however, it seemed desperately heavy and gnawed at her insides until she felt exhausted and restless.

On a whim, she ordered pizza and picked off the toppings, popping them into her mouth as she watched some teenage drama series about two feuding vampire brothers in love with the same human girl. Her wall of windows gave her a spectacular view of the city, coming alive on a Friday night as college students and work professionals shrugged off their regular identities in favor of bolder, albeit inebriated, alter egos.

For weeks, Alex had foregone drinking to avoid exacerbating her concussion, but tonight it seemed like a superb way to open up the possibility of a dreamless, coma-like sleep. She opened a bottle of Chenin blanc, the last of her stash from South Africa, and poured a generous amount into a plastic cup. She sipped the chilled liquid gingerly, letting the complexity coat her taste buds and, after a few swallows, felt the encroaching warmth and carefree relaxation brought on by good wine.

Once the cup was drained and her limbs felt heavy and obedient, she folded herself into bed, scruffy dog in one arm and her phone in the other...just in case. Her slumber, dreamless and deep, was truncated when a blaring fire engine screamed down an empty street close to midnight. She glanced at her phone screen through sticky eyes and caught the green rectangle of a missed call. *Damn.* She must have really been comatose to sleep through her phone ringing. She shakily pressed Ian's picture next to the missed call and was sent straight to voicemail. She tried again with the same result.

Desperation flooded her followed by annoyance and then a thin sliver of anger, like a white-hot shard piercing her heart. Alex knew she had hurt him, but his avoidance bordered on pathologic. She needed to hear his voice to prove to herself that she had made the right decision—to make sure that he had found his happiness once again. With that knowledge, she could establish closure. Without it, the superficial wound would heal over, but the deep chasm underneath would not granulate in. In medicine, nonhealing wounds required time, an adequate blood supply, and sometimes debridement of the dead tissue so that new cells could lay down a matrix for new skin. The anger she felt energized her, and its sharp edges would be the thing that debrided her wounds…and kickstarted the healing process.

Jets of dingy street water sprayed onto Alex's scrub pants as she schlepped down the sidewalk on the way to work. At the transition between winter and spring in Philadelphia, after the snow melts and before the delicate cherry blossoms bloomed encouragement, the incessant rain came. It created a watery landscape of dripping clouds that soaked the ground and Alex's hair, sending rivulets running off her umbrella and onto her shoulders as she stepped into the hospital lobby. She didn't mind the rain though. It matched her mood.

Once she had received the all-clear from Gibson, she had immersed herself in clinical work with a diligent fury. Arriving way before dawn, she examined every patient, reviewed every lab value, and had time to catch up on any recently published critical care literature before joining rounds. This morning, prior to rounds, a paper cup of steaming chai in her hand, she scrolled through her email and honed into one in particular from the *Journal of Pediatrics*. She clicked it open.

*Congratulations, Dr. Wilde. Your article titled "Educational Interventions and Optimization of Care Delivery for Critically Ill Children in Botswana" has been accepted for publication.*

Alex blinked and reread the email. Her first published paper. She pumped her fist in the air and let out a celebratory squeal, thankful that no one was in the office to see her. It was mid-day in Gaborone. She took a chance and dialed Dr. K.

"Hello, Dr. Alex," he boomed into the phone. His voice always made her smile. "I don't have much time."

She heard cars whizzing and honking in the background. "It's okay. I just wanted to let you know that our paper is getting published in the *Journal of Pediatrics*."

"Hot dog," he exclaimed after a brief moment of silence, and Alex couldn't help but chuckle.

"I know. I can't believe it!"

"Alex, I have not wanted to rush you with anything, especially after your terrible incident, but I would like to know your thoughts on the job."

Alex inhaled, something solidifying inside her, like pieces of a Tetris game falling into place.

"I would like to accept." The air whooshed out of her chest, her words carried on air molecules mixed with terror but also quiet relief.

"Excellent. I will be in touch soon with the details."

She heard a distinct click and the phone disconnected.


"Give twenty milliliters per kilogram of lactated ringer's and call me with the heart rate."

Alex snapped her gloves in the trash, spread alcohol foam over her hands, and set out for the next bed space all in the same smooth motion. If her intuition aligned with the full moon's premonition, she knew this Friday evening in April was turning into a very long night.

Although their shifts had ended hours ago, she, Tim, and Beth were still at the hospital putting out fires. Alex walked by a crash cart, its drawers splayed open, medication bottles littering the top, and beyond its silhouette, she saw Tim engaged in putting a breathing tube into a teenager with a poly-drug overdose. She gestured a quick thumbs-up in his direction and kept striding for the east wing of the ICU, where Beth needed her assistance with an arterial line in a tiny baby with unexplained pulmonary hypertension.

The baby, recently discharged from the neonatal ICU, had abominable lung disease at baseline and now needed a breathing tube for a viral infection she had caught from one of her siblings. The room had been converted into a mini-operating room for the procedure with sterile blue drapes covering every inch of surface that wasn't the tiny square of pale skin that Beth was poking with a needle.

"How is it going?" Alex asked from the doorway, tying a surgical mask behind her head and opening a package of sterile gloves.

"Disgustingly terrible." Beth's voice was muffled behind her own mask. "I keep getting a flash, but I can't pass the bloody wire."

"This baby is really tiny. Her arteries are probably smaller than a piece of spaghetti. Don't give up," Alex added encouragingly as she started prepping a second site.

"Son of a...ughh." Beth dropped her head as she removed a very distorted-appearing wire.

"I'll try the femoral artery. No promises, but we might be able to get it if we work together. I'll stick—you pass the wire, okay?"

Beth begrudgingly picked up the wire and nodded. Saying a silent prayer, Alex stuck once, and a pulsing stream of bright red blood shot up the needle.

"Now," she commanded Beth, and the wire glided into the vessel like it was going through melted butter on a summer sidewalk.

"Fabulous," Beth muttered and proceeded to place the catheter and suture it into place.

"Beth, what's taking so long?" shouted an irritated voice from the doorway.

"I got it," Beth grunted as she threw in the last suture.

"Good. Alex—I need a word with you," Dr. Gibson called and turned on her heel.

"Thanks," Beth said quietly.

"No problem," Alex replied. "I'll see what she wants, then let's get a drink and regroup with Tim about what's left to do."

Alex found Dr. Gibson in her office, plucking away at her laptop keyboard like she was taking over the world one email at a time. She didn't look up as she spoke.

"Sit."

Alex did as she was commanded, pulling over a spare black desk chair.

"Have you found a job?"

"Um...yes...I accepted a position in Botswana."

Her painted-on eyebrows rose as a unit. "Hmm. Did your dog die?"

"Not that I know of."

"Get evicted from your apartment? Heard that Diet Coke is no longer being mass produced?" Gibson smiled at her own joke, thin and brief, but it had happened.

"No." Alex could not figure out where this was headed.

"Then what, Dr. Wilde, is wrong with you?" She pushed back from her desk and replaced her oversized red-rimmed glasses on her face, staring at Alex with eyes the size of gourds.

*I lost the love of my life.* The thought was fleeting but real, and she sent it up, up, and away like a helium balloon in a summer breeze.

Alex threw up her hands. "I don't know, but I assume you do, so why don't you tell me."

She had never spoken this candidly to Gibson before and received a look that encompassed both admonishment and respect at the same time.

"Despite your best efforts at hiding it," she said in an authoritative tone, "you have a heart of gold. You may not always know what to do—that will come with experience—but you always know how to do it. You have a bleeding heart to a fault—kind, compassionate, thoughtful. Lately, you practice medicine like it is pure science—exact, clinical, calculable. While you made a lot of children improve, you did not impress me or your patients. So, I ask again, what happened?"

Alex could feel every single beat of hot blood shooting through her arteries and her pupils dilating from the adrenaline. "I did exactly what you said. You told me to choose what to sacrifice...so I did."

"It seems..." Gibson paused dramatically and resumed typing. "That perhaps you made the wrong choice."


Alex stomped all the way to the soda machine and then back to the office with a variety of caffeinated beverages. "Take your pick," she said, plunking the sodas down on her desk. "Apparently, I have no idea how to make choices, so I'll take what's left."

Tim and Beth, seated in identical rolling desk chairs, simultaneously glanced up at her in surprise. Tim wadded up his surgical mask and attempted a seated jump shot into the trash can. "What's up Gibson's backside?" he said nonchalantly.

Alex fell into her own chair and cracked open one of the Diet Coke bottles. "I have never worked harder in my life...despite being near graduation...despite publishing a paper...despite recovering from multisystem trauma...and she is not *impressed* with my performance." Alex made melodramatic air quotes.

"What exactly did she say?" Tim inquired as he guzzled half his Coke in record time.

Alex started slowly, attempting to explain her conversation with Gibson. "She said my work has been clinically good, but it's missing…something."

Beth, who had been strangely quiet, now piped up.

"Heart…passion…joy."

"Basically…how did you know?"

"It's what she has told me for three years. Clinically I'm, well, near perfect." She gave a simpering smile. "But I lack—how did she put it—zeal."

Alex shook her head, trying to erase the conversation like words on a chalkboard. "Six months ago, she told me to stop being distracted and make a sacrifice that would make me a better doctor. Now she tells me I'm no better—possibly worse—and I apparently chose poorly."

"Well, you did," Beth offered.

"I can't have everything, and I made a choice," Alex responded icily.

"You're wrong." Beth shook her head. "You *can* have everything…just not all at the same time."

"Who are you, and what did you do with Queen B?" Tim asked, flabbergasted.

Beth shrugged. "Boston offered me everything I dreamed of— seed money for research, opportunities for early career advancement, mentorship—but I chose Seattle for the clinical flexibility. And for the guy I've been seeing who lives there."

Tim choked on his soda with a guttural noise that mimicked a wounded animal, and Alex sat, stone-faced, staring at Beth, trying to digest the words coming out of her mouth.

"I'm not necessarily telling you to choose Ian—that plane has completely gone down in flames." Beth fluttered her dark lashes to the ceiling as Alex and Tim exchanged looks. "But I am telling you to choose love—either for someone else or—" She paused dramatically. "For you."

# TWENTY-EIGHT

More rain. Tiny tributaries streamed down the oval window to form misshapen lakes across the tarmac. *It had been raining that day too.* Alex could both see her reflection in the glass and see beyond it to the flurry of activity as airline workers scurried like ants through the torrent. Her face bordered on transparent, as if the rain was washing away her fortitude bit by bit and leaving fragility in its place.

After arriving home from the hospital just a few hours before dawn, she collapsed into her bed, unaware of the subsequent voicemails left by Janie Wilde. She had awoken with the sun already burning a hole in her eyelids and startled when she glanced at her phone. Her mom answered on the first ring. "I'm sorry to have to tell you this on the phone, honey, but John Robert died. They found him last night."

In a swirling state of shock, her voice felt mechanical. "I'll be there soon."

Alex stared into the rain streaming across her face in the airplane window and thought, ironically, how it made her look as if she was crying. *She hadn't cried that day either.*

"Mommy, it's still raining!" Alex announced, clutching her brown puppy to her chest, his soft fur tickling her chin. Their little blue house, situated on the bank of a brackish river that met the Gulf of Mexico, shuddered with the impending storm. Alex heard the roof creak in anguish with the first peal of thunder. Janie wiped her hands on a dishtowel and crouched next to her daughter in front of the window to the backyard.

"The water sure is high," she said to her daughter, and they stared together at brownish-gray waves lapping over the pier. "Come on to the table, honey. I fixed us some supper."

Alex took her seat on the wooden pullout bench, scruffy dog beside her, and obediently began poking a pile of chicken with her fork.

"When will Daddy be home?"

John Robert worked on one of the local shrimping boats and was accustomed to long, arduous days in the heat and salt-filled air. He often didn't mind rewarding himself at the end of the day with a stop at Cooter's for a drink...or seven. Janie would fix him a plate and leave it in a warm oven for him to stumble home to, receiving a snide insult or a broken dish for her gesture.

"He'll be along soon, I imagine. Now eat your broccoli too," Janie chided.

By the time Alex was brushing her long milk chocolate hair and dressed in her favorite My Little Pony pajamas, the rain had become a torrential downpour, and the wind caused the trees outside her bedroom window to kowtow to the storm. Janie appeared with a thick volume of fairy tales, and she jumped onto her twin mattress with glee, making room for her mom to slide in next to her. She cracked open the spine of the book.

"What will it be tonight, my sweet girl?"

"How about Sleeping Beauty?" Alex yawned.

Janie flipped open the threadbare book, handing it over to Alex. "You read better than I do these days. You can read to me."

Alex smiled up at her and began, "Once upon a time..."

They must have fallen asleep for several hours, snuggled together for warmth and protection against the storm that raged outside because when Alex awoke, it was pitch black in her room. She slept with her lamp on every night—a porcelain unicorn base with a pink shade that they had found in a garage sale. The bulb was dark, which meant the electricity was off. She frantically searched her bed for her mom and connected with her warm, still body, her chest rising and falling in peaceful sleep.

"Mom...Mom, wake up." Alex shook her shoulder violently.

The air felt electric like the static created in Alex's socks when they emerged from the dryer, and a gigantic flash lit up the room as aggressive God-worthy thunder rocked the floorboards underneath her bare feet. Janie flew to the window, staring into the pelting rain as if to glean wisdom for what to do next.

"Oh my God," she uttered and jerked Alex's arm toward the closet, opening it to reveal a few clothes and her only pair of shoes.

"Put your shoes on, sweetie, and get your backpack. Put your favorite thing in it and come to the kitchen."

Alex found her shoes, a pair of white trainers, and her school bag and stuffed scruffy dog in the top, zipping his head inside. When she made it to the kitchen, Janie had opened the backdoor and was busy cramming her feet into a pair of muddy rubber boots. Alex could see the surging river, black and ominous, right outside the open screen door. Even as a child, she realized the house risked being washed away with the next storm surge and a cold fear spread to her toes. They were trapped here. John Robert drove their beat-up Ford truck to work and back every day, and more than likely, it was parked right outside Cooter's bar while its owner took a last call and waited out the storm.

Janie knelt to the kitchen linoleum. "Alex, I need you to do exactly what I say. When I tell you to run—run. If I tell you to leave me—you leave me. We are going to try to outrun this river. If we can make it up the road to the fire station, they can help us."

"I'm ready, mom."

She held out her little hand to meet her mom's not much bigger one, and they stepped out into the rain.

The raindrops hit her face like shards of glass, stinging her cheeks and dripping over her eyelids. They had a small flashlight, a few photons acting as their beacon of hope in the pitch black, allowing them to see where their feet were striking the ground. Alex, hand in hand with Janie, ran without stopping—away from the rising river and, although she didn't know it at the time, away from their previous life for good.

The last mile of their journey had been through water up to Alex's knees, but she was proud that she made it the entire way running alongside her brave mother and didn't have to ask to be carried. They arrived at the fire station and collapsed on the steps, soaked to their bones and covered in a layer of mud that took Alex days to extract from her hair. The fire chief transported them to the hospital in the nearest neighboring town of Cole's Church, where they were checked out and then released the following day.

John Robert was not there to pick them up at the hospital. In fact, they didn't know whether he was even alive for several days until they saw him driving down Main Street, weaving from side to side in the blue Ford. Janie, who was not one for dishonesty, told Alex that their house and everything in it had been washed away by the river that night. A few months later, they drove by to view the site of their previous home, now a pile of splintered two by fours and haphazard shingles covered in a thick crust of earth.

Alex never saw her father again after that day except for the occasional sighting of his silhouette in his truck parked outside the liquor store or his random appearance at a high school football game a time or two. She had gone years at a time without even thinking of him, but she never able to completely bury the memories. They haunted her dreams with the smell of stale alcohol and fish guts and the sensation of water rushing past her knees.

"How was the flight, honey?" Janie asked as Alex tossed her suitcase into the bed of the cherry red truck.

"Bumpy and long," she replied. She could feel the inkling of a migraine erupting behind her left eye and leaned her head back on the leather seat.

They rode in silence, each of them processing the maelstrom of emotions that leach out when someone dies. Alex was overcome with the nausea that typically accompanied her headaches and needed a solid distraction.

"How did it happen, mom?" she asked, mostly out of medical curiosity.

"Liver cancer. Apparently, he had known for some time."

"That's not surprising with his alcohol use," Alex noted and turned the radio down to a hum. "What do we need to do?" she asked, not sure if she wanted to know the answer.

"He has no living relatives, so I said we would arrange the wake and the church service and see that he's buried."

"When is all of this happening?" Alex felt the throbbing in her head reach the red zone, wishing she could give herself a tiny craniotomy for pressure release.

"The wake is tonight at the funeral home, and the service will be at our church tomorrow."

"I'm surprised Pastor Brian agreed to do the service."

"I suppose this is an act of goodwill and kindness on his part."

"It's going to be the shortest funeral in history," Alex muttered.

Janie said nothing and refocused her eyes on the gray asphalt ahead of them and drove.

The funeral home smelled of stale coffee and despair, and Alex retreated to the bathroom with the guise of needing a moment to redo her hair. She stood in front of the overly large mirror, hands on the counter in a navy-blue wrap dress that hugged her tiny frame, and simply exhaled. Her ocean-blue eyes were accented by a violaceous hue underneath that stubbornly refused to be covered with concealer. Suddenly, Ian's words chugged through her brain like a bullet train. *Do you even know who you are, Alex? I do. No matter what I have accomplished, inside, I'm still a frightened little girl.*

"Alex, it is so good to see you. You are so grown up and absolutely beautiful," said a rich voice that made her think of sweet iced tea.

"Thank you. It's good to see you too, Pastor Brian."

"I am so sorry for your loss. I'll be praying for you and your mama," he said in a thick East Texas accent.

"That's kind of you," Alex replied.

"Your mama tells me that you are a famous doctor up in Philadelphia."

"Not the famous part," Alex smiled.

"Well, she sure is proud of you and I know your dad was proud of you too."

Alex stiffened and nodded but said nothing as her skin grew gooseflesh.

"You know I met with him once the week before he died." Alex lifted her brows. "And he wanted me to give you this." He handed her an envelope, her name scribbled on the back in a childlike script.

"Thank you, Pastor Brian, for this and for doing the service."

She hastily stuffed the envelope into her leather shoulder bag and took her place in the front of the room next to the simple pine coffin with the lid thankfully closed.

The visitation lasted a mere hour, and Alex had counted down every single minute until she could escape the constriction of that room and her pantyhose. A handful of people had stopped by, mostly scraggly fisherman in overalls who had worked with John Robert or longtime drinking buddies who kept the barstools warm at Cooter's. One particular man shuffled in and reached a dingy hand out to Alex.

"I'm awfully sorry about your papa."

"Thank you," Alex replied mechanically, as she had with every other visitor.

His face was deeply wrinkled and scattered with the signs of sun damage, and his nose, red and edematous, overly large for his face. It was the nose of someone who always kept a bottle nearby. As the whiskey vapors struck her face, Alex felt a rush of blood to her head as hundreds of tiny memory specks rose to the surface of her consciousness. A rough hand dragging her elbow through the supermarket as her bare feet struggled to keep up. The splitting sound of dishes breaking mixed with her mother sobbing and always the stench of stale alcohol as abusive words absconded from cruel lips. Her entire childhood had been dominated by terror and insecurity. She had never felt guilty for being grateful to the raging storm that night. It had been the catalyst that changed everything.

After the last straggler had paid respects, Alex retreated to the sanctuary of her mom's truck for some much-needed desensitization therapy in the quiet warmth of the front seat. Her migraine continued to pound a steady rhythm of pain behind her left eye. Her mom tapped on the truck window, and she reluctantly opened the door.

"Sorry, Mom. I just had to get out of there."

"It's okay, honey. We just need to be over at the church in a minute. The ladies have a spread set out for us."

In small-town Texas, a casserole and a Bundt cake could solve just about anything. Whenever someone died, the "ladies", who were the indomitable pillars of her childhood Baptist church, amassed a feast that could have literally fed the five thousand…with seconds. Alex surveyed the buffet of dishes with both appreciation and disdain. She didn't think her stomach could tolerate so much love in the form of cheese and mayonnaise.

The ladies bustled about in their floral dresses and sensible shoes, murmuring instructions to each other and casting smiles in her direction. Even though she and her mother had not lived with John Robert for more than two decades, the ladies acted like he had been the center of their lives with their empathetic grief and bountiful "bless your hearts". Alex knew it was for lack of knowing what else to do. This one-act play was on repeat in their town, and these ladies were the consistent actors every time a loved one was lost. They would never trade honesty for their ladylike reputations.

Alex played with a piece of pound cake on her plate, letting the buttery crumbs coat her fork and then her tongue, wishing she could astral project herself somewhere tropical. A tinny but fabulously familiar voice echoed behind her.

"Alex?"

"Natalie?"

Alex turned and spied her best friend from high school in all of her freckled strawberry blonde glory in a royal blue sheath dress, arms outstretched, ready to pull her into an embrace.

"I haven't seen you in so long."

Alex filed backward through her memory catalog as toned, tan arms wrapped around her middle. They had last seen one another at a mutual friend's baby shower, almost five years ago, right in this very fellowship hall. She looked amazing, more blonde than strawberry at this point in her life, and wearing shoes with a very signature red bottom.

"How are you doing with all this?" she said in a low voice, her eyes searching for the things Alex couldn't quite speak aloud.

"I'm okay. I guess I expected this to happen sooner or later."

She appraised Alex up and down. "You've gotten too skinny. They are working you too hard at…where are you a doctor now?"

"Philadelphia," Alex smiled. "Where are you these days?"

"Dallas…and loving it!"

"It suits you," Alex said with sincere warmth and then bit her lower lip. "I've missed you. I'm so sorry about these last few years. Time has just gotten away from me…"

Natalie rolled her eyes in the melodramatic way Alex remembered.

"Are you kidding? We'll just pick up where we left off."


They stayed up talking until almost midnight, sharing life stories and a bottle of wine Alex had managed to knab from the county line liquor store on the way home. Alex hadn't felt this connected to her past since she had left for college and never looked back. She could almost feel the roots sprouting into the earth of her soul. Natalie talked animatedly about her life in the fast-paced world of Dallas real estate, and once the wine bottle neared empty, they began reminiscing about high school.

"I can't believe we did that!" Alex wheezed with laughter and could practically feel the winter air on her bare breasts, remembering how they drove topless at top speed with the windows down through the county backroads.

"We were young...and fearless." Natalie giggled and slurped the last drops of wine from her glass. "And the time we canoed down the river in the middle of the night with Justin James so the cops wouldn't catch us drinking in the barn."

"I was just like Sacagawea," Alex sighed, the memory surging back like it was yesterday.

"Justin was so into you. He probably still is." Natalie released the uncontrollable tittering of one who has just consumed too much wine and too little dinner.

"What?" Alex asked, incredulous. "We kissed once...in your car...on the way back from a New Year's Eve pasture party. That hardly is the foundation for true love."

Natalie shrugged suggestively and cut her eyes at Alex. "Maybe that's all you need. One single perfect moment in time."

Alex threw a purple pillow in her direction, trying to push down the memory of her one perfect moment in time.


The forecast predicted a cloudless sky and luxurious sunshine on what would prove to be one of the least humid days in Cole's Church history. Not the typical day one would expect for a funeral. Alex stepped on the emergency brake in the red truck, and she and Janie walked as a unit up to the white limestone Baptist church, the church of her youth that was shaped interestingly like the Alamo. They walked up the aisle of the sanctuary and slid into the padded burgundy pew near the front joining the five other funeral-goers, one of which included Natalie who gave her a wave of encouragement.

Alex had declined to give a eulogy, asking Pastor Brian if he could deliver it instead, in addition to his short message. She tucked her black patent heels underneath the pew and smoothed the wrinkles in her black crepe sheath dress with sweaty palms. Janie, seated next to her, sat peacefully neutral during the service, and Alex couldn't help but envy her composure.

Pastor Brian droned on about forgiveness of sin at the end of one's life and how John Robert could be considered much like the criminal who was crucified next to Christ and promised a post in heaven. Alex did her best to tune out the embellished truths and outright lies of John Robert's miserable life. Instead, her mind roved to Ian and wondered how he had felt during Ryan's funeral. Had he been overwhelmed with guilt and grief? She wondered how a boy who had suffered so much could have grown into a man who could love so freely and recklessly. A man who would fly to Haiti and yank her, literally kicking and screaming, out of a medical tent. No matter how she had tried to fill her life, there remained a giant hole where Ian belonged.

The sun scattered into its various refracted particles through the stained-glass images of the story of Christ and right onto the material of Alex's black dress. By the time "Amazing Grace" was played by the pianist, she yearned to be outside, feeling the sunlight on her hair, reminding her that she hadn't died and was still expected to live her life to the fullest.

"That concludes our service," announced Pastor Brian. Alex nearly wilted in gratitude. "If anyone would like to attend the burial, John Robert has requested that he be buried in the old Stagg's road church cemetery."

Too numb to be shocked by anything at this point, Alex parked the red truck on the side of the gravel road and walked in her heels up to the rickety wooden bridge over the creek leading to the white A-frame church. Janie had declined joining her with the excuse of needing to "meet folks at the house."

Alex had always believed that, similar to birth, death needed a witness, and she was here to ensure that her father's corpse was returned to the earth. As she traversed the bridge, images of Ian and the last time she was here popped into her mind and weighed down her steps more than her pinching heels. Her shoes sunk into the ground as she trekked up to the grassy hill and the plot of freshly overturned earth marked by a simple wooden white cross. Halfway there, she removed her shoes, allowing the brown dirt particles to settle between her toes.

Wildflowers had sprouted amidst the thick grass, and she crouched to remove a few bluebonnets by their stems. They were wild types, natural products of the land, occurring every spring when the rains paused, and the sun emerged. Today, the sun shone brilliantly onto the tranquil gravesite, and Alex lifted her face upward and felt overwhelmingly alive.

She played with some of the loose dirt with one toe.

"I never thought about you after that day of the storm. I wasn't angry or sad that you made our lives miserable or left us to drown. I didn't feel anything toward you. And now that you're dead, I've decided that I am angry. And in the very moment that you can't hear a word, I've decided that I have things to say."

Alex drew a deep life-giving breath. "You made me feel worthless—like I wasn't worth loving. Every great thing I have ever done is in spite of you."

Her voice echoed off the back wall of the wooden church and gained strength as the thistles bowed, and the wind picked up around her. "My entire life, I never trusted anyone to love me, and I gave up the only real love I have ever known from a man...because of you. You have influenced all of my choices—the good and the bad—but I won't give you that power anymore. I choose to forgive you. I choose to forget you. And I choose me and my life...without your dark shadow hanging over it."

She turned, her face meeting the sun and the wind stroking her back as she strode across the bridge.

"Goodbye, John Robert."

# TWENTY-NINE

Alex sat in the driveway of Janie's white clapboard house, parked behind Peter's black Chevy pickup, unable to command her limbs to actually exit the vehicle. She couldn't bear to exhibit any more fake grief to the cluster of people perusing the house like bees in a hive. Her mom was seated in the porch swing, flanked by two longtime friends holding glasses of chilled iced tea, most likely engrossed in the therapeutic sharing of the latest gossip. With a wave of acknowledgment in her mom's direction, she started the truck engine and pulled the gear shift into reverse with no idea where she was going. At that moment, the destination seemed less important than the journey itself.

Alex drove through the single stoplight twice with the windows down, letting the beginnings of spring infiltrate her senses with its faint scent of honeysuckle and promise of renewal. Without realizing it, she found herself entering the two-lane highway on the outskirts of town where the roadside was generously dotted with tiny blue and orange wildflowers, poking their tiny heads upward from the unmown grass.

After a few miles, the next town came into view. With its well-stocked general store and franchise eateries, it was the epicenter of activity for all the surrounding towns whose dots were too small for the map. She skillfully maneuvered the truck into one of the slots at a well-established hamburger joint where she placed an order for a large vanilla Diet Coke over a crackly speaker. They had the best ice on the planet here.

Now that her radius had increased from the exact middle of nowhere, her phone gained a few bars, which was the only good thing that had happened all day. She pressed Rox's picture, which she had updated to a manicured hand boasting a sizeable yellow diamond ring.

"Hello, my dear." Rox's usual effervescence seemed flat today, a strong note of tired in her voice.

"I'm sorry to call so late, Rox."

Alex hesitated and then made a quick decision. She wasn't quite ready to fling open the door to her past and she was incredibly bored of talking and thinking about herself.

"I'm just checking in about the wedding plans," Alex said evenly. "I sent you a few dresses I found online, and I looked at the website for the venue in Provence. It's going to be beautiful." An awkward moment ensued while Alex waited for Rox to respond.

"I honestly don't know if there is going to be a wedding."

"What happened?" Alex inhaled sharply.

"Ugh...I'm surprised you don't already know. It's been all over social media."

"I've been a little out of touch." She sipped her drink and settled into the leather truck seat.

"Some trollop is blackmailing Nic. She threatened him with sending me a video of their supposed tryst. He called her bluff and told me...but now she's shared it with some sleazy magazine that's posted it on the internet."

Alex let out a groan of pure frustration. "I'm so sorry, Rox. I hate to even ask...but have you watched it? Is it Nic?"

"Of course I watched it! I'm not an ostrich type of gal."

Alex had to stifle her laughter. "And?"

She could picture Rox chewing on the end of whatever writing instrument she had in her possession. "I honestly don't know. It's dark and grainy and taken from a security camera outside some bar."

"What does Nic say?"

"That the entire thing is ridiculous. That she just wants money and attention."

"Do you believe him?"

"I want to, but I need to take a step back. Pump the brakes a bit and make sure this whole thing is what I really truly want."

"I know what you mean...except I apparently don't just put my foot on the brake, I completely transect the cables," Alex said with a wry smile. She heard the rumbling of a laugh that then erupted into a chuckle, and then explosive staccato giggles intermixed with a snort or two.

"I am crying!" Rox guffawed into the phone receiver. "And about to wee myself. I'm sorry. That was just the funniest thing I've heard in months. I have this image in my head of you and me in a convertible just flying over a cliff."

"Like Thelma and Louise?" Alex offered.

"Yesss!" Rox crowed, and they laughed like cackling hens until she sighed longingly. "I miss you, my dear."

The tug on Alex's heart was tangible.


The airport was uncomfortably chilly, and Alex zipped up her navy hoodie. "I'll be fine, mom. I promise."

Alex hugged Janie tightly around the shoulders before entering the serpentine security line at the airport. Janie waved from the expansive lobby, always a little tearful at Alex's departure but more so today. She could actually see the outer corners of her eyelids glistening from her position in line and wondered if it was because she had told her about accepting a job in Botswana. Alex knew her mom had hoped she would take a job closer to home, preferably within driving distance, but she wasn't ready to settle somewhere yet, and moving to Botswana gave her the perfect opportunity to delay that decision. The promise of adventure and self-discovery awaited her and, as an added benefit, she knew it would keep Ian close. She wanted to live in the country where they met and oversee the manifestation of his generosity.

Alex missed him, and now on an airplane without any opportunity for distractions, she closed her eyes and let herself open the neatly packed away box marked Ian. *Did he truly love her?* She knew that he did. At this moment, instead of denial, she felt the tender acceptance of such a love...and an overwhelming desire to drink in every drop and return it in magnitudes. Something wonderful and terrifying had happened to her in the last few days. Her heart had opened to the possibility of a wondrous love that knew no limits. A love that demanded vulnerability but promised intimacy. A love that demanded sacrifice but guaranteed blessings. A love that was reckless...timeless...epic. That kind of love was not just possible, it was within her reach. A love that promised freedom.

"Pardon me," uttered the lady seated next to her with snow-white hair and a classy Hermès bag. "Can I borrow a pen?"

Alex reluctantly emerged from her epiphany moment.

"Sure," she replied and dug around her powder blue leather satchel, catching sight of a sealed white envelope as she did so. "Here you go," she said and handed over the blue ballpoint.

She pulled out the envelope given to her by Pastor Brian at the wake and stared at it as if it might spontaneously combust in her hand. She opened it and pulled out a barely legible handwritten note and a cashier's check for $1287.30.

*Dear Alexandra,*
*I never was good with words. I don't have much, but it's yours. Spend it on something for you. I'm sorry. Dad*

Alex didn't know how to feel about clutching a lifetime's worth of regret and monetary savings in one fist. She shoved it down into her bag to let it marinate there out of her sight.

"Here, dear. Thank you."

The lady handed back her pen, and she noticed a giant aquamarine cocktail ring winking at her from the lady's right hand. Next to the elegant woman, Alex felt like a village peasant, dressed in yoga pants and a green Phillies baseball hat pulled low over her face.

"You're welcome." Alex smiled and dropped the pen in her purse.

The lady pursed her lips and fussed with some lint on her black pantsuit. "If I don't write things down these days, I simply just forget."

"What were you writing, if you don't mind me asking?" Alex said warmly.

"Just something I read the other day." She paused dramatically and closed her eyes. *"The very essence of romance is uncertainty."*

Alex nodded and dredged up a forgotten college English essay. "Oscar Wilde?"

"Yes, I believe so. I have always been a romantic myself. My family disapproved of my husband when we were courting, and I had to make a choice. One day I boarded a train with him and never looked back." She smiled with a far-away look in her eyes.

"Any regrets?" asked Alex.

"Only that I didn't do it sooner," she said with a wink, her age lines crinkling around glassy blue eyes.

Alex ambled off the plane, her bag in tow, down the jetway, past the novelty shops and eateries, to where she visualized the revolving exit door. Instead of exiting, she took a seat at the bookstore café and ordered a tea. The fragrant smell of chamomile mixed with a drop of honey seemed to center her a little more with every inhale.

Every memory she had of Ian flooded her consciousness. All at once, her heart nearly burst with the love blossoming inside of her that currently had no outlet. She palpated her own neck, half convinced that her pulse might have disappeared in the midst of her exploding myocardium. As she spun the warm mug in a tight circle, she decided that she had to tell him—not over the phone but in person. She wanted to hold Ian's face in her hands when she told him she was in love with him. Everything else in her life could wait.

She quickly paid for the tea and, with renewed purpose and an overwhelming sense of lunacy, strode up to a British Airways gate agent before she could change her mind.

"Pardon me," she said to a middle-aged woman with hair chopped into a trendy shag cut and a generous amount of blue eyeliner highlighting her grey eyes.

"Can I help you?" she murmured in a hint of a British accent without looking up from the keyboard where she was typing.

Alex faltered for a moment then fished the cashier's check from the bottom of her bag. "I need a seat on the next flight to London."

The agent continued making rapid keystrokes without talking for a moment, and Alex felt the bottom fall out of her stomach.

"One seat left in first class on our next flight leaving from Gate D27. Leaving in thirty minutes."

Alex felt her adrenaline spike as she scrambled to locate her passport, which, thankfully, Ian had thought to retrieve from Haiti.

"How much?"

"One thousand three hundred seventy-three dollars...and thirty cents."

Alex bundled her passport, credit card, and the cashier's check and shoved them across the counter as a unit. "I'll take it," she said, hopping from one foot to the other as the printer screeched while printing her boarding pass. With the glorious sound of ripping paper, the speculative agent handed her a pamphlet of stamped papers.

"You might want to run."

Alex weaved and dodged like a thoroughbred in the Kentucky derby, legs pumping and heart pounding, and couldn't help but think how her running addiction was finally coming in handy. When she collapsed into her plush first-class seat—the most expensive thing she had ever bought besides her brain—she accepted the mini bottle of white wine from the flight attendant and pulled out her phone to send one essential text before take-off.

*Rox—On my way to London. I'll be there in six hours.*

"I can't believe you are actually here," Rox exclaimed as she weaved through the frenetic traffic of early morning Londoners anxious to reach their destinations.

Alex yawned. "Me neither. I feel like I'm in the middle of a dream...about the Indy 500." She laughed as one only does as punch drunk and jet-lagged.

"I have clinic all day, so I am going to drop you at the flat, but I'll try to make it back early."

"Sounds good." Alex smashed her head against the chill of the passenger side window trying to will herself awake.

"Believe me, dear, I am absolutely thrilled you are here...but why are you here?"

"I need to see him, Rox."

She could feel the elegant tension in her best friend's posture.

"And why is that?" Crisp, pregnant silence filled the car.

"Because I need to tell him I'm in love with him," she said plainly and without outward fanfare, although her insides practically combusted as the words left her lips. Now that they were out in the world, heard by someone else's ears, they had become real.

Rox nearly swerved the car onto the sidewalk in celebration as her ecstatic scream rang in Alex's ears.

"I knew it...ha! I knew it."

"I need to get some sleep first, not to mention a shower. I look and smell like a homeless person."

Although Alex was breaking the bank with her level of patience, her eyes justifiably refused to open any further than slits.

"Okay. I'll pick you up right after work, and we'll track him down. Nic will know where he is today."

Alex was deposited on the sidewalk in front of a cranberry-colored brick building boasting a large archway where a wooden door and a brass doorknob held the key to her respite…literally.

After a steaming hot shower and several hours of glorious sleep in Rox and Nic's spare bedroom, Alex felt clear-headed enough to prepare to see Ian. They hadn't spoken in almost three months—not since he had left her in Texas. The few times she had allowed herself to scan the internet gossip, his photographs, so prevalent before, had still not appeared. She had remained content with the few pictures she kept on her phone of moments that seemed eternally precious now that there might not be any more of them. She felt wistful but calm, terrified but purposeful, and held on to the hope that his love for her had not waned and that she could maintain this brave new version of herself if it had.

A quick rap on the door and then it swung open to reveal a breathless Rox carrying a shopping bag.

"You're home early," Alex remarked, continuing to brush out her mildly damp hair.

"I had a few cancellations this afternoon, and I thought you might need me, so here I am."

She gave Alex a quick wink and dumped out the contents of the shopping bag onto the bed—a new pair of jeans and a long-sleeved striped Breton.

"Seriously, Rox, you spoil me." Alex held the new blouse up to her frame, thinking it would fit perfectly.

"Somebody has to," she said with an exaggerated eye roll. "I have a coat you can borrow. It's still chilly here, you know."

Alex had forgotten that the only items in her carryon were funeral attire that she wanted to toss in a dumpster the first chance she got. She couldn't stand clothes with bad memories, and she dared hope that these new ones would be associated with good ones. She pulled on the dark washed jeans, a trendy straight leg variety that hugged her calves.

"Where is Nic today?"

"He's around…practice and what not."

"How are things with you guys?" Alex asked gently, hoping for a positive response.

"Let's get going." Rox glanced at her watch. "It might take us a bit to get there. We'll talk in the car."

"Where are we going?" Alex frowned in confusion.

"Nic said Ian has been staying out at his dad's place outside London. I thought we'd try there first."

"Oh. Okay. How do I look?"

She turned around a few times and swept her hair into a high ponytail feeling very British in her Breton and trainers. She'd applied a little makeup, enough to pink her cheeks and add some shine to her lips and received a bright smile of approval from Rox.

"Smashing, dear. Your eyes are smiling even when your lips are not."

Once in the car while speeding through the London streets toward their destination of Waltham Abbey, Alex experienced a growing sense of panic as the traffic thinned out, the road widened, and the buildings dispersed into the countryside. The view was Jane Austen-worthy picturesque with rolling hills, green with the promise of spring, and Victorian homes with peaked roofs. In an honest attempt to be a good friend rather than focus on internal turmoil, Alex drew away from the window and turned to Rox.

"So, tell me what's going on with Nic."

Rox narrowed her perfectly done smoky eyelids and gripped the steering wheel a little harder. "He's bloody perfect. Giving me space and writing me love notes and leaving my dinner in a warm oven if I'm late."

"Sounds awful," Alex commiserated.

"It is!" Rox threw up her hands, and the car swerved onto the left shoulder. "It confuses me and makes me hate him...and makes me love him more."

"This is your life Rox. Just yours. And you don't have to do anything you don't want to. I learned the hard way that choosing someone takes courage, and you have more courage than anyone I've ever known...but you need to be sure that he is choosing you too."

Rox was abnormally quiet for several miles before speaking over the background hum of the engine. "He is the love of my life. I do choose him…and I know deep down that he has chosen me. But I'm terrified every day that eventually some horrible thing will crash down on us and rip us apart."

Alex pondered her words and spoke carefully. "Maybe…but don't let that stop you from living the life you imagined."

Alex had lived every day of her life expecting the horrible thing to happen, which sometimes it did. Tragedy had become predictably comfortable, not only in her job, but in her life. It was past time that she took her mom's advice and learned to live in joy. Her first order of joy would be to make sure Rox got her happy ending.

The brakes squealed, and Rox threw the car in reverse, creating a fine spray of loose rocks that aerosolized behind them.

"Damn, I almost missed the driveway."

They turned left onto a paved driveway that twisted through a well-manicured front lawn dotted with neat hedges and clusters of brightly blooming flowers. The path ended in a semicircle drive in front of a massive stone English country house that had jumped straight from the pages of *Pride and Prejudice*. The peaked roof seemed like a pair of eyebrows furrowed in interest over narrow rectangular windows. Alex imagined that the inside was filled with period furniture covered in floral patterns and tiny trinkets neatly lined up on the shelves of open cabinetry. To her astonishment, parked in the circle drive opposite the arched doorway, was a blue Corvette Stingray with the top down, like she had just returned from stretching her legs on the lonely country roads.

"That's Ian's car," Alex whispered.

"Hot dog. Nic just made it off my crap list."

Alex giggled nervously. "No one says that. Have you been binge-watching *Golden Girls* again?"

"So, what if I have?" Rox neatly pulled her car in behind the blue one. "Go on then, love. I'll wait here."

Alex felt surreal, like this entire scene threatened to disappear and she would open one eye to see the Philadelphia skyline out her apartment window. She knocked on the heavy wooden door, the sound bouncing off the arched stone entryway. Through a slim rectangle of glass, she saw a prim gray-haired woman in a navy sweater and matching slacks approach and open the door warily.

"Can I help you, dear?" she said in a kind, tinkling voice that reminded Alex of a bubbling stream.

"I'm here to see Ian. I'm Alex…a friend of his."

A look of recognition crossed her aged features, and her bird-like mouth split open in a smile. "I know who you are, dearie. I have seen Master Devall's photographs on his mobile." She opened the door wider and gestured inside, "Right this way."

Alex fiddled nervously with her lion pendant, a talisman that she rarely removed these days and wished she could siphon its courage through her fingertips. She followed the stately woman into what could only be described as a library masquerading as a parlor. It was a larger version of the one Ian had in his London home. A tufted leather sofa, worn by years of patronage, stretched across one wall while every other vertical space was lined floor to ceiling with hardback books held upright by artifacts picked up on world travels. A tray of crystal highball glasses and an expensive-looking bottle of bourbon rested on an antique sidebar. Liquor preference was obviously genetic. The room wasn't the Victorian novel come to life that she had expected. Instead, it was masculine and refined, reflecting the multiple generations that had passed without any feminine influence.

"Please be seated. Master Devall will be with you shortly."

The composed older woman extended a thin, sun-spotted hand toward the leather sofa. Alex settled into the soft leather, running her hands over the worn spots and imagining Ian sitting here with a book and a half-empty glass of bourbon. Hearing the creak of floorboards, she looked up sharply toward the doorway, heart pattering wildly, but in place of Ian, a towering, distinguished appearing older gentleman filled the doorframe. His hair was thick and white and combed to perfection over a kind, sculpted face with deep-set brown eyes and trimmed facial hair that framed his mouth. Upon seeing her, that mouth had widened into a smile displaying perfectly straight pearl-like teeth. He moved with grace for such a large man, stepping over to the sofa where Alex sat precariously on the edge of her cushion and held out a gargantuan sized hand.

"Hello Alexandra, I am George Devall, Ian's father."

He had an ironically quiet voice and a lovely British accent that made everything sound pleasurable. She grasped the outstretched hand and stood abruptly. He was much taller than Ian, and although she could see similarities in their bone structure, they did not resemble one another. However, she had seen remnants of his face before—in a faded Polaroid of a little boy with sandy hair.

"Very nice to meet you, sir. I apologize for the unexpected visit, but I came to find Ian." Alex looked expectantly into the face of George Devall, not able to conjure a more accurate depiction of refined wealth if she had tried.

He released her hand and sat down in the club chair opposite her, resting his hands on the knees of his gray houndstooth trousers. He cleared his throat delicately.

"You are as beautiful as Ian described."

Alex felt her cheeks tint pink in response.

"But I am truly sorry, my dear, that you traveled all this way. Ian has been gone for some time."

# THIRTY

*Gone?* The word pinballed around Alex's brain knocking into the various lobes as she tried to decipher its meaning. Gone as in to the store? On a run? Gone as in traveling? Gone in the most final meaning of that word? She wouldn't even consider the last possibility. Her mouth was so bone dry that she could barely evacuate a word from her lips.

"Gone?" Her voice sounded hollow and disbelieving to her own ears.

"Yes. I sent him on an assignment a few months ago, and he decided to prolong his stay."

"Can I ask where?" Alex croaked.

"Mongolia," answered Mr. Devall senior.

No wonder he had not returned her calls or been captured in the media. He was completely off the grid.

A vintage silver tray was placed on a nearby side table by the woman in navy, after which she swept out of the room without fanfare.

"Could I offer you tea, Alexandra?"

Her name sounded so regal on his lips, and she remembered how Ian had savored it that first time they had met. Regaining her composure and manners, Alex responded, "Yes. Of course."

He walked over to the table and poured two steaming cups of fragrant liquid, adding a spoonful of sugar to each. He offered one of the delicate porcelain cups painted with a blue flower border to Alex. She sniffed it, letting the aroma of hyacinth and rose clear her head.

"Have you heard from him recently?"

"No, but I suspect I will soon. He is on a path of self-discovery, I think, but he will be back before the upcoming nuptials of his

285

friends Nic and Roxanne."

"Did he tell you why he decided to stay in Mongolia?" Alex said.

"I believe it had something to do with you." Mr. Devall eyed her over his cup of tea. Alex fidgeted in her seat, wondering how many details Ian had shared with his father.

"I imagine so," she said, putting her own cup to her lips.

"He tells me that you are as inspirational as you are beautiful and that your influence resulted in a very generous grant to a lovely hospital in Gaborone. He has previously found it difficult to believe in people and their causes."

Alex smiled, remembering a similar conversation with Ian in a dim-lit bar after a very lively dart tournament.

"He told me as much. He said that was why you promoted him to chairman of the Devall foundation," she offered.

"And what reason did he share with you?"

Alex looked to the ceiling, mentally scrolling back to Ian's exact phrasing. "He said you were trying to teach him a lesson…to put him in the midst of good, selfless people hoping it would rub off on him."

"What rubbish!" Mr. Devall sipped his tea. "I placed Ian in that position to show him the good that has always been inside him. He just needed a reason to find it, and you, my lovely, opened a door that had been closed for a very long time."

Alex felt cold despite the warm tea clutched between her palms. Any words that came to mind died in her throat.

Frenetic barking filled the silence, echoing off the walls, as two eager Jack Russell terriers bounded into the room. The dogs scampered straight over to Devall senior and sat at attention, posed like statues at his feet.

"Well, hello there." He reached down to scratch the pups on their heads, and they whined in response, their tails dragging across the rug in succession. "This is Winston, and this is Clementine."

He pulled two treats out of the inner pocket of his grey jacket. The dogs gently took them from his fingers with their teeth and then ran around the behind the chair to gobble them down noisily.

"They are really well trained," said Alex, talking past the prominent lump in her throat.

"Animals are a passion of mine as they are for Ian. Do you have any special pets?"

"My dog McCartney. He's a Rhodesian Ridgeback that I rescued when I was living in Gaborone."

"Then you understand the bond between dogs and their humans is lifelong." He straightened in his chair, placing the teacup on a side table. "And I take it from the name of your canine that you are a fan of the Beatles?"

Alex nodded, providing a weak smile. He opened his mouth, a clear tenor voice filling the air around her.

"And then while I'm away, I'll write home every day and send all my loving to you."

His voice was almost as good as Ian's with perfect pitch and a warm timbre. Alex recalled Ian texting her a few choice lines from that particular song, and her heart swelled a palpable tenderness.

"I always loved that song. In fact, I used to sing it to Ian when he was a little boy. I could have been Paul, you know, had I grown up in Liverpool."

He winked mischievously and stood up, stepping over to one of the bookshelves on the far wall. He pulled out a leather-bound book and removed a folded sheet of plain white paper with ruffled edges like it was torn from a journal. "I have something that I think you might want."

Gliding over to her, he handed over the slip of paper, scribbled writing visible on one side. "I took Ian's car for a little joyride the other day, and this fell out when I reached into the glove compartment." She clutched the note to her chest as if it was a lifeline to Ian.

"Thank you. I appreciate all of this," Alex whispered as he offered his arm and helped her rise from the couch.

"I will see you out, Alexandra."

She walked through the parlor toward the front door, shafts of sunlight lighting the path of her dragging feet, dreading the moment when she would step outside and sever this newfound connection to Ian. Mr. Devall opened the door, and she stepped out into the brightest of spring days and noticed that Rox had taken up residence on a stone bench and seemed engrossed in conversation on her cell. A weighty hand rested on her shoulder.

"When the time comes, tell Ian how you feel, and most importantly, don't give up hope. He will surprise you when you least expect it."

Before she could reply, he was gone, having stepped back into his home to offer her a private moment in the portico with her precious note.

She wanted to savor this moment and hold tightly to everything here that made Ian feel real. The earth his feet had touched. The house that held his memories. The very air he had breathed. The tightly packed gravel crunched under her feet as she walked over to the blue vintage sportscar glinting in the sunlight. The metal was the exact color of his eyes. Blue like the sky. Blue like flaming copper. Before she could stop herself, she reached under the silver handle and pulled the door open, sitting down behind the wheel into a cream leather seat. She unfolded the letter, smoothing out the crinkles on the dashboard, and sat back to read.

*Alex,*

*I am writing this because I am a selfish coward. Selfish because I don't want to let you go and cowardly because I can't bring myself to say this to you in person. I am in love with you, Alex. I suppose love means doing the thing that is best for someone else. Even if it hurts. And it does hurt. Every time I take a breath. I don't know how to let you go, but if that's what is truly best for you, then I will. You are an angel and the love of my life and I will not deter you from your dreams.*

*Paul said it best--*
*"Blackbird singing in the dead of night. Take these broken wings and learn to fly. All your life. you were only waiting for this moment to arise."*

*Love always,*
*Ian*

Alex had not cried in Haiti, nor had she cried that day on the bridge when she asked Ian to let her go. She hadn't even cried at her father's graveside, but today, a mountain of despair welled up inside her and had nowhere else to go except out of her tear ducts. She laid her head on top of the steering wheel, clutching it in an embrace. An overpowering smell of leather filled her nostrils, which only expedited the tears—big fat salty tears creating twin rivers on each side of her face dripping into a rapidly expanding wet spot on her jeans. There was nothing else to do with her sense of devastating loss and numbing regret. She cried quietly, softly, and someone from afar could only have recognized it by the periodic movements of her shoulders. She cried until her seizure-like sobs were quieted by the gentle pressure of an expertly manicured hand.

The car ride back into London started out somber with Alex hunched over in her seat, face glued to the window, staring intently at the reflection of the young woman with swollen eyes and a red drippy nose. Her thoughts were circuitous, but all reached a common conclusion. This was entirely her fault—for not knowing what she wanted and for thinking she knew what she wanted and being wrong and for being too much of a coward to do this sooner...before Ian had left the country on a self-imposed mission to let her go.

She had no one to blame but herself. She had survived a broken childhood, a painful transition to adulthood, and an emotionally draining career choice all while exhibiting an inhuman amount of fortitude. No one had ever guessed her secret—that inside, she was a broken little doll. Her entire life path had been created by a terrified girl still running from the raging floodwaters. They had finally overtaken her and swept away the only thing she never wanted to let go.

"You look sexy when you cry."

Alex looked over and visualized Rox's deadpan face through misty eyes. "What?" She rubbed her nose across her shirtsleeve.

"You do. You could be *Maxim* magazine's sexiest woman alive— the sorrow edition."

Alex clapped her hand to her mouth.

"I can see you on the cover now wearing nothing but your teardrops and a very well placed handkerchief."

Rox's mouth twitched in its attempt to suppress a giggle. Alex bent in half, her face buried in her lap as her own laughter bubbled over uncontrollably.

"I am giving you exactly five more minutes to exist in your blame spiral, and then we are going to talk strategy. This isn't over, love."

The previously somber atmosphere of the car changed dramatically as bursts of laughter from both occupants bounced from the roof to the windows. Rox quieted first and asked, "Do you want to know what I was doing while you were chatting it up this afternoon?"

Alex wiped the last teardrop remnants from her lower eyelashes.

"Tell me," she said hoarsely. "I know you're dying to."

"It turns out that the trollop who was blackmailing Nic wasn't lying."

"What? That's terrible news."

Rox, appearing smug, continued, "It turns out she wasn't telling the truth either."

"I am now entirely confused."

"She and the well-proportioned backside of a young man are on the security camera outside the bar that Nic likes…and she did think it was Nic." Rox paused dramatically.

"But it wasn't?"

"It turns out that some guy who looks a heck of a lot like Nic has been using Nic's name to pick up girls at this bar for the past few months."

"How in the world did you figure this out?"

"I didn't. The guy was so proud of himself that he put a selfie on social media...at the bar...with the trollop...with the caption 'the *doppel-banger* strikes again'." Rox snorted.

"At least he's slightly clever."

"Clever my ass. That jerk almost ruined my life."

"So, the wedding is on?"

"It is." Rox smiled in the wickedly delicious way that only she could, fingering the multi-strand red Masai beads around her neck. "And I have one more thing for us to do before you go home."


The one more thing was a dreamy, ethereal morning seated in a sleek ivory armchair drinking a glass of champagne while her best friend modeled wedding gowns. The shop was located in a chic part of London that had a sign on the door that read "appointment required for entry". Once the glass doors were flung open, Alex and Rox had entered a wonderland of rustling dupioni silk and intricately embroidered Spanish lace, waves of soft celestial tulle, and bridesmaid's dresses in every color ever imagined. Alex tipped back her flute and let the bubbles caress her palate as Rox stepped out into the mirrored parlor.

"Does this one make me look top-heavy? I feel like an oversized frosted pastry."

"You look beautiful, but that's not the one." Alex playfully shooed her back into the dressing room.

"One day we'll be switching places, you know," Rox called from the dressing room. Alex pretended she didn't hear.

When Rox emerged in the second dress, a strapless mermaid style that fit her curves like a glove, she twisted and turned in the mirror while Alex cocked her head in evaluation. "It fits you really well, but it seems too...restrictive."

"I want something showier. The whole theme of the evening is understated elegance—but that doesn't apply to me."

Rox's honesty and phenomenal style were the traits Alex loved most about her.

"You keep trying on dresses, and I'll keep this bottle of champagne company." Alex grinned as her friend disappeared into the dressing room.

Rox appeared in every style of dress boasting various embellishments from brocade skirts to jeweled belts, from strapless to full-length sleeves, from empire waist to dropped waist. They were all beautiful, but nothing shouted spectacular.

"There are other shops," Alex offered. "We could stop by one of those."

Rox grumbled to herself. "This is the shop with everything. If I can't find one here, I'm probably just destined for mediocre."

"That is not a Roxanne Clark attitude," Alex said, mildly tipsy at this point from her generous use of the free champagne.

A dark-haired woman in a prim Chanel suit clicked around the corner in her stiletto heels. "I have one more in the back I would like you to try. It was meant for a certain celebrity a few years ago, but she ended up choosing something more traditional," the woman said in a lovely Polish accent. Her eyes brightened as she clasped her hands together, and Alex thought she must be picturing Rox in the dress.

"One more try then." Rox heaved a sigh as she struggled with the twelve-foot train of her most recent wedding dress reject.

When Rox exited the dressing room, Alex felt a well of emotion rising up her throat. The dress had a sweetheart neckline and dipped low in the back, nipping in at the waist with a row of tiny buttons. The skirt was something out of a fairytale with layers and layers of ivory and blush tulle that gave the dress a pink *ombre* effect. When Rox moved, she looked like the first rays of dawn gently billowing over the horizon.

"That's the one," Alex breathed and very nearly cried. Deciding to save her tears for the wedding, she let Roxanne do the crying for a change.

"I can't believe you are leaving me tomorrow. There is so much to do!" Rox was frantically flipping through magazines and simultaneously making notes in her day planner as Alex lay sprawled out next to her on the guest bed.

"You can call me anytime," Alex quipped. "Knowing me, I'll be up."

She mentally flipped through her checklist of things to do in the next month—graduate from fellowship, pack up her stuff and decide what she was taking to Botswana, say goodbye to her life in Philadelphia, prepare for her new job, and brace herself to see Ian at the wedding.

Nic waltzed in, drenched in sweat from a run, his emerald eyes alighting when he spied Rox engrossed in wedding paraphernalia. He bent down to give her a swift but luscious kiss on the lips. "What do I need to be doing?" he asked playfully.

"Besides me…just show up and be your gorgeous self," she replied, her eyes sparkling from their banter. "Now, go take a shower."

He backed out of the room slowly, looking as if he hoped she would leave her perch on the bed and join him. Their obvious adoration of one another both thrilled and pained Alex.

"I have to find the perfect dress for you. I'm thinking blush pink to match my dress. What do you think?"

"I'm sure whatever you pick will be perfect," Alex responded.

Rox mumbled to herself as she furiously flipped glossy magazine pages. "You need to stand out but not be overstated. It needs to scream *I'm in love with the best man.*"

Alex scrambled to a sitting position. "Rox, I cannot make it through an entire wedding staring at Ian's face. It's going to be torture."

"Not if you are planning to tell him you are in love with him."

"I don't know…what if he doesn't…"

"He does, and you know he does."

Alex sighed and let her head fall back on the pillows.

"Okay…what do I do?"

Rox settled in next to her, staring upward as if her vision could unfold on the ceiling. "First, we make sure you look absolutely stunning."

Alex made a face that Rox interrupted.

"He's been in Mongolia for four bloody months with nothing but sky and grass and horses. You are going to be a Goddess in his eyes."

She grabbed Alex's hand and pulled it into her own chest. "Then you let me handle the rest. I imagine a courtyard garden strung with twinkling lights. You can hear soft music in the background and occasional laughter from the guests. You turn. He is there. You pour your anxious little heart out. He strides toward you and pulls you in for a kiss. You twirl around in his arms as fireworks erupt in the night sky. Boom! Happily ever after." Rox pantomimed fireworks erupting as Alex covered her face with both hands.

"You've been watching too many romantic movies," she said in a muffled voice.

"This is going to be the most epic moment of your life. You'll see. Remind me that I need to find you a dress that will twirl."


"I'll see you in Gordes in June," Alex called through the open passenger window as she bent down to throw her bag over her shoulder.

"Only six weeks away," sung Rox in a lovely soprano.

"Love you," Alex called and blew her a kiss as she drove away.

# THIRTY-ONE

"Charge to forty joules, please." The whine of the defibrillator filled the crowded room. "Everyone clear? Okay now press shock."

The molded silicone body of the child mannequin, who the critical care trainees had affectionately dubbed *Harry Potter*, received his dose of electricity to revive his absent heart, and the monitor obligingly changed from squiggly lines to a regular heart rhythm.

"Very nice," remarked Alex as she made her way around the table clustered with newly graduated medical students that would be starting their pediatric internship in a few short weeks.

Traditionally, the graduating ICU physicians taught the weekend-long pediatric advanced life support (or PALS for short) course to the newbies who had never cared for a child on their own—much less a critically ill one. Alex remembered what it was like to have an extensive amount of knowledge but zero real experience on the frontlines of caring for a sick child. She had navigated the difficulties of gaining trust from worried parents and their little ones who were often tearful and agitated from an acute illness. During ten long years of training, Alex had received more than her share of disapproving stares and wary looks. She had practically become immune to crying after her several week stint in the pediatric emergency room during viral respiratory season.

Alex knew the exact day she had decided to choose critical care as her career path. She had been a second-year resident, on-call every third night during the winter, and the ICU was full. A six-month-old baby with bronchitis was breathing hard and going downhill quickly. The baby needed a breathing tube, and as frightened as she was, she knew that it had to be done right then. Something inside her had risen to the challenge. Some type of superhero complex where the only acceptable response is *here I come to save the day*! She saved the little boy's life and delivered him safely to the ICU, and he delivered her to her future.

It had been quite a journey from medical school to internship to residency to fellowship. Now Alex would be transitioning into her first real job, where, for the first time, she became the bottom line.

She glanced over at Tim, who was demonstrating how to visualize a pediatric airway, her heart warming at the scene. They had been through the travails of training together—bonding over long nights at many bedsides, poring over labs, dealing with the idiosyncrasies of their attendings, celebrating their successes, grieving over their failures. Tim seemed to sense her eyes on him because he looked up from where he was placing a laryngoscope into a silicone mouth and flashed her a beaming smile under a cocked eyebrow.

Alex had always been reticent to acknowledge this to herself, but he was a catch. He was handsome in a classic golden boy way, witty on his worst day and wicked smart. Alex raised her eyebrows and smirked in return, tilting her head toward the door. Maybe in a different life, she and Tim could have been more than friends. Now though, even with Ian halfway around the world *goatwalking,* probably literally as well as figuratively, her heart belonged to him. It always would. She held onto this simple truth as her constant among a life filled with variables that were all about to change.

"Be careful there," whispered a snide voice into her ear. "I hear he and Kim are a thing now, and he doesn't deserve to be your rebound." Beth slunk by in her long white lab coat and stiletto heels of all things.

"Mind your own business." Alex gritted her teeth to avoid saying something more pointed.

"It is my business," Beth continued extending out a hand to examine her newly manicured nails painted princess pink. "Whether you ever realized it or not, I am your friend."

Alex rolled her eyes and started unpacking the AEDs from a large cardboard box. "Nothing has ever happened with Tim and me, and nothing is happening now."

She grunted slightly as she lifted the heavy cases onto the table. *One and two and three and four and five.* The squeak of mannequin thoraxes receiving CPR filled in the silence around her, and she hoped that it was enough to drown out this conversation.

"Stop living in your tragic little self-centered universe and try not to break his heart too."

Her words stung as Alex watched her saunter off to the next teaching station, her ebony ponytail swishing behind her. Alex had nothing to say in return. A computer-generated voice emitted from the AED pretty much summed it up, "Shock delivered."

The end of May and graduation approached quickly like the cherry blossom trees along the Schuylkill that suddenly transitioned from barren to exploding with luscious pink blooms. Winter had vacated its frozen grasp on the city and the *twitterpated* birds swirling around the park confirmed that the world was deep into spring. Alex had thrown open the windows of her shoebox apartment to let the cleansing breeze circulate, grateful that she lived far enough above the city to dilute out some of the exhaust and the accompanying tire squeals of Philadelphia's taxicabs. With her clinical duties complete, showing up at work became optional. Therefore, today, she had opted to stay in her tiny sanctuary and give it an appropriate farewell as she deconstructed it into the army of sturdy cardboard boxes piled in the entryway.

She started in the kitchen with her modest amount of cooking utensils, wrapping a few select plates and glasses in bubble wrap and placing them neatly in reinforced boxes. She tucked her favorite set of wine glasses near the top of the box and imagined pulling them out again, hopefully unbroken, and setting them on a shelf in her new home in Gaborone. So many things would happen between now and then that she reeled for a moment. She would graduate fellowship and leave life as she knew it behind. Rox would be married and, most importantly, she would know how Ian responded to her revelation. Would the outcome be a happy one? She honestly didn't know, and it caused her insides to churn with anxiety.

A soulful voice drifted from her laptop, crooning a melody about useless desires. She winced and pressed the stop button. She continued absentmindedly wrapping small kitchen appliances and then unwrapped them, realizing that they weren't compatible with the electrical outlets in Botswana and placed them in a growing pile of donations.

A friendly blue bubble on her laptop screen saved her from her thought tornado. With one quick click of the mouse, her mom's cheerful face, flushed from being outdoors, filled the screen.

"I thought you might be packing, honey. I wish I was there to help."

"Hi, Mom." Alex blew a strand of hair out of her face and smiled widely. "I have to fit my entire life into thirty boxes, and I'm thinking at least ten of those are going to be for books."

"Don't stress, sweetheart. Anything you want to keep for later, you can mail home, and I'll tuck it away for you." Her mom clutched a sweaty glass of iced lemonade in her hand and rubbed her forehead with the back of her hand.

"Thanks, mom. I'll let you know. What have you been doing, by the way?" She received an eye roll in response.

"Mrs. Robbins down the road needed help weeding her flower garden—you know, Justin's grandmother. She asked how you were doing and couldn't believe it when I told her you were about to move to Africa for your first real doctor job. Everyone here is so proud of you, honey."

Alex felt a swell of homesickness for her town. Sometimes it seemed the more she sprouted her wings, the more she missed her roots.

"Did she mention how Justin was doing?" *Of course, she did.* Justin James was her pride and joy, and she could never let Janie one-up her with Alex's success.

"She said he was somewhere over in Afghanistan on a mission for the military that he couldn't tell her about."

Justin had joined the military after high school, and although they had not talked in years, Alex had kept tabs on him through Mrs. Robbins' addiction to loquaciousness. His talent for leadership and commitment seemed to have been recognized because he had been promoted to some elite counterterrorist unit in the Middle East.

"I hope he's okay." Alex frowned, remembering her copper-haired star athlete best friend from Cole's Church High School.

"I'm sure he's very good at what he does, honey. He always was—just like you."

They chatted for a few minutes more, and Alex got the sense that the funeral was in her mom's rearview. She hadn't mentioned it once or even asked how Alex had felt afterward. Alex also hadn't told her about the impromptu trip to London. Sometimes Janie liked to stay in the happy small-town bubble she had built for herself, and Alex just didn't feel like bursting it today.

As the afternoon wore on and the sun peaked and then retreated to the opposite side of Alex's high rise, box after box was carefully packed, taped shut, and labeled with a permanent blue sharpie. It had taken nearly ten boxes to fit Alex's books, which included volumes of medical texts plus a selection of bestselling nonfiction and a few classic novels. She tossed in *The Coming Plague* and smiled, remembering how Ian had casually reclined on a hotel bed flipping through the thick pages.

The air in her room was thick with dust from undisturbed books, leaving Alex's throat suddenly parched. She opened the refrigerator door. It rattled with the few remaining condiments she possessed as well as one precious bottle of rosé champagne she had been saving for a special occasion. This was as good an occasion as any. She popped the cork letting the vapors swirl like a tiny tornado around the mouth of the green bottle and poured a generous amount into her only remaining cup—an insulated Mickey Mouse mug she had once purchased at Disney World. She hit play on iTunes, and the unmistakable voice of Florence Welch from the band bearing her name belted out one of her latest hits.

Alex shimmied around the room with her champagne, moving her hips to the fast-paced beat of the music as one can only do while completely alone. The pile of boxes grew into a wall which evolved into an entire cardboard castle containing the totality of her belongings. The more she packed and sipped champagne, the more nostalgic she grew. By the time she discovered a framed photograph in her desk drawer of her and Ian from New Year's, and Grace Potter resounded from her computer singing about love left behind, she didn't even try to blink back the tears. She rubbed the nose threatening to drip onto the picture glass and decided to place the photo in the small suitcase that would be accompanying her to France. Her phone buzzed, and a miniature of her and Tim from St. Patrick's Day lit up her screen.

"Hey, what's up?" Alex said, a little too brightly for her current emotional state.

"I was just wondering if you wanted to go for a run or something this evening."

"I've been packing all day, and I'm deep into a bottle of way too expensive champagne. I don't know if I can walk, let alone run."

"Oh, okay. I'll be there in five. See you downstairs." He hung up.

Alex swore under her breath, but after one final swig of bubbly relief, she pulled on some shorts and tied her apartment key to her electric blue running shoes.

"This ought to be hilarious," she mumbled, walking haphazardly through the lobby and spying Tim's beaming face on the outside of the double glass doors to her building.


"Where are we going?" she said as she kept pace with Tim despite her the liquid in her stomach sloshing about as they ran down Walnut street.

"Nostalgia tour of Center City." He exuded an enthusiasm that Alex couldn't help but be infected by.

In a crowd of people, Tim was a sun, much like Roxanne, which is probably why they had been inseparable during the last few arduous years. They pounded the sidewalk while the sun sunk low in the sky and reflected her pink hue over the city hall building on Broad Street. They passed their favorite pizza place in Society Hill that served the greasiest slices of pepperoni that promised to cure any hangover and jogged past Bob and Barbara's where they had frequented the weekly drag show and half-priced beer nights. She recalled Ian's sweet serenade and then the erotic rendezvous in a shadowy corner on the way back to her apartment.

"Hey, look! Some of the cardiology folks," Tim called as they passed the open door of Monk's, another well-known pitstop for the young professionals in the city that boasted over a hundred different labels of beer.

The cardiology trainees were graduating as well and apparently out celebrating a few days early. All five of them were lined up along the bar, laughing and carousing, hugging each other between sips of their various cocktails and bites of the most delectable fries in the city. Alex and Tim peered into the open doorway and were immediately recognized by their colleagues, who motioned them inside.

"Fellowship is over," yelled one ecstatic girl in a distinct Colombian accent. "Have a drink with us."

Alex surveyed Tim, who shrugged carelessly and snatched two shots of something dark purple off a nearby tray, handing one to Alex.

"Here's to you guys. Congratulations!"

He and Alex clinked shot glasses and tipped back their heads as the cardiology fellows cheered them on. A strong smoky-sweet liquid snaked its way down Alex's esophagus, and she came up for air just in time to share a disgusted look with Tim.

"Congratulations you guys!" she called into the din and swiped the nearest basket of cheese fries while they were too busy cheering to notice.

Several minutes later, as they shared the stolen booty at the top of the art museum steps, they chuckled over the sharp glances they had received while running down JFK boulevard balancing a basket of fries. Tim reclined back on the steps made famous by Sylvester Stallone as Rocky Balboa, of whom a statue still stood in tribute, as the night settled over them. It couldn't have been more perfect, and Alex was grateful for the reprieve from her pining.

"Do you remember our first few months here?" he asked, dipping a slim fry into the last of the melted lake of cheese coating the bottom of the basket.

"I try to block it out."

"Neither of us was used to living in the city. The people and the noise and the dirt."

Alex laughed, dredging up recollections of their first year of fellowship. "I remember asking you to come over and help me get my bed to the third floor of my brownstone."

"Yeah...some genius told me to saw the wood slats of the box spring so we could fit it up your stairs by folding it in half."

Alex clutched her stomach as she reclined on the steps. "Except halfway up the first set of stairs, the thing unfolded and pinned you against the wall," she snorted.

Tim grimaced in remembrance. "There's nothing like a pointy piece of wood about to pierce your chest."

"Eh...what's a little cardiac tamponade?" Alex teased and reached over to ruffle his hair.

He grabbed her wrist unexpectedly, and her laughter faded as quickly as it had risen. His molten brown eyes searched her face for any sign of disapproval before he pulled her into his orbit and crushed his lips to hers. Alex melted a little at first when his mouth engulfed hers, perfectly molded around her bottom lip, warm and tender. The mouth that she had stared out countless times as it spouted encouragement or a sarcastic one-liner that made her laugh.

She had exactly one moment in time—one moment to decide to move her lips against his...to open them wider and let him taste her...to reach her arms around his neck and press her body to his. An entire lifetime flashed in front of her. It would be as easy as taking a breath. It would be secure and predictable...but it would never be enough.

Ian had been right the first night they met. She wanted a love that was epic...timeless. A love that burned so hot that she would be consumed by the flames. And she had found it with a complicated self-proclaimed selfish jerk with blue eyes as limitless as the sky who had chosen her when she didn't even know how to choose herself. Who had managed to fall in love with her despite her protective wall. Who had taught her that real love is worth any sacrifice.

Alex stilled and pulled away just enough to avoid encouragement but hopefully not enough to make the rejection sting too much.

"Tim...I—" She faltered, knowing that words without actions were just wasted oxygen and added insult to injury. He hung his head.

"You don't have to say anything. I knew I was rolling the dice."

Alex swallowed hard. "Things might have been different with us if..."

Tim cut her off. "No. Don't. I try not to imagine what ifs. I'm just not the guy for you...but I have an idea who is."

"I love him, Tim. I tried not to for so long, but it caught up with me, and I can't even remember what it's like not to love him."

"I know. I think I've known for a while. Lucky bastard," he said under his breath.

Alex let out a combination of a cry bordering on a laugh.

"Listen—you are one of my best friends and I love you and you are going to find the girl of your dreams in Atlanta...and you'll be the guy in hers. I want that for you more than anything."

He sighed so hard it ruffled his blond hair that had grown shaggy over the last few months. "You're impossible to follow, Alex, but I do hear southern girls can charm the dew right off the honeysuckle." He waggled his eyebrows suggestively, and Alex scrunched up her face.

"I have no idea what that even means."

They laughed together, sitting with knees touching on the top of the museum steps under a blanket of stars peeping through the city smog, and Alex put her arm around his waist and rested her head on his shoulder.

"I'm not ready to tell you goodbye," she murmured as one solitary tear slid down her cheek.

"It's not goodbye unless you've decided to never see me again," he whispered and placed a quick kiss on the top of her head, "and I don't plan on letting that happen."


"And next, we have Dr. Mona Gibson from the Division of Critical Care Medicine handing out certificates to the graduating fellowship class of 2010."

The booming twang of Dr. Stark echoed over the entire auditorium as Dr. Gibson stepped to the front of the stage with an armful of black frames and a precarious stack of books. Alex sat in the front row in her navy sheath dress, debuting the diamond earrings Ian had given her for Christmas, legs nervously crossing and uncrossing every few minutes. She wished her mom was here, but by this point, she had been through so many graduation ceremonies, she thought Janie had probably lost count of which was which.

"Elizabeth Hanson."

Beth looked stunning as she crossed the stage in a red dress, her hair in a trendy updo, and graciously shook Dr. Gibson's hand before accepting her certificate. Alex noticed a tall, slim guy with purposefully messy hair the color of deep bronze wearing stylish glasses blow her a kiss as she descended the short flight of stairs.

"Timothy Pierce."

Amid a generous whoop from the nursing cohort, to whom Tim flashed a homecoming king worthy smile, he rose from his seat. He accepted his frame after wrapping Gibson in a giant hug, which she accepted about as well as a cactus accepts a rain shower.

"Alexandra Wilde."

Alex stood stiffly, smoothing the folds of her dress, and felt every click of her heel as it made contact with the flooring. Dr. Gibson's face, ordinarily devoid of emotion, appeared amused as she grasped Alex's outstretched hand and supplied her with the ticket to her future—three long years of sub-specialty training summed up in some fancy calligraphy on a thick sheet of cardstock.

"Congratulations, Dr. Wilde," she said as she slipped something on top of her diploma. Alex made it to the bottom of the stage before she had a chance to glance at the title of the book gifted her by Dr. Gibson—*How to make life choices: a guide for idiots.*

# THIRTY-TWO

Thirty boxes leaving for Botswana. Five boxes labeled for delivery to her mom in Texas. One roller bag with a week's worth of wedding essentials and one blue leather shoulder bag. The entirety of her possessions organized and divided by destination. Empty white walls surrounded her on all sides. She would vacate this place like she had never been there, but its memories would stay with her—the late nights in her black desk chair, crouched over her laptop as she met a deadline for a grant, the early mornings arriving home from a crazy night on call with just enough energy to flop onto her bed, the brief visit from Ian last summer that was burned into her memory.

True to his promise, they had spent the entire day lounging in her bed, observing the gray storm clouds collecting over the city, and then watched as a curtain of rain fell and secluded them from the rest of the world. With takeout from her favorite French restaurant and a bottle of champagne, they had picnicked on the floor. He had torn off tiny bits of crusty bread and smeared soft cheese over the top before offering Alex a delectable bite. She had closed her eyes in bliss.

"This cheese is fantastic."

He had half-smirked. "I've seen that face before. A few times today, actually."

"Want to see it again?" she asked, emboldened by the champagne.

While the rockets burst their red glare over the Delaware, he had pressed her naked body against the glass windows of her apartment and shown her his own version of fireworks.

A brusque knock sounded on her door, and the hot to-go chai in her hands jiggled. Two burly gentlemen in blue dickies eyed her reasonable number of boxes with relief and began methodically carrying them down the corridor to the elevator. Sooner than she expected, everything was gone except for her suitcase and carry-on sitting in a lonely cluster in the middle of an empty room. She shrugged on her leather jacket, pulled her luggage into the hall, and turned out the light before closing the door to 2101 Chestnut one last time.

Driving in her rental car through the winding roads of southern France, Alex had a brief moment of regretting her career path in lieu of becoming the proprietor of a combination winery and lavender farm. At Rox's urging, she had decided to drive from Paris to Gordes along a scenic route that put the impressionist art world to shame. About an hour outside the city, the landscape changed from relatively flat to gentle rolling hills interspersed with quaint Provençal villages boasting outdoor markets selling locally grown grapes and delicate cheeses wrapped in waxy paper. From the traveling picnic in the passenger seat of her rental, Alex intermittently popped a succulent red grape in her mouth. The gentle breeze shifted with every slight twist and turn of the curated road, carrying with it the scent of lavender, delivered explicitly from the expansive fields of elegant purple blooms that curtsied to passersby.

Her phone rang with an incoming call. "Hello," she answered, "maid of honor here and completely at your service."

"Alex, where are you? I need an exact ETA! The lobster never arrived. The centerpieces are all wrong, and my makeup lady just canceled! Oh, and I hope you packed something smashing to wear tonight—my college friends are throwing a little impromptu hen party after the rehearsal dinner." She heard heavy breathing and felt Rox's angst seep into the peaceful sanctuary of her car.

"I will be there in…" She checked google maps. "Forty-seven minutes." She rounded an S-curve and crept to a stop to allow a herd of bleating white sheep complete with lambs fill the country lane in front of her. "Give or take a few minutes." She pressed end before Rox could detect the clattering of hooves.

Although the sheep had taken their sweet time ambling across the road to reach the next greenest pasture, Alex still managed to make it to the village of Gordes in less than an hour. The car groaned as it climbed the labyrinth of cobblestone streets higher and higher through white stone buildings labeled in blue cursive with their associated contents—charcuterie, olives, fromage. Finally, after a harrowing drive to the very apex of the village, a sweeping view of the Luberon valley came into view as well as the wrought-iron gate of the luxury estate where the wedding weekend was already in full swing.

A handful of slender young boys were perched on ladders in various nearby trees stringing delicate light strands between the branches. Long wooden tables and whitewashed chairs were already being set up on an outdoor stone patio overlooking the village for tonight's welcome dinner. Alex had barely yanked up the emergency brake on the powder blue Fiat before Roxanne accosted her in the parking area.

"Thank God you're here." She wrenched open the door and pulled Alex into a hug.

Alex moved her lips in response, but the sound died in the folds of the white linen shirt Rox was wearing, the pocket embroidered with *Bride* in robin's egg blue.

"Grab your bags and follow me. There is loads to do," Rox barked as she and her white espadrille wedges strode down a stone path toward the main building while Alex and her luggage struggled to keep up.

"Wow," remarked Alex on entering the villa that would house her and Rox until the wedding night when she would appropriately be usurped by Nic.

The stand-alone cottage contained four bedrooms, all with exposed beams in the ceiling painted a dreamy white, and elegant French furniture in blue and cream floral patterns. The main room led to a private enclosed patio with a lap pool and a picturesque view of the Medieval style architecture on display throughout the cliffside village.

"I know. It's perfect. Everything is bloody perfect, and I haven't enjoyed a second of it," shouted Rox from the master suite where she was emptying the contents of her suitcase onto a bed of purest white cotton linens, so white in fact that Alex wondered if they purchased new ones after each guest.

The role reversal from needing Rox to being needed by Rox shifted Alex's focus to her friend's current distress rather than her own. Briefly, she wondered if Ian was already here somewhere catching up with Nic over a beer or, more likely, a bottle of bourbon. On the flight over, she had had ample time to plan the various scenarios, running through every permutation possible, and most importantly, what she would say during the monologue of her life.

"Oh, bloody hell."

Alex suppressed a smile while she hastily hung up the few outfits she had brought and then scooted over to where Rox was examining the broken heel of her Jimmy Choo's.

"I can't believe I'm giving you orders but, come to think of it, it's what I do for a living, so listen up buttercup," Alex yelled above the din of the blow-dryer as a frazzled Rox sat motionless wrapped in a white towel on the stool in front of her. She cut off the blow-dryer.

"Give me a list—I'm ready." Alex grabbed a pen from her purse and tore a sheet of paper out of her barely used journal. "And while I am taking care of all this, you can relax, get ready in peace, and finally start to have a little fun at your own party."

Rox flashed her a look of gratitude, and exactly five minutes and thirteen to-do items later, Alex was bustling around the property armed with the explicit authority of the bride-to-be. If anything, her critical care training had prepared her well for such moments in life that required multi-tasking, precision timing, and attention to detail. By the time the servers began to distribute the place settings for tonight's welcome dinner in the garden, the lobster had arrived, the centerpieces of white and pink begonias looked terrific to her untrained eye, and she had retrieved the bridal gown from the town seamstress.

Sweat pooled on her lower back, and tendrils of hair escaped her ponytail and stuck to her face. Alex was having the time of her life. In this tiny window of freedom before returning to medicine, she lived as if the personal sacrifices of the last decade could be levied by the fullness of her joy.

Rox was staring at herself in the full-length mirror, her back to the door when Alex burst through with the highly important garment bag.

"Oh, Rox, you look absolutely beautiful!"

Her best friend was dressed in a white midi-length dress that had an off the shoulder neckline and a bodice that showed off her voluptuous curves, elegant with a hint of sexy, a subtler style than Rox usually chose.

"I feel so out of sorts. It's ridiculous really." She stepped into her shoes—a color pop of powder blue with a heel that Alex had deftly reattached with some Dermabond she had fished out of her purse.

Alex put her hands on Rox's bare shoulders and leaned in close to her. "Your happy ending starts now, so let everything else go and enjoy it. It's once in a lifetime."

Rox brushed back a tear from her lower lid with a French manicured pinkie. "I will...and I love you...but if you ruin my makeup, I might have to drown you in the pool tonight."

Breathtaking was the only word in the forefront of Alex's mind when she stepped into the courtyard amidst a cohort of beautifully dressed guests meandering around with glasses of wine in front of a backdrop of the sun setting over Provence. She spied Rox arm in arm with Nic as they greeted friends and had a brief moment to reminisce or catch up before new friends arrived and took their place. Rox gave her a frantic beckoning wave while still managing to laugh animatedly with a couple of Nic's teammates. Alex sidled up to her.

"I'm here. What can I do?"

"Can you fetch me a drink? Make that two. Then come and sit with Nic and me. Dinner should be starting soon."

As Alex retrieved a glass of chilled Sancerre for Rox and one for herself, she couldn't help but glance up periodically, hoping to see the raven-haired, blue-eyed object of her affection coasting through the crowd.

"Here you go," Alex whispered, taking her seat next to Rox near the head of the table. Rox took a generous sip leaving a delible fuchsia lipstick stain on the rim of the glass. "Better?" Alex asked.

"Much," Rox replied, and Alex saw the hint of a real smile playing on her lips.

"Do you think he's coming?" Alex tilted her head toward the empty chair next to Nic.

Rox frowned for a moment. "I know he's back, but I don't know if he decided to come tonight. Nic didn't know and, trust me, I grilled the stuffing out of him."

Alex played with her salad course. Her permutations had not included Ian not showing up at all. Rox squeezed her knee under the table. "Don't worry. Your happy ending is right around the corner."

The salad course ended, and the entrée of roasted chicken surrounded by teeny white potatoes came and then went, and by the time Alex dipped her spoon in a mound of chocolate mousse served in its own individual crystal stemware, Ian still had not arrived. The guests began filtering out of the courtyard to explore the grounds or resolve their jet lag. Rox and Nic had vacated their seats long ago to chat with extended family and friends, some of whom had traveled halfway around the world to witness their nuptials. She felt a warm pair of hands on her shoulder, which startled her out of teetering on the precipice of legitimate moping.

"Come on," said Rox, hints of strawberry on her exhaled breath. "We're meeting some gals at a hotel bar down the way."

"So which friends of yours made it tonight?" Alex asked as she curled some waves into her long layers.

"A few from college, a few of the Aussie crowd. You'll remember Celeste—she came to visit me in Botswana."

"The tall one who looks like a swimsuit model and trains dolphins for a living?"

"I think she's moved on to beluga whales but yes." Rox disappeared for a moment and returned in a snow-white mini dress embellished with tiny sequins. "What do you think?" She rotated in front of Alex checking out her reflection in the mirror.

"Sexy but elegant—seems to be your specialty." Alex smiled and smeared some light-reflecting gloss on her lips.

Rox met her eyes in the mirror. "Don't worry about Ian. He'll definitely be here tomorrow, or I will personally rotisserie him. This delay just gives us more time to make sure everything goes absolutely perfect."

"I hope you're right, Rox."

Rox fastened her collection of diamond layered necklaces that complimented her dress perfectly. "I know how this ends, Alex, and it's with you living a happy life—open to the reality of incredible love—no matter what happens with Ian."

Standing at the bar with a raucous group of Rox's schoolmates and friends, Alex gratefully faded into the melee. She sipped a champagne cocktail while listening to the girls regale stories that highlighted Rox's adventurous spirit, boldness, and above all, loyalty—all things she had been lucky enough to experience firsthand. Rox was in her element as the center of attention and was the quintessential bachelorette in her sparkling white dress and a pair of fuchsia pumps.

The bar, located on the upper level of a local luxury hotel, resembled a French parlor complete with compact sofas upholstered in green velvet and vintage knick-knacks carefully positioned on Louis XVI mahogany furniture. Once the numbers grew, they moved their estrogen-charged gaggle of tipsy bachelorettes onto the tree-covered patio where the conversation continued to flow as easily as the cocktails. Alex took a moment to rest her hands on the iron railing that separated patio from cliffside, the breeze ruffling the hem of her azure halter neck dress, the one she had worn in Paris with Ian. So much had changed since then, but she desperately hoped that some things had not.

"Hi, there! I'm Celeste. You're Alex, right?"

A tall, perfectly bronzed silhouette with a swinging blond ponytail inched toward her along the railing. Despite her tall frame, she had delicate bone structure and yardstick long tan legs emerging from a ruffled mini-skirt. She really was stunning and unnaturally perky. Alex maintained an awkward silence for a moment.

"Yes, I am. I remember you from Botswana." She smiled genuinely and received one in return. "Are you having fun tonight?" Alex asked.

"A blast." Celeste drained her wine glass. "I just wish there were more gents here, you know. It's a bachelorette party—who doesn't want to get a little crazy when they're all tarted up?"

Alex nodded in agreement and flitted her eyes to the commotion occurring inside the bar. Nic, along with his entourage bachelor crew, had arrived, and the back of one head with tousled dark hair caught Alex's gaze. He turned slightly, the sight of his flawless features in profile depriving her of any external senses like she had just jumped headfirst into a deep blue pool. She heard Celeste next to her, the soundwaves of her Australian lilt delivered to poorly functioning ears. A hand tightened on her arm.

"I knew this night wouldn't be a bust! Pardon me."

Alex watched in paralyzed horror as Celeste wedged herself among Nic's friends and struck up a lively conversation with Ian, who arched his thick brows and returned her flirtatious volleys while remaining oblivious to the rest of the guests. And by the rest of the guests, she meant herself. He looked the same—dashing and vivacious—but also different. He seemed harder somehow, less carefree, with an undertone of distress that only she would perceive.

When Celeste reached out a lean, shapely arm and squeezed his bicep, Alex gripped her crystal flute so hard that she thought it might shatter in her hand. Rox's warm body pressed up next to her.

"Do you still want to drown me in the pool?" Alex said through gritted teeth. "Because that seems like such a better option than watching this." She gestured to where Ian was tipping back a glass of bourbon as Celeste coyly wound her long ponytail around one hand.

"I'll drown her if you want, love," Rox winked.

"She's a dolphin trainer. They've probably taught her how to hold her breath indefinitely."

In a moment of melodrama, Alex drained her entire glass of champagne and then reached over and drained the glass in Rox's hand. "Oh, for the love, that was strong. What was in there?"

"St. Germain. Now go over there and cause some good bachelorette party drama...or I will," she said, sauntering over to where Nic loitered at the edge of the patio and pulled him into a cinema-worthy kiss.

Walking over to Ian felt like walking a very long plank suspended over an ocean teeming with sharks. Fuzzy from the champagne, she picked her way through the crowd of boisterous wedding guests until the only obstacle that remained between her and her target was a column of air. *Damn, he looked good from behind.* He was dressed to perfection in a crisp baby blue button-down the color of his eyes and navy slacks. She reached out a shaky hand and tapped him on his shoulder.

"I need to talk to you."

Her voice was sucked up by the laughter coursing through the bar. For a moment, she was catapulted into the depths of his blue eyes as they alighted in recognition. He leaned his ear close to her mouth—so close that she smelled his freshly showered skin and the spice of his cologne and the hint of bourbon on his breath when he spoke.

"I'm sorry I didn't hear you." He straightened, and her heart rate spiked to a dangerous pace.

"I need to talk to you." She enunciated every word carefully, willing him to suggest they go somewhere private. Instead, he opened up his stance to include her in the small section of flooring he shared with Celeste.

"Sure thing. Celeste was just about to tell me what she did on her vacation last year."

He gestured to Celeste expectantly, who was thrilled to have re-captured Ian's attention.

"I went diving out past the reef and did some deep-sea fishing." Her Australian accent made everything sound sexy and adventurous.

"That's fantastic. Did you catch anything good?" Ian asked.

"I caught a barramundi and some snapper. My mum loves fresh fish."

The blood rushed to Alex's head, and she was unsure if her inability to focus was the alcohol or torrential emotional overload.

"Alex." Ian was peering directly into her wide eyes. "Alex, don't you like to fish?" She searched for the familiar smolder but failed to find it. It wasn't longing or heartache residing in their depths. He observed her with simple amusement.

"I do," she replied slowly, wondering where he was going with this.

"And do you keep what you catch, or are you more of a catch and release type of girl?"

And there it was.

# THIRTY-THREE

"What did you say?" shouted a muffled voice from the bathroom as Rox took the day off her face and slathered it with night cream. Alex stuffed her head further into the fluffy pillow mound on the master suite bed, the room still spinning every time she tried to rise.

"If you are going to smother yourself, please do it after tomorrow," trilled a much clearer voice.

Alex flipped on her back to see her friend clothed in a white silk robe, hair in a towel, and face covered in a green mask, bearing the resemblance of a beloved Muppet.

"You look like the bride of Kermit," Alex giggled.

"Well, as long as you don't tell me I look like Miss Piggy, I won't help you finish offing yourself." The bed squeaked slightly as Rox sat down next to Alex's supine form. She gathered Alex's hands in her own velvety soft ones. "What happened after that?"

Alex scrunched up her face into a look of combination anguish and downright embarrassment. "In my head, I grabbed his face between my hands and told him I'm actually more of the catch and keep type, and then, as a romantic interlude played in the background, I confessed my undying love...we kissed passionately...roll credits."

"And in reality?"

Alex covered her face with her hands. "I froze in a state of panic, not able to comprehend that this was actually happening...and then I just backed away. I just left him there with Celeste and her blond ponytail, grinning like she had just landed the big one. I am the absolute worst."

Rox was thoughtful for a moment, then pursed her lips, moist with a sheer balm. "He's hurt Alex and torn between doing what you asked him to do and doing what he wants to do."

Alex rose to a sitting position, swinging her legs off the side of the bed. "And what is it that he wants to do?"

"He hasn't seen you for four months, Alex. Either he can't stand the sight of you, or he wants to show you what you've been missing…and I'd bet my Canadian farm that it's the latter."

"How can I make this right?" Alex whispered as a few tears threatened exposure.

"I'll take care of Ian…run the interference and all that. You just be ready to pour your Texas-sized heart out."

"Your sports references are really on point these days," she sniffed, pressing a tissue to her nose.

"I am marrying a world-class athlete. I had to up my game," Rox said, lightly dabbing the facemask with the pads of her fingers and trying not to crack her face with a smile.


The day of the wedding was postcard-perfect—a cloudless, sun-filled sky, a cool breeze to ruffle but not deconstruct the bridal up-do, and the subtle hint of lavender everywhere. Alex had woken before dawn and pounded her leftover emotions from last night into the winding cobblestone streets of the village Gordes, strengthening her resolve and shifting her heart as close to her surface as possible. Sweaty and energized, she returned to the villa to find a spread of French pastries along the kitchen island and labeled carafes of freshly squeezed juices. Picking up a still warm chocolate croissant, she went searching for Rox, who was examining her face critically in the mirror, palpating the skin of her jawline.

"Happy wedding day," Alex said brightly.

"I think that bloody mask gave me a rash."

"Let me see." Alex peered at the porcelain skin of her fair friend, and sure enough, there was a stippled erythematous rash along her jawline extending up to her temple.

"I cannot believe this," Rox grumbled, frantically opening her makeup bag and jiggling the contents. "I mean of all the days."

Alex had rarely seen her friend so frazzled. Rox usually had a neat solution for everything—beauty emergencies, fashion faux pas, babies' heads that got stuck mid-birth.

Alex's *save the day* complex surged. "I'll be right back."

A few minutes later, after thoroughly digging through her well-stocked shoulder bag, she had Rox seated on a stool applying a white paste to the periphery of her face. "Let this absorb for about fifteen minutes, then wash your face," Alex instructed, dabbing the last of the concoction on the undersurface of Rox's jaw.

"Do I want to know what's in here? Please tell me it's not some medicinal herb that you got from a voodoo priestess in Haiti." Rox cut her eyes up at Alex.

"Mongolian mare's milk actually." One horrified angry look from her friend quieted the laughter in Alex's throat, and she awkwardly spat a string of words. "Crushed aspirin mixed with hydrocortisone cream and a few drops of phenylephrine."

Rox visibly relaxed. "I always wondered what you carried around with you in that big blue bag of yours."

"I'm an ICU doctor. Disaster preparedness is my middle name."

Alex had just rounded the kitchen counter when Rox called out, "It's time to change it to Sex Goddess." She detected the distinct high notes of Rox's laughter as she crammed the last of her croissant into her mouth.


Before long, the previously quiet villa was inundated with a steady flow of well-wishing friends and wedding workers. Rox, her face back to its natural state of a well-hydrated, unblemished glow, sat in her silk robe in the middle of the fray, vacillating between sending out verbal requests and becoming beautified by a team of experts. Alex had used her nervous energy to their advantage by pouring mimosas for visitors, keeping a running list of gifts that had arrived, and frequently commenting on every stage of Rox's transformation into a blushing bride. Her blonde bob had been pinned in an elegant updo off her face and her makeup, highlighting the gold in her long-lashed hazel eyes, was a work of art. The last of the lingering friends gave their final *ooh's* and *aah's* and filtered out to their rooms to get ready themselves.

Alex, in a momentary fall from grace, had plucked Celeste's half-drunk mimosa out of her hand and suggested she give Rox "a moment" and head back to her room. After almost a full day of frenetic activity, the spacious villa was eerily quiet once again. Alex cleared away the scattered glasses, wiped down the counters, and fluffed the pillows in the master suite, hoping the continued activity would tame the errant butterflies flitting in her stomach.

"Can you help me in here?" Rox shouted from one of the guestrooms. She had unzipped her garment bag revealing billowing folds of gauzy material in candlelight white and the blushest of pinks.

"Here—I got it," Alex offered and lifted the massive dress out of the confines of the bag to hang it on the back of the door.

She turned around to see Rox holding a beautifully cut dress with lace cap sleeves, a sweetheart neckline, and a knee-length multilayered skirt of sheerest pink. Rox rotated the dress back and forth on the hanger. "It even twirls," she said, smiling brightly. A palpable warmth spread through Alex's chest at the sight of the gorgeous dress, and she put one hand to her mouth, biting her thumb a bit to stave off the tears threatening her mascara.

"I love it. It's perfect. Absolutely perfect."

After slipping the dress over her head without mussing her hair and donning a new pair of nude sandals, Alex set to work dressing Rox in her wedding gown, which proved more complicated than it sounded.

"I can barely lift this thing," Alex breathed heavily, a sheen of sweat collecting at her hairline. "I think you need to step into it, and then I can do the buttons."

Rox, in her wedding trousseau and luxe blush pink heels, stepped into the cavernous mouth that was the bodice of her wedding dress and put her arms through the straps. Alex began fastening the row of delicate buttons with nimble fingers accustomed to performing procedures in tiny babies. Once she was finished, she fluffed out the lengthy train that appeared subtly pink from the fabric underneath.

"One last thing."

She took the cathedral length veil off its hanger and carefully slid the combs into Rox's hair, letting the embroidered lace settle over the dress. She intertwined their arms, and they stared into the mirror together. Rox was remarkably silent.

"Rox," Alex gulped, lost on what else to say until the words found her. "I couldn't have asked for a better sister."

They embraced, clinging to each other for a singular moment in time until they were interrupted by a rapping on the door. A female head poked in, and a French accent wafted into the room.

"Mademoiselle Clarke, it is time."

Roxanne's thematic concept for this event had been understated elegance. In truth, there was nothing understated about it. The ceremony was to take place in a meadow overlooking the hillside below, right as the sun began to make her descent. The timing was impeccable. The pink and gold glow cast over the landscape created a heaven-sent backdrop that perfectly coordinated with the wedding colors of blush pink and muted gold. An enormous white tent had been set up for the post-ceremony reception, which would include dinner, dancing, and a well-stocked open bar. From their post on the veranda outside the estate main-house, Alex could see the guests filing to the white chairs set up in neat rows, separated down the middle by a carpeted aisle covered in pink rose petals. Rox paced nervously behind her, folds of material rustling with each step.

"I wish mum and dad were here," she said.

Rox was an only child with parents who tried to have children for a lifetime until giving up and then being blessed with an unexpected gift of a daughter. They had both passed away several years ago. Alex thought it must be the reason Rox had decided on obstetrics as a career—there was something magical in delivering a baby to her parents for the first time. Alex reached out and grabbed her hand on her next pass. "I know you do, and they would be so proud of you…just like I am."

Rox dabbed a tiny white handkerchief to her lower lids. "You are really killing me today, smalls."

"Sorry," Alex laughed. "I blame the emotional snowstorm on a certain best man."

"Speaking of…I have a plan. Just a tiny hatchling of one but it may work."

She whispered instructions in Alex's ear as the stringed quartet started up, and then they were being ushered forward by the event coordinator.

"No going back now," Rox whispered as they took their first steps onto the rose petal aisle.

Alex walked ahead of Rox, trying to ignore the crowd of guests whispering among themselves and taking solace in the fact that she was merely the appetizer while Rox was the main course. As she approached the end of the aisle, her eyes felt the pull of Ian's face, and she stole fleeting glances in his direction. He stood next to Nic, hands clasped in front of him and head cocked toward his friend, who was taking nervous gulps of air to steady himself. He wore a charcoal grey suit and blush pink tie, his dark hair longer than she remembered, its playful ends smoothed for the occasion. His face was thoughtful but unreadable, and she desperately wished she could pluck the thoughts right out of his mind.

She touched her diamond earrings for courage as she took her place next to the vacant one saved for the bride. The cellists picked up in volume and tempo as Rox began making her way toward a beaming Nic, a glorious expression on her face equaled in glory by the rest of her appearance. She was bridal perfection, and a low murmur swept through the crowd as she walked confidently toward the man of her dreams.

The ceremony was beautifully done, lengthy enough to create an aura of love everlasting and brief enough to avoid restlessness among the parched wedding patrons. During the exchange of vows, Alex caught Ian staring at her over Nic's shoulder, and for the first time in what seemed like forever, she thought she saw a flicker of the familiar heat she had grown to love.

"And now you may kiss your bride." The guests erupted in cheers as Rox and Nic collided in a lip lock that was almost too intimate for public view. Giddy with their newfound status as a married couple, they hastened down the aisle arm in arm, eager to start their new lives together with a banging party.

For the reception, Rox had elicited Alex's help in changing out of her gown into something more dance-friendly—a white halter neck floor-length gown of pure satin in a dreamy hourglass silhouette.

"Congratulations, Dr. Clarke-Brizido!"

Rox gave a small hop while shimmying into her dress. "Thank you, love. It's absolutely surreal."

"I'll take care of all this," Alex said, gesturing to the deposed wedding dress and various scattered cosmetics. "Get out there—it's your night."

"Not just mine. Good luck, sweetie." She sent Alex an air kiss.

Alex took a cleansing breath. "I've never been so nervous before…"

Rox leaned into the mirror to replace an earring and smear on a fresh layer of lipstick. "Not even when you took the helicopter into a snowstorm to get that sick cardiac baby...or the time a school fell on you in Haiti...or how about the time in high school when you and your friends got caught joyriding in the winter in just your skivvies?"

Alex shook out the complicated wedding dress and tried to stifle a giggle.

"The time you fell asleep on a camel in Mongolia, and he wandered into the wilderness?"

Now Rox was holding her abdomen, trying to suppress her laughter.

"Even the time we went shopping, and you got stuck in one of those zipperless bandage dresses, and we had to buy it so we could cut you out of it?"

The room rocked with their raucous uninhibited giggles, and Alex hoped this brief reprieve would carry her through the rest of the evening.


The white tent's interior had been transformed into a romantic wonderland of intimate tables topped with cream and blush floral arrangements and flickering candles with the entire scene draped in a constellation of twinkling lights. Dusk had come and spread a gentle glow over the gathering. Everything was obedient to Rox's wedding vision—even the elements.

By the time Alex tidied up the villa and walked into the tent, white-coated servers were already bustling about with trays of sparkling champagne and tiny appetizers wrapped in prosciutto. Rox and Nic were alone on the dance floor, swaying to a French jazz piece floating up from the onstage band while a crowd of onlookers watched with rapt attention. Nic was transfixed by her face, total adoration in his features. Alex had never seen Rox look more spectacular. In a celebratory gesture, she plucked a champagne glass from the nearest full tray and focused all of her senses on finding Ian.

After milling through the guests and offering polite conversation as she sipped her champagne, she finally spied his unmistakable silhouette in the middle of an animated group of Arsenal footballers. The music had become livelier, and she side-stepped through several couples trying to reach the dance floor.

"Pardon me," she said apologetically, her eyes glued to the back of Ian's head.

"Dr. Alex," boomed a familiar voice from over her shoulder. She turned to see the towering, lean shape of Dr. K as he made his way toward her.

"It's great to see you. I didn't know you were coming," she said.

"I did not want to miss such a blessed event. Could I offer you a dance?" He held out his hand.

She accepted it with a bright smile that attempted to hide her disappointment at being deterred from her original mission.

"I'd love to."

Dr. K whirled her around the dancefloor with an ease and grace that she felt had disappeared with her generation. He extended her arm into a turn, and her eyes found Ian, who was dancing a few couples over, arm in arm with a bronzed blond Australian.

Her distress grew by the minute as she willed herself to look away, but his eyes locked with hers over Celeste's bare shoulder. They danced as two heavenly bodies, always slightly out of each other's orbit, and when the song ended, he exited the dancefloor quickly as if escaping the inevitable gravity of Alex's nearness. She watched him carve a trajectory through the tent as he headed for its mouth until he was stopped short by the groom and his formidable bride.

Alex watched the scene unfold as if it was a silent movie. Rox gestured to the courtyard with a magnetic smile and pleading eyes. Ian shifted uncomfortably and then nodded curtly to Rox, who threw her arms around him. Once he had disappeared into the night, Rox nodded to Alex, putting her hands to her lips in silent prayer.


The velvet black-blue hue of the clear night sky sprinkled with tiny pulsating stars and a bright luminescent moon created a celestial backdrop for the scene of Ian crouched on the ground separating blades of grass.

"Lose something?" Alex asked as she tread lightly in her heels through the grass to stand next to him.

His head popped up, face contorted in consternation. "No, but apparently Rox did—some bracelet that her sister gave her. She asked me to find it."

"Oh. Did I ever mention that Rox is an only child?"

He narrowed his eyes and grunted as he stood up and brushed

off his slacks. "I don't think you did." He smirked but didn't close the distance between them. "You look stunning tonight."

"It's my fishing outfit."

Humor lit his gaze, giving Alex the courage to continue.

"It turns out that I am not a catch and release type of girl at all."

"And what kind of girl are you?"

"One that loves you."

Emotion flooded his face, but he said nothing. Alex forged ahead.

"I am in love with you, Ian. I love you, and I'm sorry I let you believe that I didn't."

Her voice shook with an emotional torrent, and she inhaled to steady herself. In that moment, she could smell the fragrance of every individual flower and pick out every star in the night sky.

"My entire life, I was waiting for something to rescue me from a dark place—a place where I felt unworthy of being loved. I thought that freedom from attachment was my salvation...but there is no freedom in a life that doesn't have you. You needed something from me that I believed I could never give you, and it tortured me every single day. But now I understand that you only needed me to choose you. I am choosing you now, and I will choose you always. I love you, Ian."

She paused to catch her breath and will the frantic sonata inside her chest to slow. His face gave nothing away, and, in the dark, his eyes reflected only starlight.

Alex waited in a patch of moonlight while he walked slowly toward her. A faint melody began in the background as the band started up again. "Dance with me?"

He pulled her close, one arm encircling her waist and another taking her hand. They moved together as a slow ballad played in the background, and when the last note died, he ran his nose over her cheek. She shivered involuntarily, her eyes closing and her lips blossoming as they waited to meet his. A gust of exhaled breath ruffled her hair as his lips connected with the top of her head.

Alex stepped out of his embrace, searching for what lay in the depths of his blue eyes. Would it be love, anger, indifference? There was only pain, a raw, primitive pain that was all too familiar. She had seen it in her own reflection for years. He tucked his chin to his chest, staring at a conjured vision in the grass that she couldn't see.

"Do you know what I have been doing these last four months?" His voice was barely a whisper.

"You were in Mongolia."

"It was beautiful there. Peaceful…spiritual…the perfect place to heal from life's many wounds."

She wondered if he meant the ones from his childhood…or the ones caused by her. He stepped back, widening the distance between them.

"I thought I loved you enough to let you go…to let you live exactly how you want. Guess what I learned?"

Alex was paralyzed into silence said none of the words that apparated into her brain.

"That I can't. And believe me, I tried."

Propelled by the hope fluttering its tiny wings in her chest, she took a tentative step toward Ian.

"I can't let you go," he said, staring upward into the silent universe, "but I can't be with you either…not when you still don't know what you want."

The night collapsed inward, suffocating her with a thick blanket of despair. She fought back, sucking every oxygen molecule from the air around her.

"I know exactly what I want, Ian."

"Maybe. But I need you to be absolutely sure…because I'm not strong enough to lose you again." His eyes implored hers and she stilled before her shaking voice filled the night's void.

"I am sure. More sure than I have been of anything…ever…and when you are ready to believe me, come find me."

# THIRTY-FOUR

There was solace in an airplane, tucked into a tiny window seat with zero communication with the world below and no social responsibility to anyone in sight. Alex had folded herself into the smallest blanket-covered ball possible, choosing to spend her fourteen-hour flight emotionally cutting by watching an endless stream of romance movies. She had been tempted to pull the protruding blade from her heart and retreat into her protective ice fortress after last night. It's what her old self would have done. Instead, she had chosen to keep her wounds fresh, maintaining her heart in a state of tender fragility—even though it meant she felt like she was hemorrhaging sadness.

On the Lilliputian-sized movie screen, Julia Roberts' flawless face and tear-filled eyes pleaded with Hugh Grant— "After all, I'm also just a girl standing in front of a boy asking him to love her."

Alex slumped in her seat and pulled the thin airplane blanket to her chin, not really caring who saw her own face, blotchy and swollen.

Last night had been exhausting in every way. After uttering her final words to Ian, she had reluctantly left him there in the dreamy moonlight. There was nothing more she could say. Only he could decide if she was worth the risk. She had been once…and she hoped beyond all hope that she would be again. As the breeze caught up with her retreating form, she thought it carried the words *I will* or maybe she imagined it. It wasn't until she made it all the way back to the celebration tent that she gave up hoping to feel a hand on her shoulder or hear her name on his lips.

She hadn't appreciated the depth of his hurt until that night when she saw the fear of abandonment written all over his face—the same face he must have had when his brother died, and his mother had left him. His mother hadn't loved him enough to choose him, but Alex would…if he would let her.

"It's this one right there."

Alex motioned out the window of the taxi to a white stucco house with bright blue shutters surrounded by an iron gate that also enclosed a small but lush green lawn. She had found this little gem purely by good fortune. It was owned by a South African couple who were spending the year traveling through Southeast Asia and had decided to rent out their fully-furnished residence, which meant that other than bed linens and personal effects, Alex wouldn't need much of anything. They had also left their black Land Rover, complete with sunroof and a passenger seat that would undoubtedly fit a full-sized Rhodesian Ridgeback.

"Home sweet home," she said, dropping her few bags in the entryway and taking a moment to survey the quaint but well-decorated interior.

The floors were a dark ebony stain that contrasted with stark white walls, white cabinets, and furniture in neutral tones of beige and gray. The kitchen was small but updated with a large central island flanked by a pair of leather stools that would be perfect for entertaining. A tiny flight of stairs led to a second story that comprised the master suite bedroom and bathroom. It held a simple four-poster bed with a matching wooden dresser and was sparsely decorated with a few carved wooden elephant statues but no personal effects. Alex presumed the thoughtful couple had packed away their things, wanting it to seem like her home, even in the short term. The large bay windows in the bedroom looked out onto a grassy field of scattered acacia trees and contained a small window seat for reading. It was perfect.

Sharp rapping on the front door sent her hurrying down the stairs. A frantic barking that devolved into a distinct whine resounded off the door as she drew nearer. She threw it open to reveal Dr. K's grandson, Leo, holding the leash to a russet colored gargantuan-sized dog. Alex was on her knees in seconds and was rewarded with wet dog kisses that left a trail of slobber across her entire cheek.

"Sorry, Dr. Alex! He has gotten so strong!"

"It's fine, Leo. Thanks for bringing him."

"It's good to have you back."

"It's great to be back." She stood and offered a quick hug that resulted in a shrug of mild embarrassment from the teenage boy.

"I better get going. This was only the first item on my grandmother's list today."

She waved goodbye and ushered McCartney into their new home.


Alex had moved more times than she could count, having changed cities for every stage of her education and medical training. She had it down to a science—a science that was both distracting and therapeutic. Her boxes from Philadelphia arrived a few at a time, each one a veritable treasure trove. She immersed herself into cleaning each item as it was unpacked and finding a place for her few kitchen items. Two of the shelves in the main room sufficed for her most important books. McCartney followed at her heels, afraid of losing sight of her, even a moment, and examined every unpacked parcel with a delicate sniff.

The weather had turned crisp, and Alex flung open her windows to let the wintry mix permeate the house. By the end of the week, the house was spotless, her things were unpacked, and McCartney was settled. Idleness was her breeding ground for negativity. She hadn't heard from Ian. She had poured every fiber of her being into that soliloquy, but he had yet to respond. By sheer force of will, she had committed to simply waiting.

McCartney snored in the corner, and as she fluffed a few pillows on the couch, her eyes connected with a pair of electric blue running shoes that sat neatly by the door. Her feet felt secure as they struck the pavement and the sun warmed her back as she turned on a familiar road that was not much more than a dusty lane. A zebra foal galloped alongside her mother, kicking up dust on the other side of a wire fence.

Alex rounded a bend and sped up her pace, but instead of metaphorically outrunning her grief, she embraced it and held it close to her chest—because accepting the bad feelings kept her heart attune to experiencing the good ones. She didn't want to lose the grasp she had on her promise to herself—to live a life of joy rather than tragedy.

Chest heaving, she pulled to a stop at a familiar spot where the grass was indented by four separate hoof prints, but her sad little donkey, the masochistic mascot of her Gaborone running highway, was gone.

As the sweat evaporated to cool and refresh her skin, she started a slow jog back into the city. She wondered if Rox and Nic were enjoying the weather in Mozambique, where they were currently on an extended honeymoon.

Alex had left Ian in the courtyard that night with nothing but his thoughts and entered the wedding tent, half-heartedly rejoining the festivities while Rox cast concerned glances in her direction. She hadn't been ready to relive the conversation with Ian and had purposefully not interrupted the new bride, who was the life of her own party. She had been stationed in the send-off line, waving her sparkler in the air like a child on the Fourth of July as Nic and Rox—in her third outfit of the night consisting of a white high waisted jumpsuit—hopped into the waiting vintage automobile that would whisk them to the airport.

Rox had rolled down the window and grabbed her wrist. "Hey—what happened?"

Alex had shaken her head and averted her eyes. "Have a wonderful time, Rox. We'll talk when you get back."

The driver gunned the car and began to pull away from the waving wedding throng. "Be ready for a phone call when I get to Mozambique," called Rox out the open window.

For the first time since Alex had known her, Rox had not called when she said she would, and as Alex kicked off her running shoes, she was not bothered in the least. She hoped Rox and Nic were tangled up somewhere in an oceanside bungalow. Her phone buzzed in the pocket of her tights, and she dug it out breathlessly, half expecting Ian's name to flash onto the screen.

"Hello Rox," Alex smiled and flopped down on the couch.
"Hello, love! It took me a few days to find a spot where my phone has signal," she shouted, and Alex could hear waves breaking in the background.

"Where are you?" Alex chuckled.

"Ibo island," she said. "It's gorgeous here. You have to come someday. The water is the most brilliant blue I've ever seen."

Alex thought of the most brilliant blue she had ever seen, and it wasn't on a beach.

"I'm dying to know what happened with Ian, so spill it before my phone is toast."

Alex filled in the missing details for Rox, who listened patiently, inserting a few *ooh's* and *hmm's* in the appropriate places.

"Have you heard from him?"

"No, and I haven't tried to call him. I put it out there, Rox. Now it's up to him to decide if I'm worth the risk."

"What are you going to do in the meantime?"

"I'm going to wait...and go back to work."

Monday morning came with an overcast sky, heavy gray clouds pregnant with rain, and Alex, zipped into her black puffer jacket, entered the parking lot of Princess Marina. She hurried inside the block of brick administrative buildings just as the first drops of rain struck her nose and eyelashes. Dr. K was seated in his office, displaying perfect posture in his oversized office chair, the phone to one ear, and his hands furiously flipping through a stack of paper. He motioned for her to come in and pointed to a leather chair in the corner. Alex sat down on the edge of the cushion.

"We will talk soon, friend, okay?" He replaced the phone on its cradle and stood up to greet Alex. "Dr. Alex," he said, making his way over to her. She stood and offered him her hand, which he shook heartily. "I was not expecting you for a few weeks."

"I'd like to start a little earlier if that's okay."

He took the chair opposite hers and interlocked his long thin fingers. "Alex, if I may be so bold, I am going to give you some perhaps fatherly advice."

Alex cocked her head to the side, wondering what potential life-altering words would come next. There were few people in the world she held in such high esteem as Dr. K.

"When I was a young man, I worked in a small shop while I attended university and then medical school. I worked early each morning and then went to school and studied late into the night. Then I got a second job as a phlebotomist working nights, and then

I was accepted into a prestigious residency...and on and on. My point is my work ethic is incomparable."

Alex straightened in her chair, nodding and gearing up for whatever arduous task Dr. K might be asking for.

"Yes, sir. I am truly inspired by you."

He pulled his glasses to the end of his nose and peered at her over the top of the wire rims. "There is plenty of time to work, Alex. Take these next few weeks and go live your life for a while."


Alex huffed and slammed the door on the Land Rover, surprising a sleeping McCartney who thrust his head into the window and sent out a string of staccato barks. She pushed open the front door and sent her keys flying into the bowl on a nearby shelf. She never minded time off, but her patience had worn into something thin and ragged, and her pining had grown from a manageable ache to a heaviness that she felt every time her heart contracted. She could fill up the next few weeks with things she loved—running, reading, taking McCartney to the park. Maybe she could take a few day trips or learn to make Bolognese or start practicing French. The central problem was that she could not do what Dr. K had asked because living the life she wanted...the life she imagined...was a life with Ian.

In the end, she decided to try her luck at baking, and she fell in love with the combination of art and science needed to create the perfect tart or the most delectable pan of brownies. There was something tangibly therapeutic about measuring ingredients and swirling them together in a bowl where they would combine to form a creamy batter that tasted as good uncooked as it did after it had puffed up in the oven.

While she baked, she caught up on the last decade of pop culture entertainment that she had ignored while her life belonged to medical training—Oscar-winning movies, popular books, binge-worthy television. She cried when Sam and Frodo were seemingly left to die together on Mount Doom and when Dumbledore was snuffed out by Snape and when Anakin descended into madness and became Darth Vader. She finally did read the entire Twilight series and could see why tweens and teens all over the planet had fallen in love with it. It had made her feel like a lovesick seventeen-year-old girl herself. She listened to music blasting her favorite Beatles from the tiny speakers of her laptop. Lately, she had been addicted to the *White Album.* "Who knows how long I've loved you...you know I love you still...will I wait a lonely lifetime...if you want me to, I will."

The grocery down the street carried a variety of hand-woven baskets piled in the front of the store, and she had loaded up the truck with as many as she could fit one day. As she perfected her baked goods, she created parcels for her neighbors, leaving them on various front doors with a note of encouragement and hoping that, as in Texas, good food was a great ice breaker.

A solid week into her bake-athon, she and a leashed McCartney were trotting back from their daily deliveries when she noticed a strange black car parked in the driveway and a not so strange blonde head poking out of the sunroof. Alex took off at a mad pace with her pup close at her heels, hurling herself into the arms of Dr. Roxanne Clarke-Brizido. They squealed like teenagers and alternated between hugging each other and calming an overly anxious McCartney who wanted some of the action.

"When did you get here?" Alex panted.

"Just now—we flew in to check on you for a couple of days, and then we are leaving for Paris." She gestured to Nic, who was sporting large black aviators while sitting behind the wheel of their rental.

"Paris?" Alex eyed her enviously.

"We're just not ready to end the honeymoon yet." She glanced back at Nic adoringly. "Anyway, we're staying at a hotel in town and we're going to Ex-Pats tonight."

"Where it all started?" Alex grinned.

"Where a lot of things started. Meet us there?"

Alex sensed that it wasn't a request and nodded excitedly. It was time for her to get out of the safe bubble of her house of perpetual pining. Rox jumped back in the car.

"Eight o'clock."

Alex waved as they jetted down the street, probably a little too quickly for her neighborhood's liking.

Ex-Pats looked and smelled exactly how Alex remembered. Jeff, the middle-aged bartender, was carefully wiping down the main bar with thick hairy arms. Tidbits of loud conversation floated through the air before the sound waves met the tiny ossicles of someone's ears and petered out. The smell of road dust mixed with leather floated into Alex's nostrils, and she inhaled deeply. She waved at Jeff, who saluted her, and then continued to the back where a screen door led to the outdoor patio.

In the middle of winter, the temperature dropped at night, but Alex always preferred outdoors despite the chill. A few small heating lamps had been turned on, and in her black cashmere sweater and jeans, she would be warm enough to wait for Rox and Nic. Motioning to the bartender, she ordered a glass of wine—a nice pinotage that could warm her from the inside and stave off the goosebumps. Swirling the ruby liquid around her glass, she stared into it, searching for the answers to all of her lingering questions in its depths.

The screen door behind her squeaked and banged closed, causing her to reflexively turn her head, and the entire world slowed on its axis. Ian stood there exactly how she remembered him on that first night they met—a black t-shirt and dark jeans, this time with his black leather jacket to keep out the winter air. He drew nearer, a pair of sky-blue eyes searching hers, and his perfect face broke into his characteristic half-smile as he leaned on the bar in the empty space next to her. So many words erupted in her head, but only a few mattered.

"What are you doing here?" she asked.

He averted his eyes downward and began tracing a pattern on the aged wood of the bar.

"One time, someone told me about this game where you try to get a stranger to kiss you."

He lifted his eyes to hers—burning flame-blue eyes. Eyes that had tormented her...seduced her...seen her at her most vulnerable...eyes that had loved her. She leaped into their flames without fear, catching fire like a phoenix. A phoenix rising up to a new plane of existence where she was liberated by joy and free to love...and be loved...like she had always wanted.

Alex leaned over and met his lips with her own in a kiss that started slowly but grew exponentially until all of the despair of the past mixed with the promise of the future. She opened her mouth and her heart to his and they kissed while, for one moment, the world revolved around them.

Suddenly Alex laughed and pulled away, breathless and flushed and filled with the most insatiable desire.

"What?" he said, his entire face lit in a smile.

"Are you done running from me?" she said with narrowed eyes.

"Are you done not knowing what you want?" he countered and she shrugged.

"I'm done not loving you."

She kissed him again, lighter but just as intense, feeling the sear of his lips on hers when they paused.

"What now? Is this the beginning of our epic love story?" Alex asked, and he pulled her close, leaning down so that his eyes bore into hers.

"It is. Now let's get out of here…because I'm pretty sure that we're due some epic makeup sex."

# ABOUT THE AUTHOR

HK Jacobs graduated from Baylor College of Medicine and has spent her life as a physician traveling the globe caring for children. She also has a Master of Public Health from the University of Texas with a concentration in global health and completed her thesis in Port au Prince, Haiti. She currently resides in Texas, where she practices pediatric critical care medicine and lives the life she imagined. *Wilde Type* is her debut novel.

*Coming Summer 2021*

The epic love story of Alex and Ian continues...

www.hkjacobs.com
Instagram: @hkjacobsauthor
Twitter: @hk_jacobs
Pinterest: Author HK Jacobs
Apple Playlist: AlexWilde

Made in the USA
Columbia, SC
23 September 2021